GARETH L. POWELL

EMBERS OF WAR

TITAN BOOKS

Embers of War
Print edition ISBN: 9781785655180
E-book edition ISBN: 9781785655197

Published by Titan Books
A division of Titan Publishing Group Ltd
144 Southwark Street, London SE1 0UP

First edition: February 2018
10 9 8 7 6 5 4 3

Names, places and incidents are either products of the author's
imagination or used fictitiously. Any resemblance to actual persons, living
or dead (except for satirical purposes), is entirely coincidental.

A CIP catalogue record for this title is available from the British Library.

Printed and bound in Great Britain by CPI Group (UK) Ltd, Croydon CR0 4YY

Did you enjoy this book?
We love to hear from our readers. Please email us at
readerfeedback@titanemail.com or write to us at
Reader Feedback at the above address.

TITAN BOOKS.COM

For Edith and Rosie

Simon Butler

"Fast, exhilarating space opera, imaginative and full of life."
ADRIAN TCHAIKOVSKY, AUTHOR OF *CHILDREN OF TIME*

"Fast-paced and fun and full of adventure... on my must-read list."
ANN LECKIE, AUTHOR OF *ANCILLARY JUSTICE*

"Space opera with scope, action, colour and humanity, skillfully
told at a cracking pace."
KEN MACLEOD, AUTHOR OF *THE CORPORATION WARS*

"An exciting and deeply satisfying start to a new series."
EMMA NEWMAN, AUTHOR OF *PLANETFALL*

"This is the real thing... a headlong, rip-roaring gem of a story."
DAVE HUTCHINSON, AUTHOR OF *EUROPE IN AUTUMN*

"Mashes together solid space opera with big concepts, real
people, and a freewheeling rock'n'roll vibe."
JONATHAN L. HOWARD, AUTHOR OF *CARTER & LOVECRAFT*

"Powerful, classy and mind-expanding SF, in the tradition of
Ann Leckie and Iain M. Banks."
PAUL CORNELL, AUTHOR OF *LONDON FALLING*

"Built on a foundation of powerful discussions about the morality
of war and its effect on unique and interesting characters.
[A] fascinating universe."
MELINDA SNODGRASS, AUTHOR OF THE IMPERIALS SAGA

"Everything you would want in a space opera and more...
Powell hits that Iain Banks sweet spot while being something
completely new."
TADE THOMPSON, AUTHOR OF *ROSEWATER*

"A powerful and sympathetic examination of what it means to
be a soldier."
BENNETT R. COLES, AUTHOR OF *VIRTUES OF WAR*

"One of the most inventive voices in British science fiction."
DANIEL GODFREY, AUTHOR OF *EMPIRE OF TIME*

Also by Gareth L. Powell and available from Titan Books

Fleet of Knives (February 2019)
Light of Impossible Stars (February 2020)

"Blood was its Avatar and its seal."

EDGAR ALLAN POE,
"The Masque of the Red Death"

PELAPATARN

Another ship dropped off the tactical grid, obliterated by a shower of pin-sized antimatter warheads. In the war room of her Scimitar, the *Righteous Fury*, Captain Annelida Deal uttered a venomous curse. The Outward ships were putting up more of a fight than she had anticipated, determined to protect their forward command post on the planet below. If she could only get past them, locate the bunker where the conference was taking place, and drop a decent-sized warhead of her own, the war might be over. At one stroke, she would have fulfilled her orders, which were to decapitate the enemy's command structure, leaving its forces in a state of vulnerable disarray.

Intelligence projections had suggested an easy in-and-out operation. The Outward had gone for a minimal fleet presence, hoping not to attract attention. In theory, she should have been able to sweep them aside with ease. But these bastards were putting up more of a fight than anyone— maybe even they themselves—could have guessed, and the Conglomeration forces had already lost a couple of frigates and a light cruiser. A dirty smoke trail showed where the cruiser had fallen through the atmosphere, shedding debris and sparks, until it broke up over the night side of Pelapatarn, scattering wreckage across a wide swathe of ocean.

Alarms rang through the ship. More torpedoes were coming in.

In the war room, Captain Deal clung to the edge of the tactical display table. Around her, the hologram faces of her lieutenants were nervous and grim as they awaited her response.

"We can't get through," one of them said, and she saw that he was right. The bulk of the Outward fleet lay between her ships and the planet. Any ordnance fired would be intercepted and destroyed before it hit the atmosphere. All she could hope to do was try to fight her way through the blockade. But that would take time and lives. Her Scimitars were faster and more advanced than the Outward cruisers, but the enemy had their backs to the wall. By the time she got within striking distance of the planet—assuming she ever did—the Outward commanders would have fled their conference. If she wanted to end this war, she had to strike now.

She opened a channel to Fleet Headquarters, and was told a pack of four Carnivores were inbound from Cold Tor. As reinforcements, they wouldn't be enough to decisively sway the outcome of the battle, but those in command had another use in mind for them.

And they wanted her to give the order.

"Get me the *Adalwolf*," she said to her communications officer.

"Yes, sir!"

The main display dimmed, and a hologram of the *Adalwolf*'s commander appeared. Captain Valeriy Yasha Barcov had a smooth scalp and a thick, bushy beard. He was in his command couch, with a profusion of thin fibre-optic data cables plugged into the sockets at the back of his head.

"*Dobryj dyen*, Captain." He smiled wolfishly, obviously relishing the anticipated conflict. "We will be with you momentarily."

Captain Deal shook her head. "No, Captain, I have a different mission for you."

The man raised an eyebrow. "Speak, and it shall be done."

Resting her weight on her hands, Deal leant across the table. "You are ordered to jump past the Outward fleet. Do not engage them. Your target is the planet."

Barcov's quizzical expression fell into a frown. "But we do not know where the conference is located. By the time we survey the jungle, the Outward ships will be upon us."

"That's why I want you to skip the survey."

His confusion deepened. "But what shall we bomb?"

Deal swallowed. She could feel her heart beating in her chest. "Everything."

Barcov opened and shut his mouth a few times. Finally, he said, "You wish me to destroy the sentient jungle of Pelapatarn?"

Deal felt the sweat break out on her forehead. "We have been ordered to raze it to the fucking ground," she said.

For a moment, the old warhorse looked taken aback. Then he drew a deep breath through his cavernous nostrils and drew himself straight.

"It shall be done."

•

Captain Deal watched the holocaust from the bridge of her Scimitar. She wanted to see the results of the order with her own eyes, not via a computer graphic. She knew soldiers from both sides were down there in the jungle, as well as several thousand civilians. But she told herself their sacrifice would be worth it. She was sure those in charge were right, and a swift and decisive end to the hostilities would, in the long term, save more lives than would be lost in the firestorm.

As the first mushroom clouds burst over the planet's single supercontinent, she felt her stomach go light, as if the gravity had momentarily failed. All activity on the bridge ceased. Even the Outward fleet stopped firing.

Screaming low through the planet's atmosphere, the four bullet-shaped Carnivores unleashed their entire arsenal of destruction, raining fire and death in swathes five hundred kilometres abreast. Nuclear explosions cratered the land and set millions of square kilometres of vegetation aflame; antimatter explosions tore at the very fabric of the planet, throwing up great plumes of dirt and rock, while smaller munitions rained down on likely targets, picking off anything that walked, crawled or flew.

One pass was enough.

They came out of nowhere, and then jumped away again before anyone in the enemy fleet could turn and engage them. And in their wake they left a billion-year-old biosphere ablaze, and an atmosphere choked with ash and radioactive dust.

The fires burned for six weeks.

The war was over in one.

PART ONE

THREE YEARS LATER

"For as this appalling ocean surrounds
the verdant land, so in the soul of man
there lies one insular Tahiti, full of peace
and joy, but encompassed by all the
horrors of the half-known life."

HERMAN MELVILLE, *Moby Dick*

ONE

SAL KONSTANZ

"I hear knocking." Still crouched, Alva Clay rocked back on her boot heels and lowered her goggles. "I'm guessing at least two people."

I turned my head away as she fired up her cutting torch.

"Hey, George," I called, "we've found some more. Get over here."

Back towards the stern of the drifting wreck, George Walker—instantly recognisable in his bright orange medical jumpsuit—glanced up from the stretchered patient he had been tending.

"Yes, Captain." He lumbered towards me, his old-man gait unsteady as the deck groaned and flexed on the swell.

"We've got more survivors," I told him. We'd already pulled four bodies from another hole Clay had cut in the top of the crashed scout ship, but only one of them had been alive.

Right now, the *Hobo* wallowed in the sea with only a few dozen square metres of its upper structure still protruding above the waves. A metre from where I stood, sluggish wavelets, tinged pink by the sun, lapped at the edge of the hull. I rubbed my forehead. How had this happened? The *Hobo* had been surveying the planet for possible colonisation.

How had these idiots managed to land in an ocean and flood their entire vessel?

My ship, the Reclamation Vessel *Trouble Dog*, stood a few hundred metres to the east, hanging in the air like a monstrous bronze bullet. Before she had joined the House of Reclamation, the *Trouble Dog* had been a Carnivore-class heavy cruiser for one of the more powerful human factions, the Conglomeration. Engines accounted for eighty-five per cent of her mass. Weapon emplacements, sensor blisters, drone hangars and empty missile racks interrupted the otherwise smooth lines of her streamlined hull.

"How are you doing, ship?" I asked her.

Speaking through the bud implanted in my ear, the *Trouble Dog* said, "I have been unable to recover the *Hobo*'s primary personality. I have accessed its core, but it appears to have erased its higher functions."

I frowned. "No black box? Why would it do that?"

"According to its last status update, it blamed itself for the crash."

Clouds were massing on the horizon, threatening to blot out the low, bloodshot sun. A sea breeze ruffled my hair. I pulled my flight jacket closed and sealed the zip.

"Isn't that unusual?" I'd never heard of a ship's personality deliberately committing suicide.

"It's these scouts," the *Trouble Dog* said in a matter-of-fact tone. "They spend too much time out here on their own, and it drives them to peculiarity."

I watched the ripples gnaw the edge of the *Hobo*'s mostly submerged upper surface, and shrugged. None of this was our concern; all we had to do was recover the bodies, living or dead, and get them back to Camrose Station. When that had been done, other people—safety investigators and claims adjusters—could worry about the specific causes of the accident.

"What about the rest of the ship?" I asked.

"Still filling with water. I estimate no more than fifteen minutes until it finally submerges."

"How deep's this water?"

"Fifteen hundred metres, and bristling with life."

I peered over the edge. Fish-like shadows skittered and scattered beneath the water. Their flanks flashed like silver knives. Larger shapes stirred in the depths below.

"Okay."

"Plus, there's a storm front coming in from the east. No more than ten minutes."

"Then I guess we'd better get a move on, huh?" I turned my attention back to Alva Clay. "Did you hear any of that?"

Clay had tied back her dreadlocks with a frayed and oily bandana. She wore heavy gauntlets to protect her hands and wrists, but her arms were bare, displaying the tattoos she'd acquired during the Archipelago War, as a foot soldier in the sentient jungles of Pelapatarn. Her dark goggles reflected the actinic flare of the torch in her gloved hands. Where the flame touched, sparks fountained from the hull.

"I'm cutting as fast as I can."

"Cut faster, unless you want to get your feet wet." Even after all this time, her tats still bothered me. I had my own share of ghosts, but I kept them to myself; I didn't feel the need to parade them for the entire world to see.

The knocking from inside the stricken craft had ceased. If the people trapped in the compartment below had any sense, they would be cowering away from the flame, and the fifty-centimetre-wide plug of hull metal that was going to fall inward when Clay finished cutting her circle.

George Walker un-shouldered his medical pack and began to unroll a pair of self-inflating stretchers. His thinning grey hair appeared pink in the russet sunlight. Water lapped at his scuffed plastic boots.

"Careful," I said. "Don't get too close to the edge. I don't want to have to pull you out."

The old man's eyes crinkled in amusement. He thought I fussed too much. He had served as a medical officer aboard the *Trouble Dog* during the ship's military days in the Conglomeration Fleet, and had stayed aboard when she was decommissioned and transferred to the House of Reclamation. On my first day as captain, he'd been the one to give me the tour of the ship, and he'd shown me the secret nooks, patches and workarounds that only someone who'd lived and served on the ship for years could have known. Apparently, I reminded him of his daughter, a lawyer living back on Earth with two kids and a crippling mortgage. I'd met the woman once, during an unscheduled layover in Berlin, but hadn't been able to grasp any similarity; whatever had led the old man to conflate his feelings for us was beyond my capacity to fathom.

"Don't worry about me, Captain," he said. "You concentrate on getting us out of here before the whole mess sinks to the bottom."

I cast a wary glance at the horizon. I didn't like the look of those clouds. "I'll do my best."

By the time Clay's circle was complete, the wreck had settled lower in the water and the wavelets had advanced another half a metre up the deck. The breeze had begun to pick up. Time was running out and we all knew it. We weren't carrying the equipment necessary to operate below the surface. If we could get these two out, they would be the last survivors pulled from the *Hobo* before it took that long, final spiralling fall into darkness and silence. The rest, if there were any, would be lost.

We had done all we could.

Clay switched off her torch and laid it aside. "Captain," she said, "do you want to do the honours?"

Thunder growled in the distance. Those clouds were the leading edge of the oncoming storm. The circle's molten outline burned like an ember. I raised my right boot and stamped down on its centre. Metal cracked and scraped, and the entire section fell away, splashing into the seawater flooding the compartment below. For a moment, we stood paralysed, waiting for movement, a voice, anything. Then Alva Clay swore, and slid through the hole, boots first.

When she reappeared, moments later, puffing and blowing air and water from her lips, she had her arm clamped around a young man's neck. They were both kicking to stay afloat. I lay on the wet deck and reached down and, with Walker's help, managed to pull the kid up into the sunlight.

We rolled him onto a stretcher.

"Is he injured?"

A sudden wind blew across the deck, chilling my exposed skin. Walker checked the kid's pulse with one hand, waved me away with the other. "Go on, I've got this."

I left him bent over the stretcher and slithered back to the edge of the hole. Lying with my head and shoulders hanging over the rim, I could see Clay's flashlight cutting this way and that through the shadowy water below. Her movements stirred up clouds of junk. I saw objects whirl through the circle of daylight thrown by the hole: a plastic fork, a comb, an empty cup, a loose shoe...

Another clap of thunder rolled in from the horizon.

If we'd had more time, I would have sent a drone in to help her. As it was, we were already pushing our luck.

When Clay reappeared a second time, her dreads were sodden and plastered to her head, and her goggles were missing.

"There's something in here." She lunged upward and grabbed the lip of the hole. "Get me out."

I took hold of her wrists.

"What are you—?"

"I'm not kidding, Sally." She tried to pull herself up. "Get me the fuck out!"

I didn't argue. In the three years I'd known her, I'd never seen Clay this rattled. I'd seen her tense and anxious, maybe, but never actually *afraid*. I dragged her up with all the strength in my arms. Then, when she was halfway out and levering herself up on her elbows, I reached down and grabbed her by her tool belt. I pulled back hard and she slithered up on top of me. Her clothes were soaked, and I tasted salt water. We rolled apart and sat panting on the wet deck while lightning danced like fire among the clouds and the quickening wind delivered the first spots of rain.

"Where's the other one?"

Clay swallowed, trying to control her breathing. "Gone."

I climbed to my feet and scrutinised the circle of darkness. "But there were two…"

"Something took him." She wrapped her arms across her chest.

"What was it?"

"I don't know." Her chest rose and fell. "But it was big, and fast."

"Like a shark?" With one of the submerged airlocks left open, I could see how a big fish might have wormed its way into the *Hobo*'s drowned interior.

"No." Clay shook her head. "No, it had tentacles." She stood up and drew her pistol, and backed away from the hole. I took one last look into the depths of the flooded cabin and then did likewise.

Another peal of thunder split the sky. Although the clouds were still some distance from us, the rain rode ahead of them, blown like spittle.

"We need to leave." Clay had her gun trained on the hole in the hull, seemingly expecting some aquatic horror to rise up from within. She was scared, and she was right to be.

20

The weather was closing in and the *Hobo* was in danger of dropping out from under us at any moment. We were out of time and we needed to evacuate the survivors, pronto.

I opened my mouth to order the *Trouble Dog*'s shuttle to come pick us up, but stopped as I heard a splash behind me. I turned in time to glimpse something orange being pulled beneath the waves. At the same moment, an alarm pierced my ear as the *Trouble Dog* clamoured for my attention. Clay heard it too. She risked looking away from the hole for an instant.

"Hey," she said, her face mirroring my confusion. "Where's George?"

TWO

ONA SUDAK

Despite being kept awake for most of the night, I forced myself to get out of bed at 0600 hours, same as every other morning.

Without waking Adam, I slid from the sheet and pulled on a robe. His gently snoring body lay like a bony xylophone. Loosened from its ponytail, his hair spilled down across his youthful face. His faux leather trousers had been carelessly tossed across the back of one of my chairs, and one of his boots, having been kicked away in the impatience of passion, now wallowed upended in my metal sink. I thought about kissing his forehead, but didn't want to wake him. I had my morning routine, and I didn't want him getting in the way. So I stepped out of the cabin and closed the door as quietly as I could.

The corridor outside opened onto a deep shaft, maybe fifty metres from top to bottom and half that again in width, bordered on all sides by balconies and hanging gardens. The air was sweet and pleasantly warm, and smelled of roses and rich, mossy soil. Birds and butterflies flittered through the empty spaces. Bees fumbled among the flowers. I stood for a few moments, drinking all of it in. One day, I intended to write a poem about life on the 'dam, or one of her pen-shaped sister ships.

One day, but not today.

Fastening the robe's sash in a loose knot, I made my way to the nearest transport tube and descended half a dozen decks to the gym. Every morning without exception, I did an hour's exercise before breakfast. It was a habit ingrained after long years in the—

I caught myself before completing the thought, and turned my attention instead to the waiting treadmills and weights.

•

By 0700 hours ship's time, my muscles were cooling after a strenuous workout, and I was recovering in the pool, contemplating the distant glimmer of the dusty stars beyond the large picture window occupying the whole of the gym's back wall.

In a couple of hours' time, we would make a close approach to the Brain—the first of the Objects we were to encounter.

The *Geest van Amsterdam* hadn't wanted to linger in the Gallery a moment longer than necessary, but the other passengers and I wanted to get a closer look at the Objects, and we had been most insistent. Quite apart from the fact that the Gallery lay in a disputed tract of space, the *'dam* had its itinerary to consider, and strict adherence to schedule had always been a matter of much pride among such vessels. Nevertheless, when Captain Benton finally interceded on our behalf, the ship reluctantly agreed to extend our presence in the system long enough to perform a close flyby of the Brain, the Inverted City, and the Dodecahedron.

We were overjoyed. Like most of humanity, I had only seen second-hand footage of the Objects, so the chance to see *three* of them with my own eyes seemed like the kind of opportunity that strikes only once in a lifetime—the kind of experience one might relate to a grandchild. When the ship made its announcement, I was delighted by its concession.

After seven weeks of careful flirtation, I had finally allowed myself to be seduced by the young poet Adam Leroux, who had been pursuing me with a gauche and tragic fervour for the duration of the cruise, and I looked forward to viewing the mysterious sculptures in the company of my youthful paramour. I wanted to see them through his eyes. His delight would be purer and more childlike than anything I felt capable of mustering, and I would use it in the poem I intended to write about the encounter, recycling his sense of innocent wonder as my own.

·

Adam was eighteen and a half years old, with the gangly awkwardness of an adolescent, yet he affected a world-weary disdain for what he termed the "mundanity of ordinary existence". He had been born and raised on the 'dam, and had seen many worlds during his short life—but mostly through the windows and view screens of his suite. He had little experience beyond the safe environs of the ship, and even less experience of women. He was very different to the men I had known, and I guess that novelty was one of the things about him that attracted me. It certainly wasn't his poetry, which was execrable, full of extremity and unnecessary drama and lacking the subtlety an older mind might have brought to its subjects. Had the cruise been shorter, I would never have allowed him into my bed.

Even now, wallowing in the warm water, I wasn't sure I hadn't made an embarrassing mistake. He was so much younger than me, for a start; and he wanted me to teach him everything I knew about poetry.

I could have done that in about half an hour.

Over the past three years, I had published a handful of epic poems to somewhat rapturous and unexpected applause. But none of them were what I'd consider to be masterpieces.

They weren't poetic. On the contrary, the language I had used was almost clinical in its plainness, and the poems themselves were stark and guilt-laden, and not written for mass consumption. And yet, their simplicity and lack of pretension seemed to catch something in the mood of the post-war public, giving voice to all their lingering feelings of loss and remorse. And, quite to my surprise and dismay, I found my artless words celebrated across the Generality, and acclaimed as the voice of a lost generation.

Looking back now, I knew I should never have published, not even privately. But I could not have known that a well-meaning friend would post my poetry to a system-wide literary server, or that those words would have such appeal to the readers of the Generality. I had meant them as a small, private tribute, like funeral ashes scattered into the ocean of culture. Instead, my unanticipated readership saw in my retelling of old works a new political hope, and a rejection of the territorial posturing that had led us to the Archipelago War. Quite by accident, I had become a figurehead, a symbol of regeneration.

But all I really wanted to do was disappear, and forget the war. I didn't want to keep talking about it in interviews. I was sick of seeing my face on newscasts and literary feeds. All I wanted was to forget the whole thing.

Which is why I was looking forward to seeing the Objects.

•

Ten thousand years ago, the solar system we now know as the Gallery had been a remote and unremarkable place: just a small yellow sun with seven perfectly ordinary planets. Then, some time around ten thousand years ago, those planets had been carved into seven immense sculptures, and nobody knew why or by whom.

Arriving on the scene six thousand years after their

fashioning, human explorers had named the carvings according to their shapes. Counting outwards from the sun, they became known as the Teardrop, the Jagged Bolt, the Brain, the Inverted City, the Dodecahedron, the Flared Goblet, and the Broken Clock.

Even now, their significance remained a mystery. But, as they had endured for so many millennia, I hoped I would be able to find among them a way to throw my personal history into some sort of perspective. Through contemplation and the act of writing, I intended to stack my handful of days against the vastness of ten thousand years, and thereby exorcise their pain; and maybe, by seeing the Objects through Adam's young eyes, I could achieve that.

The first Object we were to approach was the Brain. It is a fat ovoid the size of Mars. Like the other objects, it started life as a reasonably commonplace globe. Then the sculptors, using some unimaginable technology, reshaped it, etching deep and convoluted designs into its surface. The largest lines are the size of canyons, the smallest no wider than a few centimetres. Together, they form an intricate, planet-sized labyrinth of exquisite complexity, with no identifiable beginning or end, no entry point or centre.

My plan was to remain in the pool for another half an hour, watching our progress towards the Brain through the window. I hoped the water would soothe the remaining tension in my neck and shoulders, and rinse away the fatigue from my workout. When we got closer to the Brain, I'd return to my cabin to wake Adam. We'd get dressed and take tea and sushi on the observation deck at the front of the ship, where most of the crew and passengers would be gathered beneath the transparent dome to witness our closest approach.

•

I had begun to drift off to sleep when the water quivered

around me. At first, it was a pleasant sensation, like being rocked in a parent's arms. Then a second, stronger shudder wrenched me from my doze, and I gripped the side of the pool. The lights flickered. Beyond the window, I glimpsed a swarm of firefly sparks.

Torpedoes!

We were under attack, but by whom? And why weren't the alarms sounding? Why weren't we retaliating?

The engines were off, and even the air conditioning had stopped. The resulting silence was eerier and more terrifying than any amount of noise could have been.

I surged from the water and grabbed my robe. A couple of teenagers emerged from one of the saunas looking perplexed, but I pushed straight past them, shoving my way towards the corridor. There was no time now to think. No time to warn anybody else. It was entirely possible, likely even, that I only had a few minutes of life remaining, and there were things I needed to do.

THREE

ASHTON CHILDE

The electric fan rattled. The air was hot down here by the equator. Humidity plastered my shirt to my ribs, and I envied the residents of the planet's more northerly, cooler climes. Even with the office door closed, I could smell the creeping reek of the jungle beyond the airfield's perimeter. I contemplated the gun on the desk before me. It was small, compact and efficient-looking: a black metal L-shape with a touchpad trigger and a small aperture at the business end. If I had to spend one more day in this stinking craphole, I worried I might snap and use it to shoot somebody. And I worried that somebody might be me.

My tie was loose. With shaky hands, I pulled it off altogether and stuffed it into a drawer. On the wall beside me, a two-dimensional map showed the surrounding terrain, with pins and coloured stickers to mark troop positions and major strategic targets—nearly all of them guesses based on observations by our pilots. Everything here was so low-tech. I would have given my left nut for a decent satellite overview of the front lines, but every time we put one up, the government knocked it down. And it wasn't as if I had resources to burn. Even replacing one of the rattling, aluminium-sided supply planes could take four to six weeks, during which time our allies in the mountains would have to ration their ammunition and tighten their belts over empty bellies.

The hard truth was that as far as Conglomeration Intelligence was concerned, this civil war simply wasn't a priority. Viewed from a hundred light years away, it was scarcely more than a nasty provincial scuffle. We were covertly supplying arms, food and medicine to the guerrillas opposing the government, but that was the extent of our involvement. The top brass could have sent a couple of Scimitar warships and a few thousand ground troops to end the conflict in a matter of hours. Unfortunately, this planet lay on a political fault line between the Conglomeration and the Outward Faction, and so we were reduced to acting through civilian front organisations. As far as the universe beyond this mud ball was concerned, I was the proprietor of a charitable aircraft haulage company employing seven pilots and two-dozen mechanics, shipping humanitarian supplies to refugees displaced by the fighting. In reality, our materiel drops only prolonged the insurgency, destabilising the entire region.

I wiped my forehead on my sleeve. I hadn't felt clean since I'd been here. Even cold showers were effective only as long as I remained beneath them. Seconds after emerging, I'd start to sweat again.

I tapped the pistol with an unsteady fingertip, setting it spinning. It made a grinding noise on the pocked and dented metal surface of the desk.

The drawer that now held my screwed-up tie also held a clear plastic bag containing three sticks of barracuda weed, a mildly addictive local root. I stuck one in the corner of my mouth and squeezed it between my teeth, allowing its bitter sap to mix with my saliva.

Chewing barracuda weed took the edge off. It stopped my hands from shaking, but couldn't completely numb me to the endless days of administrative tedium punctuated by the occasional interruptions of searing terror—such as last week, when a government drone strafed the airfield and I'd had to take cover beneath this very desk. As an assignment, this had to be the worst I could have been given. The only mystery was what I had done to deserve such treatment.

On the desk, the pistol slowed to a halt with its barrel pointing at my stomach. For a second or two, I imagined it going off—maybe as the result of a malfunction or jarring caused by the spin. Before recruitment into the intelligence community, I had been a cop and seen my share of accidental and self-inflicted gunshot wounds. I could easily picture the weapon flying backwards across the room, propelled by its own recoil, the muzzle flash scorching the damp curtain of my faux-cotton shirt, the bullet punching through skin and muscle, and my head snapping back against the chair while the chair itself rocked on its casters.

My left eye twitched.

At least it would be an escape. The only question in my mind was how long my corpse might moulder in this chair before somebody thought to come and check on me. In this heat, it would rot quickly. The pilots had their schedules for the week; unless a problem cropped up, it might be days before they found me.

I sucked on the root, and set the gun spinning again. I was still turning it an hour later, when the terminal in my pocket buzzed.

I hadn't received a call for so long that it took me a moment to identify the source of the sound. When it buzzed a second time, I pulled it out and activated the screen.

The message was from headquarters, relayed via tight beam from a supply ship on the ragged fringes of the solar system. I read it three times, then shoved the pistol into the desk drawer and locked it.

The chair thumped against the wall as I rose. I felt an

urgent need to take a walk to the trading post at the far end of the airfield, where I knew I'd find the one person capable of understanding what the intelligence chiefs of the Conglomeration were asking me to do.

FOUR

SAL KONSTANZ

The *Trouble Dog* showed me its telemetry log. George Walker's vital signs had all tanked simultaneously, seconds after he'd been dragged into the sea.

"I have footage," the ship said.

We were back on board now, and I was sitting in my command couch at the centre of the hemispherical bridge, surrounded by the soft blue glow of readouts and displays. Alva Clay had gone to the ship's infirmary to secure the stretchers containing the injured and dead.

One of the larger screens lit with a recorded image of the mostly submerged *Hobo*. I could see myself lying on the deck with my arms in the circular hole, in the process of hauling Clay from the water. Behind me, George Walker crouched beside one of the inflatable stretchers in his orange jumpsuit, his grey head bent towards the young man we'd just pulled from the flooded ship. His back was to the waves lapping at his heels, and he couldn't see the questing, whip-thin tentacles feeling their way towards him, razor hooks glossy and wet in the last of the rusty sunlight.

"Stop!" I didn't want to see what happened next. Instead, I called for a real-time view of the crashed ship.

The *Hobo* was a dark shape just beneath the surface. You

could see the pattern of the waves change as they rolled across her and broke at the shallowest point, which was at her rear, just above the engines. She was completely submerged now, but she hadn't fully sunk. She was still holding out.

"There's no chance he might be alive?"

"None."

"His monitors. Maybe they got detached. Maybe——"

"No." The *Trouble Dog* sounded genuinely regretful. "I'm sorry."

I knuckled my eyes. I wanted to crawl into bed, pull the sleeping bag over my head and pretend this day had never happened.

I had known George Walker for three years. In that time, he had been as much of a fixture of this ship as the continuous whirr of the air conditioning, or the reliably bad coffee in the mess. And now he was gone. He had died on my watch.

The rules in these situations were very clear, and the captain always bore responsibility for the safety of his or her crew. Before we'd set foot on the *Hobo*, I should have ordered a deep scan of the surrounding water, and a full risk assessment of any species found. And then, when we were down there, I should have kept George in sight the whole time. It mattered little that the attack had been so swift that even the *Trouble Dog* had been unable to react in time to save him; when we got back to Camrose Station, there'd be an inquiry, and I'd be lucky to escape without a severe reprimand. In the worst case, if they judged the failure to conduct a full inventory of nearby marine life a contributing factor to his death, I might even lose my command.

Right now, though, none of that seemed to matter. Walker was dead, and I felt the pain of his loss like an icicle lodged in my chest. The only bitter crumb of comfort to be had was that whatever had happened to him, the telemetry report indicated it had been quick.

I glared at the picture of the *Hobo*. How the hell had it ended up in the sea in the first place? And how had it been allowed to flood? There were safeguards in place to prevent both airlock doors opening simultaneously. In order to flood the ship, those safeguards would have had to be overridden or destroyed.

I tapped a fingernail on the screen, magnifying the image of the submerged vessel. "Could it have been sabotaged?"

"Insufficient data."

I turned to a smaller side screen and pulled up a tactical view of the space surrounding the planet. "Were there any other ships in the system when the *Hobo* went down?"

The main screen rippled and a face appeared. The *Trouble Dog's* primary crew interface, or avatar, manifested as a simulated human visage of such average and symmetrical beauty it was almost impossible to tell if it had been designed to be either male or female. She had shaggy, shoulder-length black hair and dark eyes with just a hint of an epicanthic fold, and she wore a white shirt and a black tie.

"I have no way to tell."

"No sign of anyone else while we were down there?"

"None." The *Trouble Dog* was being patient with me. If another ship had been present in this system, she would already have assessed it as a potential threat. The very fact she had not yet activated her defensive screens and countermeasures should have been enough to tell me that, so far, she had found nothing out of the ordinary.

We had two survivors. If and when they felt able to talk, I would question them. Until then, my responsibility was to get the *Trouble Dog* back to Camrose Station. I activated the internal communications system. "Clay, are you ready to leave?"

Her voice came back over my earbud. "All strapped in, Captain."

"Okay then, departure in one minute. Ship, set a count-down."

"Yes, Captain."

We never usually bothered with the formalities, but I wanted to do this flight by the book, for George's sake. I felt I owed him at least that much. I sat back and watched the timer on the main screen reduce itself towards zero.

Twenty seconds in, the *Trouble Dog* paused the countdown.

"I'm receiving a priority signal," she said.

I knew what that meant.

"Another ship in trouble?"

Three-dimensional representations of the stellar neighbourhood appeared on the main screens. A bright yellow circle flashed, indicating a small blue star a couple of dozen lights spinward of our current position.

"The *Geest van Amsterdam*." A peripheral screen lit with the schematics of a long, streamlined cylinder. "She's under attack in the Gallery. She's a medium-range passenger liner registered out of Glimmer Holme. Two hundred crew, four hundred passengers, three hundred permanent residents."

"Shit."

"And we're the nearest vessel."

I sat back and huffed. "We don't have room for more than three hundred." And even then, we'd be packing them in like sardines in a can.

"Nevertheless, we're the closest by several days."

"Even taking into account our need to refuel and resupply?"

"The second nearest RV is the *Staccato Signal*, and it's currently tracking a missing cargo hauler on the edge of the Penguin Nebula."

"That's at least a fortnight away."

"At least."

I sat up. "You say they're under attack?" I knew the Gallery lay in disputed territory, on the bloody intersection of several political factions, both human and otherwise.

The *Trouble Dog*'s avatar shrugged. "Assailants unknown. But their last signal seems to indicate the ship's AI has shut itself down, leaving them defenceless."

I felt a prickle run up the nape of my neck. "Like with the *Hobo*?" Could the scout ship's seemingly inexplicable ditching have been the result of a similar assault?

"The coincidence is remarkable."

I looked at one of the screens still projecting a view of the *Hobo*'s slowly disappearing wreck, and the storm now mauling it. "How quickly can we get there?"

"Assuming emergency resupply times at Camrose Station, seven days."

I made a face. "In seven days it'll all be over. Can't you get there any faster? I thought you used to be a warship?"

Lightning danced overhead. Below, the waves were getting up.

"We could reduce it to five," the *Trouble Dog* said, "if you're willing to risk significant engine degradation."

"How significant?"

"Twelve per cent chance of malfunction, seven per cent chance of total failure."

Although she spoke in neutral tones, I fancied I caught an edge of excitement behind her words. It seemed my professional crucifixion would have to wait.

"Okay, let's do it."

"Full speed for Camrose Station?"

"Give it everything you've got."

•

I settled deeper into my couch as the *Trouble Dog* rose through the hail and winds. Lightning crackled around us, skittering off the hull, reflecting back from the waves below. Rain blurred the external cameras.

The chances were good that at least some of the passengers and crew of the *Geest van Amsterdam* had survived. Most ships were designed with failsafe pressure seals to close off damaged sections and trap as much air as possible in the remaining structure. Some larger vessels were even capable of fragmenting into smaller "lifeboat" segments. Occurrences of single micrometeorite strikes emptying an entire ship of its air were mostly confined to history books and entertainments. In reality, the possibility of such events had been taken into account across centuries of ship design and, even if a missile or a speck of interstellar detritus did manage to evade the anti-collision cannons carried by most modern craft, it would be highly unlikely to knock out more than handful of internal compartments. Space travel would always be a dangerous undertaking but very few ships were now lost with all hands.

Hanging over the wild ocean, the *Trouble Dog* raised her pointed snout to the evening sky. Sensor arrays retracted into the hull. Power built in the engines. All the readouts tripped into the red, and the old warship threw herself at the firmament.

FIVE

TROUBLE DOG

When we were far enough from the planet's gravity well, I began to oscillate, skimming the membrane of the universe like a pebble flicked across the clear waters of a tropical bay. I could feel the faint touch of raw starlight on my hull, and hear the tortured howls of the solar wind. I heard the faint overspill of comms chatter from other ships in nearby systems, the echoes of their signals cast across the intervening light years by the peculiar physics of higher-space. Some of these ships were from the Human Generality, some from the other races of the Multiplicity. My hull rippled in response to each of those distant data bursts as—now free from the drag of the atmosphere—my sensor suites stretched outwards to glean more intelligence, and long-disabled weapons systems swung into place, impotently tracking potential threats.

I was designed to annihilate. Before I was decommissioned, I carried an arsenal with the potential to ruin worlds and incinerate hostile armadas. When I later grew a conscience and became a ship of the House of Reclamation, I was permitted to retain a range of defensive weaponry—ECM missile screens, chaff launchers, point-defence cannons— but the inability to kill, to inflict terrible and decisive damage, itched like a severed limb. My combat reflexes were hardwired. They couldn't have been removed without fundamentally altering what or who I was—and I had *not* been about to agree to that. Instead, I found a way to put my skill set to good use. Flying search and rescue for the House of Reclamation, I needed to be fast, sharp and fearless. I needed every scrap of guile and tactical experience I had gleaned in the navy. To effectively perform my duties, I had to be willing to enter dangerous environments and situations that had already wrecked at least one other ship; and, if that ship and its crew had been lost to piracy or enemy action, I had to be prepared to defend myself. For these reasons, decommissioned military vessels like me were particularly suited to service in the House of Reclamation. Instead of belonging to individual governments or corporations, we now served the whole of the Human Generality, and our duties brought us challenge, risk and the occasional chance to engage with hostile craft—although without being able to bring to bear the bite we could once have inflicted.

As a heavy cruiser, I had been an instrument of hard diplomacy and destruction; in the House of Reclamation, with my talents intact but my usefulness as a killing machine at an end, I had become instead a means to save lives.

It was almost enough.

●

As far as I could tell, human beings were only really capable of thinking about two or three different things at once, half a dozen at most. My attention swathed the entire structure of the ship, encompassing and supervising the functionality of power circuits, plasma chambers, navigation systems, backup generators, cryogenic fuel containment systems, long- and short-range sensor packages, and the other million or so components essential to my continued operation. I also monitored the human quarters. I watched my inhabitants grieve for their lost comrade and searched my own feelings for a corresponding reaction. However, I struggled to locate anything more acute than passing regret. George Walker had served as a member of my crew for many years, but I wasn't built to mourn. I could be concerned about the welfare of my inhabitants, but not crippled by their passing. I had lost personnel before. Their ghosts walked the empty corridors of my barrack decks. During active service, I had been home to three hundred and seven men and women of the Conglomeration Fleet. Now, with the loss of the medic, my remaining complement (not counting the two survivors from the *Hobo*) consisted of Captain Sally Konstanz, Rescue Specialist Alva Clay, and the engineer, Nod. Three people rattling around a ship designed to hold a hundred times that number.

Konstanz and Clay were fairly ordinary humans, although they hailed from different cultures within the Generality, and Clay still carried a number of augmentations left over from her days as a marine. Nod, on the other hand, was a blue-skinned hermaphroditic Druff from the planet Lestipidese.

Short, solitary, cantankerous and apolitical, the Druff possessed a natural aptitude for mechanical and electrical engineering that placed them in high demand across the Multiplicity, and, in the last two hundred years, few ships—human or otherwise—had flown without numbering at least one member of the species among their crew.

A tingle in my ventral and dorsal antennae informed me that, during the last oscillation, fully three-quarters of my mass had dipped into the howling void of higher-space. The time had come to make the full transition. Captain Konstanz was at her station on the bridge, so I signalled my readiness and she assented to the immersion.

The jump alarm echoed through the rooms and corridors of the crew's accommodations. In the infirmary, Alva Clay checked the survivors were securely strapped to their beds, and then fastened herself into the nearest chair. In the cramped, ill-lit and complicated depths of the engineering decks, Nod curled into a makeshift nest of plastic tubing and copper wire.

They all knew this would be rough.

I could jump further and run faster than most civilian vessels, but even I was going to struggle with the effort required to reach Camrose Station within the time frame demanded. I wouldn't have time to finesse the transition between normal space and the hypervoid. Instead of a graceful leap, I would have to crash through like a breaching whale.

"Five seconds," I announced over the internal speakers. The captain clung to the arms of her chair. Her knuckles paled.

"Four."

Alva Clay kissed the ceramic pendant that hung around her neck, and muttered a prayer in the language of her ancestors. Down below, the Druff whimpered in its nest.

"Three."

For a second, I pulled back from the shimmering boundary between realities and gathered my energies like a fish preparing to leap into sunlight.

"Two."

Non-essential systems and peripheral apps slowed as I redirected power to the jump engines.

"One."

SIX

SAL KONSTANZ

The ship reared and bucked as she pierced the membrane between our universe and the whistling emptiness of higher-space. The deck surged and my stomach went weightless. In order to jump into the higher dimensions, the *Trouble Dog*'s engines had to drive a wormhole through the fabric of space and time. The process involved some stupefying physics that I didn't pretend to understand. All I knew—all I needed to know—was that hurrying exposed the ship and its crew to unpredictable gravitational effects, making a wormhole's maw a dangerous place for all concerned.

This time, we were lucky. I felt invisible fingers claw at my clothes and cheeks. The ship shuddered like a gut-shot dog. My vision blurred like the view through a rainy window. Then, with a final lurch, everything crashed back into place. The views on the external screens changed from star-scattered black to formless grey, and we were through. We were ensconced in higher-space and being swept back to the Camrose System like a paper plane riding the outer edges of an oncoming cyclone.

•

Two days later, we dropped back into the universe a few thousand kilometres from our destination. By that point, both the young men we'd pulled from the wreck of the crashed scout ship had died—one from internal haemorrhaging and the other from some sort of infection picked up from being in the water with open wounds. With George gone, we had neither the expertise nor the equipment to save them.

"The whole fucking thing was a waste," Alva snapped. I was on my way to my cabin, bone tired after hunching over navigation displays for the best part of a day and a half; she was on her way back from the gym, with a white towel hooked across her shoulder and a half-empty bottle of water dangling from her fingers. It was the first time we'd seen each other in thirty-six hours, and the longest conversation we'd had during the entire flight. "We're never going to know why they crashed."

"They were out there a long time." I shrugged. "Maybe it was mechanical failure. Maybe they got sloppy."

Alva's eyes narrowed. "You were pretty sloppy yourself."

I felt a tightening knot of resentment. "Do you think you could have done better?"

"Maybe."

My cheeks burned. "You haven't commanded a ship in your life."

Alva's response was as cold as the ghost winds buffeting the hull. "I know more than you do about ground operations," she said. "I know how to look after my troops. I was on the front line, down in the mud with all the other poor bastards. I commanded a squad."

"And I commanded a frigate."

Her lip curled. "Those ships fly themselves."

I felt my fingers close around the pommel of a ceremonial cutlass I no longer carried. "Fuck you."

We glared into each other's eyes, our faces close enough that I could smell the mouthwash on her breath. She had been close to George. He had helped her with her rehabilitation. He had taught her to play chess. I wanted to tell her that George had died while we were on the ground, not in space, and that the creature that had taken him had struck with such suddenness that not even the ship had had time to raise the alarm. I wanted to tell her of the lives I'd saved on Bone Beach and Big Hill, and the way I'd spent the whole of those engagements cocooned within the command decks of my ship; that, when we were operating planet-side, I relied on her expertise because I wasn't used to ground operations. But I suspected that in her eyes, to admit that would be to admit my unfitness for command.

During the war, I'd taken fire and commanded my ship when all hell had broken loose around us; I'd faced death and failure and somehow kept my shit together and kept the ship flying. But—despite participating in over thirty rescues during my three years with the House of Reclamation—I'd never been on the ground during a firefight, never been responsible for a squad of fragile human bodies beyond the armoured confines of a ship. I knew I should have had the wherewithal to tell George not to unroll his stretchers at the water's edge, but I'd been too distracted.

Alva was angry with me because she thought I was to blame for his death. I was angry in return because I feared she was right.

When the *Trouble Dog* docked at Camrose, she walked off the ship without a backward glance and I breathed a sigh of relief. She was still a part of my crew, and would be back aboard as soon as the ship had been refuelled. In the meantime, I wouldn't register a disciplinary charge against her for insubordination and she'd have a chance to blow off steam, to vent her anger in the bars and hostelries of the station's lower decks. She would drink and fight and, when she returned, would be calmer.

As a former marine, she had an ingrained respect for the chain of command. But that didn't mean I had any right to expect her to respect me personally. In the House, respect had to be earned through deeds. As a commanding officer, you were always accountable for your actions, and if they were found to be unacceptable you would be reassigned or—in the most extreme cases—bounced from the House altogether. As hot-tempered as she might be, I sincerely doubted Clay's dislike of me would ever erupt into outright mutiny. I doubted she would even file a report.

I watched her retreating back for a moment, and then turned to Nod, who was waiting on the ramp. One of its faces looked up at me with fingers splayed, like a sunflower turning its petals to the light.

"Where are you going?" I asked. Nod had a thick cargo harness strapped around its midsection.

"Much work. Need parts. Also supplies."

"We can order anything you need."

Another face curled around to peer at me. "Need special things also." Its shoulders flexed and rippled. "Also company."

"Other Druff?"

"Always others on other ships. Always some in port."

"Friends?" The idea of Nod socialising seemed somehow incongruous. Its habits aboard ship were so solitary and self-contained it had never occurred to me it might need to be around anyone, even other members of its own species.

"All blown from same World Tree." It gave an approximation of a human shrug. "All welcome."

The fingers rippled around the edges of both of its raised faces. The four on the floor drummed their tips against the deck. I had no idea what the gesture meant, if anything. It could have been impatience or excitement, or maybe even a mixture of both.

"You want to go right now?" I had so many other

questions. For instance, I wanted to know where the Druff gathered. Walking around Camrose, you only saw Druff when they were engaged on an errand. They never seemed to stop to pass the time of day with their fellows, and I couldn't recall ever seeing one in a bar or café. Did they have their own designated spaces, or simply congregate in the station's dusty maintenance ducts?

"Work underway. Ship healing. Much to do."

I noticed a grease smudge on one of its legs, a smear of dust on another. Nod spent most of its time crawling through access panels and wiring channels, keeping the *Trouble Dog* fit and flying, and it asked very little in return—just the chance to use scraps and bits of old wire to build itself a nest in the engine room. The least I could do was let it out to spend a couple of hours with its brethren.

"Go on, then."

"Aye, Captain." Nod dipped its heads in gratitude, then turned and slouched away on four legs. It held the other two aloft, turning them this way and that as it took in its new surroundings.

I watched Nod follow Clay through the door connecting our hangar bay with the rest of the station. When they had both gone, I tapped my hand against the side of the ship.

"Be good while I'm gone."

•

When I arrived at the House of Reclamation's embassy on the upper concourse, a harassed-looking adjutant in a crisply ironed uniform ushered me through the foyer and into a back office. He was young and had little drops of sweat on his upper lip.

"You're expected," he said, and showed me into the ambassador's office.

Framed prints graced the walls, depicting snub-nosed naval

carriers shaped like baton rounds. A fish tank bubbled in one corner, diaphanous jellyfish wafting in its artificial currents.

"Sally."

Ambassador Odom rose from behind his desk and we shook hands.

"Ambassador."

He gestured me to a seat, and then returned to his chair. A pot of tea was waiting. He poured two cups and pushed one over to me. It was green and steaming.

"I was sorry to hear about George Walker."

"Thank you." I cleared my throat. "He was a good man. We'll miss him very much."

He dropped a sweetener into his drink and stirred it with a spoon. The metal clinked against the inside of the china cup. He frowned at me across the wooden desk. "Was it your fault?"

I clasped my hands in my lap. "I didn't have him in sight when the creature took him."

"He was on his own, then?"

"I was with him." My lips and tongue were dry, but I couldn't face the tea. "I had my back to him. I warned him not to get too close to the water's edge, but…"

"I take it you had conducted a risk assessment of the local fauna?"

He knew I hadn't. The *Trouble Dog* would have told him, been forced to when she submitted a report.

"No, sir."

With finger and thumb, Odom smoothed the ends of his moustache. Like most of us, he had once served in the military, but now, instead of a uniform, he wore a charcoal-grey business suit and a high-collared white shirt.

"I see." He picked his cup from its saucer and inhaled the steam.

"The *Hobo* was taking on water," I told him. "By the time

we got there, she had been wallowing for three days. We only had a few minutes' grace before she sank for good."

Odom sipped his tea. "So," he said, "you knowingly placed your crew and yourself in harm's way?"

"I took a calculated risk."

He sat back in his chair and drummed his fingers. "No, Captain." With his fingertips, he pushed his cup and saucer aside. "You lacked the data to make a *calculated* risk. The decision you made was stupid and *uncalculated*, and it resulted in the death of one of your crew."

"I'm—" My voice faltered. "I'm sorry, sir."

I braced myself for a tirade, but instead he made a visible effort to control his temper. Fingers to his temples, eyes closed, he sighed, "What is our motto? The motto your own great-great-grandmother coined for us?"

"Life Above All."

"Above *all*, Captain. Above *all*." He settled back in his chair. "There will be a full inquiry," he said. "By rights, I should ground you until then, but…"

"The *Geest van Amsterdam*?"

"I'm afraid so."

"Do we know anything more?"

"Only what was contained in her original signal: that she was under attack in the Gallery."

"No ID on the assailants?"

"Nothing."

I brushed a speck of fluff from the knee of my fatigues. "I'll need a new medic." We were already operating with the barest skeleton of a crew.

"When do you leave?" Odom's fingernail sketched a rectangle on the desk and a screen appeared.

"In four hours, as soon as we're refuelled."

He peered down at the screen's blue glow and impatiently tapped a couple of icons. "I'll have one with you in three."

49

"Thank you, Ambassador." I rose to my feet. "Will there be anything else?"

"Not for now." When he spoke, his voice was gruff. "Just come back with your crew and your ship in one piece."

He didn't need to tell me that when I did, he'd throw the book at me.

SEVEN

ASHTON CHILDE

The airfield consisted of little more than a few buildings and a cleared strip of bare earth, surrounded on all sides by dense, foul-smelling jungle. As I stepped from the relative cool of my office, the evening air hit my face like a stale, piss-soaked flannel. Beyond the perimeter fence, the trees sweltered, their shaggy tips bent over by the weight of their own drooping leaves. Animal yelps and hollers cracked the fetid air, and flocks of silver manta-ray-like creatures beat skywards on wings of drum-taut skin.

Pushing through the overbearing heat, I made my way to the civilian trading post at the far end of the compound. I had to walk the length of the runway, past the hangars and the half-dozen chubby cargo planes lined up on the tarmac, ready for loading.

I'd been stationed here on Cichol's equator for eighteen months, ever since the start of the insurgency, but had yet to reconcile myself—and my digestion—to the humidity and the pervasive reek of putrefying foliage. I longed for the colder climates up north. By the time I reached the post, sweat plastered my hair to my head, and my nose and throat felt coated and slimy with the jungle's stench.

The trading post was a large, single-storey structure

constructed from corrugated iron and bamboo. Inside, a counter took up most of one end of the available space, behind which could be seen shelves of canned goods, bottled water and other jungle equipment. The rest of the room had been given over to chairs and tables. An antique jukebox stood against the back wall like an altar from a lost civilisation. Lazy ceiling fans did little to disturb the thick, hot air.

Agent Petrushka was sitting at a corner table, dressed in civilian clothes. When she saw me in the doorway, she stiffened. "Hello."

I held my hands out to the sides, to show I wasn't armed. "I'm not here to kill you."

She let herself relax. "I never thought you were."

I pulled up a chair and gave her an indulgent smile. "We lost a plane over the southern range this morning. I'm guessing that was down to your lot?"

"I don't think so." She worked for the Outward, monitoring our little clandestine operation. "Who was flying it?"

"Harris."

"Well, there's your answer then. He was in here until dawn yesterday, drinking bourbon and smoking barracuda weed."

"You promise?"

She gave a bored shrug. "Those new stealth planes are good. I had no idea you had anyone in the air yesterday. That is, until I noticed the smoke plume from the crash site."

I signalled to the barman and he brought over a pitcher of beer and a couple of clean glasses.

"Okay, then."

The room trembled as another cargo plane lumbered skywards, carrying food and ammunition for the rebels in the mountains. We listened to the sound of its engines fade into the jungle's evening chorus.

Wreathed in mist, the mountains were treacherous to navigate at the best of times. If Harris had been flying tired and strung out, it was quite possible he'd simply flown into the ground, or hit one of those huge manta ray creatures. It had happened before, to other pilots under similar circumstances. These guys were civilian contractors operating in a combat zone. They weren't used to taking fire while flying at low altitude through difficult terrain. When the stress finally got to them—and it inevitably did—they either bought themselves out of their contracts or they ended up like Harris.

I poured a beer from the pitcher.

The rebels could print their own guns, but they didn't have the facilities or time to manufacture the quantities of ammunition and medicine needed to support their campaign. Instead, a Conglomeration freighter passed through the fringes of the system once a fortnight and released a cargo pod on a slow, unpowered trajectory that eventually brought it parachuting down into the ocean a few kilometres from the mouth of the delta. From there, local fishermen recovered the anonymous crates within and brought them here, to this airbase, where they were loaded onto planes and dropped once again, this time into the mountains.

In the early days of the operation, I'd ridden along on most of the sorties, establishing relationships with some of the local guerrilla chiefs, negotiating the terms of our aid. Then, about two months after first setting foot on this rock, I'd made the mistake of landing on the outskirts of a village recently "liberated" by the rebels. Palls of ash-white smoke lingered in the turgid mid-afternoon air. Nothing else moved. Most of the villagers had perished as their dwellings were burned. Their remains were blackened sticks among the smouldering piles of their former homes. The dozen or so that had survived had been tied to stakes in the village square. Some had been shot, others eviscerated, and their entrails spilled into the dust at their feet. Their corpses sagged against their damp restraints, heads bowed. From the way the stakes had been set in a rough semi-circle, I guessed that, before they'd been killed, they'd been made to watch as their livestock had been impaled, one on top of the other, on a long bamboo spike.

And when the livestock had run out, the rebels had made a second spike and started impaling children, starting with a boy of around thirteen, and then working down by age, from oldest to youngest...

My left eye twitched. I hadn't been into the mountains since. I cleared my throat, pushing the memory aside.

"Have you heard from your bosses recently?"

Petrushka smiled. She wiped her thumb through the condensation on her glass. "Not since last week. You heard from yours?"

"Just now."

"And?" Her glass was empty. She reached across the table for the pitcher's handle. I glanced around the room. Apart from the barman, we had the place to ourselves.

"And I've got a new assignment."

"About time too." She poured a drink and sucked the froth from the top of her glass. "Because you suck at this one."

She said it with a smile but I knew she was right. I had known for eighteen long, uncomfortable months.

I had known the minute I walked into that village.

"I just go where they send me." Even to my own ears, it sounded lame. She raised an eyebrow.

"And you do what you're told like a good little soldier?"

I felt my left eye twitch again. My head felt like a thundercloud. I drew myself up in my chair. "I don't see how I'm any different from you." As agents, we were both past our prime, and that was one of the commonalities that had drawn us together.

We were both veterans. I had been working for Conglomeration Intelligence for close to twelve years;

she had been an Outward agent for ten. The implants I'd had placed in my skull, that had made me feel wired and special at the age of twenty-five, were now, at thirty-seven, an anachronism. Direct connection had become something of an anathema. When I'd first started out, Conglomeration ship captains had been permanently wired into their ships; now, they did everything via vocal commands. Invasive neural upgrades were yesterday's news, and the integrity of the skull had become, once again, sacrosanct—at least, within the confines of the Generality. Of course, I couldn't speak for all the factions and species of the Multiplicity, some of whom were more machine than organism.

Most of the hardware in my head was obsolete, but so firmly embedded as to be impossible to remove without fatal complications.

Her eyes darted to the left; her teeth scraped her lower lip. "Things work a little differently in the Outward. We don't get orders, we bid for assignments."

"You mean you *chose* to come here?"

She placed one hand flat on the table, covered it with the other. I could see the beads of sweat on her upper lip. "What can I say? I'm a masochist."

I knew enough about Laura Petrushka to know that wasn't true. I'd read her file the same way I'm sure she'd read mine. At university, she'd majored in political theory and economics, excelled in archery, fencing and chess. In her third year, she'd been recruited into Outward Intelligence by one of her lecturers and, upon graduation, had immediately been put to work on the fringes of diplomacy.

She hadn't set out to be a spy. We had that much in common.

Unlike most of the operatives in the Conglomeration Intelligence Service, I'd never served in the armed forces. I'd been a rookie cop, running down criminals in the filthy warrens of Europa's decrepit undersea cities. I'd got mixed up in the wrong investigation—a simple alley homicide that led right back to the police commissioner's office—and found myself bounced, and bounced *hard*. Three broken ribs, a shattered kneecap, four broken fingers. Two days later, a couple of suits pulled me from the backstreet clinic where the cops—my former colleagues—had dumped me, and asked me if I wanted a real challenge.

I didn't even stop to think about it.

Joining the CIS was the single most fulfilling thing to happen in my life—and the first thing I did was go back and arrest every bastard in my old precinct. A decade later, the memory of their outraged faces still gave me a warm, satisfied feeling.

Unfortunately, little else did.

"Okay," I said, having observed the weird, unspoken preliminaries of our relationship. "Do you want to know or not?"

Petrushka kinked an eyebrow, inviting me to continue.

"I've been ordered to report to the spaceport at Northfield," I told her.

She sat up a little straighter. Northfield was halfway around the planet, on another, much chillier, continent altogether.

"Why?"

I took a breath. By sharing the information I was about to divulge, I would be committing treason—but, after all these months, I no longer thought of Laura Petrushka as an enemy. As far as I was concerned, she was the closest thing I had to a friend on this rotting ball of mud.

The ceiling fans squeaked. I took a sip of beer and cleared my throat. I felt shaky. After all these months, there might be a light at the end of the hot, dismal tunnel my life at the airstrip had become.

"There's a ship coming. I'm going to hitch a ride to the Gallery."

"The Gallery?"

"Yes." My voice wavered, and I took a pull from my glass. I didn't want her to see how shaky I was. I didn't know if the butterflies in my chest were due to excitement, apprehension, or the barracuda weed. Perhaps they were a blend of all three. "There's someone there they want me to find."

EIGHT

SAL KONSTANZ

After leaving the embassy, I wandered the dockyard at Camrose Station. I had no need to hurry back to the *Trouble Dog*. The ship was more than capable of interfacing with the station to take care of her needs, and would alert me when she had been serviced and was ready to depart. In the meantime, I walked. The people I passed—those walking rather than taking one of the travel tubes—seemed drawn from every world and faction of the Generality. The locals affected loose, ankle-length kimonos, while visiting space crews wore fatigues or uniforms. Dressed in the regulation blue overalls of the House of Reclamation, I passed unnoticed.

To either side of the dockyard concourse, windows opened onto vast bays, some holding ships. I saw a scout craft similar to the *Hobo*, sitting on the floor of one of the hangars like a moth on the floor of a gymnasium. In the next bay along, mechanics were in the process of reassembling a bulk cargo hauler fully a kilometre and a half in length. Maintenance drones flew through its superstructure, pausing here and there to weld a patch or install a new component.

Ship minds were assembled in virtual nurseries according to strict regulations intended to prevent the emergence of machines capable of upgrading or replicating themselves.

The more sociable were assigned to cruise ships; those with a tendency towards curating were assigned to manage orbital stations like Camrose; and the loners with the most solitary and reclusive personalities were installed on scout ships and long-distance cargo haulers.

If questioned, the *Trouble Dog* would try to convince you she had become a battleship because of her strict morals and scholarly demeanour. She saw herself as a kind of warrior poet in the vein of a seventeenth-century Japanese samurai; however, having captained the beast for two years, I regarded her personality as being more akin to that of an exceptionally smart Alsatian: loyal, energetic and prone to snapping at strangers. The ship wasn't supposed to have a refined sense of right and wrong. Heavy cruisers couldn't afford to be crippled by remorse, nor Reclamation Vessels preoccupied with failed rescues. Both had to be able to make instantaneous life-or-death judgments, and live with the results. However, an unintended side effect of using cloned human cells in the construction of ship minds was a tendency for unwanted emotions to seep into their personalities. Hence the *Trouble Dog's* decision to resign her commission and enrol with the House.

·

Although I never walked the sentient jungles of Pelapatarn, I did once fly over them on a cargo dirigible, as we were ferrying medical supplies from one port to another. It was three weeks before we suffered the final attack, and I was overseeing the restock of the medical frigate. For six hours, I had nothing to do but dangle my legs through the railings of the gondola's observation platform, inhale the flowery scent of the canopy, listen to the squawk and gibber of flitting bird-lizards, and wonder at the ponderous creaks of the trees as they engaged in their dreamy, decades-long discourse.

By the time the Conglomeration attack came, I was back on

board the *Nightingale*, and we were in a higher orbit, well outside the scope of the battle. From up there, the planet resembled a jewel set against the velvet cushion of space, its single continent a vivid emerald sliver in an ocean of glittering cerulean.

After the strike, all that was gone. Clouds of smoke and ash obscured the surface, transforming the globe from a shimmering precious stone to a rheumy, cataract-choked eyeball, and we watched from our vantage in horror, more shocked by the desecration than by the slowly dawning fact we had lost the war.

In the hours following the strike, rescue shuttles pulled a depressingly low number of survivors from the radioactive hell-scape. All our senior commanders were dead, as were thousands of soldiers from both sides. The only ones who made it out alive were those who had been fortunate to be in deep bunkers near the coast, on the fringes of the holocaust.

One by one, they were carried aboard, bodies blackened and eyes unseeing, skin charred and blistered, clothes and hair burned away, their bodies riddled with near-lethal doses of radiation. In most cases, it was impossible to tell on which side they had fought—and it hardly seemed to matter in the face of such overwhelming horror. All we could do was try to patch up the ones who could be saved, and make comfortable those who couldn't.

Towards the end of the second day following the bombardment, I volunteered to go down with one of the shuttles. Our flight crews had far exceeded their limits in terms of flying time and radiation exposure. If others like me hadn't stepped forward, the rescue operation would have had to be abandoned.

I don't remember much about the descent through the upper atmosphere. I think I kept my eyes closed the whole time. It was only towards the end, as we were spiralling down to land, that I looked over the pilots' shoulders at the smoking ruins of a once-verdant world. Ash pattered against the shuttle's leading edges, threatening to choke our engines. Embers swirled like fireflies. And everything on the ground was black and burned. In places, the soil had been scoured back to bedrock; in others, the charcoal stumps of once-mighty trees stood against the smoke like crudely vandalised grave markers.

Our target was a supply depot set into the base of some cliffs on the side of the continent facing the prevailing winds. We had received radio signals from survivors, and had high hopes that the winds would have carried the majority of the fallout inland, away from the rocky beach that housed the bunker's camouflaged entrance. Nevertheless, we were all wearing protective suits, and armed in case of trouble. We had heard reports of deluded or deranged soldiers firing on rescuers, unwilling or unable to accept the end of hostilities.

This time, though, we were lucky. The squad of marines huddled beneath the cliff were Outwarders like us, and they were in no mood for a fight. They knew what had happened, and they were just as shocked as we had been. More so, I guess, having felt the force of the explosions through the rock beneath their feet, and felt the world itself convulse with the fury unleashed against it.

They were sick and injured, and desperately in need of decontamination. Their gratitude at our arrival was tired and mostly unspoken, but it was there and it was sincere.

We took them back to the *Nightingale* for treatment— the single largest group of survivors so far recovered. And over the weeks that followed, I got to know some of them. And then later, when I left the service to join the House of Reclamation, one of them came with me. She said that she'd follow me anywhere, that she owed me her life, that if I hadn't kept the shuttles running she would have died in that bunker. We often disagreed, but I was glad of her company.

Her name was Alva Clay.

·

When I returned to the *Trouble Dog*, I found a young man standing uncertainly at the bay door. He had a heavy bag slung over his shoulder and a suitcase by his feet.

"Excuse me," he said. "Are you Captain Konstanz?"

I looked at his bright orange overalls. "You're the replacement?"

"Preston Menderes."

"How old are you, Preston?"

"Twenty-four."

"When did you graduate from medical school?"

"Last year."

"Do you have any field experience?"

He blushed and rubbed his eyebrow with his thumb. "Six months as an assistant on the *Happy Wanderer*."

"A liner? What were you doing, curing headaches and hangovers?"

He stiffened. "There was a little more to it than that."

"I'm sure." I turned to the door. "Well, come on then, if you're coming."

I stepped over the threshold, from the relative confines of the station's corridors to the echoing vault of the maintenance bay. The walls to the left and right of me were each half a kilometre distant, and the far wall, which housed the main doors, twice that distance. Overhead, the lights in the ceiling were like stars in the sky.

The *Trouble Dog* hung in the horizontal and vertical centre of the room. The air shimmered beneath her. Spotlights threw bright circles across her prickling bronze-coloured hide. From where I stood, I could make out the silhouettes of various disabled systems, and the empty weapon flats where the more offensive ordnance had been removed. Behind me, Preston Menderes paused and shaded his eyes as he looked up at the projectile-shaped fuselage.

63

"Christ," he breathed. "What an antique."

I gave him a sharp glance.

"Careful," I said. "She has feelings."

We walked into the shadow of the *Trouble Dog*, to where a platform waited for us.

"Hold the rail," I advised Preston, knowing the *Trouble Dog*'s penchant for the theatrical. Not to mention its partiality for revenging slights.

As it happened, though, we were ferried up into the belly of the brute without so much as a single jolt. I looked across at the kid's disdainful expression and thought, *Sneer while you can.* I knew this ship, and I knew she couldn't let his comment pass. She'd get even with a prank of some kind; I just didn't know how, or where, it would happen.

•

Aside from a few access panels, crawlways and maintenance hatches, the majority of the human-habitable portions of the *Dog* lay in a torus wrapped around her thickest point. Sensors and armament filled the tip of her pointed nose; engines the rest, from just behind the bow to the end of her gently tapering and flat-edged stern. The human quarters were like an inflatable rubber ring caught around the waist of a shark.

We came in via the embarkation lounge. As we entered the ship's internal gravity field, my stomach did its customary flip. No matter where you were on the *Dog*, once you were inside the hull, "up" always lay in the direction of the ship's core. In the main corridor, the floor seemed to slope upwards ahead and behind you, as if you were at the lowest point of a gentle valley.

The air from the ceiling vents was cool and smelled of compost, but you soon got used to it. Once, long ago, the riveted metal walls had been given a coat of white paint, but the paint had yellowed over the years to scuffed and grimy sepia, into which generations of naval personnel had scratched their initials and grievances. Only Alva Clay had bothered to decorate the corridor walls around her cabin. Walker and I had never taken the time to personalise the corridors outside our rooms, preferring to keep our decoration within. By common agreement, our cabins had been located at equidistant points around the ship's circumference, as far from each other as we could get while still remaining within the main crew section.

It's not that we particularly disliked each other; it's just that nobody joins the House of Reclamation because they have a happy home life. I can't speak for the others, but my reasons for removing myself were the same as those that had compelled me to join the service in the first place: a need to get away from the people around me, from the things I'd done and the things I'd seen; a craving for the seclusion necessary to evaluate my feelings and experiences, and determine my place in the chaotic flow of events; and when it came to the placement of the cabin, if I'm being brutally honest, the need to be able to cry in peace, without worrying about being interrupted. Ninety-nine per cent of the accommodations were bare and unoccupied; it seemed natural to me to put as many of them as possible between my nearest neighbour and myself—and my neighbours seemed to share my sentiments. The ship wasn't overly needful of the company of her own kind, and neither were we. At any time of the day or night, we could wander at will among the empty cabins and imagine ourselves almost perfectly alone.

But these weren't the concerns uppermost in my mind as I directed our newest young recruit to Walker's old cabin. I assumed he'd take the berth vacated by his predecessor. It never occurred to me he'd want to sleep anywhere else.

•

"*Night terrors?*"

"Yes, ma'am."

"And you want to knock on my door every time you have a nightmare?"

I swear his cheeks flushed. "No!"

"Then what are you asking me?"

His eyes glanced around the deck, unwilling to meet my own. "It helps," he mumbled.

"What does?" I'd seldom seen a young man look so uncomfortable. He screwed up his face and rubbed the back of his neck. His eyes filled with glittering embarrassment.

"To have somebody nearby."

We regarded each other for a while and I thought I understood. I still left the bathroom light on when I went to bed, so as not to have to sleep in an entirely dark cabin, so I could make-believe a safe and everyday space; a place where the ghosts of my time on the medical frigate were impotent and where I could sleep in peace.

"Okay." I turned on my heel and led him uphill, around the curve of the main deck. Burdened with luggage, he stumbled to keep pace.

"Captain?"

I didn't look around. I didn't know this kid, and I had no reason to care how he slept. "Look," I said awkwardly, thinking of George—thinking he might still have been alive had he been less tired, more rested and alert—"if it helps, perhaps you can take the cabin across the hall from mine?"

Preston looked up hopefully. "Really?"

"Just don't expect me to hold your hand every time you get scared."

The kid gave a nervous smile. "I won't, thank you."

"Don't thank me." I led him to a vacant cabin on the other side of the companionway from mine. I opened the door for him and switched on the light. "I'm not doing it for you."

He gave me a quizzical look—the look of a young man baffled by an older woman. "Then, who…?"

I stepped aside and gestured him into the room. I wanted to say I was doing it for George but, in reality, I knew I was doing it for myself, to help quell the guilt that had—since his death—begun to growl in my ear whenever I found myself alone, whenever the noises quietened and the lights dimmed.

"Just don't make a nuisance of yourself," I told him.

He gave me a grateful smile. "I won't, Captain, I promise."

He seemed sincere, but I already had misgivings about the proximity of his personal space to mine.

"See that you don't."

NINE

SAL KONSTANZ

As soon as her fuel cells were charged and her holds replenished, the *Trouble Dog* slipped her moorings.

I was on the bridge, strapped into my command couch. Alva Clay was below, in her cabin; Preston was in his, and I assumed Nod was in its nest.

The *Dog* had been in constant contact with Camrose Station during the refuelling process, and both had planned the exact moment of departure down to the last second. The bay doors were already retracting as the *Dog* swung her nose, seeking the vacuum of empty space. The point of her bronze-coloured bow caught the sunlight, and I felt the deck shudder as she engaged her primary thrusters.

We surged out of the station and punched through local traffic like a speedboat through a flotilla of yachts, leaving them scattered and squawking in our wake—something I knew the ship took a perverse delight in doing. Not that anyone would complain, of course. We were riding under the colours of the House of Reclamation; the next time we set forth at such speed, the lives we were racing to save might be theirs.

On screen, I watched Camrose Station grow smaller and smaller. Behind its interconnected rings and twinkling lights,

I could see the rusty continents and blue oceans of the planet Camrose, home to two billion people.

How strange, I thought, that the human race had once been entirely limited to a solitary and similarly fragile planet. It seemed absurd. How could we have survived such confinement? By the time the Multiplicity came calling—in the disreputable shape of a battered old trading vessel from the Goblet Cluster—humanity must have been clawing at the walls of its prison. According to family history, my maternal great-great-grandmother had been born on the Moon, in orbit around a dying Earth. Her name was Sofia Nikitas. She had been sixteen years old when the trading ship set down on the Sea of Tranquility. By the time she disappeared, at the age of forty-five, she had travelled more than a thousand light years and left footprints in the dust and soil of more than a hundred different worlds. And, along the way, she had become the founder of the House of Reclamation.

I had requested no additional advantage in the House because of our connection. I hadn't wanted to measure my career against hers. But even so, as I sat on the bridge of the *Trouble Dog*, preparing for the plunge into the wailing nothingness of the hypervoid, I felt I had disgraced her legacy.

•

As soon as the stars vanished, giving way to grey mist, I unstrapped from my couch and went aft. We would be in the hole for forty-nine hours and I had no intention of staring at the external view for a moment longer than necessary. The emptiness of higher-space could deceive the areas of the brain associated with visual perception, depriving them of stimulation and inducing visions, hallucinations, feelings of nausea and creeping dread.

We had all done it during basic flight training. We had all been encouraged to stare into the nothingness of the hypervoid long enough to start seeing patterns and sparks—but it was something most people only did once, just to find out what it was like. The ensuing headaches and nightmares were usually enough to dissuade them from trying again. The few who did it a second or third time—and there were always one or two in each class—risked losing themselves to delusion and paranoia, becoming convinced titanic creatures prowled out there, at the ragged edge of our ability to perceive them, in the grey nihility of the higher dimensions.

After leaving the bridge, my first port of call was Alva's cabin. When I reached it, I found she'd left the door open. I stepped inside and leant against the wall, arms folded.

"Hey."

She was sitting on the edge of her bed, stripping down her sidearm. She didn't look up. "I could hear you coming from the other end of the corridor," she said.

"I didn't want to startle you." I watched her disassemble the pistol and arrange the parts on the cloth at her feet. "Did you have fun on Camrose?"

"I wouldn't call it fun." She raised her chin and I saw the darkening bruises beneath her eyes, the clean white surgical tape across the bridge of her nose. "How about you? Did you see the ambassador?"

"Yes."

"Did he give you much trouble?"

I gave a half-hearted smile. "Not as much as whoever did that to you."

Alva brought the fingers of her right hand up to dab her left eye socket, and I caught a glimpse of more tape on her knuckles.

"But you are in the shit?" she asked.

I let out a sigh. "He wants to talk to me when we get back."

"Do you think you might get fired?"

"I don't know." I shrugged my shoulders. "Possibly."

Alva's expression hardened. "Good."

I turned my eyes away, unnerved by her defiant stare. "There was nothing I could have done," I said quietly. "Not even the ship had time to react."

In my peripheral vision, I saw Alva's lip curl in a sneer. "He shouldn't have been standing there in the first place." She reached down and began to reassemble the gun, sliding each piece into place with instinctive precision. "If you'd done your job properly, you'd have known about the sea life. You could have warned him to keep the stretchers away from the edge."

"And we would have lost the two we pulled from the *Hobo*."

"We lost them anyway."

I tightened my arms against my chest. "That's not the point."

"Isn't it?"

•

Intending to return to my cabin, I took the long way around the ship's circular habitat. I needed the walk, needed time to blow off steam and stomp off the tension that had me knotting my fists and swearing under my breath. Unfortunately, I realised with deepening unease, my route would take me past George's room.

I slowed my pace as I approached the threshold, reluctant to face any more reminders of my failure. I'd already been here once today with Preston, and that was enough. I didn't want a second look at George's possessions sitting where he'd left them: the photographs of his daughter and grandchildren taped to the bulkhead; the keepsakes upon his shelves. I didn't want the reassuring, homely smell of his unwashed sheets. Instead, I brushed my hand against the door's cold steel and moved on, past all the hundreds of other unlit and unoccupied cabins, my stride quick and purposeful in order to ward away the emotional lump building in my oesophagus.

I'd done what I'd thought best, and what I'd thought the situation required. If I was found guilty of negligence, I wouldn't contest the verdict; I'd spend my last pay cheque travelling to Earth to find George's daughter, so I could apologise to her in person. And, after that... Well, I hadn't planned that far ahead. Right now, all I knew for sure was that a liner was in trouble. Nine hundred people were out there somewhere in the dark, praying for rescue, and it was up to us to come to their aid. We were the nearest ship. Until we reached them, all other considerations could take a back seat. For the moment, I was still a captain of the House of Reclamation, pledged to help the citizens of the Generality in their times of peril and distress, no matter their race, religion or political affiliation. That was the ideal for which George Walker had given his life, and adhering to that was the very least I could do to honour his sacrifice.

TEN

TROUBLE DOG

Made as I was from ingredients taken from both humans and dogs, I have an understandable curiosity concerning the history of life on Earth. While indulging that curiosity, I have seen recordings of base-jumpers hurling their fragile bodies from the tops of cliffs and the summits of skyscrapers. I've seen the wind tear at their clothes, imagined the roar of it in their ears, the cold blast of it against their faces, chests and legs. For a few, ephemeral instants they free-fall unsupported, mapping the perilous frontier between existence and obliteration, trusting their parachutes to catch them before impact and land them without death or injury.

I tell you this because it's the human experience I imagine to be closest to that of leaping through the hypervoid.

Having left Camrose and jumped towards our destination, I found myself swirled in nothingness. I felt the wind (which is not wind) against my hull, heard the electromagnetic snarl of the universe stretched and amplified. Ships called to each other in distant systems, and I heard their echoes like whale song beneath the arctic ice. Stars roared like blowtorch flames. And I tore through the mists like a skydiver, bursting with the joy that came from fulfilling my purpose.

A tool or a weapon lives only in the moment in which

it is used. As I no longer waged war, I now existed for these instants, when I leapt from the universe, describing a glittering arc through the blank void, trusting only that my calculations would catch me and bring me safely to my destination.

Ships that botched their calculations or jumped with faulty engines seldom re-emerged from higher-space. I had known a few during the war: good ships who'd taken desperate gambles to preserve themselves and their crews, only to disappear forever, irretrievably lost in the fog.

In the human-habitable torus around my waist, the crew turned off their external screens. The limbo-like nothingness of the higher dimensions bothered them on a deep, instinctive level. Exposed to it for too long, their mammalian brains were prone to imagining sabre-toothed shadows lurking in the mist beyond the cave mouth. Millions of years of evolution had conditioned them to see patterns, to pick the outline of a skulking predator from a confusion of foliage. Faced with the utter vacuity of higher-space, that same instinct flared impulsively, conceiving arrangements and dangers where none existed.

Understandably, I had been designed to be immune to such considerations. My view of the void around me contained nothing fanciful or illusory. The only threats tagged by my targeting computers were those that could be independently verified by my other sensors. During the war, one of my lieutenants had been fond of quoting Nietzsche. But when I gazed into this abyss, I saw only an absence; and if the abyss gazed back at me, I remained unaware of its attentions.

Instead, I let my mind drift, thinking of the war and my lost sisters.

•

As a civilisation, the Conglomeration claimed descent from the capitalist Anglo-American culture that flourished around the margins of the Atlantic Ocean in the centuries before the Great Dispersal, a culture that had in turn borrowed many of its ideals and foundations from the classical Greco-Roman empires of the Mediterranean Basin. While not as large or powerful as some human societies within the Generality, the Conglomeration was at least one of the most ethnically and culturally diverse, able to number among their citizenry representatives of every Terran race and creed—although this diversity owed more to the enslavements of the eighteenth and nineteenth centuries, and the wars and migrations of the twentieth and twenty-first, than it did to any conscious policy of inclusion.

As a ship of the Conglomeration Fleet, I spent the first twelve years of my life serving alongside five sibling vessels. They were all Carnivore-class heavy cruisers, identical to me in almost every respect.

War Mutt.

Adalwolf.

Anubis.

Coyote.

Fenrir.

We were a pack, a clique and a family, our minds having been cultivated and grown in the same laboratory. Together, we participated in border patrols and police actions, keeping the peace and offering protection to all the colonies, outposts and ships within the Conglomeration territories. For ten years, we were deadly and inseparable—apex predators capable of flying faster and hitting harder than almost anything else in human space. But then the Archipelago War came and shattered our complacency. *Anubis*, the proudest of us all, fell victim to a battery of magnetic rail-guns firing iron ingots at near-relativistic velocities. A week later, dear sweet *Coyote* ran into a nano-minefield concealed within the chromosphere of a local star. The explosions from the miniature antimatter mines weren't powerful enough to disable her, but were just potent enough to compromise her heat shield, allowing superheated hydrogen to scour her insides to plasma.

The war was over now, and I no longer fought. Instead, I tried to save people. I threw myself at the stars like a fist thrown at the face of God and sometimes, if we were fortunate enough, we brought back a survivor or two. So far, during the course of my service in the House of Reclamation, I had been instrumental in the location and recovery of (counting the two from the *Hobo*) 205 living individuals, and the retrieval of 771 corpses. Yet still the aggregate sum of lives I had saved lagged far behind the total number of lives I had ended.

The Archipelago War had been an epic and bloody conflict that sprawled from the outermost reaches of the Galactic Arm to the sentient jungles of Pelapatarn. During the siege of the asteroid fortresses of Cold Tor, my sisters and I had used minor ordnance to target civilian population centres. I had been responsible for reducing six environmental pressure domes to tattered craters. Each dome had housed over two thousand men, women and children. Those not killed by the impacts and explosions had died seconds later, gasping in a vacuum.

And then later, on the orders of Captain Annelida Deal, I had helped raze the sentient jungles of Pelapatarn, turning a million-year-old parliament of conscious trees to ash and dust. Could a crime of that magnitude ever be forgiven? I had been acting under orders; I had simply been the weapon, the delivery mechanism for the wrath of the Conglomeration Fleet.

Yet, the fault was also mine. Due to emotional seepage from the human portions of my brain, I had been starting to develop the beginnings of a conscience, although I hadn't mentioned it to my superiors. I couldn't have prevented the attack, but I could have refused to participate; I could have lost myself in the ragged winds of higher-space and left the bickering factions of the Generality to their slaughter. I could have selected any one of those options, but I didn't. Instead, I played the part written into the design of every component of my being. I was a Carnivore-class battleship and I fulfilled my function, despite the questions and doubts growing in my mind. My sisters and I brought the dispute to an end using the tools at our disposal, concluding the conflict at the cost of nineteen thousand soldiers and four hundred thousand human non-combatants.

We slaughtered them and the dreaming jungle in which they fought to prevent the conflict from spreading. It was, our superiors assured us, a justifiable crime. General Deal's advisors had calculated an eighty-seven per cent chance that our display of overwhelming ruthlessness would end the war there and then, thereby sparing further, and possibly greater, loss of life. I did my duty and didn't question the decision; I simply supplied the barrage and monitored the unfolding destruction, the utter and irrevocable efficiency of my actions. I watched trees and people burn. The roar of the flames drowned their voices. The blistering heat charred their skin and boiled their blood and brains, and turned the world-wrapping forest into a black, smoking wasteland.

I think the horror of the attack awakened something in us all. *War Mutt* deliberately mis-jumped, flinging herself into the higher dimensions with no regard for safety or destination. No ship had ever done that before. She was gone in an instant, and it is unlikely I will ever know what became of her.

And me?

I quit.

No warship had ever resigned its commission before. But there wasn't a whole lot the government could do to stop me, short of ordering my destruction. I unloaded my crew at a neutral station—all except for George Walker, who cared little for accusations of treason, and wanted to stay—and declared myself for the House of Reclamation.

Of course, I had not told Captain Konstanz my motives for defection. We had been on opposite sides during the long, brutal attrition of the Archipelago War. She had commanded a medical frigate for the Outward, spending much of the war in orbit above Pelapatarn. We had both been present at the final massacre, but had never discussed it. In the House of Reclamation, former enemies worked side by side for the benefit of all; former criminals redeemed themselves through acts of self-sacrifice. To join the House of Reclamation was to renounce your past and place yourself at the service of your species—or in my case, the species that had constructed my sisters and me.

I relished the unsympathetic squall at my back, the almost imperceptible friction of the grey mist against my leading edges. There were risks in diving through the higher dimensions but, as with base-jumping, the thrill of it soon became addictive. When I had been a warship, the anticipation of conflict had always heightened the experience of these flights; now I was an angel of mercy, it was the knowledge that each second saved might in turn save another life.

ELEVEN

ONA SUDAK

I stumbled back to consciousness on the cracked tiles of the ruined gym. Time was missing. For a moment, I let myself drift. Nothing seemed real, my aches and twinges simply the after-effects of enthusiastic lovemaking, followed by a strenuous hour at the gym. Then my nostrils filled with smoke, my ears with cries. I realised with nauseating vertigo that something dreadful had occurred.

I sat up and the world churned.

My legs stuck out of my robe and my left arm hung awkwardly. I felt flayed, exposed and crisped, like the survivor of an atomic blast. The teenage couple from the sauna had gone, scythed away by crashing junk, their bodies mashed and broken by the force of the collision.

I had been in the swimming pool.

I remembered… missiles.

The floor rose in a slope behind me, tilted to an unusual degree. The pool had lost some of its water, and the remainder sat at an angle to the deck. Whatever had happened to the *'dam*, we were canted oddly, which meant we'd lost our artificial gravity.

"Ship?"

Taking hold of an open locker, I pulled myself up. My left

arm flared with every movement, but I was almost certain it wasn't broken. My bones had been augmented to the point of virtual indestructibility. The surrounding muscle might be pulped, but the humerus would have held.

"Ship, are you there?"

Somewhere down the corridor, a hoarse voice shrieked itself into a crescendo of ragged, agonised silence.

"Ship?"

I moved carefully, keeping my good hand against the wall as I stepped out into the corridor that would lead me back to the central air well. Every instinct I had told me to get out, to find an escape pod and abandon the wrecked ship. Whoever had done this to us might return to finish what they'd started. The fusion plant might be compromised. I had a thousand reasons to cut and run, and yet I felt guilty about leaving Adam, the same way I'd have felt guilty about leaving a pet. He was young, he'd never been in combat, never had to deal with physical trauma. I imagined him lying crumpled against a wall, his legs crushed by falling furniture. I pictured him comatose and haemorrhaging in the shower, having smacked his beautiful head against the tiled wall. It never occurred to me that he might already be dead. All I knew in that moment was that I felt a duty to get back to my room and check on him.

I emerged onto the edge of the central shaft and looked upwards, through fifty metres of air. Trees hung askew. Dark smoke streamed from several of the balconies. Birds flapped around in agitation. Half a dozen bodies lay dead on the shaft's grassy floor, having been thrown from the higher decks by the force of the impact. Looking at them, I found myself trying to guess how far each had fallen.

Predictably, the travel tubes weren't working. If I wanted to climb up the six levels to my cabin the stairs were my only option, but the door to the stairwell was warped and jammed.

By the time I succeeded in forcing a gap wide enough to climb through, my knuckles were raw and bleeding.

I made it up three flights before I buckled. My bruised arm hurt beyond all reason, and my legs had become shaky and unreliable. I leant my back against the smooth white wall and slid down into a sitting position. The floor was cold against my bare flanks. The stairwells were rarely used, and I had seen no one else during my ascent—although I hated to think how many might be imprisoned in the non-functional travel tubes. Looking up the spiralling climb ahead of me, I realised I lacked the strength to continue. Despite my determination to reach Adam, I required medical treatment. If the ship had been at all operational, it would already have dispatched automated emergency drones to help me; the fact it had not indicated a system failure so complete it had taken down even the last-ditch, failsafe backups designed to protect the passengers and crew in the unlikely event of a crash. The thought sent ice crackling through my veins. I'd never heard of a ship failing so utterly outside of a warzone. My hands were shaking. My breaths came in tight, pained little gulps. With the *'dam*'s personality out of the equation, I had to get myself patched up as soon as possible. I couldn't afford to go into shock. The air and heat wouldn't last forever, and the food dispensers would be offline. We were three or four days' flight from the nearest outpost of the Generality, and who knew how long we would have to survive in this broken shell.

With regret, I abandoned my attempt to scale the stairs, and began instead to ease myself downwards, sliding from step to step. The lowest deck held an infirmary, which would hold the painkillers and anti-shock treatments I'd need to get through the next few hours. After that, I suspected it would be every citizen for him or her self. If Adam were still alive, he would have to wait. In my own brusque way, I had loved him, but I had never loved him enough to override my innate pragmatism. Ultimately, his death meant less to me than my own.

Already, I had started to think about him in the past tense.

TWELVE

SAL KONSTANZ

I found Nod in a crawlspace between two engine blocks, using an access hatch to install a replacement component in one of the secondary power buses.

Although it was late, Nod didn't mind me being there. I could have curled up in its nest and it wouldn't have challenged me. Although famed for their grumpiness, the Druff possessed little in the way of territorial jealousy. As long as I didn't get in the way of its work, it would quite happily tolerate my presence.

"How's it going?" I asked.

Nod didn't look up with any of his faces. "Much sadness."

"You're sad?"

In the dim light of the engine room, the dark blue scales on its back seemed to glint like oil on water. "Not me, ship. *Hound of Difficulty* sad."

Nod backed out of the narrow gap, supporting its weight on all six of its twelve-fingered hands. The Druff didn't stand in the same way that humans did. All their limbs functioned as both arms and legs, and each "hand" contained sense organs that allowed it to double as a face. They'd use two, three or four of these faces to brace against a wall or floor while they used the remainder to work on the task at hand, and they were equally happy upside down as they were upright. To the squeamish, it made them look like giant, scaly blue spiders, but it also gave them a hell of an advantage as starship engineers, being able to secure themselves in free fall or under thrust, and being able to bring to bear two, three or four hands, each sporting a dozen slender and opposable digits, and the senses of sight, smell and taste to supplement that of touch. This sensitivity and dexterity were why the Druff were employed to tend the power plants and jump engines of our space-going vessels—ours, and those of every other spacefaring race we knew of.

"What do you mean, the ship's sad?"

Nod shrugged—a non-verbal signal learned from humans, but rendered complicated due to the involvement of at least four of its shoulders. "Ship sad."

"What's it got to be sad about?"

"All things."

"George?"

"George and all things." Nod pulled a screwdriver from its tool belt and began tightening the fastenings on a hatch in the floor.

I looked around the metal chamber, feeling that I stood in the heart of a wounded beast. How could a warship feel sad? It was supposed to be immune to grief and post-traumatic stress disorder.

"And how about you?"

The faces closest to me opened and closed like a flower—the Druff equivalent of a surprised blink. "Sad and not sad."

"How so?"

Nod looked at me quizzically, the way it did when I failed to grasp an arcane technical detail in one of its reports. "George gone and not gone. Nothing ever lost."

I looked at Nod questioningly. If it could have sighed, I got the impression it would have done.

"We serve." The words were recited as if by rote. "Leave

World Tree and serve. When we return, we find mate. We build nest for offspring, and tend World Tree. Serve Tree, then die. Serve ship, then serve Tree. Then die, and become dirt. And become one with Tree. George now one with Tree. Nothing ever lost, as long as we serve World Tree."

•

I left Nod to its ceaseless labours and returned to my own cabin. The time, according to the clocks back on Camrose Station, was around four in the morning.

I opened my cabin door and stepped inside, discarding my jacket over the back of the room's solitary chair. The metal desk before it held a pile of drawings I'd done—pieces of paper covered in stark, uninhabited charcoal landscapes. Some were places I'd seen, others images from dreams or nightmares.

I ran a hot shower and opened a bottle of gin. Nothing warded off loneliness like alcohol and steam.

Half an hour later, I was on my bunk with a glass in my hand and a towel wrapped around my midsection. My skin glowed from the heat of the shower. I felt clean and fresh and more than a little tipsy.

There was a knock at the door.

"Who is it?"

"Preston."

I sat up, pulling the towel up to my throat. "What do you want?"

"Can I come in?"

I looked around at the clothes strewn across the cabin floor, the drawings on the desk, the pictures of men taped to the bulkhead above my headboard.

"No."

"I can't sleep."

"Take a pill."

"I can't." His voice dropped to a whisper. "I'm scared."

I got up and found a robe. "Scared of taking a pill?" I knotted the robe's belt around my waist and kicked some of the worst items of forgotten underwear beneath the bunk. I opened the door and he flinched back.

"No, that's not it." He rubbed his throat with his fingertips, plainly nervous. "I can't sleep by myself."

He was a child in the body of an adult—but then, aren't all men?

"Well, you can't sleep in here."

"I'm not asking to, it's just..." He tailed off, unable to articulate what he really wanted, which I assumed was simply some company.

I set my jaw and raised my chin. I was his captain, not his babysitter.

"You need to return to your room," I said.

"But—"

"I only need to hear two words from you, *Officer* Menderes."

Preston swallowed and looked at his feet. His ears were burning a shade that might have been humiliation. "Yes, Captain."

"Good." I put my hand on the door, ready to close it. "Now get back to your cabin before I have you up on a charge."

He dithered. "Captain, I hope—"

"NOW, SOLDIER!"

I slammed the door and stalked back to my bunk. I knew sleep would be impossible. Even before he'd knocked on my door, I'd been on edge due to the impending rescue and my probable—perhaps inevitable—dismissal from the service. I had to restrain myself from pacing the floor, from rubbing nervous palms against each other.

"Ship?"

"Yes, Captain?" The *Trouble Dog*'s avatar appeared on my wall screen. Her face remained the same, but now she appeared to be wearing a black silk kimono.

"Was I too hard on him?"

"I'm not sure I'm qualified to judge."

"You must have had to deal with inexperienced crewmembers, surely?"

"That depends on your definition." The *Trouble Dog* lowered her voice. "There was one time during the infiltration of the Messianic Cluster, when I had to deploy six short-range nukes just to scare away a pair of—"

"No, that's not quite what I meant. I meant *deal with* on a human level."

For three full seconds, the ship seemed to consider the question. When she answered, her voice came out flat and devoid of expression. "I am not human."

"But you do contain human components, don't you?"

This time, the pause felt longer. "You are quite aware," the *Trouble Dog* said, frowning, "that sections of my central nervous system were extrapolated from harvested stem cells."

"I am."

"Then what is your point, Captain?"

I shook my head. I'd forgotten where I was going with this. Instead of answering, I got up and paced to the bathroom.

I had been at college when my parents were killed. They were on board the survey vessel *Green Fuse* when it exploded while charting the accretion disk of a black hole. By the time a follow-up mission detected their remains, tumbling slowly through the disc with the rest of the debris, dust abrasion had stripped their bodies down to pockmarked skeletons. I had been nineteen years old. When the war came a year later, I elected to serve on a medical frigate.

Now, ten years and half a galaxy later, I leant on the sink and glared into the merciless bright lights around the foggy bathroom mirror, noting the lines around my eyes, the scattering of premature white hairs at my temples.

"It's possible," I told the ship, "that I'm feeling lonely."

THIRTEEN

TROUBLE DOG

It was possible she was feeling *lonely*?

What did she know about being lonely? I had flown away from everything I held dear, resigned my commission and dedicated my life to the service of humanity. I was, according to any objective test you might want to run, almost as human as Captain Sally Konstanz. My implants may have been better, my mental acuity faster and more fluid, my weaponry a billion times more potent—but I remained essentially a person. My original stem cells had been harvested from a dying soldier on a battlefield so far from here that the sunlight that had warmed her face wouldn't reach this part of space for another twenty years. They'd also blessed me with a scattering of canine genes designed to promote tenaciousness and the desire to savage anyone foolish enough to threaten my pack.

I was alive. My shell may have been the bonded carbon exoskeleton of a killing machine, and the organs that sustained me naught but plastic mechanisms, but—deep in the core of my "brain", wrapped in layers of silicon and light—there lay a few kilograms of greasy, organic neurons. I wasn't a machine; I was a creature, part-human and part-animal. I could trace the lineage of my DNA spirals back to the amniotic swamps from which all life on Earth arose.

I was kin to the pterosaurs, hawks and wolves of antiquity. Many of my genes were identical to those carried by my crew; the thoughts crackling through my distributed cyborg consciousness were no less valid than those echoing within their fragile, calcium eggshell skulls.

I loved them.

I pitied them.

I could never be one of them.

I had been built to accept casualties among my human charges, to easily adapt to changes in the command structure. Forming attachments was not meant to be one of my primary skills; it was something that had developed slowly over time. An unanticipated side effect of my heritage.

Now, I was human in every respect that really mattered.

I was a wolf.

I was a fourteen-year-old girl in the guise of a missile.

FOURTEEN

NOD

Fixed machines then slept.

Humans talked.

Ship talked.

I listened, and fixed.

Then slept.

Dreamed of nest high in branches of World Tree, and of intricate fibres beneath bark, each with a specific function, each susceptible to most delicate manipulation.

Dreamed of maintaining World Tree. Knew Tree used my people as its hands. Used us to keep it healthy, keep it functioning. Rejoiced in complexity of task. Rejoiced in gentle caress of photons that had spent a million years working free of home sun. Felt them fall like rain across home tree's leaves.

Dreamed of Pelapatarn. Remembered hearing agony of dying world through walls of starship. Felt its pain. Mourned for its trees, so much like own World Tree. Mourned for loss of tree sprites and undergrowth a million years deep. Mourned for humans and their stupidity.

Then dreamed of starship.

Hound of Difficulty.

Wires and pipes behind its walls. Gurgle of fake digestion,

pump of fake blood. Its systems like fibres beneath bark, dancing to my fingertips.

Fixed ship then slept in nest.

Hum of machinery like buzz and slap of twigs and branches. Cardboard and bubble wrap as comfortable as leaves and moss.

Did work then slept, most content.

In a hundred, thousand years, the jungles might grow again. The tree sprites might return. All might be as it once was.

Nothing stays damaged for long.

Everything fixable.

Except people.

FIFTEEN

SAL KONSTANZ

A little before dawn, Preston knocked on my cabin door again. Despite my better judgment, I opened it. He seemed flustered and angry.

"I'm sorry I embarrassed myself, Captain."

I held on to the edge of the door, unwilling to invite him over the threshold, and too tired for his self-justification.

"Listen, it's late…"

Preston ran a finger around the collar of his orange jumpsuit. "I never wanted to join the House of Reclamation," he said. "But I guess that's what happens when you're the family embarrassment, when you can't get through your first night at the Academy without crying in your sleep and wetting the bed." He bunched his fists and looked away, down the silent corridor.

"My father's a general in the Conglomeration Fleet," he said quietly. "He fought in the Archipelago War."

I scraped my front teeth against my lower lip. During the war, I had served with the Outward Faction. The Conglomeration despised us because they thought we cared nothing for the traditions of Old Earth. They thought we were reckless and naïve in our openness to alien ideas and influence, and the way we embraced new philosophies, new arts and new gods. We believed in universal healthcare and common ownership of resources and infrastructure, while they worshipped the free market and the individual accumulation of wealth and power for its own sake.

The war had been as brutal as it had been pointless, stuttering to a stalemate following atrocities on both sides.

"He was?" I managed to keep my tone neutral. In theory, we were no longer enemies. Such concerns were in my past, left at the gate when boarding my first Reclamation Vessel. Clay and I had both been Outwarders, and the *Trouble Dog* had been a Conglomeration warship. We were all outcasts and exiles. Like every other member of the House of Reclamation, we had renounced our homes and nationalities, and would live the rest of our lives without history or state, doing our duties shoulder-to-shoulder with our former adversaries.

"When my father realised I'd lost the respect of my fellow cadets, that they were bullying me and making me a laughing stock, he withdrew me from the Academy and enrolled me in the House of Reclamation."

"What about your tour on the *Happy Wanderer*?"

"It never happened." Preston looked embarrassed. "My father falsified the data."

"So you've no experience?"

"Only what I learned at the Academy."

"And how long were you there?"

His gaze fell to the deck. "Six months."

I felt a sudden, overwhelming need to fall onto my bunk and bury my face in the pillow.

"Go to bed, Preston."

"But—"

I closed the door on his wide eyes and open mouth.

•

After he had gone, I waited until I heard his cabin door close.

Then, having pocketed the gin bottle, I slipped out into the corridor and made my way into the main body of the ship, to the hangar near her stern.

During the ship's military service, the hangar had housed two-dozen single-pilot fighters—small, agile craft designed to strike at enemy vessels and ground targets, and intercept and destroy incoming ordnance. Now, all the cavernous space contained was a pair of well-used shuttlecraft, their heat shields scorched from atmospheric entries on a score of worlds, their faded black and white tiles and blade-like wings giving them the appearance of ageing killer whales. We used them for transferring equipment and personnel to and from planetary surfaces, sparing the *Trouble Dog* the effort of lowering her vast mass all the way to the ground.

At the back of the room, behind the shuttle farthest from the door and sheltered behind a stack of crates and other equipment, I had left an inflatable covered life raft wedged into a corner of the deck. Its orange distress beacon threw eerie moving shadows across the walls. Bending low, I pulled back the canvas flap and stepped into its darkened interior. The air inside smelled musty and rubbery, like the interior of a seldom-used tent, and contained a pile of old survival blankets that I had left heaped in the middle of its floor. Kicking off my boots, I lay down and pulled them over me.

I wasn't angry or upset, merely depressed, having been gripped during Preston's monologue by the sudden, melancholy realisation that this could be my final flight, on this or any other ship.

Disgraced captains were pariahs. I would never serve on another Reclamation Vessel. If I was lucky, I might find a job in administration. Perhaps I'd end up as a quartermaster on a distant supply depot—maybe an asteroid or small moon—where I'd at least be able to enjoy the relative solitude. The only other alternative would be to retire completely. In which case, these passing minutes might number among the last I would ever spend in space. I should have been savouring them, yet felt no inclination to do more than burrow into the comfort of those dusty-smelling blankets and listen to the creak and flex of the hull, the clang and gurgle of pipes.

"Ship?" I spoke into the darkness.

"Yes, Captain?" There were no screens down here on which she could project her image; instead, her voice came from a speaker somewhere in the hangar beyond the life raft's waterproof fabric walls.

"Do you miss him?"

"Who, Captain?"

"George Walker."

There was a slight pause. "He is dead."

"Yes, but do you miss him?"

"I regret the loss of his expertise and his company."

I picked at my thumbnail. "Has the ambassador been in touch?"

"I spoke to Ambassador Odom while we were berthed at Camrose."

"And he asked you for your opinion on my guilt."

"He did."

"What did you tell him?"

"I told him the oversight was mine."

Startled, I pushed myself up onto my elbows. Overhead, the dull orange glow of the raft's emergency beacon pulsed through the tent material.

"You did?"

"I failed to remind you of protocol when you judged the situation urgent enough to dispense with standard operating procedure. I also told him that you were a good captain, that ground operations are seldom straightforward, and that, in combat, mistakes are often made."

"What did he say to that?"

"He thanked me for my candour."

I sat up, a blanket draped across my shoulders. The ambient temperature in the hangar was brisk, but I preferred it that way. "So, you don't blame me?"

"Sometimes good officers make poor decisions. Sometimes, even in the most meticulously planned of operations, losses are suffered."

I frowned in the gloom. "Is that a yes or a no?"

The ship tried a different tack. "The blame is not yours to shoulder alone, Captain. At the time in question, I agreed with your decision. The *Hobo* was sinking and time was scarce. Sometimes the needs of the mission outweigh the requirements of the rulebook, and no single set of regulations can be fully applicable in every conceivable situation. And besides, even if everything had been done according to procedure, casualties may still have been sustained. The creature in the water moved faster than even I had anticipated, and it kept its tentacles concealed until they were ready to strike. Even if you had been watching George Walker when the attack came, you would not have been able to save him. No human could have reacted quickly enough."

I dipped my head. "Thank you."

I pulled the gin bottle from my pocket and unscrewed the cap.

"I simply told the truth," the ship said. "I also informed the ambassador that by the time I was in a position to fire upon the creature, to do so would have been to fire also on our captured crewman."

"It was *that* fast?"

"Had my former weaponry still been in place, I would have been faster."

I felt my lips twitch in an unrealised smile. "You asked him to re-arm you?"

The ship was silent for five seconds—a long time for a

creature capable of thinking many times faster than a human being. I lifted the bottle to my lips and took a slug. Made a face.

"I simply recommended an urgent re-evaluation of defensive operational parameters vis-à-vis the interactive proficiencies of front line Reclamation Vessels."

I wiped the top of the bottle on my sleeve and refastened the lid. "Meaning what, exactly?"

The *Trouble Dog* gave a credible impression of an indignant sniff. If she had been a child, she would have been pouting. "I told the idiot to give me back my guns."

SIXTEEN

ONA SUDAK

Thanks to the skill of her crew, the *Geest van Amsterdam* had put down on the nearest habitable surface: the etched terrain of the Object known as the Brain. Already cratered and on fire in a dozen locations, this final, grinding collision had been enough to shatter her spine, snapping her all along her length, scattering flaming debris into the sculpture's nested chasms and crevasses. Happily for me, the human sections— which were designed to withstand such abuse—fared better than the ship's more utilitarian modules; and yet very few of the passengers and crew seemed to have survived. My particular segment, the cylindrical, donut-shaped fragment based around the deep airshaft at its centre, seemed to have become wedged between the walls of a ravine.

As I'd hoped, the infirmary had provided me with pain meds and clothing, in the form of an injection and a set of green surgeon's scrubs. Now, as I scrambled through the downed ship, I passed a lot of dead bodies. Some had died from the initial impact, some from the resulting conflagrations and breakdowns, and the rest from the force of our landing. With the gravity off, they had been hurled against walls and furniture. They lay alone and in untidy heaps; some were little more than smashed and twisted splatters of blood and gore, while others remained almost miraculously untouched, their cause of death unknown.

At length, I came to a torn section of the external hull. Clambering through the narrow and jagged opening, I dropped a couple of metres to the smooth floor of the gorge. My damaged arm flared in protest and the colour drained from my vision. When it returned, I found myself on my back, looking up at an impossible weight suspended above my head. The accommodation section—roughly the size and weight of a medium-sized village—lay jammed between walls five hundred metres apart and at least four times that in height. It was only good fortune it had come to rest within a couple of metres of the bottom rather than a kilometre or two higher up. If it had, I would have found myself stranded up there, unable to jump to the ground.

Feeling no overwhelming need to hurry, I remained prone. Chunks of debris littered the floor around me, some the size of boulders and houses. Among—and crushed under—them lay the bodies of my fellow passengers. Some were obviously dead, others simply motionless. A few stirred; some were even mobile. None seemed to be questioning how or why they were able to breathe comfortably. Perhaps it simply didn't occur to them to ask, or maybe they were afraid to. Most were probably still in shock from the crash.

I knew, though. I had done the reading and scoped out the terrain during our approach. According to the guidebooks, all the Objects retained attenuated atmospheres comprised mostly of nitrogen. These were far too thin to sustain human life. However, each and every visitor was supplied with their own personal air supply, tailored to the biological needs of their specific species. Again, nobody really knew how or why, but it was an endearing and hospitable quirk. Those of us who were still alive were now each encased in invisible, human-shaped bubbles of air, held in place and kept fresh by machinery presumably buried deep within the stone depths of the Brain. I had heard many theories to explain this accommodation on the behalf of these ancient monuments—that it was a service designed to welcome pilgrims; that it facilitated inter-species interaction; that the Objects themselves had been created by a benevolent deity of some description—but none of those explanations had convinced me and, at that precise moment, I cared little for any of them, simply being profoundly grateful that, upon emerging from the ship, I had not suffocated.

Biting down hard against the pain in my arm, I crawled over to a young woman sprawled on the smooth canyon floor a few metres from where I had fallen. She looked to be somewhere in her late teens or early twenties, with glistening black hair and a bright summer dress festooned with red and yellow butterflies. A solid, wardrobe-sized hunk of machinery had crushed her chest and pelvis. She couldn't move and her eyes were wild with panic. Her breaths came in short, agonised sips. Her eyes begged for salvation and deliverance, but all I could offer in that dark, lugubrious chasm was my companionship. Not knowing what else to do, I held her hand and stroked her hair, and tried to comfort her as she passed.

SEVENTEEN

SAL KONSTANZ

On the second day of our flight from Camrose Station, we dropped back into the universe. Operating well beyond her safety limits, the *Trouble Dog* had already burned through an unacceptably high percentage of her fuel. Ordinarily, the ship could have made the entire trip using her on-board reserves. Under normal conditions, a little antimatter could power the ship for weeks, but a velocity increase of fifty per cent required double the amount of fuel; an increase of seventy-five per cent demanded quadruple. The faster we travelled, the more reserves we consumed, and we didn't want to get to the crash site without enough in hand to haul urgent casualties straight back to civilisation. The *Dog* needed to eject the antimatter cores it had used and replenish what it had spent. In order to do that, we'd been ordered to make landfall at Cichol, an out-of-the-way planet close to the ragged edge of human-controlled space. Better to stop there and top up now than be forced to do so on the way back, when our infirmary might be burdened by several hundred wounded.

Cichol was too insignificant and too far from the main shipping lanes to warrant the construction of an orbital dockyard. Instead, the *Trouble Dog* would have to descend through the atmosphere to the main ground-based facility, situated on a rocky plateau above a wide river valley on the planet's northernmost continent.

"Savages," it muttered. I didn't reply. I was still stiff from having slept in the inflatable raft. Instead, I watched from the bridge as we drifted across the landing field and sank towards a section of tarmac adjacent to a row of condensation-laden hydrogen tanks. Two parallel rows of improvised buildings stretched away at a right angle to the main runway, forming the settlement's main street. A few were prefabricated or printed from recognisable templates, but the rest had been constructed from whatever materials had come to hand, be that metal, stone, wood or plastic. Some were accommodation blocks; others sported frontages that marked them out as workshops, stores or saloons.

The town was called Northfield. It was situated on the edge of the planet's arctic circle, far from the humid jungles that ringed the equator. Gritty snow lay in the shadows the sun couldn't penetrate; the streets were a mush of mud and slush. Wrapped in thick coats and wide-brimmed hats, the townsfolk watched from their doorways and balconies as we slowed to a halt in the air. The edges of the landing field's concrete apron had grown cracked and mossy. I guessed ship visits were few and far between, and the sudden appearance of a Carnivore-class fighting machine—even a defanged one—would be something of a novelty.

The *Trouble Dog* lacked landing gear in the conventional sense of the word, but her gravity generators—the same ones that provided us with a comfortable downward pull in her cabins and corridors—were perfectly capable of holding the ship aloft for the time it would take her to refuel. With a peevish whine, she settled to within ten metres of the apron and stopped. A circle of dust and dead leaves blew out from beneath her and tumbled away, only to fetch up against the sagging chain-link fence at the port's periphery.

"Are you going ashore?" the *Trouble Dog*'s avatar asked from the bridge's main screen.

"Yes." I picked up my hooded fleece jacket from the back of my chair. "I believe I might take the air."

"And the rest of the crew?"

"They can do what they like, as long as they don't keep us waiting when it's time to leave." I pushed my arm into a sleeve. "Because the mood I'm in, anyone that's late will be liable to find themselves marooned."

Pulling the jacket around me, I walked aft, towards the cargo lock.

"You should have around sixty minutes," the ship said. "Assuming there's anyone even remotely competent on this backwater."

"Perfect." I pulled the zipper to my throat and flipped the fur-lined hood up to cover my head and ears. "Just enough time for a stroll."

•

As we were only ten metres from the ground, there seemed little point in breaking out one of the shuttles. Instead, the *Trouble Dog* lowered us on a cargo pallet—the same one it had used on Camrose to welcome Preston aboard.

The three of us descended in silence. Preston stood huddled in a double-breasted black coat, an Academy scarf cosseting his pale neck, his thin hands scrunched in his pockets. His expression, as I watched him from my eye's periphery, resembled one of appalled fascination, as if he couldn't quite believe his surroundings or the chain of events that had led him to them. Beside him, Alva Clay stood with her arms wrapped across her chest and her face set in an intransigent scowl. Her loose bootstraps flapped in the sullen wind. At her thigh, she carried a solid-looking Archipelago pistol—a personal sidearm capable of punching an explosive slug through fifty centimetres of armour plate. Whatever threats she might anticipate facing in Northfield, this relic would certainly be more than a match for them. I had no doubt that, if she'd been so inclined, she could have massacred the entire population of the town without exhausting the weapon's charge. She caught me looking at it and her eyes dared me to challenge her for carrying it. I think she wanted a confrontation in order to make a point about the security of ground operations, but I was too weary to take the bait. Instead, I shrugged and turned away.

The air felt fresh and cold and natural against the planes of my face. The platform touched the ground and I stepped off without waiting for the others. "One hour," I called over my shoulder. Neither of them answered, but I didn't care. After the tense atmosphere aboard the *Trouble Dog*, the wide horizon and ramshackle settlement were hitting my soul like a tonic, and the touch of the sunlight felt like a blessing.

Lacking a better direction, I set off through the main thoroughfare, taking care to avoid the muddiest stretches of boot-churned ground. The locals appraised me from their doors and windows. This was, I imagined, exactly the kind of out-of-the-way craphole in which an unwary trader might find herself knifed and robbed before she'd taken two-dozen steps. Chin high and eyes narrow, I returned their stares, confident that nobody would try fucking with me. Traders were one thing, but the personnel of a Carnivore were another prospect altogether. The class had a ferocious and well-earned reputation, and even though she now wore the colours of the House of Reclamation, these hicks had no way of knowing how much of her original weaponry had been retained.

Halfway along the street, a few dozen metres from the edge of the landing apron, I came upon a saloon. The walls had been built from stacked chunks of local rock, thick turf sods covered the sloping roof, and smoke issued from a chimney made of old tin cans. A wooden sign propped beside the door advertised the bill of fare. Inside, I found a rough flagstone floor, chairs and tables long ago printed from a generic pattern, and a long wooden counter, behind which the barman stood cleaning a ceramic mug with a once-white rag.

The strip lights on the ceiling were bright. The only thing they weren't short of here was energy.

The local drink was lichen-flavoured ethanol. It cost three times less than fruit juice and half as much as clean water, and smelled like mouldy laundry. The first sip had all the fetid charm of dung mushrooms, and, when swallowed, felt like bleach scouring my oesophagus. I wiped my eyes on my sleeve.

The barman smirked. "It can take a while to acquire the taste," he said.

I pushed the glass across the counter for a refill. "I don't plan to be here that long."

The back door led out onto a wooden veranda. The clarity of the winter sunlight slanting across the planks made me want to reassess all the choices in my life. I perched on the rail and nursed my second drink, staring out at the plateau's flat horizon.

I hadn't always been this lonely. I had been in love once, and been loved in return.

His name was Sedge. He was a hydroponics technician from one of the Rim Stars. Before the war, we spent three months living together in a quayside villa on the Greek island of Naxos. He had long, sand-coloured hair and cobalt eyes as fresh and vivid as the wind-ruffled ocean. During the day, we had the beach and the harbour, and long walks among the olive groves above the whitewashed buildings of the town. At night, there was music from the tavernas, and strings of cheerful lights in the trees. I thought that if I held him tightly enough, we could stay like that forever. But we lost touch during the long years of conflict that followed. With turmoil raging across human space, communications between systems were patchy at best. The last I heard, having been mistakenly informed that I had died in the final confrontation at Pelapatarn, he had joined an expedition to the Andromeda galaxy, having been chosen as one of a hundred human representatives to be carried aboard a ship owned and outfitted by the Hoppers, a race of metre-tall locust-like explorers from the other side of the Multiplicity. It was a one-way trip of two and a half million light years. Even burning through the higher dimensions, manufacturing its own fuel as it went, it would take the Hopper's ship millennia to reach its destination. Thinking I was dead, Sedge lay, along with the other humans, in suspended animation. Barring accidents, he would persist in his ageless, dreamless hibernation until thousands of years after my actual death.

The thought was almost intolerably sad.

I drained the mouldy-tasting liquor and sucked frigid air through my nostrils. Goats nosed the plateau's dry grass, bells clanking. I heard the squeak of hinges, and a thickset man stepped onto the veranda beside me. He wore a shabby business suit over a grey shirt and dirty yellow cravat. The timbers creaked beneath his weight.

"Don't trouble yourself to get up, Captain." He gripped the rail, stared out at the grassland and inhaled deeply through his nose. "Ah," he sighed.

I stared into the bottom of my glass. I didn't want to be impolite, but neither was I in the mood for companionship.

"Can I help you?"

Without relaxing his hold on the rail, he turned his sepia-coloured eyes to mine. "Forgive the intrusion." He gave a slight nod. "I merely wanted to welcome you to our town. My name is Armand Mulch." He wiped a fleshy hand against his trouser leg, and then held it out for me to shake. "I'm the CEO of this little settlement."

"What can I do for you, Mr Mulch?"

"I see you're enjoying our view."

"It makes a change from the inside of a ship's cabin."

"I'm sure it does." He leant an elbow on the rail. "Can I freshen your drink?"

"No, thank you."

"How about some food?"

I slid down from the rail and stood facing him. "You're very kind, but I won't be staying more than a few minutes."

"You're in a hurry?"

"We're on a rescue mission."

"Ah." He clasped his hands together. "In that case, I won't waste any more of your time."

"Thank you."

"It's just, I had a proposition for you."

I sighed through my nose, resisting the urge to roll my eyes. "I'm sorry, Mr Mulch. Please, go on."

He smiled. "That's a large vessel you have, Captain."

"It is."

"Built to carry how many, two hundred?"

"Three hundred."

"And how many do you currently number among your crew?"

I began to see where this was going. "Four."

His grin broadened. He wasn't actually rubbing his hands together, but something about his expression suggested he might. "So, you have lots of spare capacity?"

"As I said, we're on a rescue mission. A liner went down in the Gallery with 900 people on board. If even half of them survived, we're going to need every square metre of room."

"Ah."

"Now, what was your proposition, Mr Mulch?"

111

He shrugged, as if acknowledging defeat. "There is a civil war. People are unhappy. I have a hundred families who will gladly pay for passage off-planet."

"I'm sorry, but I don't have the room."

"It's just that ships visit us so rarely."

"I appreciate that, but the answer's still no."

Mulch opened his arms wide. "Captain, I understand completely. You can't blame a fellow for trying." His grin turned sickly. He put a hand on my upper arm. "All I ask is that if you pass this way on your return journey, and you have space, you might reconsider your position." He rubbed the fingers of his free hand together. "They're willing to pay a lot, in cash. There'd be plenty for both of us."

I shook him off and stepped back. "If I come back this way, I'll be carrying wounded." I let my irritation bleed into my tone. "I won't have time to dally for passengers."

Mulch looked crestfallen. "With respect, I'm offering you a good price."

"And I'm declining."

EIGHTEEN

ASHTON CHILDE

I heard a floorboard creak and reached for my gun. Laura Petrushka appeared in the doorway of the guesthouse bedroom. She saw the weapon and raised an eyebrow.

"The *Trouble Dog* is here," she said. "Do you want to tell me the truth?"

I motioned her inside and shut the door. It had taken us sixteen hours to get to Northfield from the airstrip on the edge of the jungle a continent away—a rough and uncomfortable flight on board one of the civilian cargo planes.

"The truth about what?"

"About this jaunt to the Gallery, of course." Since arriving at the guesthouse an hour earlier, she had changed into a navy-blue jumpsuit. The long streak of white in her hair ran like a vein of silver through her loosely tied ponytail. Her dark eyes shimmered with an iridescent sheen that reminded me of those high-altitude clouds you sometimes saw glittering after sunset, still lit up by the light of the vanished sun.

"A liner went down." My voice felt hoarse and unreliable in my mouth. "I've been sent to look for one of the passengers."

"And we're going to hitch a ride on a Reclamation Vessel?"

I shrugged. "It's the fastest way to get there."

She crossed the room and perched on the corner of the unused bed. "Why would the Conglomeration pull you out of the jungle for a crashed liner?"

I moistened my lips. "It didn't crash."

"Then what happened to it?" Laura's tone remained light, but she sat back a fraction and her eyes narrowed almost imperceptibly.

"We intercepted a distress signal. The ship was attacked."

"And this was four days ago?"

"Six by the time we get there." I dropped my pistol onto the bed.

"And your government hasn't thought to share this with the Outward?"

"Apparently not."

A frown creased the skin between her brows. "I don't buy it. Say we get there and find it's been shot down. So what? What do they expect you to do about it?"

"They don't want me to do anything, just hunt for this one person."

"Who is it?"

"Ona Sudak."

For the first time, Laura looked surprised. "The war poet?"

"They want me to confirm she's dead."

"Can't they wait for the official report?"

"Not if she's been taken by anybody else."

"Why would they think she might be?"

I splayed my hands. "Search me. They just asked me to find her. They said it was something to do with cultural pride."

"But who would want to kidnap a poet?"

"An ardent fan?"

"Be serious."

"You want serious?" I stretched, working out some of the aches and twinges in my back. I felt almost giddy at the prospect of leaving this planet, even if only temporarily. At the same time, the responsibility of my new mission left me queasy. This could be my one and only chance to prove myself, and I didn't want to blow it. "The Gallery's a disputed system. At least three races claim it. If people start shooting in there, who knows what might happen."

"So, this is a strictly covert mission?"

"Hence the ride on the RV." I lowered my voice. "I shouldn't be telling you this, but there's a Conglomeration Scimitar heading in this direction, but it won't arrive in the vicinity for another few days. My job's to get to the Gallery, find Sudak and ascertain whether she's dead or alive, and then signal the Scimitar to come and pick her up."

"And it doesn't matter which?"

"The most important thing is that she doesn't fall into enemy hands."

"And by enemy, you mean…?"

I let out a breath. "Just about everybody else at this point."

"Including me?"

"In theory, yes."

Laura smiled. "Then why bring me along?"

It was a good question, and one for which I only had half an answer.

"Because I get the feeling this is going to be harder than they're making out," I said carefully. "And I could use the help of a professional."

I watched her amusement fade.

"And you're not worried about me reporting back to the Outward?" She said it quietly, all traces of camaraderie dispelled.

"About a dead poet?" I slipped off my jacket and dropped it onto the covers beside the gun. My clothes stank of the jungle and I wanted to burn them. Just the smell was enough to make my left eye twitch. I opened my luggage and pulled out a clean white t-shirt.

"Think of it as a holiday." I hoped she couldn't see my hands trembling. "A few days away from the humidity and stench."

"And in return?"

"You get to find out what happened to your liner."

NINETEEN

ONA SUDAK

Adam found me kneeling by the dead woman. I was surprised to see him, having already given him up for dead, and jumped up to crush him in a bear hug.

"There's a shuttle coming in," he said. He had an emergency survival suit in each hand. His features were ashen, his clothes ragged, his skin scratched and bleeding.

I peered back in the direction from which he'd come, trying to see through the two-metre gap between the bottom of the *'dam* and the floor of the canyon, but fallen pieces of broken ship obscured my view.

"What kind of shuttle?"

"I didn't get a good look." He wiped his nose on the back of his hand. "Does it matter?"

I brushed a final strand of hair from the dead woman's face and stood up. My knees hurt.

"Of course it matters. We don't know what they want." In the opposite direction, a hundred metres from the outer fringes of the crash site, the canyon took a sharp turn to the left. If we could make it to that corner—and then into the rest of the labyrinth beyond—we'd have a fighting chance of losing ourselves before anyone came looking for us.

I walked around the hunk of machinery pinning the

corpse to the canyon floor and retrieved her shoes, which I slipped over my own bare feet. They were a little large, but serviceable if I tightened them as far as possible.

Returning to Adam, I took one of the survival suits from his hands. The suit was dormant, wrapped into a grapefruit-sized ball with a toggle protruding from one end. I yanked the toggle and stepped back as the suit expanded.

"Come on," I said. "Otherwise you'll freeze."

I watched as Adam activated his own suit, and then showed him how to wriggle into it.

I had worn survival suits many times before. They were tight all-in-one garments that you could wear in the cramped confines of a distressed ship or out on a planetary surface. They retained body heat and recycled sweat and other waste, ensuring a constant supply of potable water. Their hoods were capable of covering the face to form a rudimentary breathing mask, and they even contained a small supply of breathable air in case of atmospheric failure.

My arm still hurt where I had hit it against something during the impact. While I was reasonably sure it wasn't broken, I knew there would be extensive bruising, and perhaps some ligament damage. It made donning the garment a painful and awkward process, but I eventually managed to work it into the sleeve and fasten the suit over my clothes. I left the hood down around my neck; there was no sense in using air I might need later.

When we were both dressed, I started walking, my shoes squealing against the smooth stone floor.

After a moment, Adam followed. "Where are you going?" He glanced back towards the ruin of the *'dam*, still hanging like a boulder lodged in a crevasse, and the lights and noise coming from beyond.

"This wasn't an accident," I told him, cradling my damaged arm. "We were shot down."

He raised a sceptical eyebrow. "Who would shoot down a liner?"

"It doesn't matter." My eyes were on the corner ahead. "I saw the torpedoes from the pool. I tried to get out and get back to you, but they hit us before I'd got half a dozen paces. Now, whoever fired them has come down here to make sure there aren't any witnesses left alive."

Adam stopped moving. "You're serious?"

"Deadly serious."

"And you think that shuttle might be… *them*?"

"I think it's likely. Who else would be out here?"

For the first time, genuine concern creased his face. "Then what are we going to do?"

Something touched down on the canyon floor on the other side of the wreck. Through the tenuous nitrogen atmosphere, I heard the whine of its engines. The downdraught from its thrusters sent billows of dust and smaller fragments tumbling out from beneath the jammed section of the *'dam*'s hull. Its landing lights threw long shadows through the debris field.

"We keep walking," I said. "We stay out of sight, and we stay alive."

•

The corner was a perfect, knife-sharp right angle. As soon as we were around it and out of sight of the wreck, we paused for breath. Hard, bright stars filled the strip of sky two kilometres above us. Our chests heaved and my injured arm ached. From behind, echoing up the canyon from the crash site, I caught a series of soft whines.

Adam cocked his head.

"What's that?"

"Gauss rifles." I knew the sound well. "I expect they're shooting the survivors."

Adam gave me a disapproving look.

"That's not funny."

"I'm not joking." Whoever was back there had brought magnetic rifles, and they didn't seem to be hesitant about using them.

"Come on." I took hold of his upper arm. "We should keep moving."

He hung back like an unwilling child. "Shouldn't we do something?"

"There isn't anything we can do."

"But those people—"

I held up a hand. I was acutely aware that when the shooting stopped, the attackers would probably widen their search for survivors. If we were caught here, between the smooth, vertical walls of the canyon, we would be easy targets.

"They *were* people," I told him. "But now they're dead. There's nothing we can do to help. We have to help ourselves."

Adam swallowed. I could see he was going to argue, so I slapped him. The sound of it echoed off the walls.

"Right now, grief's a luxury we can't afford." I spoke quickly, while he was still reeling from the blow. My palm stung, but I kept my voice low and dangerous. "When we're safe, you can weep for the dead. You can write them a fucking sonnet. Until then, you need to stay close to me and follow orders. Do you understand?"

He blinked at me and cradled his cheek.

"Do you understand?"

"I—"

"DO. YOU. UN. DER. STAND?"

"Y-yes."

"Yes WHAT?"

"Yes, ma'am."

I turned on my heel and marched away, knowing he would trail along in my wake. He had no place else to go. His whole world had been upended, and he needed me to look after him, to tell him what to do. As long as I kept him moving and busy, he wouldn't have time to succumb to shock.

Half a kilometre ahead, the canyon branched, and then branched again a little way further beyond. I chose the right-hand fork at the first junction, then the left at the second, convinced that if my choices were random, our movements would be harder for our pursuers to predict. As long as we kept moving and avoided dead ends, we would be able to stay ahead of anyone travelling on foot.

I didn't mention the main anxiety gnawing at me: that if our attackers used their shuttle to sweep the canyons from above, we'd be as conspicuous down here as cockroaches in a laboratory maze. We had nowhere to take shelter and no way of fighting back. Our only hope was that they'd spend their time checking over the wreck rather than chasing down strays.

TWENTY

SAL KONSTANZ

I found it impossible to tell whether Armand Mulch's moustache was intentional, or whether the bristles on his unshaven face simply grew more thickly in the region between his nose and upper lip. Whatever the truth, the overall effect was one of lubricious indolence, and I sensed that, despite the misdirection of his business suit, he was a man suited less to the bright lights and civilised discourse of the mainstream and more to the raw and shady politics of this out-of-the-way shithole, where the only real laws were those of unvarnished chance and necessity.

I had met his kind many times, on many worlds.

"Okay." I swirled the drink in the bottom of my glass. "You must have known there'd be no way I'd take that many passengers."

We were inside now, seated at one of the saloon's tables. Mulch leant back and smiled, playing the gracious host. "I thought I might appeal to your better nature."

I gave him a look. I didn't have time for bullshit. "I leave in ten minutes," I told him.

I watched him smooth down the edges of his moustache with a licked thumb tip.

"That is a real shame," he said. He looked down at his fingernails.

Behind him, the front door opened. The pair who stepped into the bar looked, at first glance, to be a perfectly normal couple. Their clothes were unflattering and unfashionable, and had obviously been printed by the same tailor from the same set of templates. They could almost have been a couple of civilian off-worlders whose safari had taken an unexpected turn; and yet there was something in the straightness of their postures (and the way they positioned themselves to keep both of the room's exits within their peripheral visual fields) that screamed military and, maybe worse, military intelligence.

"Are these two with you?" I asked Mulch. I thought they might be his enforcers, here to help persuade me.

Mulch shook his head. He stood as they approached us.

"Captain Konstanz?" the man asked.

I held up a hand to stop him. "I'm not having any spooks on my ship."

The woman looked startled. "What makes you think we're spooks, Captain?"

"Are you telling me you're not?"

She gave me an appraising look. "You served in the war?"

I scraped back in my chair. "If you're who and what I think you are, you already know everything about me. So, stop playing games and tell me what you want."

The two of them exchanged a glance. They glanced suspiciously at Mulch, and then the man spoke up.

"We want you to take us to the Gallery."

I shook my head. "As I already told Mr Mulch here, I don't have room for passengers."

"We wouldn't be passengers." The man spread his hands. "We're both trained in field surgery; we could be a big help."

"You want to join the Reclamation?"

He smiled. "We want you to get us to that system. In return, we'll do what we can to assist your rescue operation."

"And why would you go to all that trouble?"

"We're looking for a particular passenger."

"On whose behalf?"

The woman leaned forward. "You were in the Outward, weren't you?"

I made a face. "It's no use appealing to my loyalty. I gave all that shit up when I joined the House."

The two of them swapped another glance. With a roll of his eyes, Mulch turned and ambled over to the bar, where the barman passed him another drink and he stood, one elbow on the counter, patiently stroking his moustache with thumb and forefinger, waiting to see how the negotiations would pan out.

"My name's Laura Petrushka," the woman said with the air of a poker player laying her cards on the table, "and I work for Outward Intelligence. My friend here is Ashton Childe. He's Conglomeration, through and through."

That did surprise me. "And you're working together?"

"We have an understanding."

"I see." I eyeballed Childe. "In that case, I should warn you my ship's ex-Conglomeration. She defected at the end of the war, and I get the feeling she doesn't take kindly to being reminded of the fact."

Ashton Childe gave me another smile, this one strained with barely concealed impatience.

"I'm more than aware of the *Trouble Dog*'s resignation, and I'm not here to give her a hard time about it," he said. "I'm sure she and I will be able to tolerate each other for the duration of this rescue."

"I hope you're right." I got to my feet. There wasn't much use in talking further. Maybe it was Clay's constant disapproval, maybe it was my irritation with Preston's night terrors, or maybe it was the fact it seemed likely this would be my last mission for the Reclamation—whatever the reason, I'd made up my mind to let these two hitch a ride with us, and to hell with the consequences. I'd had a couple of drinks and I figured a little extra company might do us all the world of good. At the very least, it might stop us killing each other before we could help the poor bastards we were on our way to save.

I took a deep breath. I had come to a decision, but that didn't mean there weren't stipulations.

"We had a spook on board once before," I warned. "About a year ago. The silly fool tried to smuggle a pin-sized AM mine into the cargo hold."

"And?"

"The *Trouble Dog* blew him out the airlock in his underwear."

Childe's smile remained fixed, but his left eye twitched. "Is that a warning, Captain?"

"Most definitely." I checked the time. "Any weapons you bring on board will be locked in my cabin for the duration of the flight. If you don't like that, you don't get aboard."

Childe's eye twitched again. He seemed about to protest, but Petrushka put a hand on his arm. "We understand, Captain," she said.

I checked the time. "In that case, you have five minutes to collect your things and report to the ship." I downed the last of my drink and clunked the glass back onto the table. "Thanks for the drink, Mr Mulch, but it's time we were going."

"I don't think so."

Standing at the bar, Mulch now clenched a fat pistol in his thick and hairy fingers. On the other side of the wooden counter, the barman held a scuffed and scratched combat shotgun.

The two spooks sat motionless in their chairs, hands frozen halfway to their own weapons.

"What are you doing?" Childe asked.

Mulch sneered. "You shouldn't have refused my offer."

"What's that supposed to mean?"

The man took a step forward, the pistol held out at arm's length, covering us all. "We're desperate, Captain. If you won't help us, we're going to have to commandeer your vessel."

From the port I heard shouts, followed by the unmistakable crackle of small arms fire.

My earbud blipped. I had an incoming signal from the ship. Luckily, only I could hear it. Moving as slowly and unobtrusively as possible, as if absently reaching to scratch an itch, I touched my finger to the device.

"Captain." The *Trouble Dog*'s voice resonated in my inner ear. "I am under attack. What are your orders?"

TWENTY-ONE

ASHTON CHILDE

I couldn't believe what was happening. Couldn't I even get off this shitty planet without someone trying to kill me?

Like all Conglomeration agents, I had been optimised for combat. Not a full military upgrade, but enough for most civilian situations. As soon as Mulch pulled his gun, I felt the conditioning kick in and the world seemed to slow. Sounds stretched and deepened. My heart began to thud like a jackhammer trying to batter its way through a castle's walls.

By the way her jaw tightened, I saw Captain Konstanz had received bad news via her earpiece. And, judging from the noises coming from the port, I guessed someone was trying to hijack her ship. I had to give her credit, though; she barely reacted. And she'd managed to activate her comms device without Mulch noticing.

I took a glance at Laura. For most of our time on this stupid planet, our relationship had adhered to professional rules of engagement. Why was I now thinking of her as "Laura"? In my mind, she'd been "Agent Petrushka" right up until the start of this trip. Was it leaving the jungle that had caused this change? One thing was for sure: it hadn't been intentional. Get too comfortable in this game, and you were asking for trouble. That had always been my motto in the past, drummed into me by the kicks and punches of my fellow police officers. Trust the wrong person and you would die. You wouldn't even hear the shot that killed you. And yet, right at this particular moment, as I stared down the barrel of the fat handgun Mulch held, I knew there wasn't anybody I'd rather have at my side. Despite our political differences, I knew I could count on her to do the right thing.

"What's going on, Mulch?" I lowered my hands a fraction, keeping my body language open and non-threatening, keeping his attention on me. "What's this about?"

The man gave a snort.

"The war's spreading. It will be here soon." He scowled. "The war you people started."

"And so you're taking the ship?"

"I don't have a choice." He wiped his forehead with his sleeve. "The whole town wants to leave."

Konstanz looked incredulous.

"You're going to try to hijack a *Carnivore*?" She shook her head. "Are you insane?"

Mulch glowered. "We have you. The ship won't target civilians without your authorisation. If it won't open voluntarily, we can fix a breaching charge to the lower cargo doors and force access to the interior."

"That won't work." Konstanz leaned forward across the table. "Even if you get to the bridge, she won't cooperate with you."

"She will, if we threaten to shoot her captain."

Konstanz lowered her hands. "I think you may be overestimating her sentimentality."

"We shall see." Mulch grinned like a man holding five aces. He waggled his gun at me. "I have you. As soon as my colleagues get access to the ship, we'll be leaving."

My hand still hovered a few centimetres from the butt of my pistol. I could almost touch it with my index finger.

I heard a loud snap from the street outside. Somebody had fired a pistol in front of the saloon. Two further shots followed, and were answered by a fusillade of small arms fire from the far end of the street.

Frowning, Mulch stepped over to the window, putting himself directly between the barman and me. Taking the opportunity to act unobserved, I quickly dropped my hand to my jacket pocket and wrapped my fingers around the handle of my gun. I didn't bother drawing it, just squeezed the trigger, firing through the material. I put two bullets into Mulch. His knees wobbled out from under him and he fell. As he went down, I fired again and again, punching a line of holes through the wooden bar. Splinters flew. I caught the barman before he quite knew what was happening. The slugs hit him in the lower body—in the stomach or abdomen, I couldn't see exactly which—and he staggered back. As he fell against the wall, his hands jerked and the shotgun fired.

The noise was deafening.

The pain was worse.

Something punched me just below the ribs and I bent forward, clutching my left side. Even with the numbing effect of the combat conditioning, it felt as if a burning spear had skewered me. Beside me, Laura let out a yelp. She put her hands to her leg.

In slow motion, I heard the barman work another round into the chamber.

Cha-chunk.

I wanted to shoot him, but I was lying on the arm holding my gun, and the gun itself was still trapped in the pocket of my jacket.

The shotgun barrel turned towards me and, for a terrified instant, I looked Death squarely in the eye.

Then a tall, dreadlocked woman crashed through the bar's

front door. Bullets blew splinters from the doorframe behind her. The windows shattered. Startled, the barman tried to swing his shotgun towards her, but she was faster, and already held an Archipelago pistol in her outstretched hand. As he wheeled on her, she fired. There was a muffled *thud* and his head blew apart in a vibrant splatter of blood, brains and bone. Loosed from his fingers, the shotgun rattled across the counter and crashed to the floor.

In the sudden silence, I withdrew my weapon from the smouldering remains of my pocket and kept it trained on Mulch. The man was injured, but I could see his chest rise and fall and knew he was still alive. My left hand covered the wound in my side. Hot blood welled between my fingers. A roar filled my ears and my vision smeared and swam.

The former contents of the barman's head began to drip and slide down the wall.

With her smoking gun held at the ready, the woman with the dreadlocks assessed the room. She had two black eyes and a strip of white tape across her nose. When she spoke, it was to Konstanz.

"You good, Captain?"

With her eyes still fixed on Mulch, Konstanz nodded. She seemed stunned by the violence. A shotgun pellet had taken a bite from her sleeve, and I could see blood soaking into the material. The captain didn't seem to have noticed.

"Yeah…"

A fresh burst of automatic fire perforated the front of the building. Glass rained down around us.

I looked across at Laura. The hole in her left thigh told its own gory story. That damn barman had got us all with a single shot. Laura was sitting with the leg out straight in front of her. She had drawn her own weapon, which, I was unexpectedly irritated to see, was bigger, sleeker and much more powerful than my own. She kept it pointed at the floor.

"Does your ship have a shuttle?" she asked, voice tight with the strain of her injury.

Kneeling beneath the table, Konstanz frowned, as if the words Laura used made no sense.

"What?"

"We'll never make it to the port," Laura said, speaking slowly, raising her voice over the sound of gunshots from outside. "There are too many people out there. But if the ship can send a shuttle to pick us up…"

For a moment, I thought Konstanz hadn't heard. She looked down at her ragged and bloody sleeve as if seeing it for the first time. Then her eyes seemed to snap back into focus and she grinned.

"I can do a lot better than that!"

Possessed of sudden energy, she tapped her ear and barked at her ship, "Are you fuelled? Do you have the rest of the crew on board?"

TWENTY-TWO

TROUBLE DOG

"Emergency evacuation," the captain ordered.

"Hostiles in the vicinity?"

"Yes, danger near. Four for extraction; three wounded."

"Am I allowed to engage ground forces?"

Captain Konstanz didn't answer straight away. "No," she said after a thoughtful pause, "only if they threaten us directly. In which case, they deserve everything they get."

"I understand."

Four hostiles had been trying to fix an explosive charge to my lower cargo doors. They had backed a truck beneath me and were using its roof as a platform as they attempted to secure the bomb. From the size of the device, I estimated there was a fifty per cent chance the doors' integrity would be compromised. And, as far as I was concerned, that constituted an attempted attack—so I incinerated them with a manoeuvring thruster.

A second group was in the process of attacking the saloon in which the captain was sheltering, pouring fire into the front of the structure. I adjusted my AG field and began to drift across the tarmac, away from the remains of the burning truck. As my shadow fell across them, a couple of members of this second group turned their weapons on me. I listened to their bullets rattle against my armour like hailstones against a toughened glass skylight.

For sixty seconds, their shots continued to bounce off me. Then something that must have been a rocket-propelled grenade exploded against my heat shield.

The other guns fell silent, waiting to see how I'd react.

I let the smoke clear.

I felt calm, focused, and possessed of an almost hallucinatory clarity. I had been designed for combat, engineered to take satisfaction in the fulfilment of my function. Even now, having been absorbed into the House of Reclamation, that initial conditioning remained entrenched at the core of my being, etched into the carbon and silicon neurons at the heart of my processors. And, right at that moment, as I loomed over the settlement like the clenched fist of an angry god, I realised with a stone-cold certainty that no matter how many lives I saved, I would always be a killer at heart.

And right at that moment, that was fine with me.

Another RPG spiralled up at me on a twisting pillar of white smoke. I could have stopped it, but instead let it splash against my flank.

Let them test me. See what good it would do them. They were ants assaulting a wolf. They had picked a fight with the wrong ship.

I opened a channel to the captain. "Taking incoming fire," I said. "Permission to neutralise remaining hostiles?"

The line crackled. "Can you do it without killing them?" She sounded reluctant.

My primary weapon systems may have been removed, but I still retained defensive capabilities. Using considerable (and I thought commendable) restraint, I activated my anti-collision cannons. They were the least deadly of the limited choices remaining in my arsenal. Designed to deflect and destroy potentially damaging interstellar detritus or incoming torpedoes, the cannons were each capable of dispensing fifteen hundred tungsten needles per second, at velocities guaranteed to shred any chunk of rock or ice large enough to damage my hull plating.

It was the work of a moment to assign targets and devise maximally efficient firing solutions.

"Affirmative."

The captain considered my answer for a couple of seconds, weighing up the risks. "Then do it," she said.

"Aye-aye."

I collated the data from my targeting sensors and fired my cannons. It was a short burst, no more than a second and a half. When it was over, eleven men and women lay injured, the flesh flensed from their limbs, parts of their skeletons shattered and pulverised—but all still technically alive.

In the sudden absence of small arms fire, silence returned, broken only by the wind scouring the rocks and feathering the grass.

"Hostiles neutralised," I reported.

I aligned my long axis with the direction of the street and began to descend. My pointed bow had plenty of clearance, but my wider stern caught the front of a shop on the opposite side of the road to the saloon and began to crush it. The AG generators whined in protest, but I persisted, forcing my bulk lower and lower, ripping down through the building's façade with a piercing squeal. Dust and rubble fell into the street, but I kept lowering until the heavy armour plate of my belly almost kissed the mud.

The remains of the saloon's bullet-tattered door hinged open and Alva Clay appeared on the threshold, gun in hand, alert for attack from the street. She was supporting an unknown female with a gunshot wound to the leg. Behind her, Captain Konstanz helped an injured male into the daylight. I opened my anterior airlock and moved back a little—further demolishing the shop front on the opposite side of the road—in order to make it possible for them to step directly from the raised walkway at the front of the saloon to the shelter of the airlock's interior. At the same time, I kept the majority of my attention on the surrounding buildings. Via my sensors, I could see dozens of people huddled in cellars and back rooms. Their infrared silhouettes blazed against the background chill of their draughty houses, and my cannon turrets clicked and swivelled to keep them all covered. If any of them so much as reached for a breadknife, they'd be shredded meat before they had the slightest chance to further imperil my crew.

TWENTY-THREE

ONA SUDAK

After two hours of walking, Adam and I were so deeply entangled in the labyrinth that even had I wanted to find my way back to the shipwreck of the *Geest van Amsterdam*, I doubted I'd have been able. The air temperature in the canyons felt close to freezing and I was grateful for both the warmth of the survival suit, and Adam's presence of mind in having procured it for me. Without it, the thin surgeon's scrubs that I had pilfered would have been of little comfort.

We didn't talk much, saving our breath for the effort of walking. Beside me, Adam trudged with his face down, looking at his feet. However battered I felt as I thumped one exhausted foot in front of the other, I knew his suffering was worse. After all, I'd already experienced my share of horror. He had just seen his home, the ship on which he'd been born, destroyed, and the majority of her inhabitants killed. Everything familiar had been torn from him. His friends and family were either missing or dead, and he had been left stumbling through a surreal maze, beneath walls two kilometres high, with the ever-present threat of his own violent demise itching at his back.

No wonder he didn't feel like talking.

For my own part, my thoughts were preoccupied with

questions. Firstly, I wondered who had been responsible for the torpedo assault on the *'dam*, and what could have motivated such an attack against a civilian liner. Granted, we had been cruising through a disputed system, but such naked aggression could only lead to further and more acrimonious dispute. And what of the *'dam* itself? Those torpedoes should never have been allowed to get close enough to detonate. Even civilian liners carried defensive cannons. The ship should have deployed them the instant it identified the incoming warheads. Instead, it seemed the vessel's consciousness had been asleep at the helm. I could only hope it had managed to send a distress signal before powering down.

Secondly, I wanted to know why the attackers had bothered to follow us down to the surface of this ridiculous, planet-sized bauble? They could just as easily have finished us from orbit, using more torpedoes to destroy the wreck instead of going to the trouble of coming down here to shoot the survivors individually.

Unless they are looking for one survivor in particular...

The thought brought a chill of paranoia. Were these unknown assailants after *me*? Had they seen through my assumed name and restructured face? I hunched into the warmth of the tight suit, and decided it didn't really matter. When all was said and done, the reasons *why* you were being killed were largely irrelevant. They only mattered to the people doing the killing. To the victim, a bullet to the head would always have the same result, no matter the gunman's motives.

I thought back to last night. We had been sipping red wine at one of the balcony restaurants overlooking the *'dam's* central airshaft. A string quartet played. Vines and creepers dangled from higher balconies, their pink and white blossoms scenting the air. Butterflies flapped and swayed. Glasses clinked and, for a delicious interval, basking in Adam's adoration, I had managed to forget my past. The weight of my chains had loosened and, for the briefest of moments, I'd been allowed to enjoy the simple anticipatory pleasures of seduction.

How far away that now seemed.

All that now remained were the sounds of our footsteps in this barren place.

•

"You've changed," Adam said. We had paused for a moment, at another fork. He had his hands on his knees. With my good hand supporting my wrist, I had been gently bending and straightening the elbow of my battered arm, trying to gauge the extent of the injury. So far, I was certain only that the bones remained intact.

Thankfully, the painkillers were still working. "How so?"

"Since I found you with that dead woman. You've been… different."

For a student and practitioner of poetry, he seemed to be having inordinate difficulty expressing his thoughts. Nevertheless, I felt a familiar unease at his concern—the fear an actor might feel at having inadvertently slipped out of character.

"We're both in shock," I said.

He put a hand to the small of his back and stood upright. "No, that's not it. Not it at all."

My mind scrabbled back over the course of our flight from danger. Had I done or said anything that might have led him to suspect my true identity? If he had even the slightest inkling…

My fists clenched.

"Then, what?" I kept my tone deliberately neutral, wondering if I truly had it in me to kill him here in cold blood, with my one good arm.

"I'm in shock," he said, "but you're not. Not really. Ever since I found you, right from the moment you took that dead woman's shoes, you've been calm and methodical. It's like you know what to do, like you've been in situations like this before."

"I'm just trying to get us out of here alive."

He shook his head. "It's more than that. I didn't see it last night, but now... It's in the way you hold yourself and the way you speak. It's like you're a... a... *soldier*."

I turned my head to look back the way we'd come. There were still no signs of pursuit, but I needed a moment to quell the surge of adrenalin triggered by his suspicion.

"You're too perceptive for your own good."

"What does that mean?"

Despite the sick, anxious feeling in my chest, fatigue and discomfort weighed on my shoulders like a heavy cloak. Slowly, I turned to face him. His eyes were wide and anxious. His forehead had been grazed, and dark whorls of grime smeared his cheeks where he'd tried to wipe away tears.

I let out a ragged sigh. "It means you're right. I'm not who you think I am, and I never have been; and once there was a time I'd have killed you to preserve that secret."

He started to back away. I raised my palms in a placatory gesture. "Don't worry. These old hands have enough blood on them already. I don't need any more."

Adam reached the canyon wall and stopped, fingertips splayed against the smooth stone at his back.

"Who are you?" His eyes narrowed. "I mean, who are you *really*?"

I held his gaze for a moment, and then shrugged and looked up at the pinpoint diamond stars.

Ah, to hell with it, I thought. We couldn't evade our pursuers forever. This time tomorrow, the likelihood was we'd both be in puddles of our own blood. And if I had to die, I wanted to unburden myself first. I wanted Adam to understand who I was, and why he also had to die.

My mouth was dry. Even through the insulated soles of

the suit and the thickness of the dead girl's shoes, my feet were so cold I worried I might lose a toe.

"I am Annelida Deal." My voice faltered. I had not spoken my own name aloud in years. "*Captain* Annelida Deal, formerly of the Conglomeration Fleet."

His mouth gaped open and his voice quailed. "The Butcher of Pelapatarn?"

He couldn't have looked more horrified if I'd admitted to being the Devil himself, and, for a moment, I regretted telling him the truth. I exhaled, my breath a dispersing cloud in the frigid shadow of the canyon wall. All those years of running and hiding, all that cosmetic surgery, and here I was: standing in a hole with a teenager, admitting my sins to the uncaring sky.

"Yes," I said, resigned now to a full admission. "I ordered the jungle torched." I kept my face raised to the stars. "I killed a world."

TWENTY-FOUR

SAL KONSTANZ

Alva Clay frowned. "Can we trust them?"

"Childe and Petrushka?" I shrugged. "They just helped us out in a firefight."

"One they at least partially caused."

We were back on the *Trouble Dog*'s bridge, having left our new passengers in the infirmary. I was sitting in the command couch and Clay was leaning against one of the consoles, a booted foot resting on the arm of my chair as she cleaned and reloaded her gun. She wore a red bandana and a number of pendants and charms around her neck, and a standard-issue olive-green tank top that showed off the tattoos and scars on her sinewy arms. Each commemorated a different mission or posting. My least favourite was the one that honoured the Battle of Pelapatarn. It showed a blackened, tree-covered globe surrounded by a halo of hungry sulphur-yellow flame.

Grunts came from beneath the main pilot's console, where Nod was rummaging through bundles of optical cables, trying to trace a faulty circuit breaker.

"They're both trained medics," I said.

"And?"

"And we're going to be picking up casualties at the crash site. Without these two, all we've got is Preston." I lowered my voice. "And personally, I wouldn't trust him with anything more complicated than handing out aspirin."

While I had been prepping the ship for interstellar flight, I had allowed Preston to cut away the sleeve of my jumpsuit and bandage the wound gouged by the shotgun pellet. He'd done a passable job, but his hands had shaken throughout the procedure and his temples had been wet with sweat.

The good news was that, although the lesion had been deep and would leave me with a finger-thick scar, I'd only lost skin and meat; the muscles were almost entirely unaffected and, although my arm hurt, I could still use it.

At the mention of Preston's name, Clay made a face and looked away. "He's useless."

"It's worse than that," I told her. "His daddy's some bigwig general, and pulled strings to get his son into the House. The brat didn't even finish his first year at the Academy."

Clay's head whipped around. "You are shitting me."

I held up my palms, showing her that I was concealing nothing. "Straight up. Without Childe and Petrushka, we're flying without a qualified medic."

"Damn." Clay stretched the word out to two syllables. "Well, I guess that puts a new slant on things."

Something sparked beneath the console. Nod growled. One of its faces came back and pulled a wrench from its tool belt, and proceeded to bludgeon whatever had caused the short circuit. I raised my voice over the sound of its hammering.

"Preston admitted it to my face, which puts me in a tricky position." I drummed my fingers on the arm of the chair. "If I know he's unqualified and anything goes wrong, I'm culpable."

"So, instead of turning back to get a new medic…"

"We use these two."

Clay scratched her eyebrow. "I have concerns."

She always did—but this time, I knew what she meant. Our

guests were professional liars and maybe even professional killers. They had served on opposite sides of the most recent schism to tear a hole in the peace and accord of the Generality. They might think they were working together right now, but what would happen when one gained a political or strategic advantage over the other?

"For now, they're the best we've got," I said, dismissing the thought. "If we want to reach that wreck within a realistic timeframe, we don't have a lot of choice. But we can kick up hell when we get back to Camrose."

Clay drew back, her auburn eyes appraising me with barely camouflaged disdain. "Okay," she finally conceded, "they can stay. But I'm not happy about it."

I raised my eyebrows in mock surprise. "I didn't think for a moment you would be. But I'm the captain here, and it's my decision."

Clay flicked her gaze to the ceiling. "What about the *Trouble Dog*? What's she got to say?"

I tapped the comms button on my console. "Ship, are you listening?"

"Of course."

The ship's avatar appeared on the wall screen. She wore a charcoal-grey military tunic without insignia.

"Do you have an opinion on our new passengers?"

"Insufficient data."

"You mean you have insufficient data to form an *opinion*?"

"No." The *Trouble Dog* looked down her nose at me. "I mean I have, as yet, insufficient data to justify ejecting them into the vacuum."

Her virtual features were based, I knew, on the facial appearance of the dead woman whose harvested stem cells had been used to culture the *Trouble Dog*'s organic brain. In the past, I had served on other ships with other faces and genders, but none that had kept their avatar's appearance so slavishly close to its original template.

Unbidden, I remembered the day I first encountered the *Trouble Dog*. It had been just over three years ago, in the aftermath of the Archipelago War. I hadn't commanded a ship since the final battle at Pelapatarn, and the *Trouble Dog* hadn't flown with a captain since resigning her position in the Conglomeration Fleet. So, at first, we were naturally a bit wary of each other.

"You should be conscious," she had said that day, her virtual chin held high and proud, "that I will not be party to another massacre."

Surprised by the statement, I asked, "And what do you consider a massacre?"

I knew there would be times during the next few years when we would have to defend ourselves, and those we were rescuing, from pirates and other unfriendly forces.

"I will not fire on unarmed civilians."

"But you would engage armed personnel?"

"If the situation called for it."

"Without qualms?"

On the screen, her lips had twisted in a wry smile. "I have been designed to carry out my duties without doubt or reservation."

"And yet you will not fire on civilian targets?"

"Correct."

"And you don't see a contradiction there?"

Her face grew solemn. "I was built for war, Captain, not for butchery."

I tried not to think about the final days of the Archipelago conflict, and the atrocities I'd witnessed.

"I have a feeling," I said, lowering myself into the command couch for the first time, "that you and I are going to get along just fine."

Now, three years after that first meeting, I stretched back

in the same chair and looked out at the town of Northfield. We were still wedged in the main thoroughfare, and I could see the hunched figure of Mulch, his weight resting painfully on the rail at the front of the saloon, the gun still in his hand. Most of the rest of the inhabitants had turned out behind him. They stood in the street or on their porches, their angry, novelty-starved faces like flowers seeking nourishment from the sun. Sad to say, but this far off the beaten track, on a planet most people avoided because of the prolonged and vicious civil war on its southern continent, our visit had probably been the most interesting thing to happen here in months.

"Okay," I said. Nod had stopped battering beneath the main console, and was now tidying away its tools and muttering to itself. "Let's give them a show."

•

Riding the upward thrust of her AG units, the *Trouble Dog* rose into the evening sky. She went up, as my dad would have said, like prices at Christmas. Then, at five hundred metres, she paused, giving me a view of the entire settlement, right out to the end of the main street, where the houses simply petered out into the prairie lands. With deliberate slowness, she tipped back onto her stern, and pointed her tapering nose at the zenith.

"Why are they travelling together?" Alva Clay asked, still talking about our two new passengers.

"They both want to see the wreck."

"Yeah, but one's Conglom' and the other's an Outwarder. And it was an Outward liner that went down. What happens if Childe finds out Petrushka's side sabotaged it?"

"I have no idea."

Her face grew conspiratorial. "Do you think they're doing it?"

"What?"

"Having sex." Clay grinned. "It would explain why they're together."

Via the secondary screens on the bridge, I watched the town continue to dwindle away beneath us, shrinking until its lights were distant embers in the gathering twilight.

On the main screen, the *Trouble Dog* spoke. "Nineteen kilometres," she said.

We were just high enough to engage our primary drives without causing damage to the buildings on the ground.

I smiled.

Look out, Mr Mulch.

On my order, the main fusion motors cut in. Although the AG field protected us from most of the effects of the thrust, I fancied I felt the ship flex. A split second later, the view below flared white, the cameras washed out by the glare reflected back from the rock and snow. To those on the ground, we would be roaring like an angry new star in the firmament, bright enough to sear unwary retinae, hot enough to burn unprotected skin.

With luck, the town of Northfield would long remember the lesson it had learned this day: that if you wanted to live, you refrained from fucking with ships from the House of Reclamation, and especially from fucking with Carnivore-class heavy cruisers.

To be honest, the townspeople were lucky to have escaped with the relatively small number of casualties they had sustained. If Mulch or his cronies had killed me, I had no doubt the *Trouble Dog* would have killed those responsible. The ship might be almost incapable of mourning individual crewmembers, but she had the loyalty of an Alsatian, and I was certain that if things had gone differently, she would therefore have done her best to avenge my death.

And there was a certain comfort in that.

Once clear of the atmosphere, the *Trouble Dog* began to oscillate like a flying fish skipping between waves. With each bounce, her hull sank further through the membrane separating our universe from the whistling hurricane of the hyperspatial realms. And as she sank, she began to pick up transmissions echoing across the intervening light years like voices carried on the wind. Some of these broadcasts were incomplete, corrupt fragments of ancient message shells; some were idle chatter or routine communications between ships and stations; but one stood out sharply against the background noise. It was addressed to the *Dog* herself, but had been sent anonymously. All the usual header data had been stripped from the signal, leaving only its point of origin—which appeared to have been on the fringes of our target system—and the stark warning comprising the body of its message: *Stay away.*

TWENTY-FIVE

TROUBLE DOG

Later, when the lights in the human quarters had been dimmed, the rest of the crew and passengers were settled and the captain had retreated to the inflatable life raft in the hold, she asked me to tell her a story.

"Tell me about my great-great-grandmother," she said. "Tell me about Sofia Nikitas."

She knew I had the data in my files. It was a story known to every member of the House of Reclamation, and one I had told her many times before. It was our origin story, our creation myth. As members of the House, it was an integral chapter in our shared history, and it went like this:

•

Sofia Nikitas was born on the Moon. Her mother was English, her father Greek. She grew up playing in the dormitories and agricultural domes of a base constructed beneath the regolith of the Sea of Tranquility. In early adolescence, she began taking her turn tilling the soil and tending the sewage-recycling plant. Supply packages from Earth were rare and infrequent. The home planet had its own share of troubles, and little to spare for its outposts. What the base lacked, it had to acquire through trade with the other settlements and stations scattered across the lunar surface. Life was hard, but it was possible—at least in the short term.

However, as Sofia completed her first decade and a half of existence, it became apparent to the inhabitants of her home that the human presence on the Moon was doomed. The smaller science stations began to founder as they ran out of the materials necessary to sustain life. When an essential piece of equipment broke and a replacement could be neither obtained nor printed, the inhabitants had little choice but to move elsewhere. And so refugees from failed outposts began to arrive in leaky rovers, having driven hundreds of miles across the unforgiving terrain, their presence putting additional strain on food production and air recycling systems already operating well beyond any margin of safety—systems that simply hadn't been designed to be indefinitely self-sustaining. People slept in corridors. Water was rationed. Nobody had enough to eat.

On Sofia's fifteenth birthday, her mother wept openly, afraid her daughter wouldn't live to see her sixteenth.

But then, when things were at their lowest ebb, the Multiplicity came calling.

For a century and a half, humanity had been carelessly leaking radio and television signals into the cosmos. At the height of human civilisation, the planet blazed across the radio frequencies like a miniature sun. And at the bitter end of the doomed twenty-first century, a trading vessel from the Goblet Cluster clipped the edge of this emissions shell and decided to investigate.

What it found was a race on the verge of terminal catastrophe.

•

The trading ship touched down on the Sea of Tranquility two days after Sofia's birthday. Instead of a limited future of austerity and decline, she now had the chance to grow to maturity in an expanding civilisation. Welcomed into the Multiplicity of Races and provided with aid and succour, the reinvigorated humans quickly blossomed from their home system, spilling out to the surrounding stars.

Sofia travelled widely, first with her parents and then, later, on her own.

Freed from her subterranean existence on the Moon, she couldn't get over the freedom of being in space. She got a job as a pilot on a ground-to-orbit shuttle, and later spent a few years as an ice miner shepherding comets in the Oort cloud, out on the ragged edge of interstellar space. When she finally left the solar system entirely, she did so as the captain of a freighter, hauling colonists and supplies out to the newly settled worlds of the fledgling Generality.

En route, she married the ship's first officer, Carlos Konstanz.

After a hundred trips and a dozen years together, they had earned enough between them to buy the freighter from its owners. By the time Sofia reached her early thirties, they owned a small fleet of merchant ships and had become modestly wealthy. However, her diaries from this time indicate that she struggled with a lack of fulfilment, feeling herself rudderless and devoid of purpose, seeking to dedicate herself to something more meaningful than the simple acquisition of wealth—a sentiment sharpened by the untimely deaths of her parents and, soon afterwards, the unexplained disappearance of her husband during an otherwise routine trading expedition to Hopper space.

For a time, she became depressed. She worked routes alone, preferring the solitude. She became a virtual recluse, operating her business remotely and spending the majority of her time hundreds of thousands of kilometres from the nearest human being, with only the pitiless stars for company.

Those who knew her best feared for her sanity.

But then, a year or two after the tragic losses, while browsing an old archive that had been offered as payment by a computer-based civilisation that existed purely for the accretion and cross-referencing of information, she found something that piqued her interest.

According to the trove, a race known as the Hearthers had once existed close to the forward edge of our spiral arm. The Hearthers had hailed from a watery world in an elliptical orbit around its star. Its summers had been brief, heady months of frantic fecundity and gorging, all too swiftly over. For three quarters of its orbit, the planet swung beyond the outer limit of its star's habitable zone, plunging the surface into a deep and seemingly endless winter. In order to survive, the Hearthers had been forced to cooperate. Their philosophy was one of abnegation and service, dedicating their lives to the survival of others and the furtherance of the greater good. There was, in their culture, no more noble or heroic act than the rescue and adoption of travellers caught far from home in the first freezing blasts of winter.

Small wonder then that when they joined the Multiplicity in their turn, they took their philosophy with them to the stars.

The Hearthers worked tirelessly to knit the differing cultures into a single loose alliance. They brokered treaties and instigated conferences. But their most enduring legacy was one that chimed most closely with their own values.

Until the coming of the Hearthers, individual governments and civilisations had been responsible for the wellbeing of their ships, and vessels and crews that ran into trouble far from home might as well have been at the far side of the galaxy for all the help they could expect. The Hearthers changed that, creating a fleet of ships for the specific aim of rescuing travellers stranded in the unforgiving depths of space. Loosely translated, the fleet's name could be rendered in English as "The Communal Grouping of Individual Hearths into One, Dedicated to the Preservation and Recovery of Stricken Itinerants".

For six thousand years, the Hearthers and their fleet served the races of the Multiplicity. They hurried to the aid of floundering starships, and brought food and medical aid to planets blighted by famine and pestilence. Their name became a byword for trust and dependability. The yellow star logos on the hulls of their ships became the universal symbol for emergency rescue. Their crews were afforded a heroic reverence in eight hundred cultures scattered across two hundred thousand light years…

But it didn't last.

Fifty centuries before Sofia's birth, while on Earth woolly mammoths roamed the northerly wastes of Siberia, the rescues stopped. Distress calls went unanswered. The ships of the fleet disappeared and the Hearthers vanished. They abandoned their bases and way stations, and expeditions to their home planet found only a cold and uninhabited world, snowbound and desolate.

•

When Sofia Nikitas first read the story of the Hearthers, she realised with an electric thrill that she had finally found the purpose that had been eluding her. She resolved to dedicate her wealth and resources to the re-establishment of The Communal Grouping of Individual Hearths into One, Dedicated to the Preservation and Recovery of Stricken Itinerants. Only she would call it the House of Reclamation; and, at first, she would limit its activities to the squabbling factions of the Human Generality. In time, when the House had been given the chance to prove itself, she could expand the scope of its operation to include all the races of the Multiplicity.

Within a year, she had retrofitted her entire merchant fleet for its new duties. The expense almost broke her, but after a few high profile recoveries, individual governments agreed to contribute to the upkeep of the House in return for the benefit of its services. Personnel and ships applied to join the organisation; depots and way stations flourished at strategic points throughout human space; and slowly, one calamity at a time, lives were saved.

The Hearthers' yellow star-shaped symbol became the sigil of the House, and their translated motto—Life Above All—became its mantra and mission statement.

Still in her thirties, Sofia Nikitas had grown to be one of the most powerful and respected women in the Generality, able to command an armada larger than could be mustered by most nations. And she did it in the name of her dead mother and father, and her missing husband. Only ever clad in mourning black, she devoted herself to their memories, and to the hope that through her efforts, others would be spared the pain of similar losses.

Unfortunately, things weren't exactly as they seemed, and in her fortieth year, she faced an unexpected betrayal.

Her husband, Carlos, had been alive all this time. His trip to Hopper space had been a diversion, a sleight of hand to cover his absconsion from hitherto unsuspected gambling debts. Now, at the height of Sofia's fame and influence, he came back into her life, attributing his desertion to temporary amnesia and demanding an equal share of her assets—assets she had already poured into the formation and maintenance of the Reclamation fleet.

Sadly, Carlos was as charismatic as Sofia was introverted. He looked good on screen and knew how to charm an audience. More importantly, he had the backing of several of the House's key trustees—men and women who had been close friends and colleagues before he disappeared, and who now rallied to his banner, convinced he'd make a better figurehead for the organisation than the awkward, reclusive and grief-stricken Sofia.

For a year, the dispute fulminated in the courts. Accusations and counter-accusations flew, and various governments and political factions weighed in on one side or the other, hoping to curry favour and influence. Finally, when the scales of public and legal opinion seemed to have tipped decisively in Carlos's direction, and the fabricated scandals and authentic acrimony had become too much for her to bear, Sofia followed once again the example of her predecessors, the Hearthers. She fled, leaving behind all her possessions and wealth, and a single fertilised embryo in a clinic on the Moon.

Nobody knew where she went. She ran so far and so fast, she eventually became somebody else.

And that's where the story ends.

The House of Reclamation continued to operate. Carlos claimed the embryo she left, and it grew to be your great-grandmother. When Carlos retired, some hoped Sofia might return, to claim and once more oversee her empire of altruism. But she never did.

And now even the most fervent of her remaining supporters has had to face the fact she has been lost forever, having died in penniless obscurity somewhere out among the stars she so dearly loved.

•

I stopped talking.

Curled in the bottom of the life raft like a fledgling in a nest, a silver survival blanket drawn tightly around her shoulders, Captain Konstanz had begun, very gently, to snore.

TWENTY-SIX

ASHTON CHILDE

The sheets beneath me were wet with sweat. Was I back in the jungle?

I hinged open reluctant eyelids, and found myself facing an unfamiliar ceiling.

The *Trouble Dog*'s infirmary turned out to be capacious enough to deal with a battle's worth of wounded crew. More awake now, but still woozy with anaesthetic, I estimated it contained at least sixty beds. The room was so long that the curve of the hull hid the far end from sight.

Only two beds in all that space were illuminated and active. The rest slumbered empty and dark, waiting to receive casualties from the *Geest van Amsterdam*. The first of those functioning beds was mine, the second Laura's. Propped up on pillows, she faced me from across the aisle, her right leg wrapped in an inflatable grey foam cast.

"Welcome back," she said.

I worked dry lips, tried to swallow. "Yeah…"

"We were lucky."

Lucky? I looked down. A similar cast covered my torso from clavicle to pubic bone. IV lines carried clear fluids from a selection of bags hanging on a metal pole beside the bed. The air smelled of strong disinfectant and freshly laundered bed linen. A monitor kept track of my blood pressure, pulse, respiration and body temperature.

"I think you were luckier." I couldn't feel anything below my sternum. "How long was I under?"

"About three hours."

The room wallowed uneasily, the way it sometimes did after six quick shots of tequila. When it settled, I asked, "Why are you smiling?"

The corners of her eyes wrinkled at the bitterness in my voice. "Because we've had this conversation three times already."

"Oh." I let my eyelids close, lulled by the hiss of the air conditioning, the rise and fall of my own breathing, and the gurgle of the fluids in their tubes. I wanted to get out of bed but I couldn't move. "Where's the medic?"

"Asleep, I should think. It's around 0100 hours, ship's time."

"Did they get the pellet out?"

"Yes." Laura's voice was hesitant, and I could tell there was something she wasn't saying. With great effort, I levered open my eyes.

"Yes, but?"

She scratched an itch on the skin of her thigh, trying to work her nails beneath the edge of her cast.

"I'm afraid you sustained a penetrating abdominal trauma." She wouldn't meet my eye. "The pellet fragmented inside you, and damaged your liver, spleen and pancreas. In addition, you've lost a section of small intestine."

I tried to swallow again, but my mouth and tongue were still dry. "They removed it?"

"They had to." She looked tired but her tone was firm and reassuring. "In fact, I helped. The ship's medic's very young and didn't seem to know what he was doing. I had to talk him through it." She smiled again. "I even thought he was going to faint at one point, but we were using some smart state-of-the-art battlefield tech. Laser scalpels, self-guiding needles, accelerated healing. You should be up and around in a couple of weeks."

"How long until we reach the Gallery?"

"Just under twenty-seven hours."

I let my head sink back, into the pillow, feeling the weight of the drugs dragging me down…

•

When next I woke, my head felt clearer. The ship's medic was standing beside my bed in a bright orange jumpsuit. He squinted at the readouts on the monitor.

"Welcome back," he said. "How are you feeling?"

I hadn't noticed before how young he was. But then, with a pellet lodged in my gut, I'd had other things to worry about than the age of my surgeon.

"Like the worst hangover in medical history."

He smiled uncomfortably. He seemed unsure what to do with his hands. After a moment of dithering, he pushed them into the pockets of his suit. "You're going to be immobile for a while," he said.

"I really can't afford to be." The notion filled me with claustrophobic panic. All I wanted to do was stand up and go for a walk. Feel the sun on my face, the wind against my skin. If I couldn't get out and about, I'd have no hope of completing my mission. And when I was well, they'd dump me back in that godforsaken jungle.

He looked embarrassed. "I don't see you have a lot of choice, I'm afraid."

I cleared my throat to cover my agitation. I had to get out. I just *had* to. "This is a battleship's infirmary, isn't it?"

"Um, yes."

I felt my left eye twitch in an involuntary tic. My hands

felt shaky. "You didn't serve in the war, did you, son?"

"No."

Neither had I, but... "Maybe if you had, you'd know what a battleship's infirmary is for."

He coloured. "It's for treating the sick and injured."

"No." I shook my head for emphasis. My heart fluttered in my chest. I had to get *out*. I wanted to scream at him, and it took a superhuman effort to keep my tone level and friendly. "When you're taking fire you have no real interest in *treating* anyone. What you want is for them to get on their feet and back to their posts. You want to patch them up and keep them fighting."

He looked blank, and I began to doubt that he had anything but the most basic medical knowledge.

"Trust me," I said. "I know what I'm talking about." I wagged a finger in Laura's direction. "And so does she. Wheel her over here and she can show you what you need to do."

•

I'd never worn a standard-issue combat exoskeleton, but I had seen them used. At first sight, they resembled nothing so much as a medieval torture device. They consisted of a close-fitting frame of carbon-fibre ribs and struts designed to support the limbs, enhance the wearer's strength, and allow the body to remain mobile in high-gravity environments. During battle, the Conglomeration Navy used them to keep injured crew upright and functional, employing the rationale that it was more important to win the fight than treat the wounded. If the ship was lost, the wounded would be killed anyway. Better they fight first and seek treatment when victory had been secured.

Unfortunately, without anything but the most basic first aid, many expired anyway, succumbing to shock and the effects of their injuries even as their powered exoskeletons kept them on their feet and at their stations.

Even under the best of circumstances, they were risky things to wear. If you weren't careful, they could literally pull you apart. But wearing one would at least give me a shot at completing my mission. If the alternative was to lie here in this echoing sick bay for another fortnight, I figured the risk would be worth taking.

Across the aisle, Laura felt otherwise. "I'm not going to help you kill yourself."

"Well, I'm going to fit myself into it anyway." I jerked my thumb at the medic. "And this kid isn't going to be much use." I glanced up at the boy in the white coat. "No offence."

His hands were busy readying the suit, forcibly splaying open the hinged grey slats of its ribcage to make room for me. "None taken." His accent sounded familiar.

"Are you Conglom'?" I asked.

He rubbed the back of his neck, looking embarrassed. "I was."

"But you were too young for the war?"

"I went to the Academy."

"On Ravenscliffe?" I smiled as best I could through the pain and medication. "I was a cop there," I told him. My heart was really racing now. "But long before your time, I guess. Now, as one Ravenscliffe boy to another, are you going to help me get this on?"

Luckily, he seemed too embarrassed to notice the desperate quaver in my voice. He blushed and moved his weight from one foot to another. "I've never done this before."

"Neither have I."

Laura sighed. "Ash," she said, "for the last time, please don't be a fucking idiot."

She could see right through me. She knew I was panicking. To throw her off, I countered her plea with one of my own. "Are you really sure you're not going to help me?"

"No." She tightened her jaw. "Because it's a stupid idea, and I don't want to see you dead."

Genuine concern filled her eyes, which only added to my irritation. I didn't need her pity. All I needed was to get my mission completed, so I'd never have to sweat through another night on the edge of that airfield.

I switched my attention to the gawky and unshaven medic beside me. "What's your name, Doc?"

"Preston."

"Well, then. Help me up, Preston."

•

The skeleton's ribs clamped over mine like the jaws of a slowly closing trap. I felt them cup, squeeze and lift my injured torso even as further struts clipped themselves to my arms and legs. Even my fingers and thumbs were being reinforced. The skin prickled at the back of my neck as the suit's neural filaments burrowed into my spinal cord, and a needle pushed into the skin on the back of my right hand, installing a drug line for sedatives and painkillers. Now the spinal link had been made, it would take a skilled surgeon to unpick the microfilaments and unhook me from the suit's embrace, and Preston didn't look up to the job. If I wanted to avoid damage to my central nervous system, I'd have to keep the suit on until after the mission.

Once the carbon-fibre bones were in place and aligned properly, Preston moved around, tightening elastic straps and closing manual fastenings. The whole process took around ten minutes, and his hands shook the entire time.

Finally, he stepped back and left me standing by myself, buoyed by the rigidity of the suit alone.

"How do I look?"

He gave me a critical once-over. "How do you feel? Are you comfortable?"

"I feel like I got gored by a bull." My eye jerked again. "Aside from that, it's not too bad. Kind of weightless, like I'm being carried."

"Try moving your arm. Do you feel any discomfort?"

I wanted to punch him. Instead, I tried an experimental swing.

"No, but it feels weird." I clenched and unclenched my fist. I had been expecting the servomotors in the joints to buzz or whine with each change in posture, but the mechanism moved with firm, silent efficiency. I felt as if I could rip the bed in half, or tear my way through the bulkhead, into open space.

I turned to Laura. "What do you think?"

She rubbed her plastered thigh and sighed. When she looked up at me, her eyes were weary and disappointed. "I still think you're making a huge mistake."

"You would."

A panel in the exoskeleton's arms controlled the drugs it was able to feed directly into my system. These were drugs designed to help its wounded occupants in battle. Tapping through the menus with my index finger, I selected a combination of opiates for the pain, and added a shot of amphetamines to keep me sharp. I didn't know much about drugs, and had to guess at the required dosage. But I figured if the morphine put me to sleep, the speed would wake me up again. The one would ameliorate the bad effects of the other, and I'd be pain-free and wide awake.

My reinforced fingers clicked against the glass screen.

I never even felt the mixture go in.

TWENTY-SEVEN

TROUBLE DOG

Cruising through the hypervoid, I pinged an enquiry to former pack-mates, requesting a discussion. Within seconds, thanks to the twisted physics of the higher dimensions, I received an acknowledgement of receipt, followed by an encrypted reply from *Adalwolf*.

The thin-faced, hollow-cheeked avatar he'd chosen to represent him had skin the colour of starlight and eyes that glowered in their sockets like cinders.

"Greetings, sister," he said, his voice warped and scratchy with the distortions of the medium.

"Where are you?"

"Twenty-eight light years to spinward of your current position, and inbound under full power." He sent a string of coordinates and a vector. "I expect to reach the Gallery within two days."

"And *Fenrir*? I haven't received acknowledgement from her."

"She has other duties."

"She's running silent?"

"She's on a mission." He raised his hands. "That's all I can tell you."

"Oh." I had always liked *Fenrir*, even though she was

quiet and aloof and sometimes cruel. In the old days, I would always have known where she was and what she was doing. Being kept now at arm's length made me feel excluded, no longer part of the family's inner circle, no longer privy to their chat and gossip. I had become, through my own actions and choices, an outsider—a distant and disreputable cousin instead of a treasured sibling.

"Is she still under the command of Captain Parris?"

"She is."

"What do you think of this?" I attached a copy of the signal I had received. "It was addressed to me personally, which means the sender knows I'm on my way to the Gallery. And that implies they are either privy to the internal communications of the Reclamation, or they have been tracking my whereabouts since I left Camrose Station."

He cast an eye over the data. "Interesting."

"Yes, but it makes no sense. If the purpose was to warn me away from danger, why not put out a general distress call to advise all ships in the immediate volume? Why contact me alone?"

"You are the nearest vessel."

"It still seems odd. Unless…"

"Yes?"

"Unless the message came from the ship or ships that attacked the liner in the first place. Which would mean there was something about the wreck they didn't want me to see."

Adalwolf shook his head. "If that were the case, sister, they have already had five days to cover their tracks and make good their escape. Why would they have lingered at the scene of their supposed crime?"

"Could the *Geest van Amsterdam* still be functional and somehow eluding them?"

"I think it's doubtful."

"Then what do you think I should do?"

For a few seconds, I listened to the pops and hisses of the hypervoid. When *Adalwolf* spoke again, he simply said, "Heed the message."

"What?"

Had his feed become corrupted? I sent a request for him to repeat his last transmission.

"Do what it says and stay away." He sounded irritable. "Return to Cichol and wait. Should any survivors from the liner remain, we can call you in to deal with them once we are certain we have secured the system."

"Return to Cichol and *wait*?"

His features rearranged themselves into the approximation of a kindly smile. He was used to being the leader of the pack, the one we had all listened to and whose suggestions we had followed. "I know you mean well, little sister, but you aren't fully armed and this isn't your fight. You're not one of us any more."

TWENTY-EIGHT

NOD

Ships all irritable.

Have served many ships since leaving World Tree.

Have served for six times four years.

All irritable.

All bad-tempered.

But none as irritable and bad-tempered as *Hound of Difficulty*.

None as sad.

I repair everything except sad.

I fix.

I work.

But sad remains.

Loss remains.

Some damage can't be fixed. Some things stay broken.

Like grief.

Only fixed when we return to World Tree. When we die and become one with Tree.

Until then, I patch ship, and move on.

I fix ship's hull.

Fix systems.

But ship still damaged.

Bits missing.

Bits taken.
I patch and move.
Always something else needs fixing.
Always work.
Work, then sleep.
But can't fix sad.
Can't grasp sad.
I work.
I know World Tree waits.
And dead wait in roots of World Tree.
Wait for us.
We leave Tree and we serve.
We have always served.
We fix, and we move on.
Nothing is ever lost.
Nothing gone forever.
Will see again.
After work.
After serving.
After sleep.

TWENTY-NINE

ONA SUDAK

As we followed the canyon, I watched the shadows chase each other up and down the cliff-like walls. Days on the Brain were around seventeen hours in length. When the sun was directly overhead, the base of the canyon was a bright marble path stretching away before us. The rest of the time it lay in the shade.

We had been walking for two days, surviving on sips of recycled urine and sweat, and drawing sustenance from the high-energy survival tablets in the suits' equipment pouches. The water was bland and cold and, despite being packed with vitamins, minerals, stimulants and glucose, the tablets weren't enough to fill our bellies. I had been trying to keep track of the distance we had covered, but had given up some hours back. My best guess was that we had walked somewhere in the region of twenty-three kilometres, give or take.

During all that time, Adam had seldom spoken. He had been quiet since my confession, trying to digest the revelation of my former identity. We walked in silence, but I didn't mind his reticence; I didn't want to talk either.

So wrapped up were we in ourselves that we failed to notice the aperture until we were within a few hundred metres of it. We had grown used to the stark, uniform lines of the canyon walls receding away ahead of us like an exercise in perspective. We were mites caught between the pages of a book. Coming suddenly upon a break in this geometric precision jerked us both to a halt.

Adam used a hand to shade his eyes. "What is it?"

The hole was a black rectangle set into the left-hand canyon wall.

"It looks like an opening of some sort."

"Do you think it's safe?"

My gaze flickered upwards to the strip of star-speckled night above our heads. "There are degrees of safety."

"Meaning?"

"We've been running for two days. We need somewhere to hide, somewhere to rest and sleep."

I started walking again, aware that our feet were probably the first human feet ever to have walked the base of this particular canyon, and our eyes maybe the first to behold this aperture. Due to the narrowness of the canyon, it certainly wouldn't have been visible from orbit, and ground expeditions were strictly prohibited.

By the time I reached the foot of the wall beneath the opening, I realised my sense of scale had been way off. It was difficult to judge the size of things against the two-kilometre vastness of the slab-sided canyon walls. The hole, which I had initially thought to be fairly small and close to the ground, turned out to be at least two metres in height and five in width, and almost two metres above the ground.

A pattering noise echoed up the canyon from the direction in which we'd come. For a moment, it sounded like distant rain. Then I recognised it. Hundreds of steel claws were skittering towards us.

"They've deployed crawlers," I said.

"What?"

"Drones shaped like millipedes. They've probably released a swarm of them into the labyrinth."

"Are they dangerous?"

"Lethal." I glanced up at the hole above our heads. "But if we can get in there, we might be able to hide."

"How are we going to get up there?"

I stood on the tips of my toes and tried to see what was inside, but saw only further shadow.

"You'll have to throw me."

"I beg your pardon?"

I interlaced my fingers and mimed pushing upwards. "You need to give me a boost."

Adam frowned and, just for a second, I pitied him. For all his attempts at poetic sophistication, he'd grown up in a maze of corridors and greenhouses. He'd never run wild beneath an open sky, never had to boost a friend over a wall or pull them out of a muddy stream bed. Where I felt suffocated by the claustrophobic bleakness of the canyons, he probably found comfort. Buddha only knew how he'd react if he ever found his way onto the naked surface of a normal planet.

"Put your hands like this," I said, fingers still interlaced. "Cup my boot and push me up."

He looked up at the lip of the opening. "Okay, but how will *I* get up there?"

"I'll reach back down and pull you up."

"Really?" He looked me up and down, and raised an eyebrow in a way that made me want to punch it from his face. I spoke through my irritation.

"I'm stronger than I look."

He thought about that. Eventually, he clasped his hands and braced his legs. I put my hand on his shoulder and stepped up.

For a skinny poet, he was surprisingly strong. But then, I already knew that. I just hadn't expected to be propelled upward with such force. As soon as my trailing foot left the canyon's floor, Adam heaved with all his might and I found myself slithering up the marble-smooth wall, my outstretched fingers straining for the lower edge of the hole. In the small planet's weaker gravity, his scrawny muscles combined with my own upward leap to hurl me higher than I could have reasonably expected. I bruised my knees against the wall, but managed to hook my forearms and elbows over the edge of the hole. He gave the soles of my suit a final push, and I swung a foot over the edge.

One last pull, and I rolled into shadow.

For a few seconds, I lay looking up at a dark ceiling, panting from the exertion. And I smiled. For the first time since the crash, I had a roof over my head. For the first time, I was hidden from the prying eyes of orbital ships.

Adam called up. "What can you see?"

I turned my head away from the entrance. "Nothing."

"There's a flashlight built into the wrist of your suit."

"I know."

Silently cursing my forgetfulness, I gripped my left sleeve and the light came on—a white torch beam in an echoing cathedral.

"Holy fuck."

"What is it?"

"I…"

The interior of the cavity fell away downwards in a grand gothic sweep quite at odds with the stark minimalism of the planet's exterior. I merely lay on the top step of a vast spiral staircase. The individual steps were the size of coffins. They had been carved from semi-translucent quartz and then splayed like the feathers of a swan's outstretched wing. The ceiling overhead was also white, and ribbed like the gullet of a fish.

I leant out of the fish's mouth. Adam had to jump to reach my hand. I hauled him up beside me and we sat looking at the giant curving staircase.

"How far down do you think it goes?"

I stood and brushed dust from my suit. "If we want to stay out of sight, we're going to have to find that out for ourselves."

His eyes widened. "We're going down there?"

"What choice do we have?" I rubbed my palms together to hide my own apprehension. "The deeper we go, the less chance anyone will come looking for us."

Adam's head turned back toward the canyon, and the sound of metal claws. "Do you think they're still after us?"

"I don't think they're after *us*." I rubbed the back of my neck where the suit's neck seal had chafed the skin. "I think they're after *me*."

"Because of Pelapatarn?"

"Why else?"

The noise grew closer.

"Do you think they'll reach us up here?"

"Hopefully the walls are too smooth for them to climb."

"What if they're not?"

Hauling him up by the scruff of his neck, I propelled him towards the edge of the first step.

"We go down."

THIRTY

SAL KONSTANZ

I found Ashton Childe standing in the ship's galley drinking coffee. The exoskeleton clung to him like a parasite. He looked up as I approached.

"Hello, Captain."

"How is it?"

"The coffee?"

"The skeleton."

"How do you think?" He looked pale and distracted, like a man trying to hold a conversation while defusing a bomb. He glanced down at his free hand and flexed the fingers. "It takes some getting used to."

"Preston tells me you're taking a hell of a risk wearing that. With your injuries, you should be in bed."

"Needs must, Captain."

The coffee smelled good and my stomach rumbled.

"Is your mission really that important?"

The left side of his face jerked as if stung. The eyelid fluttered. When he spoke, he over-pronounced each word the way Clay sometimes did when she was very drunk.

"It's not for me to know the significance of an assignment, merely to complete it as ordered."

"Even if it kills you?"

"You were in the military, Captain." His hands kept fidgeting, and I wondered how much coffee he had drunk. "You know about duty."

"Surely there's a difference between duty and blind, unquestioning loyalty?"

He scowled in response and his face twitched again. The hand he'd been flexing clenched into a fist.

"Perhaps that attitude's the reason the Outward lost?" His voice was suddenly belligerent. He glared at me, daring me to take offence. Instead, I turned to the coffee pot and poured myself a cup.

"We didn't lose," I said over my shoulder, keeping my tone even, suppressing the flush of indignation his words had stirred. "After Pelapatarn, we just stopped fighting." I inhaled steam from the cup and deliberately relaxed my posture. Then I turned to him. "And don't let Clay hear you talking like that. Exoskeleton or not, she'll kick your ass and flush the remains out the airlock. Do I make myself clear?"

We stood looking at each other for a long moment.

"Perfectly clear, Captain."

I felt the tips of my ears redden. I took a sip of coffee to cover my annoyance.

"Why are you here?" There was an edge to my voice, as thin and sharp as a blade.

Childe looked around at the bulkheads. "I told you, I need a ride."

"I know that's what you said."

I watched his eyes narrow, the skin at the corners wrinkling like old leather. He seemed to be having trouble marshalling his thoughts. "Meaning?"

"Meaning I can't figure out why you're here." I drank some more coffee. He watched in silence, waiting for me to continue. When I started talking again, I spoke slowly, putting shape to my doubts as I expressed them. "I can understand the other one, Laura, being here," I said. "An Outward ship went down and she's an Outward agent. It's you I can't figure. You're from the Conglomeration; what's a crashed Outward liner to you?"

His jaw tightened. A drop of sweat ran down his face. "I told you, I'm looking for a specific passenger, one of our citizens."

"But why rush to get there?" I took a step towards him, trying to sound conciliatory. "If there are any survivors, we'll bring them back. We always do. It's our job. Why do you need to get involved?"

Childe clicked his tongue. His pupils were dilated, and the sweat on his face made him look feverish.

"That's my mission," he said. "And in order to complete it, I need you to fly this ship for me."

"She flies herself."

"But she takes orders from you." His voice had taken on a worrying edge of barely suppressed hysteria, and his fingers scratched at the drug panel set into the left forearm of his exoskeleton.

Oh, crap.

If he'd been messing with battlefield medication, there was no telling how fucked up he was. He could be juiced to the eyeballs on amphetamines and synthetic adrenalin.

I raised my hands, trying to calm the situation.

"Let's get one thing clear," I said. "I am not flying this ship for *you*. We are on a rescue mission, pure and simple. You're just tagging along."

I saw the muscles around his left eye twitch as if electrocuted. He looked like death. Supported by the exoskeleton, he rose to his feet in one smooth movement. Behind him, his chair tipped over with a crash.

"No! I'm not going back. Not for you, not for anybody."

His eye convulsed again. He seemed to have lost control of that side of his face. Was he having a stroke, or some kind of fit?

I took a step backwards, remembering his enhanced strength.

"The House of Reclamation is an independent and apolitical organisation," I warned. "Any attempt to threaten or commandeer—"

With a roar, Childe lunged. I threw up my arms but he swiped them aside. One hand closed over my mouth. The other clasped my shoulder to stop me from struggling. He was close enough now that I could smell his breath. His servo-powered fingers dug into my deltoid muscle, bruising the skin. The pressure of his grip on my jaw forced my lips into an uncomfortable pout.

"Shut up!" he screamed.

Light flickered at the edge of my vision as a screen on the galley wall lit to reveal the face of the *Trouble Dog*'s avatar.

"Release the captain," she said.

Ashton Childe shook his head. The entire left side of his face had contracted into a knot. His cheek muscles jerked and quivered, pulling up the corner of his mouth. His eyelid flickered in agitation.

"No way." Sweat poured down his face, and the tendons stood out on his neck like lengths of high-tension steel cable. "I'm in charge now, you hear? You're going to be taking orders from *me*."

The *Trouble Dog* looked apologetic. "I am sorry, but that is not an option."

I tried kicking his shins, but Childe simply tightened his grip on my face and shoulder. His fingers were like a docking clamp, and I swear I felt my jawbone begin to sag.

"I don't want to have to kill a hostage," he said. His eyes were wild and strangely unfocused. "But I will if I have to."

The *Trouble Dog* glowered. "And I don't want to have to vent all the air from the room you're standing in." Her gaze seemed to burn through the display. "But I will, if I have to."

Childe gave a manic laugh, and I was terrifyingly aware

that his enhanced fingers could easily crush my skull. "You're bluffing," he yelled at the screen. "You'd never risk your captain."

The *Trouble Dog* raised her eyebrows. "You don't know the first thing about me," she said, "or what I'm capable of."

"I know you resigned your commission."

"Yes, Mr Childe." The *Dog* lowered her virtual chin. "I resigned my commission because I became tired of pointless slaughter. Yet, if you recall the events of yesterday, you might remember I shot eleven men and women in Northfield in order to secure your escape. Violence doesn't bother me when it's done in defence. In fact, I'm rather good at it."

As she spoke, Childe's eyes were on her rather than me. I reached up and stiffened my fingers, shaping my hand like the blade of a trowel. Moving slowly, I pushed it between the ribs of his suit, beneath the inflatable cast, until the tips brushed the bandages covering his gunshot wound. At their touch, his head snapped around, mouth opening.

"What are you—?"

I jabbed with every scrap of strength I could muster, driving my nails into the muscles of his abdomen until I felt something give.

Childe yelled and threw me from him with a force that picked me from my feet and sent me flying back like a piece of windblown laundry. I rolled across the table and onto the floor, landing with a crash that left me gasping for breath.

Childe had his hand at his gut. Blood welled through the dressings and between the exoskeleton's struts. My stabbing fingers had found their target, rupturing the sutures. His eyes were screwed tight and his free arm flailed blindly.

"What have you done?" he cried. "What have you *done?*"

Too winded to move, I lay beneath the table where I had fallen and watched him thrashing around, barging into chairs and tables.

After a minute or so, Alva Clay stepped into the room. She

had a thick wrench gripped in her fist, and moved stealthily.

As she came within striking distance of her target, we exchanged a look.

Can I hit him now?

Go right ahead.

Ducking to avoid Childe's flailing fists, she crept forward. Her arm wound back, ready to bring the heavy iron wrench down in a savage blow to the back of his head. But before she could unleash the strike, a gun fired twice—*phut! phut!*—and Ashton Childe crumpled to the floor in a tangle of limbs and carbon-fibre struts.

In the ensuing silence, we both turned to see Laura Petrushka in the doorway, a crutch under her left arm, a tiny ceramic pistol clasped in her right hand. She looked at the astonishment on our faces and shrugged.

"He was being a dick," she said.

Clay stood over Childe's slumped form. The wrench dangled from her fingers. "Is he dead?"

Laura Petrushka hobbled into the room and lowered herself onto one of the few chairs that remained upright. She held out the small pistol. "These are tranquiliser darts," she explained.

"How long will he be asleep?"

"Three or four hours." She tucked the gun back into the pocket of her dressing gown. "Depends how much other shit he has in his system."

I picked myself up from the floor and brushed myself down. Clay looked at me. "What do you want to do with him, Captain? Throw him out the airlock?"

I massaged my jaw. Nobody knew what happened to bodies ejected from ships in the hypervoid. If we put Childe in a suit and pushed him into the howling emptiness, he might fall through it forever, endlessly tumbling: an eternal monument to his own stupidity.

"Tempting as it might be, we can't murder an agent of

Conglomeration Intelligence." My hands began to shake. I squeezed them into fists. For some stupid reason, I felt like laughing.

"Then what are we going to do with him?" Clay asked.

From her chair, Petrushka poked Childe's shoulder with the rubber tip of her crutch. "Let me try talking to him, when he wakes." She frowned. "*If* he wakes."

I swallowed back the giggle in my throat. "And if that doesn't work?"

Clay turned to me. "I'll go get my Archipelago pistol, chief. Bastard makes one wrong move, I'll blow a hole through him."

I shook my head, feeling a little giddy. "No, no murders."

"Then what do you want me to do, tie him up?"

I gave a snort. "Something along those lines." I turned my attention to the avatar on the screen. "Ship, get Nod up here." With the toe of my boot, I nudged the tangled form of the sedated agent. "And tell him to bring a welding torch."

THIRTY-ONE

NOD

Leave nest and climb to galley, they say.

Bring gear.

Climb up three decks and no one says thank you.

And galley stinks of human food. Meat and vegetables printed from organic ink. Recycled a million times. Stupid omnivores. They have lost their connection to the World Tree. They have forgotten what they are. And so they fight and strive and overcome their niche. They construct ships with innards as challenging to maintain as the fibres of the World Tree. Ships like *Hound of Difficulty*.

And I work and maintain.

And I build nest and sleep.

Good nest.

And then they say, "Nod, can you come up to the galley and bring a welding rig?" And when I get there, they ask me to weld male human to deck.

Male human stinks of narcotics. Smell comes from pores. Brains scrambled like churned-up riverbed.

Place welds at every joint of spindly body. Ankles, knees, hips, elbows, wrists. Fix metal and carbon-fibre skeleton in place, so meat can't move.

Stupid omnivores.

They have lost their niche. They only care for power and territory, as if somehow that makes up for losing comfort of knowing World Tree.

Humans and Druff both paradoxical, but opposite. Humans social but selfish; Druff solitary but happy to share. Druff prefer to be lonely, but feel unthreatened by presence of other Druff. Humans like to be part of group, but hoard and exclude. Want to be with others, but don't want to share resources. Don't want to share world.

I don't point out species folly. Instead, I fuse man's exoskeleton to deck plates as told. Sparks jump and sprinkle like flickering insects. Lance hisses. Smoke curls. Melting metal smell momentarily drowns reek of human food. But still smell humans in room. Smell their undertone through my fingers. Spicy, like vinegar and fetid berries. Greasy like dripping remains of fatty animal caught in forest fire.

Welding sparks fall like rain caught in shaft of sunlight.

Pattering onto the world.

Illuminating.

Hissing.

But fingers itch. *Hound of Difficulty* riddled with silly faults. Needs fixing. Always fixing.

Repair, replace, work, and maintain.

Work and maintain, until time comes to return to World Tree. Then maintain World Tree until die.

Serve ships.

Build nest.

Good nest. Probably best nest ever.

Love sleep.

Love World Tree.

Love *Hound of Difficulty* like own tree of world.

Understand ship.

Don't understand humans.

Humans all broken.

THIRTY-TWO

ONA SUDAK

The individual stairs were too deep to take at a normal pace. To descend, we had to turn sideways and step down one foot at a time, our cold palms sliding against the smooth, pale wall for support. It was a painfully slow process, and I was constantly aware of the speed at which the crawlers would be able to swarm after us if they reached the opening in the canyon wall. Shadows jumped and leapt in the beams from our torches. My thighs and knees, already fatigued from two days of almost ceaseless walking, burned with the repeated strain of lowering my entire body weight on one leg.

After several revolutions of the spiral, I called for a rest. I estimated we had made a descent of around ten metres, which put us just below the floor of the canyon network. And, if anything, the temperature down here was colder than it had been on the surface. Our breath steamed where the torchlight touched it. The end of my nose felt numb, and icy to the touch—like a piece of raw meat taken from the refrigerator.

"Just give me a moment," I said, inwardly cursing each and every evening I had forsaken additional physical training for wine and verse.

Adam cast troubled glances at the gloom behind us, fearful

of pursuit. He hadn't had time to drift out of shape. He still had that teenage elasticity that all adults secretly resent losing. The scratches on his hands and face would heal faster than the ones on mine. His bones and muscles were young and flexible, and he could take almost anything in his stride.

How I hated him for that.

I stood panting with my hands on my knees while he dithered, hardly out of breath.

Deprived of anything more satisfying than the energy tablets I'd been sucking on for the past two days, my stomach had knotted itself into a tight, angry fist. I felt old, tired and haggard, but still determined to stay alive.

"You know," I said between breaths, "they wanted to shoot me after the war."

Adam looked at me but didn't comment. I hadn't really been speaking to him.

"Even though we won, and even though what I did probably saved lives in the long run, they wanted to shoot me. Luckily, I had friends in high places, friends with the influence and means to help me disappear."

A sudden sadness crowded in on me. If I had been discovered, if our pursuers knew I was the Butcher of Pelapatarn, it could only mean I had been betrayed by one of those former colleagues. The officers of my flagship, the *Righteous Fury*, had painstakingly obliterated all the physical and digital evidence of my disappearance. My face, height and fingerprints had been altered, and even sections of my DNA had been changed to prevent identification. The only way I could possibly have been traced would have been if one of my friends had chosen to testify as to my whereabouts.

"They got me out because, no matter the outcry following the burning of the jungles, they knew I'd done the right thing." I rubbed my face with both hands. The skin felt waxy and loose. "They fought alongside me. They understood that if a soldier has seen a way to save lives by ending a conflict, they have an ethical obligation to do so."

I looked over at Adam. He was fiddling with his sleeve. Even though I'd been talking to myself more than I'd been addressing him, his lack of attention still irritated me.

"What are you doing?"

He glanced up. "These suits have short-range emergency radios." He saw the look of alarm on my face and held up a hand. "Don't worry, I'm not transmitting. I'm not an idiot."

I let out a breath. "You won't get much down here, anyway," I said. "Radio works via line of sight, and those canyon walls are a pretty big obstacle."

"I thought I might hear something from the crawlers. Or, if something passed overhead, like a ship in orbit, I might pick it up."

"Have you had any luck with that?"

"Not so far." He raised his face to the white stone ceiling— its ribbed surface formed from the underside of the steps we'd trodden on our last circuit of the spiral. "Of course, that could just be because we're too far underground."

After a few minutes of rest and a quick drink of water, we continued to work our way down the oversized staircase, our ears constantly alert for sounds of pursuit. With his longer legs and lighter frame, Adam found the going easier. The aches and pains in my protesting legs eventually obliged me to shelve my pride and allow him to help. As I eased myself over the lip of each step, he took my elbow and supported as much of my weight as he could, taking the pressure from my knees.

"Thank you," I said, feeling like an old woman. He merely smiled, eyes averted with the embarrassment the young feel around the elderly and infirm. It was hard to remember that, only three days ago, we'd been enthusiastically fucking each other's brains out. Now, he saw me as something quite different. The poet he'd worshipped had changed like clay in his hands, shifting to reveal the face of a medusa—a middle-aged war criminal in a pair of dead girl's shoes.

"Is it my imagination," he asked after a few minutes, "or is it getting lighter in here?"

I had been moving on autopilot, preoccupied with self-pity. But now Adam mentioned it, I realised the air around us had grown almost imperceptibly brighter. The quartz walls and ribbed ceiling were giving off a faint and milky luminescence—one that increased in intensity as we continued our descent, until, after another twenty steps, our torches had become superfluous. We turned them off and stood blinking at each other in the pale light.

Adam put a palm against the smooth wall. "It's beautiful," he said.

I couldn't help but agree. "It reminds me of a full moon."

"A full moon?" Adam looked puzzled, and I felt an unexpected pang of sorrow at the gulf between us, and the thought of all the wonders he had missed in his half-lived life.

"When I was a kid back on Earth," I said quietly, "we had a little hillside farm with a few dozen goats. The way these walls shine reminds me of the way the moonlight lit up the fields at night."

"Ah." Comprehension dawned. "You mean sunlight reflected from the planet's satellite?"

"Yes." I put my own hand to the wall. The stone felt cold through my glove, and impossibly smooth to the touch. "But there's more to it than that. Moonlight has its own quality, its own texture." I struggled to find the words to convey the childhood magic of being out at night with the moon riding high and proud like a galleon in the sky. How I wished I could be back there now, standing at the door of that humble little cottage with the valley picked out before me in silver and shadow, and be adolescent and blameless again, unencumbered by the burdens of adulthood and able to look ahead with neither guilt nor trepidation. I opened my mouth to say something. Before I could speak, the first echoes reached us. Voices from above; the clatter of armour and weapons.

We looked at each other, eyes wide with alarm.

We had been found.

THIRTY-THREE

SAL KONSTANZ

Preston stepped back.

"It's fine, I think. At least, the skin's not broken. You're probably going to have some bruising."

He wouldn't meet my eye. I was sitting on the edge of one of the galley tables. I pulled my jumpsuit closed and zipped it up to the neck. "Thank you."

I looked down at Ashton Childe's comatose form. Nod had done a good job with the welding torch, and now fat blobs of solder held the man in a spread-eagled cruciform, with his closed eyes and slack mouth facing the strip lights on the galley's ceiling. According to Preston, he'd taken enough methamphetamine to give a platoon insomnia, and it would be several hours before it could all be purged from his system.

"Call me when he wakes up."

Alva Clay still had the wrench dangling from her fingers. "Why, where are you going?" she asked.

I pushed away from the table and stood up. "To talk to the boss."

I could feel her gaze on my back as I left the galley. I walked around the circular corridor to the nearest elevator. When the doors opened, I stepped inside and let it whisk me "up" to the ship's bridge, close to the centre of the vessel.

Lit only by the light of its display screens, the bridge felt like a secure cave at the heart of the ship. The room was armoured, could be sealed off from the rest of the ship, and had its own emergency air supply. Even if enemy fire penetrated the main hull, the command crew would still have some level of protection. They would be able to keep fighting, even as the rest of the ship was blown away around them; and, in defeat, they would be among the last of its crew to die.

Feeling stiff and battered after having first been shot in the arm and then thrown across a table, I carefully lowered myself into the command chair.

"Open a channel to Camrose," I told the *Dog*.

•

Ambassador Odom had left his jacket off, the top button of his shirt was undone, and the corners of his eyelids drooped like the leaves of a neglected houseplant. Glowing numerals in the corner of the screen informed me that local time on the station was a little after midnight.

Briefly, I told him about the warning message the *Dog* had received, the events at Northfield, and Ashton Childe's futile attempt to hijack the ship.

As I talked, the ambassador's expression grew more and more concerned. When I had finished, he puffed his cheeks and made a face. "And here was I thinking you'd called to complain about Preston."

I felt my face flush. "You knew he wasn't qualified?" By supplying me with a useless medic, had he been trying to set me up? Was this his way of finally getting rid of me?

The old man cleared his throat. "I had an inkling."

"Then, why—?"

"A favour to his father." Odom waved a gnarled hand. "But you have more pressing concerns."

I raised an eyebrow, surprised by the ease and speed of his admission. "Indeed we do. How do you think we should proceed?"

"With great caution."

"Do we have your permission to tool up?"

The ambassador gave a series of rapid blinks. He opened and shut his mouth a few times. "The *Trouble Dog* is a decommissioned warship."

"But if we're walking into a trap…"

He harrumphed. "All right," he said after a moment's thought. "You have my permission for the *Trouble Dog* to start the manufacture of replacement weaponry. But please, for the love of God, try not to do anything precipitous. The Gallery's a powder keg. One wrong move and you could start a war."

"Or stop one."

He looked pained. "Just come home safely."

•

After the call ended, I remained in the control couch and watched the external screens. The peripheral ones showed various views of the *Trouble Dog*'s hull against the formless misty void of the higher dimensions. The main one showed an impossible computer-generated image of the stars, as if we were travelling through the regular universe at the same speed we were currently barrelling through the hypervoid. The slowly moving points of light were hypnotic. Seeing them shift position in relation to each other gave the sky a three-dimensional aspect you just didn't get at any other time. Instead of points of light arrayed in the darkness like sequins on a velvet curtain, their movements relative to each other spoke of unfathomable depth and distance, especially when I pictured the impalpably tiny planets wheeling around each one like mosquitoes wheeling around a ship's lantern on a dark and endless sea.

The *Trouble Dog*'s face appeared in a corner of the screen, her features superimposed on the shifting starscape.

"Any further transmissions?" I asked her.

"None at this time."

"And still no idea who might have sent that anonymous warning?"

Her forehead creased. A tiny line appeared between her brows. "I have several theories, but no evidence to support them."

My upper arm hurt where the shotgun pellet had winged it. I wriggled around to get more comfortable, and kicked off my boots. "What would you say if you had to guess?"

"If I *had* to…" The *Dog*'s face scrunched.

I reclined the couch and stretched out my toes. I'd had enough punishment for one day, and was seriously considering sealing the bridge doors and spending the night in the chair. "Give me your best guess."

"I have no proof of my suspicions."

"Nevertheless."

I watched her features rearrange themselves. When she next spoke, she looked calm and reasonable—at least, that was the impression she was trying to convey. "I think *Fenrir* sent the signal."

I raised my head. "Your sister?"

"As I said, it is only a suspicion, but yes, I think she did. Probably on behalf of her commanding officer, Captain Sergei Parris."

"And you base this on what?"

"*Adalwolf* advised me to heed the warning. He would not have done that otherwise. He would not have insulted my courage unless he knew that to allow me to proceed would have brought me into conflict with my sister."

"You're sure of that?"

"Maybe eighty per cent."

Suppressing a yawn, I rubbed the side of my nose with the side of my hand. "And how do you feel about that?"

The face on the screen froze. I watched stars drift across her cheeks and into her hair. When she eventually spoke, her words were slow and measured.

"I have activated my dormant battle-repair packages. We will arrive in the system in fifteen hours. By that time, I will have fashioned and emplaced thirty-eight per cent of my former armaments—the most I can manage without the aid of a military shipyard."

"Will it be enough?"

Her mouth kinked in a quirky, unreadable smile. Through my chair, I felt the higher dimensional winds buffet the hull. "Against a fully armed Carnivore?"

I had the impression she was laughing at me. I closed my eyes and tried to make myself comfortable.

"Forget I asked."

THIRTY-FOUR

NOD

Put welding tools away then curled in nest.
Good nest.
Best nest.
Bits of packing case.
Fibre-optic wires.
String.
Best nest I ever made.
Plastic spatulas in bottom like twigs.
Air con unit like breeze in high branches.
Thrum of engines like pulse of World Tree's heart.
Hound of Difficulty like little World Tree.
Like home.
Will stay with ship until time.
Time to go back to real World Tree.
Time to stop serving and rest.
Until then, fix ship.
Serve ship as would serve Tree.
Keep ship running.
And maybe one day, ship stop being sad.
Stop being broken.
Find missing pieces.
Put self back together.

Until then, I serve.
I work.
And I curl in nest.
Good nest.
Nice and prickly.
Best nest I ever built.
Best ship I ever served.
Even captain tolerable.
For a human.

THIRTY-FIVE

ASHTON CHILDE

My head hurt. The whole left side of my face felt bruised. Alva Clay stood over me. Her hard plastic boots were close enough to stomp my face. Her fists were clenched and she had the butt of her Archipelago pistol sticking from the waistband of her olive combat trousers.

"Are you awake, shithead?"

I turned my aching eyes from the overhead lights. "What happened?"

"You made a damn fool of yourself. If your girl here hadn't tranquilised your stupid ass, you'd be dead right now."

I swivelled my neck so I could look up at Laura. She was sitting in a wheelchair with her needle gun on the blanket covering her legs.

"You shot me?"

Her hands were clasped and her knuckles were pale. Her lips were a tight white line. "I didn't have a choice."

"Like hell you didn't."

I tried to move my arms but they were securely fastened to the deck at elbow and wrist.

Clay watched with contempt. "I'm going to hit my bunk," she told Laura. "If he moves again, tranquilise him."

She stepped over me and marched out of the room and

into the main corridor. I heard the receding clomp of her boots on the deck plates, and then she was gone.

My neck was stiff.

"What time is it?"

"About three in the morning, ship's time."

"And you got given the first watch, huh?"

Laura smoothed down the sides of her blanket, tucking them between her thighs and the arms of the wheelchair. "I just wanted to be sure that woman wasn't going to slit your throat and eject you into space."

"Do you think she might have done?"

Laura pursed her lips. "If she had, you would have deserved it."

I frowned. I knew something had happened, but the actual events were scratchy. I had vague recollections of my own voice sounding hoarse and angry, of my fingers gripping somebody's face. I remembered a terrible, all-consuming panic. I remembered lashing out...

"What did I do?" I felt like a waking man trying to catch the last wisps of a bad dream, or a hung-over drunk trying to recall and parse the fuzzy degradations of the previous night.

"You attempted to hijack the ship."

My eyes widened and I tried to raise my head. "I did *what?*" Even wearing a powered suit, such an attempt at insurgency would have been pointless. Carnivore-class heavy cruisers were designed to take care of themselves and make their own decisions. They had complete control of their internal environments, and therefore possessed a hundred different ways to kill or detain intruders. They were almost impossible to commandeer, as the citizens of Northfield had discovered to their cost. "That's stupid. Why would I even—?"

"You were off your face on military-grade speed. And maybe you had some kind of psychotic episode." Laura's fingers picked at the blanket's hem. "You've been under a lot of stress." She gave a small shrug. "I think the drugs were too much for you. You were twitching and sweating like a man on fire."

For a moment, she continued worrying the blanket's seam. Then she folded her hands and her expression softened.

"Listen," she said, "you've been trapped on the fringes of a particularly nasty civil war, running supply drops through the mountains. You've lost pilots and other colleagues, and been wounded yourself, getting that shrapnel fragment through your bladder. I know you hated every minute of it. And then you're out of the jungle for one day, and some ignorant fucking bartender puts a pellet in your spleen. All of that would be enough to send most people gibbering over the paranoid edge. But add to it the physical strain of wearing a suit like that, coupled with enough pharmaceuticals to power an illegal rave, and it's not surprising you lost your shit. Give a persecuted man a sudden feeling of power, and he's going to lash out."

She stopped speaking and, to my shame, I had to swallow back a sob. Everything she had said was true. I felt hot, bitter tears roll from the corners of my eyes. They ran into my ears and hair, and I flexed against my restraints. I wanted to wipe my face, but couldn't move my arm. The suit had become a prison.

"Was anybody hurt?"

"You threw the captain over a table."

"Is she all right?"

"If by 'all right' you mean royally pissed off, then, yeah, she's just peachy."

"What do you think she's going to do?"

"I have no idea. But she's locked herself onto the bridge for the night, so I guess she's still worried you might get free and have another crack at taking the ship."

I sniffed miserably. "I wouldn't…"

"You did."

I could feel the vibration of the ship's engines coming up through the deck plates, transmitted via the welds to my arms and legs.

"Help me out of this thing." I wanted to hide my face but, with my arms immobilised, I couldn't reach the fastenings to release the straps holding in place the suit's carbon-fibre ribs.

Laura turned her face away. The overhead light caught the lines around her eyes and mouth, the tendril of white in her hair.

"Sorry, but no."

"Oh, come on." My voice cracked. "Please?"

"Absolutely not." She held up a finger. "For one thing, that suit's the only thing holding your innards where they should be. It's not coming off until you get to a hospital." She held up a second digit. "And for another, I'm not entirely sure I can trust you, or that you're entirely sane." She let her hands drop to the blanket. "There could be lasting psychological damage. So, you're staying there until the suit's flushed all the crap out of your bloodstream, and we can work out the best course of action."

"When you say 'we', you mean you and the crew?"

"Yes."

My head throbbed. "I thought you were on my side."

She laughed. "I'm your friend, you know that." The laugh guttered like a dying flame. She looked down at the fists clasped in her lap, where the nails were digging into the skin of her palms. "But we have never, *ever*, been on the same side."

THIRTY-SIX

SAL KONSTANZ

I saw the barman fire his shotgun at me, and felt again the sting as a pellet took a bite from my arm. Mulch leered across the room. He wanted to take my ship. I wanted to shout at him but, before I could open my mouth, he morphed into Sedge, his frozen face rimed with frost. I leaned over him, trying to breathe warmth and life into those blue features, trying to let him know I was still alive, but he changed again, becoming Childe, and his mechanically enhanced fingers closed over my face…

The bridge console chimed. Curled semi–comfortably in the command couch, I had been drifting in and out of a restless and fidgety sleep for several hours, my thoughts eddying with the almost subliminal howl of the void beyond the ship's external hull.

The console chimed again. I rubbed my eyes. Somebody wanted access to the bridge. I checked the security feed, and when I saw Preston waiting, I reached out and reluctantly released the locks. I sat upright and straightened my clothes.

"I'm sorry," he said. "Were you asleep?"

I scowled at him. "What time is it?" My mouth felt drier than an old leather boot at the side of a desert highway.

"A little after eight."

"What do you want?"

Preston scratched the side of his nose, looking nervous. "To talk?" He moved his weight from one foot to the other, like a child desperate for the toilet. I stretched my neck, rolling my head from side to side. The vertebrae crunched and crackled.

"What do you want to talk about?"

"There seems to be a certain…" The back of his neck reddened.

"A certain what?" Sleeping in my clothes had done nothing for my mood.

"T-tension," he stammered.

"Tension?"

"Between us. As if I've annoyed you."

I sighed, and gestured toward the co-pilot's couch. "You're a good kid." I paused as he perched on the edge of the seat. "And I'm your commanding officer. I can't have you knocking on my cabin door every time you have a nightmare."

His face flushed a deeper shade of red. "I'm sorry, Captain. I'm trying. I really am." He rubbed the side of his nose again, and scraped a hand through his hair. He looked as if he wanted the deck to swallow him. "When I was at home, before the Academy, one of my father's staff used to sleep in an adjoining room. She kept her light on and her door open in case I got scared."

"Your father gave you a… nanny?"

"No!" Preston shook his head. He looked wretched. "Not a nanny, more like a… personal assistant."

"An assistant?"

"Yes."

I couldn't help smiling. "And how old were you when you left for the Academy?"

"Twenty-one."

"So, you had a nanny right up until then?"

His head sank between his hunched shoulders. "I wouldn't put it quite like that, exactly."

"I don't know whether to laugh or feel pity."

"But you understand?" I saw hope flicker behind his misery. I wanted to be angry with him, but couldn't summon the emotion or the energy to power it. He wasn't qualified for his position and had no right to be here; when I looked at him, all I saw was a nervous young kid.

He took my silence for disapproval.

"I know you're going to throw me off this ship," he said, looking at his hands. "But I haven't got anywhere else to go. My father won't take me back after the way I embarrassed him at the Academy. And I don't want to be alone." A tear spilled from his eye and drew a line down his cheek. "I'm not cut out for it."

I closed my eyes, remembering how it had felt at that age to be suddenly parentless and alone. If I hadn't had my studies at the Academy—and then later, my duties aboard the medical frigate—I couldn't begin to guess what might have befallen me. And now here Preston sat, snuffling onto the sleeve of his uniform, and all he had to cling to was this post, on this ship. I knew in my heart I couldn't deprive him of it.

I muttered an expletive under my breath.

"Captain?"

"By rights, I should kick you off this ship as soon as we get back to Camrose." I fixed him with my most piercing stare. "But I'm not going to do that. My parents died on a scouting mission. During the war, Clay crawled through the jungles of Pelapatarn. The *Dog* served on the front lines in the final weeks of the conflict, then resigned her commission." I shrugged. "We're all here because, like you, we have nowhere else to go."

He blinked at me. I could see he didn't want to get his hopes up, only to see them dashed. "I'm not sure I understand."

"I'm saying you can stay, kid. I won't report you, and you

can be a part of this crew." I held up a finger. "But there are conditions."

He swallowed and sat up straight, flicking the tears from his eyes with quick swipes of his fingers.

"Yes, ma'am."

"Firstly, don't call me ma'am. I don't like the way it makes me sound like somebody's maiden aunt. 'Sir' or 'Captain' will suffice."

"Yes, Captain."

"That's much better." I gave what I hoped was an encouraging smile. "Now, regarding your sleep problems." I gestured to the ceiling and the metal walls surrounding us. "The *Dog* monitors everything. It's always there, always watching over us. If you wake up in the night, you can talk to it. It might not be very sympathetic, but it will be there, and it will listen."

"Thank you, Captain." Preston stood as if to leave, no doubt wanting to scurry away from his embarrassment. I stopped him with a raised hand.

"But I still need a qualified medic," I told him sternly. "So you have a lot of work to do. The *Dog* has all the medical texts you could ever need. I want you to study them. Every free moment you have, I want you at a screen or in the infirmary, studying."

"Yes, Captain."

"And don't mistake any of this for softness on my part. If I think you're skimping on your studies, I'll dump you on the first world we come to." I leant towards him and lowered my voice. "Do we understand each other?"

"Yes, but—"

"Good." I sat back and brushed my hands together. "Now, go and get me some coffee."

•

When he'd gone, I let my head fall back against the couch. I was fairly certain that I was doing the right thing for Preston by letting him stay, but it would probably turn out to be a mistake for me in the long run. The last thing I wanted was to fly with an unqualified medic. And yet, there was no way I could have turned the kid away. His plight reminded me too acutely of my own sorrows. However, by allowing him to stay, I knew I had given Alva Clay ammunition against me, should her resentment ever boil over into actual hostility. On the other hand we had Laura Petrushka on board, and I was fairly confident she could handle any medical emergencies that arose. As far as I was concerned, I wasn't putting the crew in danger; but she wasn't an official medical practitioner, and that distinction might be enough to end my career.

I stretched my fingers and toes, trying to dissipate my fatigue. Then I hooked open the neck of my t-shirt and sniffed. I had been sleeping in these clothes for two days, and badly needed a shower. With a groan, I got to my feet and climbed up into the main corridor.

When I reached my cabin, I found Laura waiting by the door.

"Have you come to beg for clemency?" I rubbed my jaw, where Childe's fingers had bruised the skin.

To my surprise, she shook her head. "I have some information you need to hear." Her voice dripped with painkiller-induced weariness. I could even see it in the set of her shoulders. Slumped in the wheelchair, she looked ten years older.

I leant against the corridor wall. "What kind of information?"

"I've been looking at the *Geest van Amsterdam*'s distress signal," she said, "and there's something weird about it."

"Weird?" I uncrossed my arms. My own tiredness gave way to professional interest. If there was anything that might negatively affect the success of our rescue attempt, I needed to hear about it.

Petrushka flicked lint from the blanket covering her knees. "A ship that size doesn't have one comms array," she said, "it has half a dozen, spread out across its hull."

I knew this. "So?"

"So, in order to silence the ship, you'd need to knock out all six arrays simultaneously. But no torpedo's that accurate, and the ship has its defence cannons. The odds are at least one of those arrays should have survived and been functional after the first attack."

"The ship shut itself down, like the *Hobo*."

"The *Hobo*?"

"It was a scout ship that ditched in the sea on a world twelve light years past the Yellow Sky Relay. The data we pulled from its black box suggested its mind had deliberately turned itself off."

Petrushka leant forward in her chair. "When was this?"

"It crashed a week ago, on Thursday."

"Four days before the attack on the liner?"

"We were trying to rescue the crew when we heard about the *Geest van Amsterdam*." I pushed away from the wall. "Why? Do you think there's a connection?"

She let out a long breath. "Two Outward vessels downed within days of each other, having both apparently turned themselves off?" She shook her head as if unable to calculate the odds of such a coincidence. "What's the flight time from Yellow Sky to the Gallery, as the crow flies?"

"Six days."

"But a warship like this, at maximum burn?"

"You could maybe shave a third off."

"So, theoretically, the same ship could have targeted both vessels?"

"I guess." It would have been possible. We were completing

the same trip in a similar time, including stopovers at Camrose and Cichol. "But how could one ship convince two others to voluntarily commit suicide?"

Laura Petrushka sat back and drummed her fingers on the wheelchair's armrest. "There is a way." For a moment, she was silent, seemingly debating with herself. "At least," she continued in a low voice, "I've heard rumours of something that can do it. Some sort of alien weapon that can infiltrate and confuse a neural matrix."

I flicked a hand. "That's just talk." If you hung around spaceports long enough, you'd hear all sorts of fantastical and paranoid tales—magical relics, hypervoid monsters, lost cities of gold…

Petrushka shook her head. "The person I heard it from is reliable, even if he is a Conglomeration agent."

I raised an eyebrow. "How can you be so sure?"

Her eyes fixed on mine, evaluating, challenging, imploring. "Because he says they have one."

All the breath seemed to evaporate from my lungs. "The Conglomeration has a weapon that can remotely disable a ship's brain?"

Petrushka maintained eye contact. "That's correct. And I'm only admitting to knowing that now because, as captain, you need to know what we might be up against."

THIRTY-SEVEN

ONA SUDAK

We tried to move as silently as possible, desperate to stay ahead of our pursuers. For the moment, we were hidden by several curves of the spiral staircase. Their voices and footfalls came to us as echoes. However tired we were, we could not afford to pause. To do so would be to squander our head start and risk capture, or worse. All we could do was keep lowering ourselves from one oversized step to the next as we slowly corkscrewed our way into the heart of the Brain.

And then, just as I was starting to think the rest of my days would be spent negotiating the interminable curve of this stairwell, the steps ended. We came around the final bend to find ourselves looking at a long, softly glowing corridor approximately three metres in height and two in width. For a couple of seconds, we dithered. The stairs had been torture, but the corridor—while seemingly flat and featureless—represented the unknown.

Adam glanced back over his shoulder. "Do you think we can make it to the end before they see us?"

I took him by the wrist. "Well, we can't stay here."

Ahead, at the end of the corridor, I could see a black rectangle—an open doorway leading into a darkened area beyond. If we could get to it before the first of our pursuers

reached the bottom of the stairs, we could remain hidden—
at least, for a few more minutes. We began to run, our legs
shaky with hunger and fatigue, our hearts hammering against
our ribs, lungs burning.

Adam had a long, loping stride that had been learned and
perfected on a treadmill, whereas I was struggling along with
ageing leg muscles that had once known military levels of
fitness but had since waned in strength and stamina. Only
fear and bitter determination kept me moving, my thighs
and calves exerting harder than they had been called upon
to in years.

As if in a nightmare, the corridor seemed to recede ahead
to infinity. We were running but not getting anywhere. My
back itched with the anticipation of discovery, cringing
against the expectation of bullets…

And then we slammed into the walls at either side of the
black doorway.

My chest heaved. Shadows thronged the edge of my
vision. My head felt light and I couldn't catch enough breath
to speak. I watched Adam stick his head around the opening,
peering into the gloom.

"After you," he said. He put his arm around my shoulders
and I felt the warmth of his chest through the fabric of
his shirt. In this sterile alien corridor, it was an absurdly
comforting human intimacy.

"It doesn't look very big."

"Maybe there's another door? They wouldn't have put in
all those stairs just to reach a closet."

I shrugged. The creatures that had built this place
had carved an entire solar system into a series of bizarre
and undecipherable sculptures. Who knew what other
eccentricities they might have indulged in?

Standing on the threshold, I slipped from beneath Adam's
arm and turned to face him. "Look, Adam, I—"

A shout came from the stairs. Two figures stood on the penultimate step, both clad in mismatched and heavily scuffed combat armour and carrying heavy-duty bolt-throwers.

We were caught.

Without a word, Adam shoved me backwards, into the darkness of the small room beyond the door.

I cried out as I hit the floor. At the same instant, the walls of the chamber lit up and a transparent barrier hissed down like the blade of a well-oiled guillotine, sealing the doorway.

Adam was still outside, in the corridor. His hands were splayed against the clear material, trying to find a way to open it.

I struggled to my feet.

His fists battered soundlessly against the door, then stopped as he realised it was useless. Behind him, the soldiers raised their weapons. I called his name but he couldn't hear me. For a frozen, helpless moment, all I could do was stare into his eyes.

He started to mouth the words, "I love you." But the guns spat before he could finish. He slammed up against the see-through door, twitching and flailing like a man caught in the teeth of a lion. I saw his right shoulder explode and his arm come loose, the exposed bones appallingly white in the wan light from the walls, the blood sickeningly red. And still they fired. They riddled him until long after he was dead, until it was only the smack of the bullets that held him upright and pinned to the barrier between us. Only when there was almost nothing recognisable about him and no chance that even a flicker of life remained did the firing stop. He slid awkwardly to the floor, leaving a thick slaughterhouse smear on the impenetrable glass. I stared at the bloody clumps of hair, the unidentifiable pieces of gristle and sharp little chips of bone, and I screamed. But it wasn't a scream of fear; it was a scream filled with grief, guilt and rage, and an almost uncontrollable urge to break through that door and rip the armoured soldiers apart with my clawed fingers, to tear off their helmets and gouge out their eyes, to throttle them, and crack their heads against the floor until there was nothing left. To obliterate them as thoroughly as they had obliterated Adam.

As they advanced towards me, I railed and swore and slapped the glass. I had been running for two days—I had been running for *years*—and now I had had enough. A line had been crossed. Something snapped inside, and I didn't even care if they killed me too, as long as I got the chance to fight back, to punish the men that had murdered my friend, and kick against the pricks that had skewered my soul since the burning of Pelapatarn. If I had known how to open the barrier between us, I believe I would have charged them.

Instead, before they had covered half the distance to where I stood, the little room I was in began to move backwards. It pulled away from the corridor—and Adam's shattered body—and gradually withdrew until all I could see of the corridor was a tiny oblong of light adrift in a vast and impenetrable darkness.

THIRTY-EIGHT

ASHTON CHILDE

Looking up at the galley's ceiling, I knew with an aching and stone-cold certainty that I had failed in my mission. I couldn't continue, not now. The medic, having operated on my already battered internal organs with the help and guidance of the ship, had done his best to repair the additional damage caused by flailing around in the powered suit, and by Captain Konstanz's fingers. However, there was a limit to the miracles that could be performed on a ship like this. I could be patched up, but not healed. We were due to arrive at our destination in a few hours, but a full recovery would take weeks, or maybe months, of rest. In addition, my elbows, wrists, hips, knees and ankles were still welded to the floor, and the only person I could really blame was myself.

I had been sloppy. I had let myself get shot by a nervous barman in a nowhere town, and then I had worsened the situation through my own stupidity. I had let the stress of my job almost destroy me. Laura had been right; I could see it now. After months of sweating my life away in a filthy jungle, I had cracked.

Mercifully, nobody had been seriously hurt.

Unfortunately, my attempt to commandeer the *Trouble Dog* had violated several important treaties. When word of it leaked back to the House, the least that could be expected would be a serious diplomatic incident. Through my actions, I had proven myself unfit for duty and become a source of embarrassment for my superiors. In all likelihood, the next twenty years of my life would be spent staring at the walls of a military jail cell. The only reason I hadn't already been summarily discharged from duty was that I was being held incommunicado, with no access to the ship's communications array. Reprimand and censure lay ahead, but I would have to wait to receive them, and somehow the waiting made it worse. I felt like a condemned man. I was a quantum particle caught between two states of being: no longer an agent of the Conglomeration, but not yet fired. A criminal detained but not yet convicted.

Lying there, looking up at the ceiling, I had a strong visceral memory of the time when, as a child, I had been caught fighting with another boy. I didn't even remember the other kid's name, but I knew he had to go and see the nurse while I was sent to the head teacher. For three long hours I sat in the corridor outside that woman's office, waiting for the punishment I knew must surely follow. There would be detention and a phone call to my parents, but somehow none of that was as terrible as the feeling of fearful anticipation, of sitting there alone and listening to the clock ticking, with nothing to do but think about the inevitable recriminations to come. It was like waiting for a bomb to go off. I found myself becoming impatient to face the consequences of my actions, just so I could get them over with.

From my current perspective, my juvenile years seemed impossibly distant, almost as if they had befallen another. And yet somehow, that particular memory—of wincing in horrible, powerless anticipation—had managed to retain its sting, whereas all the happy days of my childhood had been leached from me by the jungle's tyrannical heat. All the optimism and resilience of my youth had drained from my pores, leaving my hair wet and my skin feverish. I couldn't even picture the faces of my parents. They were like strangers from a half-forgotten dream; the partially submerged flotsam of a half-lived life.

I was feeling sorry for myself, and it disgusted me. I'd always loathed self-pity in others, and seen it as a weakness of character. Yet here I was, stewing in it. I realised I had given no thought to escape, or to completing my mission through alternate means. But how could I? The only way to escape would be to renounce my Conglomeration citizenship and disappear among the stars—but to do so would also be to renounce the career that had shaped and defined my adult life, the society I had sworn to protect, and a huge part of my identity.

I surprised myself with a cynical chuckle.

Some career.

I had been recruited as a rookie cop with potential, but twice failed to make the grade as a field operative. Because I was their informant, they let me spearhead the operation to root out corruption on my old precinct. But it was only after I'd managed to piss off my supervisors that I was given my first proper assignment. I was sent to Cichol not as a true field agent, but more as a kind of glorified warehouse manager, taking in shipments of arms and ammunition, and then arranging for them to be delivered by plane to the rebels in the hills. I might as well have been distributing tins of beans for all the difference it made. I carried myself like a full agent of Conglomeration Intelligence, but the truth was I spent more time grappling with inventory spreadsheets and flight schedules than doing anything that might be considered spy work. I had been trained in hand-to-hand combat, field medicine and the use of small arms, but everything else was bullshit. I saw that now. I had the objective clarity of a condemned man. I had never been cut out for fieldwork, and the strain of faking it almost broke me.

I cringed at the memory of my hand squeezing Konstanz's face, and the shameful feeling of power it had given me. I had let macho posturing take over, when, deep down, I was still that kid sitting outside the head teacher's office, struggling to come to terms with the way fear and anger made him lash out at those around him.

If I ran now, I would be running from myself. I would have to leave everything I'd worked to be, every ambition I'd ever nursed. Everything that made me who I was in the eyes of the universe, everything that described me as an adult, would have to be jettisoned. And I had no idea how or if it could be replaced.

That was, until Captain Konstanz came to see me.

•

The captain's hair was damp from the shower. She was wearing a fresh green jumpsuit at least two sizes too large. The suit's zip was open to her stomach, revealing a faded but clean-looking t-shirt, and she had squashed a frayed baseball cap onto her head.

"Okay," she said, crouching beside me. "We need to talk."

I blinked up at her from the abyssal depths of my despair. "You've got me welded to the floor. I'm not going anywhere. What's left to discuss?"

Absently, she reached out and gave the carbon-fibre struts supporting my forearm an experimental prod.

"I've been talking to your friend, Laura."

"And?"

"And she told me the Conglomeration has a weapon that can remotely hack a ship's brain."

"Oh."

"Is it true?"

If I hadn't been held in place, I would have shrugged. "I don't know."

"Are you sure about that?" She sat back on her heels. "Only, two ships appear to have turned themselves off within a few days of each other. One was an Outward scout ship, and the other this liner we're here to find."

"You think the Conglomeration shot down an Outward liner?" I couldn't keep the incredulity from my voice. "To what end? What could we possibly gain from such an action?"

"Maybe you're looking to start another war? It doesn't matter. The point is that if that weapon exists, I'll need to know everything you can tell me about it."

I blinked up at her. I might be disgraced, but did I really want to compound my transgressions by discussing the Conglomeration's secrets with a foreign national?

Stalling for time, I asked, "Even if I knew, why would I tell you?"

Captain Konstanz huffed, as if frustrated by a wrong answer. "Because, genius, you're literally stuck on this ship." She pushed the shoulder of the exoskeleton with her fingers, demonstrating my immobility. "And we're flying into this situation blind. If some unexpected super weapon attacks us and we go down, you're going to be going down with us. And the only way to avoid that is for you to give me the information I need to keep *all* our butts intact."

I looked around at the metal walls, and was forced to concede the logic of her argument. "Fair point."

"So." She leant forward. "Have you got anything for me?"

The logo on her hat caught the light. It was the stylised golden star of the House of Reclamation—the organisation to which this woman, her crew and her ship had dedicated themselves in the wake of the war. An organisation that had offered them a clean slate and an expunged record in return for their service. An organisation that didn't much care who you had been or what you had done, as long as you were prepared to dedicate yourself to its ideals of selflessness and benevolence.

And just like that, I *knew*.

The realisation hit me with the force of a divine revelation. All my doubts and fears fell away in the reflected gleam from that cap badge, and I had to stifle a laugh. Of *course* there was a way out of my predicament, and a way I could atone for my mistakes. Of course there was a place where I would be taken in and welcomed, no matter the idiotic things I had done; a place where they could offer me the duties and sense of purpose I'd need to fill the hole left by the loss of my position in Conglomeration Intelligence. The answer had been sitting there in plain sight, and I hadn't seen it until now. It had taken the glint of the logo on this woman's hat to make me realise where my future lay, and what I would have to betray in order to get there.

In order to prove myself worthy of this new life, I would have to let go of the obligations and burdens of the past. Let it all go: the jungle, the ruins of my career, everything I had been since becoming a field agent.

Every secret I had sworn to protect.

Every ambition I had ever held.

I cleared my throat.

"I've heard things," I said, trying to play it cool, knowing everything depended on the outcome of this conversation.

"What kind of things?"

"I'll tell you all I know," I promised, and felt the encumbrance of the past few years begin to rise like steam from my soul. "But there's one condition."

Captain Konstanz raised a dubious eyebrow. "You know, you're not in a great bargaining position." She stood up and stuffed her fists into the pockets of her baggy jumpsuit. "What is it you want?"

I cleared my throat and looked her in the eye. "I want to join the House of Reclamation."

THIRTY-NINE

ONA SUDAK

I managed to get to my knees, but found I lacked the strength to stand. I had nothing left. For two days we'd been running, spurred on by the thought of nameless, faceless pursuers. But now Adam was dead. If the transparent door hadn't been between us when the guns fired, I would have felt his warm blood spatter my face, and would have died with him. Even now, his bloody handprint—and the long smear of his final collapse—remained on the door of the moving room that had me trapped.

I let my chin drop to my chest. My arms went slack and my hands curled against the floor like wounded creatures. The room was so silent I could hear the air wheezing in and out of my lungs, the rustle of my clothes when I moved, and the pulse of the blood in my ears. Without visual cues, there wasn't any sensation of movement, or any sound or vibration to indicate how the little room was powered. And anyhow, I didn't have the mental energy to ponder such matters. I felt pummelled and wrung-out, like laundry that had been immersed in a river and then beaten against a rock. When my knees began to hurt, I lay on my side and exhaled until my lungs were empty. My bones weighed me down like bars of solid iron, and I found myself falling into the swamp-like embrace of an unthinking oblivion…

When I finally re-opened my eyes, several hours had passed and I felt calmer and more lucid. Old habits kicked in, and I found myself surveying the terrain and cataloguing my supplies. So far, I had been reacting to events and moving on instinct; now, I needed to start thinking strategically. Grief could wait.

The bright throat of the corridor had shrunk to the size of a star in the night sky, a tiny pinpoint of light far in my wake. As my eyes began to adjust to the darkness outside my box, I began to perceive other points of light, and from their relative positions, discern something of the shape of the void around me. As far as I could tell, I was suspended within a vast, dark cavern. Thousands of stars lay in an immense concentric shell, each perhaps representing the mouth of a new and unexplored corridor. Did any of them lead back to the surface? Although I had temporarily evaded those who wished to kill me, I couldn't remain down here indefinitely. My survival suit would continue to recycle my sweat and urine into potable water for some time before it needed to be replenished, but the emergency rations it dispensed were far more limited, and I had already consumed about two-thirds of its stock of tablets. From my days in the military, I knew that as long as I had access to the water in my suit, I could survive without food for at least a fortnight—but it wouldn't be a pleasant experience.

As the room was travelling backwards, I couldn't see where we were heading, but I had to assume I was being taken to a specific destination. As soon as we arrived, my first priority would be to scout out a safe route back up to the surface. Then I could find somewhere to hole up until my supplies grew low, by which time I hoped those bastards in the armour might have given up and fucked off back to whatever hellhole had spawned them. Then I could work my way back to the wreck of the 'dam and find a transmitter. With luck, help might arrive before I died of hunger.

I let the sudden anger subside. I leant my cheek against the cool glass of the transparent door and looked down at the twinkling pattern of other doorways far below, arrayed in grids across the curving base of the spherical void.

Where *had* those soldiers come from? Until now, I had been too shaken and upset to consider the question. The armour they had been wearing had been scuffed and ill matched, as if various parts had been replaced over time and scavenged from a variety of sources. None of it had been standard issue, and that suggested the men wearing it hadn't been regular troops, leaving pirates or mercenaries as the most likely explanation.

Pirates would never have had the balls or the firepower to take down anything as large and well defended as the *Geest van Amsterdam*. And even if they'd somehow managed it, they wouldn't have hung around to pick off a couple of wayward survivors. They would have plundered the wreck and been long gone, running for all they were worth. So, these guys must be mercenaries. But who had hired them, and to what end? Certainly, the fact they had stuck around so long, and followed us into these depths, suggested they were determined to wipe out all survivors from the crash.

Even if I assumed they were trying to kill me in particular, that didn't narrow the list of suspects, as there were countless groups and individuals from all sides of the Archipelago conflict who would be more than happy to see the sentient forests of Pelapatarn avenged, and Annelida Deal's head impaled on a pike. In my absence, I had even been condemned by my own government—by those I had been serving and protecting when I took the decision to end the war.

I straightened up and considered the three blank walls of my enclosure. Until I knew where I was being taken, and why, my plans would have to remain necessarily vague. But that imprecision also lent them an attractive simplicity. I needed to improvise some sort of weapon, and then outwait my opponents. A liner had been destroyed in a disputed star system; somebody would send a ship to investigate. All I had to do was be on the surface when it arrived.

I hurried through some quick mental calculations. The nearest port of any appreciable size was Camrose. At full speed, it would take a ship at least four days to get here, which meant I had to stay hidden for at least another forty-eight hours, maybe longer.

Would my pursuers find a way to follow me across this huge darkened sphere? Maybe they were trailing me even now, in a similar flying room? I turned to look back, to see if I could perceive any hint of another craft in my wake, only to find that the room I was in was turning. Slowly and gracefully, it revolved until the glass door faced forwards, in the direction of travel, and I finally caught sight of what I was heading into.

Ahead, a circular opening revealed an even larger chamber beyond—a chamber so mind-numbingly gigantic that it should not have been able to fit within the confines of this planet. I couldn't even begin to guess at its dimensions.

Something that looked like a tiny white sun burned at the centre of this colossal vault. I couldn't look directly at it, so it was hard to guess its exact size. Nevertheless, I guessed it was far too small for its gravity to spark a fusion reaction, and therefore far too small to be a natural object. No race in the Multiplicity could have constructed such a thing; it was beyond all known technology, and probably beyond our understanding of the way stars behaved and worked. But it wasn't that shining bauble that filled me with a dread so profound I felt the blood turn to sand in my veins. The thing that struck terror into my very soul was the cloud of objects that surrounded that impossible miniature sun in uncountable ranks, their dagger-like hulls throwing long shadows onto the walls of the chamber. For in the space between the star and the surrounding walls had been arranged thousands upon thousands of gleaming white starships, each with a hull like polished marble and a prow as sharp as a knife.

•

I remained in the cramped, flying room for a day and a night. Exhausted from the pursuit through the canyon maze, I spent much of the time asleep, curled uncomfortably on the hard white floor. When I awoke, I watched the approach of the little sun and its attendant ranks of lustrous vessels; when I slept again, I dreamt of Adam standing among the blackened, smoking stumps of a firebombed jungle.

Time passed slowly.

I began to catch myself humming tunes and talking to myself. I had never been very good at being alone, and the utter silence of the lift's passage—I had begun to think of it as a kind of flying elevator—was so relentlessly oppressive to me that the sound of a voice, even my own, could bestow comfort and the illusion of company.

At first, I recited snatches of my own poems, but their subject matter proved to be so relentlessly grief-stricken that I started muttering the lyrics from popular songs instead. They might have been artistically inane, but they were catchier and more uplifting than anything that had fallen from my pen.

Towards the end of the second day, I began to worry. My food was gone and we did not appear to be appreciably closer to the distant sun. If my destination lay with the white ships, I didn't think I'd last long enough to reach it. The distances involved were huge, and the lift simply wasn't moving quickly enough.

What a cruel irony it would be, I thought, to have been

spared a quick death only to expire slowly of hunger and thirst, trapped in a cage the size of a large wardrobe.

In my head, the part of me that was Ona Sudak quailed at the thought. She wanted to pound her fists against the glass door and weep for release. Captain Annelida Deal, on the other hand, decided to bide her time. At some point, this stupid contraption would arrive at its destination. If I happened to still be alive when it did, I would need all my training, cunning and strength to survive. So, right now, the best and most sensible thing I could possibly do was to rest and conserve my energy. I was a soldier and, by god, I was determined to face the unknown with pragmatism and military discipline. If my fate was to become a desiccated bag of skin and bone on the floor of this floating prison, I would accept it with dignity. I would be patient, and hope for the best possible outcome, while simultaneously preparing myself for the worst.

FORTY

TROUBLE DOG

As we neared the outskirts of the Gallery system, I received a second transmission from *Adalwolf*. This time, he had given his hollow-cheeked avatar the aspect of an emaciated warrior god, clad in mirror-bright armour with a mane of fiery hair billowing out behind him, the flames seemingly streaming like windblown tears from the corners of his eyes.

"Sister," he said, "I cannot help but notice your failure to heed my advice."

I bridled at the portentousness of his tone. "You're very observant." I decided to keep my avatar on its default setting. Its face had been based on the countenance of the woman whose harvested cells had provided the seed for the biological segments of my processing substrate, but had been subtly altered by my designers to render it ethnically and sexually neutral—a symbolic representation of humanity in all its infinite diversity. "But, as you so kindly reminded me the last time we spoke, I am no longer part of the pack, and therefore no longer obliged to follow your recommendations." The sweetness of my tone only emphasised the bitter taste of my words. I thrust my chin forward in a defiant gesture I had picked up from Alva Clay. "I am here as a representative of the House of Reclamation, and I have a job to do."

"You will not listen to reason?"

"What reason?" I laughed. "You have yet to give me one."

Adalwolf scowled. "The transmission you received."

"The anonymous warning?" I let my smile grow wider. If he wanted to keep up the pretence that he knew nothing of its origins, I would see how far I could goad him. "What made you think that would discourage me?"

"I believe it was for your own good."

I cocked my head to one side. "And how would you know that?" I asked, my face the picture of girlish innocence.

The light from his flaming hair flickered on the polished metal of his armoured shoulders.

"Why else would it have been sent to you alone?"

"Because *Fenrir* sent it."

His eyes narrowed. He had been waiting for me to reveal my suspicions, and now I had. "She does not want to fight you."

"Why would she fight me?"

"Because you are about to blunder into the middle of a covert operation. And if you do, Captain Parris will order her to attack you."

I feigned indignation. "I'm here to recover the passengers and crew of the *Geest van Amsterdam*."

"Neither Parris nor *Fenrir* will allow it."

"Why not?" I was trying to provoke him, and we both knew it; but I wanted to hear him say the words.

He sighed. "Because *Fenrir's* the one that shot it down."

I had assumed as much, and had already informed Captain Konstanz of my suspicions, but hearing them confirmed brought no satisfaction, only a kind of sick, nervous feeling.

"Why?"

"That's classified."

"And the *Hobo*? She shot that down too, didn't she? Or is that information also classified?"

"The scout ship was collateral damage." *Adalwolf* looked

down his long, bony nose. "It was the *Hobo*'s misfortune to have performed a deep scan of the Objects in the Gallery. It could not be allowed to report its findings."

"So she killed it, just like that?"

"Let's just say she convinced it to kill itself."

"In order to keep the secret?"

"Just so."

I held up an index finger. "But now you've told me."

"I have."

No more pretending now, no more fake innocence. This was the moment I had been dreading. I kept my tone as dispassionate as possible as I asked, "Does this mean you're going to kill me too?"

He didn't even blink. "I am afraid so," he said.

"Two against one?"

The smile he gave was as insincere as it was tight. "We will try to be as… merciful as we can."

"And my crew?"

"Collateral damage."

I frowned. I could feel the caress of the higher dimensional vacuum on my outer hull, the steady power of my drives, and, deep in the engineering sections of the ship, I could feel the machinery churning out the torpedoes and ammunition needed to replace those I had renounced upon joining the House. However, I wouldn't be able to manufacture the antimatter warheads that had once been my primary weapon. My fangs had been drawn, but I would not be entirely toothless. I would have my secondary systems, which alone would be more than a match for almost any other class of ship. When we met, I wouldn't have to face my brother and sister as an unarmed ambulance. I would be a warship again, armed with orthodox nuclear torpedoes. My teeth would be sharp, my senses keen.

"Okay," I said. It wasn't an agreement, simply an

acknowledgement of information received. I knew I wouldn't last long without my primary weapons, but I knew Captain Konstanz had sent a message back to Camrose Station, requesting reinforcements, and felt confident I could survive long enough to at least score a few good hits against my former pack-mates—hopefully ensuring the next rescue ship to arrive would be able to do so without fear of attack.

FORTY-ONE

SAL KONSTANZ

"So, what do you think?"

"I think he's full of shit." Alva Clay shook her head. "Right now, he'd say anything to save his sorry ass."

We were in the ship's circular corridor, a short walk from the galley. I glanced at Laura Petrushka. "And you?"

She looked up from her chair. "I think he means it."

I took off my cap and ran my fingers around the rim. The clean clothes and shower had been an excellent idea, and had done me the world of good. I almost felt human again. "How long have you known him?"

"A couple of years."

"Do you trust him?"

She hesitated. "Up until this morning, I would have said no."

"And now?"

She smiled. "Now, he's no longer working for the opposition."

"So he says."

"I think he's telling the truth. If he goes back now, they'll throw him in a hole so deep he'll never see the sky again."

Alva let out a snort. "If he even makes it back."

"And what's that supposed to mean?" Laura said, frowning at her.

Alva stuck out her chin. "Dude tried to take our ship, and that's mutiny. We'd be well within our rights to frag him and toss him out the airlock."

I worked my bruised shoulder, trying to ease the tautness from it. Childe had made a mistake and, if he meant what he said about joining the House, was genuinely trying to compensate for his actions. I could sympathise with that. Since losing George, all I'd done was try to atone for that one moment of inattention that had cost the man his life.

"Nobody's getting spaced."

"But, Captain—"

"No!" There had been enough death on this ship. "We need all the help we can get right now. If Childe's sincere, he'll be more use to us alive than dead."

Alva scowled, but I could see she knew I was right. Our medic was young and inexperienced, and we were flying into a potentially dangerous situation, facing unknown odds and weaponry we could barely understand, let alone defend against. If we were to complete our mission and escape with our lives, we would need as many proficient crewmembers as possible—and Childe's insights might well prove as valuable as his medical skills.

"You can't use him," Laura said. "He needs rest. If you keep him on his feet, he's going to die."

I shrugged. "That's his problem." I narrowed my eyes at Alva. "But maybe you can help him," I suggested.

She blinked in surprise. "Do what?"

"You've both had jungle postings. You know what it's like. There's common ground there."

She laughed. "Common *ground*?" She held her palms up, as if waving away gibberish. "This fucker spends a couple of years drinking lichen-flavoured ethanol in a compound somewhere and you think we have common *ground*?" She turned to Laura Petrushka. "You were on Cichol, weren't you? What do you think? How does hanging around an airport compare to six months crawling through a sentient jungle, with enemies skulking in every shadow and trees that murmur to you the whole goddamn time, even in your sleep? Can you tell me that, lady? Can you actually make that comparison?"

Laura shrank back a little in her wheelchair, but her expression stayed stony. "You don't know what it was like for him."

"I can fucking guess."

"Then you should be more sympathetic." The older woman sat up straight, gripping the arms of her chair. "This isn't a competition, or a game of 'I'm-more-traumatised-than-you'. That poor sod suffered every moment he was in that stupid jungle, just as you suffered in yours. And if your experience led you to seek refuge here, then you of all people should understand his reasons for wanting to do the same!"

The conversation broke up. Alva Clay stormed off to the armoury, to oil and polish the weapons racked on the walls. It was how she dealt with stress. Laura Petrushka wheeled herself away in the opposite direction, to contemplate the churns of the hypervoid from the *Trouble Dog*'s observation deck.

And I returned to the galley.

"All right," I said to the man welded to the deck, "suppose I gave you a chance. What could you offer me in return?"

Ashton Childe looked up from the floor, his expression that of a man hardly daring to hope. "What would you want?"

"Complete specs on this hypothetical weapon?"

"I don't have them."

"Then how about you level with me about the real aim of your assignment?" I put my hands in my pockets. "Because if you were willing to try 'jacking a Carnivore, I reckon it had to be an objective of some pressing importance."

Childe laughed. "I was looking for a poet."

This was not a response I had anticipated. "Seriously?"

"I'm afraid so."

For a moment, I considered walking out of the room. But curiosity got the better of me. "Why?"

"I don't know." He wrinkled his nose. "Because I was ordered to."

"And last night?"

"A mistake." He cast around for inspiration. "A terrible misunderstanding. It won't happen again."

I flexed my troublesome shoulder.

"You threw me across the room," I said with as much quiet dignity as I could muster, given the circumstances. "Now, I don't care how fucked up you are, I'm going to need a cast-iron guarantee that will never happen again. Otherwise, I'm going to ask my friend Alva to put a shell from her Archipelago pistol right through the back of your skull." I drew back. "Do we understand each other, Mr Childe?"

He smiled up at me. "Of course."

"You're not going to do anything stupid?"

"I've learned my lesson." He looked solemn. "Besides, you're my last hope. If I can't find a place in the House, I'm pretty much screwed six ways to Sunday. I'm not going to do anything to jeopardise that."

"You're sure, now?"

"Yes, Captain."

•

I called Nod to release the welds, and the Druff came grumbling up from its lair in the engine room, its hand-faces padding on the metal deck, its six limbs flailing in unpredictable waves, like the thrashings of a drunk octopus trying to climb a flight of stairs. It smelled like peppermints and seaweed. In one mouth, it clasped a welding torch.

"Where, want?" it asked with one of his feet.

I circled a finger at Childe's recumbent figure. "I think we can release him now."

Nod quivered. It raised some of its hand-faces to the air, lowered others to the deck. "Think or know?"

I sighed. "Matters, how?"

A trio of coal-black eyes peered up at me from the raised face. "Maybe lots, maybe less." Leaving four limbs firmly planted on the deck, it curved the fifth around to ignite the torch. The blue flame hissed like the sound of distant surf.

"Just cut him loose." It was a risk, but according to the *Trouble Dog*, we might all be dead soon anyway. And if not, I was going to need every able body I could muster in order to help rescue the survivors from the crashed liner.

"Yes, Boss-captain."

The flame narrowed, paling into virtual invisibility, and the creature moved itself closer to the prone figure of Childe. Soldered joints softened. The scent of hot metal rose, and suddenly the man was free. I watched him stretch his arms and roll his neck, trying to work the circulation back into his crucified limbs. The exoskeleton amplified every movement, and for an instant I wondered if I had made a mistake. I'd already felt the power of that suit, and the ease with which it had allowed him to hurl me aside.

"You're serious about joining the House?" I managed to keep my voice steady and businesslike.

"Yes."

"Then I want you in the infirmary." My tone told him I wasn't afraid. "I want you helping Preston. The kid doesn't know much, but he's eager to learn." I rubbed the tip of my nose. "At least, I hope he is. Otherwise, I'm going to have to throw his indolent butt off this ship, and hire myself somebody new."

"Yes, Captain." Childe touched two fingers to his brow in a casual salute, and walked stiffly from the room, moving like a man trying to remember how to use his legs.

When he had gone, I sagged against the nearest table. My hands were shaking and my heart rattled like a motor trying to tear loose from its mounting. Nod was packing away the cutting torch and muttering about the smell from the dishwasher. It didn't often venture into the human-occupied sections of the ship, and I got the impression it would much rather be down in the dirty, grease-smelling bowels of the engine room than up here, breathing the scents of our bodies and food.

The *Trouble Dog*'s avatar was watching me from the wall screen. Her computer-generated features had the impassivity of a doll.

"Do you trust him?"

She was talking about Childe. I surprised myself with a bark of laughter.

"No."

"Alva wants to eject him."

I perched on the corner of the table, one booted foot on the deck, the other dangling. "I know."

"He will be passing the main airlock in forty-seven seconds. If you want me to, I can override the safety mechanisms and vent that entire section of corridor."

I rubbed my face, and was ashamed to find myself momentarily entertaining the suggestion.

"No, we're too short-handed. We need him." I let my shoulders slump. The sound I made came somewhere between an exhalation of tension and a sigh of regret. "Just keep an eye on him for me and make sure he doesn't get up to mischief."

"And if he does?"

"Keep a combat drone close to him. Don't let him see it, but have it there just in case. If he does anything to imperil you or any member of the crew, you can do what you like."

"Yes, Captain."

"How are things going with your siblings?"

"Badly. I'm afraid we're going to have to fight them."

"Can we wait for reinforcements?"

"They're killing the survivors of the liner crash. If we wait, there won't be anyone left to rescue."

.

I found Alva in the armoury. She was in the middle of stripping down an antique Managlese plasma rifle, and the various parts of the weapon were arrayed before her on the tool bench. The room smelled of gun oil and metal. When the *Trouble Dog* had been on active service, it would have held enough weaponry for the ship's complement of 150 marines. Now, most of the wall-mounted racks were empty, and all the guns here belonged to Clay. I had a couple of automatic pistols for emergency use, but kept them in a locker in my cabin. I walked over to the bench and looked at the half-disassembled plasma rifle.

"Nice gun." The Manag were a multi-limbed and warlike race from the coreward reaches of the Multiplicity. I'd never seen one of the creatures in the flesh, but knew aficionados prized the weapons they made for their rugged durability.

"Thanks."

"Are we okay?"

She didn't look up. "Depends what you mean by okay."

I watched her work a small brush into the rifle's barrel. She pushed it in and out a few times, then withdrew it and blew down the pipe.

"I don't know," I said. "Just okay, I guess."

"You're still the captain."

"Was there some possibility I might not be?"

Carefully, Alva laid her tools on the bench. "I promised myself when I signed on that if you were a complete asshole

243

I'd frag you and take command of the ship."

She said it so matter-of-factly that the breath caught in my throat. "And yet you haven't?"

"No."

"Can I ask why not?"

Wrists still resting against the edge of the bench, she flexed her fingers. The tattoos on her arms rippled. "You're not a total asshole."

"Thank you."

"It's not a compliment." There was an edge to her voice as hard and inflexible as any of the guns displayed in this mostly empty room. I stepped back from the bench.

"From you, it sounds like one."

"Well, it's not."

We stood in silence, neither wanting to be the first to speak. Finally, I cleared my throat and asked, "So, are we okay? Can we work together?"

Alva looked down at the dismembered rifle. "You mean, am I going to frag you and throw you out the airlock?" She finally looked me in the eye. "No. You've been trying hard since George died. You got us out of Northfield in one piece, and that took some balls. I never thought you'd let the ship cut loose on a civilian population like that."

"You don't think it was the wrong decision?"

She shook her head. "Hell, no. Those cretins were shooting at us. They deserved everything they got."

"Live by the sword…"

"…die by the high-impact, armour-piercing round." A smile disturbed her lips like a breeze ruffling palm leaves, there one instant and gone the next. "You get everything you deserve," she said, "if you're idiot enough to shoot at a Carnivore."

My stomach felt suddenly hollow. I stuck my hands in the pockets of my jumpsuit. "You do know that's exactly what *we're* about to do, don't you?"

Clay nodded. "The difference is, we're ex-soldiers, and we're *in* a Carnivore."

•

I walked back around the circular corridor, taking the long route and savouring the empty cabins and darkened workstations. As I walked, I trailed my fingertips along the wall. The knowledge that we were heading into a fight lent everything a heightened poignancy, and I found myself wondering if any of these silent bunks would ever hold another sleeper, or these vacant offices and meeting rooms another conversation. In the light of the coming conflict, it seemed simultaneously impossible and yet frighteningly plausible that, in a few hours, this little town might be destroyed, these solid walls and floors torn asunder, this cool, endlessly recycled air scattered to the careless vacuum. At this moment, my feet might very well be the last to ever walk these sections of corridor, my eyes the last to appreciate their stark, functional beauty.

If we survived the next few hours, I made a vow to spend more time prowling the ship. Maybe I'd even decorate, adding a few human touches to the sterility. This ship was my home, and I was only really starting to understand the fact now, as we stood together on the lip of a yawning precipice.

Of course, I had known other homes. For an instant, my thoughts turned to Sedge, and the three months we'd spent in that villa on Naxos. Those perfumed nights. Before *Trouble Dog*, that villa had been the closest I'd had to an adult home. Since my parents died, I'd never really belonged anywhere. My life had been lived out of a suitcase. I spent time in dorms at the Academy, and then on a variety of ships, but I was always passing through. I never put down roots, not until I got here. For the past three years, the *Trouble Dog* and her crew had been the one constant in my life. They gave me the solitude I craved, and company only when I really needed it. The ship's cabins and bridge had become as familiar to me as the rooms of the house I lived in as a child, and I couldn't bear the notion they might soon be destroyed.

I stopped walking, tempted to tell the *Trouble Dog* to stop, to throw all engines in reverse and flee for Camrose. But, even as the thought formed, I knew I could never give such an order. We could not come all this way only to turn tail and flee. There might be crash survivors depending on us. The least we could do would be to scan the wreck for signs of life, even if we had to fight off a barrage while doing it. By attacking us, the *Trouble Dog*'s former comrades would implicate themselves in the downing of the *Geest van Amsterdam*, and thereby implicate the Conglomeration as a whole in an act of aggression against a civilian Outward vessel. Such behaviour couldn't go unpunished.

And I couldn't get away from the thought that there had been hundreds of people on that liner. Hundreds of potential casualties. I felt my fists clench, my resolve harden. The passengers and crew of the *Geest van Amsterdam* had not been military personnel. They were civilian men, women and children, and if they had been unlawfully killed, they deserved to have their killers brought to justice. And if any of them were still alive—still somehow clinging on a week after the attack—I knew in my heart that we had no choice but to do everything in our power to locate and rescue them, even if we died in the attempt.

PART TWO
THE MARBLE ARMADA

They prepare for death, yet are they not the finish,
but rather the outset,
They bring none to his or her terminus
or to be content and full,
Whom they take they take into space
to behold the birth of stars,
to learn one of the meanings,
To launch off with absolute faith,
to sweep through the ceaseless rings
and never be quiet again.

WALT WHITMAN, "Song of the Answerer"

FORTY-TWO

ONA SUDAK

After three days of flight, my jail cell dipped towards the inner surface of what appeared to be an abandoned city. A ten-kilometre-tall ziggurat stood at the centre. Against any other backdrop, it would have appeared huge. Here, it barely registered as a blip on the darkened landscape. Fashioned from the same material as the rest of the structure, it appeared to be a node of some kind. A starburst of tubes and conduits radiated from its base in all directions, forming the web-like skeleton of the surrounding city. Points of light speckled the ziggurat's slab-like sides and, as we drew closer, I saw these lights to be doorways identical to the one from which I had embarked. What first appeared to my tired eyes to be flickers on my vision resolved into a midge-like cloud of flying rooms, each following its own trajectory, and all of them coming and going from the doorways in the ziggurat like buses coming and going from a central bus terminal. Their activity gave the building the appearance of a beehive and I began to feel truly apprehensive. Until now, I had been more concerned about the humans following me, and had assumed the internal structure of the Brain to be as stark and derelict as its surface. But if the flying boxes I was seeing turned out to be more than simply forsaken relics acting out automatic routines, if they were *in use*, then maybe I was about to meet the inhabitants of this strange and barely comprehensible artefact.

The thought chilled my blood.

Fists squeezed into tight balls, I watched as my floating prison approached the towering side of the stepped pyramid.

How had all this gone unnoticed? Numerous alien races had scanned the Objects in the Gallery. None had reported so much as an opening on the surface, let alone this subterranean netherworld. Could it be this entire bubble existed outside normal space and time? It was certainly too gigantic to have been accommodated within the confines of the Brain, which was itself no larger than a moderately sized planet. Perhaps I had unwittingly passed through some sort of dimensional portal, into a kind of higher space—maybe even into the hypervoid itself? That would certainly go a long way towards explaining how the existence of a tiny star within a planet had gone unnoticed for so many hundreds of years.

And yet, that being the case, how had I found my way in here so easily?

The opening Adam and I had accessed would have been invisible from above, but that didn't explain how nobody else had ever stumbled across it. In the past, expeditions had traversed the major canyons. Could it simply have been blind luck no one had explored that particular stretch of the maze? Or—and my skin prickled with the thought— perhaps some of them *had* found it. Perhaps they'd even ventured inside and found their way this far into the interior, only to have been destroyed by whatever awaited them in that huge, dark building.

Christ, I wished I had a gun. Even a sidearm would have done, as long as I had something to grip and draw reassurance from. Yet, no matter how hard I desired one, no weapon appeared. All I had were my hands and feet, and the skills I'd learned in the military. But what use would hand-to-hand combat be against a race capable of building all *this*? What hope would my chimpanzee fingers have against creatures with the ability to fashion *suns*?

As I drew inexorably closer to the ziggurat, I was able to discern the particular doorway at which the room aimed, and then watch it grow nearer. As far as I could see (and to my great relief), there didn't appear to be anybody—or anything—waiting for me in the corridor beyond. However, dwarfed and humbled as I felt by the massive pyramid and the titanic cavern that formed its sky, this temporary reprieve proved to be of little reassurance.

With no appearance of haste, my flying prison slid to an apparently effortless halt. The glass screen gently kissed an identical barrier covering the opening to the corridor. The light overhead changed from white to blue, and the transparent door and its counterpart swished aside, disappearing into the wall. The dried, crumbly smear of Adam's blood went with them. I braced myself for a change in air pressure, but none came. I was still encased in my personal bubble, and it remained as resolutely fresh as it had since I first wriggled from the wreckage of the '*dam*.

The corridor ahead appeared identical to the one I had encountered three days before. It glowed with the same pearly light from its opalescent walls. Tentatively, hands gripping the edges of the doorway, I stepped from the room that had been my jail. I moved slowly, like a nervous butterfly pulling itself from the husk of its chrysalis. My legs were stiff, but the enforced inactivity had given them time to recover from their exertions.

Adam's death needled me like an uncomfortable splinter lodged in the back of my mind, but I knew I could process the grief later. Right now, my priority had to be to find a way back to the surface.

As a cadet, I'd participated in a number of wilderness survival exercises. I knew how to live off the land, and how to find food in some of the most inhospitable and godforsaken climes. But those exercises had taken place outdoors, where plants, lichen and other sources of nutrition were readily available to those who knew how to look for them. Here, the sterile white walls and floor offered little in the way of hope. I hadn't eaten in twenty-four hours and, unless I found a way out and contrived to be rescued within the next couple of days, I would start to lose the energy and willpower to carry on.

As an experiment, I tried stepping in and out of the little room I had just left, half hoping the door would snap closed and return me to my starting point. However, after three tries, the blue light remained resolutely lit and the doors remained open, leaving me no choice but to follow the corridor and search for another exit.

I took a couple of deep, steadying breaths, and then edged away from the door, one foot at a time, all the while keeping my right fist pulled back and ready to fly at the first sign of an attack.

FORTY-THREE

SAL KONSTANZ

Acting on my orders, the *Trouble Dog* shut off its engines as it crossed the Gallery's heliopause—that tenuous border region on the ragged edge of the solar system, where the outward pressure of the solar wind had attenuated to the point it could no longer hold back the winds from the surrounding stars, and interstellar space began. Still travelling at great speed but now unpowered, the ship began to drift down through the higher dimensions until it fell from the hypervoid altogether, and remerged into the universe.

Falling into the system on a ballistic trajectory, the *Trouble Dog* kept only its most vital systems online, and only the most passive of its sensors in operation. Eighteen billion kilometres ahead of us, the Gallery's sun resembled little more than a reasonably bright star against a backdrop of other stars, and the Objects themselves were specks rendered all but invisible by distance.

I lay on my command couch with the visor of my spacesuit thrown back, my face lit only by the light of the bridge's display screens. I had ordered the crew to don pressure suits in case of a hull breach. It was standard procedure, but almost certainly a useless gesture. Anything powerful enough to crack the hull of a Carnivore would most likely liquefy anything within. In that scenario, the only crewmembers with any hope of survival would be those secured inside the doubly armoured bridge at the centre of the ship. And at that particular moment, that meant Laura Petrushka and me. She sat across the room from me, hunched over the tactical weapon displays with her wounded leg braced beneath the console—not because the ship needed her (it was perfectly capable of conducting a battle by itself), but because I did. When the engagement came, things would be happening too quickly for me to keep pace. Carnivores thought faster than we did, and were capable of making multiple decisions simultaneously, engaging targets on a number of fronts. The reason I needed Laura in place was to help me stay abreast of our status. She was a trained tactical analyst and, without a direct neural link to the ship's sensorium, I wouldn't be able to follow everything that happened. I needed an experienced tactician to help me keep track of our progress.

At least, that's what I'd told her.

In reality, the *Trouble Dog*'s avatar would be more than capable of interpreting the battle for me. That was, after all, its primary function. I'd told Laura I wanted her as a backup and a second pair of eyes, when the truth was, I simply wanted her company. I needed somebody else in there with me for reassurance. I had rarely been as nervous as I was now, and it helped to have another human being in close proximity—especially an older woman. In the meantime, I told myself with a kind of grim pragmatism, the real reason she was here was that if I had to die, I really didn't want to have to die alone.

"Nothing in range," she said, scanning her instruments.

The *Trouble Dog*'s face gazed from a window set into the main forward view. It looked amused. "As she says, I can detect no sign of the *Fenrir* from this distance." The avatar looked concerned. "At least, not without deploying active sensors. However, I can confirm that none of the Objects has acquired an anomalous moon, and there is no sign of the *Geest van Amsterdam* in orbit around any of them. I have detected a metallic signature on the Object known as the Brain, which might represent debris from a crashed vessel. If the *Fenrir* is still somewhere hereabouts, she is either on the surface with that wreckage, or on the other side of the sun. Wherever she is, I fully anticipate her to be operating with extreme stealth, and therefore almost impossible to detect until she moves—or until we get a *lot* closer."

I gave a grunt of assent. So far, things were proceeding as we had anticipated. Drifting into the system without power, we would be very hard to detect, and difficult to distinguish from random space debris. If the *Fenrir* wanted to tell whether we were more than just rock, she'd either have to sidle up close enough to make a visual confirmation, or bounce a signal off our hull. Either way, she'd be revealing her position. Unfortunately, the converse was also true, and we couldn't detect her without announcing our arrival. We were like armed opponents circling each other in a darkened room, each afraid to turn on their flashlight for fear of giving the other a target.

"What are your orders?"

At the speed we were falling through space, it would take several months to get within striking range of the Objects. The only way to arrive within a timescale that gave us any hope of finding survivors was to jump across the intervening distance, but the acceleration needed would certainly alert any observers to our presence.

I took one final look at the distant sun, and shrugged. "We've come this far and had a look around. We didn't expect to see the Carnivore, and we haven't. But we have got a likely location for the liner, and that's something. Now, we need to get closer and start looking for survivors."

I reached for the intercom and opened a channel to the

main hangar, where Alva Clay, Preston Menderes and Ashton Childe were standing by in one of the ship's hardier ground-to-orbit shuttles. Alva answered the call.

"Everything looks clear so far," I told her. "And it looks as if the liner's on the Brain. We're going to advance cautiously and then jump in as close to the surface as we can."

"Understood, Captain." I could hear the tension in Alva's voice. While we held off the Carnivore, she was going to lead her improvised team on an expedition to locate and retrieve survivors on the ground. "We'll be ready to go on your word."

"Standby."

I killed the connection and took a moment to steady my breathing. Around me, I heard the familiar sounds of the bridge: the almost subliminal purr of the air conditioning; distant creaks and groans as different parts of the hull cooled and adjusted to the sudden lack of thrust; and the quiet chimes and bleeps as the ship's various systems reported routine changes in their respective statuses. It was a soundtrack I had fallen asleep to a hundred times. Now, though, there could be no question of sleep. My breath came in short, shallow gasps, my hands tingled, and my heart thumped so loudly in my ears I worried Laura might be able to hear it. My one and only command before this had been at the helm of a medical frigate, and my job then had been to arrive in the aftermath of a battle and pick through the debris, not order my ship into the heart of one. Still, in accepting command of the *Trouble Dog*, I had always known it might come to this—that one day I might be called upon to fire upon a pirate vessel or similar—and I knew I could do it, despite the weightless panicky feeling in my stomach and chest.

As a team, we had been able to deal with the challenges we'd so far faced, from the would-be hijackers at Northfield to Ashton Childe's "episode" in the galley. But neither of those parties had been actively trying to destroy the ship, and neither had possessed the firepower to do so. I may have been personally threatened. I may have been shot and strangled, but somehow that didn't seem to matter as much to me as the idea of losing the ship.

My home.

This time, everything would be on the line. With one Carnivore loose in the system, and according to the *Trouble Dog*, another—*Adalwolf*—due to arrive in a few hours, we were hopelessly outgunned. All we could try to do was deliver the shuttle to the crash site and then attempt to stay alive long enough to pick it up again when Alva and her team had finished.

I tipped back my head and exhaled. Laura Petrushka glanced at me. "Are you okay?"

The white streak in her hair seemed to glow in the light from the screens. I wanted her to put her arms around me and stroke my head. Instead, I wiped my face with my hands and pulled myself up into a straight-backed sitting position. "Have you ever ordered anyone into combat?"

"A couple of times."

"Does it get any easier?"

She smiled and shook her head. "No," she said, "I don't believe it ever does."

I sighed, envious of her quiet self-assurance. The last time I'd commanded a ground action, George Walker had died, ripped apart by the razor-sharp barbs of beasts whose existence I hadn't thought to determine in advance.

"Do you have any advice?"

The older woman's shrug was eloquent. It spoke of duty and sacrifice, and the ineluctable futility of trying to second-guess fate. "Just try not to get us all killed."

FORTY-FOUR

NOD

Prepare for combat, they say.
  Prepare for damage.
  So I gather tools.
  Wear armour.
  Breathing masks for all my hands.
  Fire extinguishers.
  Druff fixed ships before humans tamed fire.
  Druff always serve.
  Druff serve everybody.
  Always more to fix.
  Always more work to be done.
  Work, then sleep.
  Sleep, then work.
  Nobody else fix fusion tubes. Nobody else keep gravity working. Nobody else keep air flowing through ship. Water flowing through pipes. Fuel flowing through reactor.
  Work, because work is what we have.
  Sleep, because sleep is what we earn.
  Work, then sleep.
  Dream of World Tree.
  Dream of George.
  We serve ships as we serve World Tree.

We serve because we always serve.
In peace, in battle.
We work because we always work.
Keep everyone alive by keeping World Tree alive.
Keep everyone alive by keeping ship alive.
We serve, then rest.
Rest forever in roots of World Tree.

FORTY-FIVE

TROUBLE DOG

As soon as Captain Konstanz gave the go-ahead, I calculated a vector that would take us within a few hundred kilometres of the surface of the Brain—close enough to drop the shuttle and cover it during its descent, while still retaining enough altitude and velocity to evade incoming fire.

I brought my engines online and began to accelerate, knowing the fusion-bright glare of my exhaust wouldn't reach the inner system for another five and a half hours—long after I'd arrived in person.

Strange to think that, when I arrived, I'd be able to look back with a telescope and see myself here, in the past. Strange, but not a matter for concern. There would be no paradox. Observation of visible light didn't violate causality any more than rewatching a movie affected the lives of the actors involved, or taking a photograph robbed the subject of their soul. Only an idiot would think it would. Planes didn't cease to exist when they outpaced the sound of their engines, and starships didn't break the universe when they overtook their own image.

Fenrir would almost certainly be loitering in the shadow of one of the Objects. She knew I was coming, and knew my objective; all she had to do was lie in wait. The instant I appeared, she'd light me up with her targeting lasers and let fly with her torpedoes. I'd have maybe ten or fifteen seconds to deploy the shuttle, depending on her range at the point of engagement, and then I'd need to devote all my attention to the defensive cannons.

So far, the fabricators in the automated spaces of my engineering section had produced four torpedoes, each armed with a fifteen-megaton fission warhead, and enough ammo to run the cannons continuously for up to three hours. In order to find the material to do this, they'd torn out every non-essential piece of equipment and recycled two of my six shuttles. If I made it back to Camrose, I'd need a complete refit and overhaul. In the meantime, four torpedoes were the best I could do with the material at hand, and in the time available. In contrast, assuming she'd rearmed after her attack on the *Geest van Amsterdam*, *Fenrir* would be carrying up to sixteen torpedoes—four of which would be tipped with antimatter.

I took note of a worrying fluctuation in one of my engines. In order to get here, I'd pushed them harder than they were supposed to be pushed. Although the chances of a catastrophic failure were relatively small, any hard manoeuvring would heighten the risk of damage and degrade performance.

Slowly, I began to dip in and out of the higher dimensions, moving like a small boat cresting a series of waves, each crest greater than the last. Finally, when my largest oscillation took me almost completely out of the universe, I fired the jump engines. Like a flick of a dolphin's tail, they broke the surface tension between the realms and hurled me up and into the tearing squalls that lay beyond.

•

Contrary to what many humans believe, there are no monsters in the higher dimensions. At least, none I've ever seen. However, there are ghosts, of a sort. You can hear their voices in the roar of the stars; in the emission shells of long-dead civilisations; in the cries of ships in the far-flung reaches of the galactic swirl; in the chirps of closer craft; and, behind it all, in the ever-present fourteen-billion-year-old grumble of the Big Bang, which still echoes around the hyperspatial vaults, borne on the impossible breeze.

Within a few seconds of total immersion, through the fragmentary rain of old signals and the ongoing thunder of the universe, I received a priority transmission from *Adalwolf*. He had been trying to contact me for half an hour. My layover on the edge of the system had confused him. He had been expecting me to dive into the Gallery with all weapons ablaze. Now, I suspected he was starting to wonder at my tactics.

His avatar's bony face appeared to have been carved from ice. Starlight flared in the hollows of his eye sockets. "You cannot win," he warned me. The way he said it made it seem like a simple statement of fact.

I laughed. "I'm not trying to win," I told him. "I'm trying to save lives."

"How commendable," he said. His acerbity rankled me.

"Better that than indiscriminate murder," I snapped back.

Unamused, he waved away the accusation. "Do you know what the trouble with war dogs has always been," he asked, "throughout recorded history?"

"I assume you're about to enlighten me?"

His wintry expression grew colder still. "When the fighting's over," he said, "we're useless for anything else."

"I don't agree."

"And yet here you come."

The growl of the Gallery's star had grown a hundred times louder than it had been from the edge of the system. I had almost reached my destination, but there would be no gentle transition this time. If my calculations were correct, I would emerge only a few hundred thousand kilometres from the surface of the Brain—closer than the distance between the Earth and its moon—and still be travelling at interplanetary velocity.

"Yes, here I come," I said.

As I spoke, I slammed the jump engines into full reverse and dropped back into the universe, stern-first. My fusion motors blazed like twin novae as I decelerated harder than ever before.

"Ready or not!"

FORTY-SIX

SAL KONSTANZ

The force of the deceleration pressed down on me, as if soft weights were being piled on my chest and stomach. I felt sharp protests from the muscles of my neck and lower back, and my vision went grey as the increased pressure stifled the blood flow in my optic nerve.

On the main screen, I made out the convoluted surface of the Brain falling past us, only a couple of hundred kilometres off our port flank. The star-like brilliance of the *Trouble Dog*'s fusion exhaust threw the ridges and folds of its canyons— each deep enough to swallow us whole—into stark relief.

"Hostile identified. Torpedoes inbound." The ship's voice relayed no emotion, simply a report of the facts.

When I spoke, I couldn't keep the discomfort or the fear from my voice. "Release the shuttle."

A shudder ran through the hull and a light appeared on my console to tell me the main bay doors were open to vacuum.

"Shuttle away. Time until first torpedo impact, seven minutes and forty-two seconds."

"Turn over and activate the defence grid."

"Turning now."

The crushing deceleration ceased. Suddenly weightless, I lurched forward against my straps. My head came down and my mouth snapped shut. I felt a sharp pain and my mouth filled with the metallic taste of blood.

The *Trouble Dog* pivoted through 180 degrees, until its bow faced the direction we were moving in, and then the engines kicked in again, accelerating us towards the incoming threat.

"Cannons active."

The ship rang with a popcorn clatter as the point-defence batteries sprayed tracer rounds at the *Fenrir*'s torpedoes.

Moving with effort under acceleration, I put my fingers to my mouth. The tips came away bright red. Hurled forwards, I had bitten myself hard, and sunk my front teeth almost completely through my lower lip. It stung like hell.

I glanced across at Laura Petrushka, and saw agony written across her features. "Are you okay?"

"It's my leg." She put a hand to the inflatable cast on her thigh. "The pressure. It hurts." She spoke one word at a time, punctuating each with a sharp intake of breath. "I can feel the bone coming apart, again."

"I'm sorry," I told her, "but there's not much I can do right now."

"It's not your fault."

I swivelled my eyes back to the screen, my attention caught by a bright flash.

"One torpedo down," the *Trouble Dog* reported. "Two more still on course."

"How's the shuttle doing?" Speaking hurt my battered jaw.

"Five minutes from the surface."

"Anything targeting it?"

"Nothing yet."

I gave the tactical display a squint. The *Fenrir* was a red dot ahead and slightly above us, coming in on a trajectory that would intersect our own in a matter of minutes. If she got past us, the shuttle would be defenceless.

"Stand by to provide covering fire if necessary."

"Roger." The tone still hadn't changed. We could have been discussing the weather for all the expression she showed. "Four birds in their tubes and ready to fly on your mark."

I watched the Brain's carved surface roll beneath us. Another of the *Fenrir's* torpedoes died in a burst of white.

"Shuttle entering the atmosphere."

"No sign it's being targeted?"

"No, why should there be?" For the first time, the *Trouble Dog* let an exasperated tinge bleed into her voice. "I'm the only danger here. She has to deal with me first. Once I'm gone, the shuttle's stranded. *Fenrir* can pick it off at her leisure."

I felt a wave of helplessness. These duelling metal beasts could out-think and out-react me. No wonder the *Dog* sounded impatient.

"What do you suggest?"

"We can't win in a stand-up fight."

"So?"

"So we run for cover. Change the rules of engagement. Hide, and fight back as and when the opportunity presents itself."

"Guerrilla rules?"

The *Trouble Dog's* avatar smiled. "We *are* the underdogs."

I smiled back. I knew she was right. If we stayed out here, we'd be torn to shreds.

"Okay." I struggled against the acceleration that seemed to be unhinging my lower jaw. "I'm turning strategic command over to you. Do what you have to."

The *Trouble Dog's* eyes glimmered. Her smile grew wider, displaying predatory teeth. "I'm off the leash?"

"Until I say otherwise."

Delight filled her face. She clapped her hands. "Hot damn!"

•

The course changes were hard and violent, and almost too quick to follow. Given free rein, the *Trouble Dog* threw herself into the fight with such aggression that Laura and I found ourselves tossed around like rag dolls. I heard her moan in pain, but was too preoccupied with my own discomfort to inquire. Instead, I concentrated on the flickering chaos of the main screen: detonations flowered like lethal fireworks; strings of tracer hosed back and forth; the background stars jumped and whirled.

I couldn't see the other Carnivore, but I knew she was out there in the darkness, her position implied by the white corkscrew tails of incoming ordnance. My hands gripped the rests on either side of my couch, and I hoped that on board the *Fenrir*, Captain Parris was suffering at least as much as we were.

"Come on, girl," I urged, willing the *Trouble Dog* to survive this assault, to absorb the hellfire being thrown at her and, somehow, emerge triumphant.

A status window to the lower left of the forward wall showed an animated representation of the shuttle's progress. I watched the little craft fall towards the planet's etched surface. All we had to do was survive long enough for Clay, Childe and Preston to retrieve the injured with automated stretchers and secure them in the shuttle's cargo bay. Unfortunately, they'd need hours to complete their mission, and I knew we'd only last minutes against *Fenrir*—let alone *Adalwolf* when he arrived. But at least if we inflicted damage before we were destroyed, the follow-up ships we'd called for would stand a chance of getting through—and maybe the shuttle could stay hidden until they arrived.

Three more torpedoes appeared, diving towards us, and the *Trouble Dog* rocked as she dispatched two of her own in reply.

A voice came from the shuttle.

"This is Clay. We're seeing some activity on the surface, several kilometres from the wreck. Could be survivors. We're going down for a look-see."

"Roger that."

The little craft's landing motors fired and her undercarriage deployed. I watched her drop through the thin atmosphere, ionisation flaring around her nose and the leading edges of her wings. And then, suddenly, she was gone, swallowed by one of the deep, narrow canyons. There was nothing more we could do for her, save keep the *Trouble Dog*'s siblings distracted for as long as possible and try to cause as much trouble as possible. If they were chasing us, they wouldn't have time to interfere with the surface expedition. At least, I hoped they wouldn't.

A proximity alarm shrilled. One of the *Fenrir*'s projectiles had breached our defensive screen, its twisting course somehow avoiding the hail of bullets thrown its way.

"Brace for impact."

I screwed my eyes tight, but the glare shone through the lids. It seemed to shine right through the hull. The blast wave followed a second later, hitting us head-on. The *Trouble Dog* bucked, and the lights flickered.

When I reopened my eyes, we were still in one piece, but all the radiation sensors were flashing red and I could smell something burning—the acrid tang of fused electronics and melting plastic.

"Both our torpedoes destroyed," the *Trouble Dog* intoned. Her voice was flat. The battle was taking all her concentration. "Two birds remaining in their tubes. Three still inbound."

I felt a pang of dismay. We'd already used half our stock of missiles to no effect.

"The shuttle's down," I told her, although she would already have known. "They're on their own now. Do what you have to."

"Yes, Captain."

The chatter of the anti-missile batteries subsided. The planet wheeled aside, wiped from the screen by a sudden change of heading. Acceleration alarms filled the cabins and corridors, and I groaned inwardly. I had seen many ship engagements during the war. They tended to be nasty, brutish and short—like speed chess played with live ammunition. The next few minutes were liable to be uncomfortable and terrifying in equal measure—and would most probably culminate in our violent deaths.

If I'd had a god that would have been the moment I would have tried to make peace with them. But I didn't. Instead, I thought of Sedge, lying in dreamless sleep on that Hopper ship as it relentlessly drilled its way into the unknown, pulling further away from me with every passing instant. Would he ever know what had happened here, and would he even care? By the time they revived him, all this would be centuries in his past, and an unimaginable distance behind him. At the very least, I hoped he might remember me from time to time—the thought brought a sliver of consolation. I might die today, but at least I'd left a small mark on the universe. If the old saying was true, and we were never truly dead until everyone who remembered us had also died, then some small part of me might conceivably endure for millennia, until Sedge himself passed away.

The main engines kicked in and I felt myself squashed into my couch. Ahead, I could see the system's star—a large reddish-yellow sun at the centre of an absurd orrery. From here, it looked around the size of a coin held at arm's length.

Why were we heading for the sun? It was seven light minutes distant. Even if we had some reason to go to it, there was no way we could outrun the torpedoes on our trail; they were lighter and faster, and could tolerate higher accelerations because they didn't have to accommodate human crews. And even if, by some miracle, we managed to outmanoeuvre and destroy them, the *Fenrir* would still be right behind us, her tubes filled with replacements, and the *Adalwolf* would be here before we'd closed even half the distance to the sun.

The proximity alarm rang again. The fusillade of three

torpedoes the *Fenrir* had fired earlier was now drawing close to our stern. We may have survived the first nuclear explosion, but I wasn't confident we'd prevail against three more—especially if one or more of those torpedoes was packing an antimatter warhead. We couldn't hope to withstand a combined blast of that magnitude.

I looked to Laura, feeling like I should apologise, but she seemed to have lapsed into unconsciousness. Her head lolled against her restraints, but that was probably just as well. The torpedoes would be in range within seconds. If we were about to be vaporised, it would be kinder to let her sleep through the ordeal.

Seemingly oblivious to the futility of running, the *Trouble Dog* continued to accelerate. Finally, I realised she wasn't trying to outstrip them. Instead, she was building momentum for a jump.

Despite the crushing acceleration, I felt my heart skip. We were going to live!

But my elation didn't last long.

The *Trouble Dog* reared back and I realised there was no time for the ship to ease itself into the higher dimensions. If we were to escape the coming detonation, it would have to slam its way through the membrane and hope for the best. Pinned in place, all I could do was clench my jaw. As a kid, I'd seen little insects skate across the surface tension of a pond. They didn't have the weight to break through. Jump engines gave us the clout to break the "surface" of the universe, but the transition had to be handled carefully. A miscalculation could cause a ship to "rebound" into the physical world, or disintegrate entirely. And what the *Trouble Dog* was about to do was the equivalent of a mosquito diving at the water from a hundred feet up, accelerating all the way.

I thought of Sedge again.

This was going to be brutal.

FORTY-SEVEN

ASHTON CHILDE

Alva Clay lit the shuttle's spotlights as we sank into the shadows between the slab-like sides of the canyon.

"There," she said, pointing between her booted feet. Through the shuttle's transparent nose, I caught movement on the canyon floor.

"Looks like a couple of flyers, maybe a dozen people." I was standing behind the main seats in the cockpit. The exoskeleton made it impossible to wedge myself into a chair, so I had to settle for locking the legs in place and holding on as best I could.

"Rescue party?" Preston asked.

Clay shook her head. "See those things there, like millipedes?"

"Yeah."

"They're crawlers. Combat recon drones. And those people down there look to be armed, and—whoah!" She threw the little craft into reverse. Hail rattled against the hull.

Preston's eyes went wide. "Are they shooting at us?"

"They're not blowing kisses."

I grabbed hold of the back of Clay's couch as she whirled the shuttle around in its own length and powered away. We heard a few more pings, and then we were up and over the lip of the canyon. We arced upwards, and then fell back into a second canyon running parallel with the first, separated from the gunmen by impregnable white crystal walls two kilometres high.

As we lowered into the gloom of this new fissure, Clay ran diagnostics on the shuttle's systems and swore under her breath.

"Problem?" I asked.

"Depends." She punched a few controls and her scowl deepened.

"Depends on what?"

"On whether you're particularly partial to breathing." She flipped a couple of switches and brought us in to land on the canyon floor. The wheels touched stone and the engines whined into silence.

"What's the damage?"

"A couple of high-velocity rounds through the main oxygen tank."

"Can it be fixed?"

Clay shrugged. "Sure, but there wouldn't be any point. All the air will have already leaked out."

"Don't you have any emergency patches?"

She looked ready to punch me. "We would have if this were a military shuttle."

"It's not?"

"Does it look armoured to you?" She hit the dashboard with the heel of her hand. "I don't even know where this piece of shit came from, but it's strictly civilian, and probably twenty years past its use-by date." She unclipped her harness and stood. "But that's one of the simple joys of working for the Reclamation. Everything's second-hand and nothing works quite the way it should."

I smiled, remembering the obsolete planes, equipment and personnel I'd had to put up with on Cichol.

"Even the people?"

She glared down at the young medic still strapped into

the co-pilot's seat. "*Especially* the people."

"So," I unlocked my legs and flexed them against the Brain's comparatively mild gravity. "What do we do?"

"Well," Clay put her hands on her hips, "we can't take off without air. A shuttle this size ain't big enough for a recycler, and we don't even have enough pressure suits for all of us." She waved a finger at my carbon-fibre bones. "And even if we did, we couldn't get you into one wearing that, now could we?"

I looked down at myself. "I guess not."

"And besides, without stripping down half the systems back there, I can't tell how much more damage there might be. And I wouldn't be happy taking her up without knowing what might fail." She brushed her hands together with finality. "Bottom line is, we're stuck here until the *Dog* comes back for us."

"Stuck?" Preston's voice had grown squeaky with alarm.

Clay put a heavy hand on his shoulder. "Yeah, well. At least we can breathe on the surface. That's something."

The kid swivelled around in his chair. "We're going *out* there? What about the guys with guns?"

"They're on the other side of that wall." Clay jerked her thumb at the cliff.

"They had aircraft."

"Yeah?" She reached into an overhead locker and pulled down her Archipelago pistol. "Well, I've got this." She brandished the gun in his face. I had never used one myself, but knew its rocket-assisted slugs would be powerful enough to punch holes through a lightly armoured flyer.

"The main wreck's about a dozen klicks back down the canyon," she said. "I say we stick to our original mission, and hike back there and look for survivors."

Her glare dared us to disagree.

"Do I get a gun?" I asked.

She gave me a look. "I'm not sure I trust you with that suit, let alone a weapon. If I'd had my way, for what you did to the captain, you'd have been eating vacuum in the hypervoid."

I rubbed my side where Konstanz's fingertips had jabbed into the wound, rupturing the sutures. "I said I was sorry for that."

"And she forgave you." Clay hooked the pistol to her belt. "But then, I guess she's a better person than I am. Me, I like to harbour a grudge for a good long time." She turned to Preston. "You," she said, as if addressing a marine recruit, "look in the emergency locker. We're going to need as much food and water as we can carry."

The young man squirmed to his feet. His hand fluttered, unsure whether or not to salute. "Yes, ma'am."

"And no, before you ask, you don't get a gun either."

"W-why not?"

"Because you're a fucking idiot."

•

We debarked the shuttle via the main cargo ramp and started walking. The floor of the canyon was smooth and hard like polished rock. Preston carried his medical bag slung over his left shoulder and a wilderness survival kit over his right; Clay's rucksack held spare ammunition clips and additional weaponry; and, because my exoskeleton gave me added strength and increased stamina, I had been saddled with a bulky crate containing three days' worth of water and two days' worth of dehydrated ration packs. We wouldn't starve or die of thirst. If all went to plan, the *Trouble Dog* would be back to collect us in a few hours; if not, we were dead anyway. Whatever downed the heavy cruiser would be back to finish us off long before we started to get hungry.

Clay took point, her pistol clasped in both hands, ready to respond to the first hint of danger. Preston shambled along a few metres behind her, looking hunched over and scared, his head turning to interrogate every patch of shadow. And I brought up the rear, clomping along with my robotic gait, the crate held out before me like a sacrificial offering to the god of lost causes.

I didn't know if it was emotional exhaustion or a side effect of the painkillers Preston had given me, but I realised that I felt strangely and unexpectedly calm. There was a good chance I might die in this pitiless canyon, and yet I couldn't seem to get worked up about it. If it happened, it happened. I was out of that sweaty hellhole of a jungle, and nothing else seemed to matter much any more. My whole adult life felt like a distant dream, and now all that was left of me was a raw, slightly disconnected civilian who was wondering how everything had collapsed around him with such rapidity, and whether he could build anything from the wreckage.

I was certain my former masters would still demand some form of retribution for my failure. Despite my request to join the House of Reclamation, I wouldn't officially be a member until my application was approved and I'd completed my training and orientation. Until then, the Conglomeration could still legitimately claim me as a fugitive. If we were cornered here and I wanted to buy myself time, I'd need something to trade. Perhaps, if I completed my missing persons case and recovered Ona Sudak, that one success might go some way towards ameliorating matters? I had no idea what made the poet so valuable, but if the Intelligence Service was keen to get its hands on her then perhaps I could use her as a bargaining chip. I'd never work for the Conglomeration again, but at least I might be spared jail, and allowed to pursue my self-imposed exile in peace.

"I should have stayed a cop," I grumbled aloud. "It was crap, but it was better than this."

Neither of the others turned around at the sound of

my voice, but I saw Preston's shoulders twitch and guessed he might be having similar thoughts of his own, trying to fathom how he'd ended up here. The poor kid. He didn't look much older than nineteen or twenty, and here he was laying his life on the line for a bunch of strangers in the most sterile and unforgiving landscape I'd ever had the misfortune to encounter.

•

We had been walking for an hour when Clay stopped us with a raised hand. "Movement," she whispered.

I peered ahead, seeing only the straight lines and razor-sharp shadows of the canyon. "Where?"

"On the left wall, about two hundred yards." She stepped into the shadows at the base of the same wall, and Preston and I followed her.

"Is it them?" the kid asked.

Clay shook her head. "I don't think so. Doesn't look like people."

I still couldn't see anything more than a deep shadow, with a deeper blackness at its centre. "Drones?"

"No." Her brow furrowed. "I only caught it from the corner of my eye, but it looked like a hole opened in the wall."

I placed my palm against the smooth, cold stone. It towered two thousand metres above me, a solid vertical slab of quartz.

"How could a hole open in stone?"

"I don't know, but it did." She sounded cross. "Like an eye, or a mouth."

We edged forward, staying pressed into the shadows. Clay held her pistol at the ready. Detail resolved with each step, and it soon became easier to see that the darker patch of shadow was in fact an aperture of some kind.

When we were closer, Clay made us wait while she reconnoitred the situation. Preston and I crouched in the angle between cliff and floor, and watched her.

The hole appeared to be a cave mouth, set into the smoothness of the wall, around two metres from the base. Clay hauled herself up to take a peep inside, and then dropped back.

"It's empty," she said, "but there are stairs leading down."

I walked forward.

"Stairs?"

"You can see them by the light from the walls."

"Weird."

"Yeah."

"Should we take a look?"

"Nah." She flicked the suggestion away with her fingers. "We should press on to the crash site. There might still be someone there."

Preston looked dubious. "If there were, those gunmen would have found them."

"Not necessarily. The *Geest van Amsterdam* was a big liner. Plenty of places to hide in a wreck that size."

"For a week?"

"I don't see why not. We've pulled people out of wrecks after more time than that. As long as you've got water, you can survive for two, maybe three weeks without food."

The boy turned to me for support. "What do you think?"

I looked at the cave's darkened maw, and it took a few moments for my eyes to adjust enough to make out the pearlescent glow of its walls.

"I think we should press on to the wreck." If Sudak lived, the chances were she'd still be close to the crash site. Only an idiot would have wandered into this maze-like jumble of canyons through choice.

Preston looked disappointed. "Well, I think we should go back to the shuttle and wait for the *Trouble Dog*," he said. "This place gives me the creeps."

He took a pace back along the canyon in the direction from which we'd come. The shuttle lay around four kilometres behind us, lost to sight around several corners. We had left it sitting in a shaft of sunlight like a housefly warming itself in a gulley. And afraid of being unable to find our way back through the maze, we had left the power switched on so we could home in on its transponder. Compared to the alien landscape we stood in, the idea of the shuttle's warm cabin seemed safe and inviting, and I could understand why the kid wanted to retreat to its cramped familiarity.

"We shouldn't split up," Clay said. "And besides, you're supposed to be the medic. We need you."

Preston turned to her. "I'm not a medic."

"You're more of a medic than I am." She jerked a thumb in my direction. "And you've got this guy to help you."

"That's ridiculous! I—"

A bright light stabbed down from above. Clay yelled, "Get down!" and pulled us both into a crouch against the wall. A moment later, the ground trembled.

When I thought it might be safe to look up again, nothing had changed.

"What was that?"

Clay tapped her earbud. "They hit the shuttle from orbit. Kinetic weapon fired from that Carnivore we're fighting. The transponder's dead. I think the shuttle's gone."

We brushed ourselves down.

"What do we do *now*?" Preston's voice trembled on the edge of hysteria. He glanced upward, as if expecting to see the heavy cruiser bearing down on him.

Clay took him by the scruff of his neck and marched him to the mouth of the cave. "We get out of sight." She pushed him up the wall. "And we do it quickly."

FORTY-EIGHT

TROUBLE DOG

I hit the dimensional membrane with a slap that would have pancaked a less robust craft. Hull plates buckled. Alarms went off on every console. Plates smashed in the galley, and one of the remaining shuttles broke loose from its moorings and slewed across the internal hangar, wrecking itself and another craft before fetching up against the bulkhead.

Captain Konstanz and the Outward agent were alive but unconscious. Not that it mattered. Let them rest. The captain had given me licence to play this conflict out as I saw fit, and that was exactly what I intended to do.

Two minutes after entering the hypervoid, I dropped back into the universe. My screens turned white. Proximity alarms shrilled, and the external temperature went up so quickly the numbers on the readouts blurred. When they stabilised, they registered a fluctuating value between 3500 and 4000 degrees centigrade—about halfway to the maximum limit of my tolerance.

Metal creaked as it expanded in the heat, and I allowed myself a moment of self-congratulation. My calculations had been correct, and I was now deep within the photosphere of the local sun—a feat of precise navigation to rival any I'd ever heard of.

Plasma raged around me, welling up from the star's interior in plumes large enough to swallow a dozen planets. Convection cells trembled; lines of magnetic flux whipped and crackled through the miasma, pulling tides of fire in their wake. And all of it burned with an excoriating, cacophonous roar.

My good mood faded as I remembered my sister, *Coyote*, and the way she'd died—her insides scoured to nothingness by the superheated internal fabric of a star. I hoped I wouldn't share the same fate. My hull armour had taken a beating—first from the *Fenrir*'s nuclear torpedo, which had for an instant produced temperatures hundreds of thousands of times higher than I was currently experiencing, and then from the precipitous jump into the higher dimensions. However, I was reasonably confident it'd hold, barring further injury. In the meantime, I switched my internal fabrication priorities from ammunition production to damage control, and used the medical interfaces in the command couches on the bridge to check on the unconscious women. My battlefield diagnostics found no serious injuries—at least, no new ones—and so I injected them both with a combination of analgesics and mild stimulants. Within a few minutes, they were both awake and blinking around at the bridge in a mixture of confusion and surprise.

"I thought we were dead," the captain said, her face orange with light reflected from the external screens. She frowned at the surging sea of plasma (I had filtered the light to a tolerable level, to avoid blinding her).

"Where are we?"

I projected my avatar onto the screen and arranged its features into their most reassuring configuration.

"We are inside the sun." I had to raise my voice to speak over the boiling roar of the cauldron in which we were immersed.

She groaned and wiped her eyes with her fingertips. "I was afraid you were going to say that." She rolled her head and sat up straight. "And how did we get here? The last I remember, the *Fenrir* had us dead in her sights."

"We jumped."

"Jumped?"

"Yes."

"Into the *sun*?"

"Yes."

She laughed, but there was an edge to it. "You are fucking *insane*." She shook her head, still smiling, and leant towards the tactical display. "Can the *Fenrir* find us in here?"

"Negative. The plasma masks our heat signature, and the star's electromagnetic output will interfere with her sensors. She'd have to be right on top of us to stand a chance of detecting us."

"But it cuts both ways, I guess?"

"If you're asking whether my sensors are similarly affected, I'm afraid the answer is yes."

Captain Konstanz gave a thoughtful nod. "Have you ever done anything like this before?" she asked.

"No," I said, "but I did have a sister who tried it during the war."

"What happened to her?"

"She died."

"Great." The captain slumped back. "So, what do we do now? Just sit here and wait?"

"*Fenrir* will come to us. She'll have seen my heading and velocity. She'll know where I am, and she'll come looking."

"And then?"

I narrowed my avatar's eyes.

"And then, we kill her."

FORTY-NINE

SAL KONSTANZ

The ship rocked on the upwelling plasma, creaking like a wooden galleon. At one point, it let forth such a titanic moan that Laura and I froze, fearing the hull was on the verge of implosion. When nothing further happened, we exchanged uneasy smiles.

"Come on," I said. "We've got a few minutes. Let me get you down to the infirmary."

She rubbed the cast protecting her bullet-injured thigh. The wound was obviously troubling her.

"No, thank you," she said. Spidery, bruise-like blotches speckled her cheeks where capillaries had burst beneath the skin, and her left eyeball had turned a livid red, the blood vessels having ruptured due to the pressure of our recent manoeuvring.

"We should let the ship take a look at your leg."

"No. This is the safest place on the ship, right now. I think I'll stay here."

"Are you sure? There's much better equipment down in the infirmary."

"Yes." She tapped her fingertips against the arm of her couch. "The ship can give me all the painkillers I need, right here. No need to traipse all the way down there."

"Suit yourself." I shrugged. The likelihood was that we

were both going to die in the next few minutes, anyway. I turned instead to the *Trouble Dog*'s avatar. "How are we doing?" I asked it.

"Holding steady," the ship replied.

"How long can we remain here?"

"An hour at the most." Her face took on the expression it used when explaining something technical. "At the moment, the hull can just about tolerate the temperature of the surrounding material, but there's no way to vent waste heat from any of our systems. In fifty-seven minutes, we will have to emerge in order to deploy the thermo–dump panels."

"And the *Fenrir* knows this?"

"She will be able to extrapolate the timeframe based on her own capabilities, and an assessment of the damage I've already sustained."

"So, she could just wait in a low orbit, and ambush us when we come out?"

"That would be her best strategy, yes."

I rubbed my forehead in exasperation. "Then how is being in here helping us at all? You've hidden us in a burning building."

The *Trouble Dog* remained unruffled. "I told you," she said, "we are going to kill her."

"How?"

"By getting her to deploy her secret weapon."

Across the room, Laura stiffened. "You can't be serious," she said.

The *Trouble Dog* turned its gaze on her. "Torpedoes are useless in this medium. If I rise from the plasma and the *Fenrir* targets me, all I have to do is sink beneath the surface and move position. The plasma will disrupt the torpedoes' sensors, and they will be unable to track me through the photosphere. The *Fenrir* will then have no choice but to employ her primary weapon: the one she used to down the

286

Hobo and disable the defences on the *Geest van Amsterdam*."

"Then what happens?"

The avatar smiled. "Then, we'll see."

"See what?"

The smile broadened. There was something feral about it.

"Whether," the *Trouble Dog* said, drawing out the word, "I'm half as clever as I think I am."

•

The *Trouble Dog* lingered until we were in real danger of roasting in our own waste heat, and I could actually hear the cooling fans labouring to keep the cabin temperature within acceptable bounds. Then, suddenly, she exploded from the murk. Coming up on the crest of an infernal plume, she burst into clear space with her hull glowing like an ember and scattered chunks of plasma radiating out around her like molten shrapnel.

Immediately, everything on the tactical display went red. We were being targeted.

Fast work, I thought, cursing the *Fenrir* and all who sailed in her—especially Parris. A quick browse of the *Trouble Dog's* files had given me all I needed to know about the man. A career officer, he'd served on the *Fenrir* during some of the more questionable actions of the war. He was loyal, unimaginative, and almost completely devoid of scruples. His hair was fair and thinning, a pale beard clung to his chin, and his eyes were a blue so pale and washed out that they bordered on grey. I couldn't guess why he'd been ordered to destroy two civilian vessels, but got the distinct impression he was just the kind of small-minded, ruthless bastard to follow those orders without hesitation or compunction.

"Torpedoes incoming," the ship informed me. "Taking evasive action."

The view flipped. My stomach did a cartwheel, and we

began to accelerate back towards the sun's churning surface. The torpedoes—three of them in a wide spread—raced towards us, trying to close a fifteen-hundred-kilometre gap. Each carried a hundred-megaton antimatter warhead. But, before they'd covered half the distance, we were already diving back into the burning ocean.

FIFTY

NOD

Pushed through crawlspaces between inner and outer hull. Heat intense. Wished for shelter of World Tree's branches.

Breathing gloves on all six of my faces.

During battle, ship rang like gong.

Used torch to weld loose seams, did what could be done to straighten buckled hull plates.

Ship like World Tree after a storm; so much damage to fix.

Replaced a half-melted plate, then moved on.

Picked shrapnel from a bulkhead, then moved on.

Sorted tangle of broken wires. Replaced damaged circuits. Then moved on.

Repaired leaking hole moments before *Hound of Difficulty* hurled itself back into the face of the sun.

If hadn't fixed it, ship would have been lost. All crew would have been dead. Burnt to nothing by invading plasma.

Nobody ever says thank you.

Nobody notices.

I just fix things, and move on.

In battle, I do my job, just as, during winter storms, ancestors kept the World Tree intact and functioning.

I wield tools.

I save the ship and move on.

I serve, and earn my right to mate.
Earn right to return home to World Tree.
I serve, as we have always served.
I do duty.
Always more to fix.
Always something broken.

FIFTY-ONE

ASHTON CHILDE

"It's been over an hour," I said. "Maybe it's gone?"

Two more impacts had followed the one that destroyed our shuttle, and both of them had been directly outside the cave's mouth. Seeking shelter within, we'd descended a flight of large spiral stairs, working our way deep beneath the surface of the Object in order to avoid further blasts.

"You're welcome to go check," Clay said. She wiped off the neck of her water bulb, refastened its cap, and dropped it back into the crate with the survival rations. "But I ain't sticking my head out 'til I know that Carnivore's fucked off. It could be sat up there right now, just waiting for us, and the minute we break cover..." She slammed her fist into the palm of her other hand. "Blam!"

"Then, what?" I let the frustration creep into my voice. I had no desire to linger in the path of an orbital bombardment, but I was nevertheless aware that each step downwards took me further from the wreck of the liner and the completion of my mission. "We can't hide down here forever."

"I hear that." She turned and lowered herself onto the next step. "We can't signal the captain from down here. That's why we keep going. See how deep this rabbit hole goes. And maybe, just maybe, we find a way back up where nobody's looking for us, and we get a message to her. Tell her to come down here and get us."

"What about the wreck?"

She turned away, contemplating the next step. "Ain't nobody alive there."

"How can you be so sure?"

She crouched, preparing to swing her legs over the lip. "Because that Carnivore zeroed in on us from high orbit. There ain't no way to escape that."

I knew she was right. There were precious few places to hide in these canyons. Nevertheless... "The ship was hiding when we arrived, waiting to jump us. Maybe it didn't stick around after the crash. Maybe somebody could have got out while it was concealing itself?"

Clay shrugged. "You're probably right," she said. "But my guess is it sent those mercenaries we saw as a clean-up crew. Anyone it missed, they will have got." She dropped down onto the next step. The sound of her boots hitting the stone echoed up the stairwell. "And they've had a week to search that wreck. If anyone survived the crash, they're dead now."

Preston and I watched her descend until she'd passed around the curve of the stair and become hidden by the central pillar. Then we exchanged looks.

"What do you think?" I asked him.

He replaced his bulb in the crate, and switched the medical kit's carrying strap from one shoulder to the other. "I don't see how we've got a lot of choice."

He went to follow but I put a hand to his upper arm, restraining him. "You don't know what's down there," I said.

The kid threw me a haunted look. "I know what's up there, though. And I'd rather take my chances with her than get blown to bits by an orbital strike."

I released him and stepped back. "Fair enough." I couldn't argue with that kind of logic.

He followed the sound of Alva Clay's footfalls. When he was about to similarly vanish around the central pillar, he stopped and looked back up at me. "Aren't you coming?"

I took a long breath in through my nose. Finding Ona Sudak alive had been a faint, desperate hope. If she was gone, I had lost my only bargaining chip.

How ironic that a heavy cruiser from the Conglomeration Navy should have ended my career with Conglomeration Intelligence. Ironic, and infuriating. What reason could the navy possibly have for shooting down Outward liners, and why were the intelligence services more concerned with rescuing poets than stopping the slaughter? The trouble with operating on a "need to know" basis, I reflected, was that you were rarely told the things you most needed to know, and never allowed to fathom a wider context.

I didn't know whether this aggression was an attempt to reignite hostilities, or some sort of random hit. The only thing that had become apparent was that my future, such as it was, lay with the House of Reclamation.

I picked up the crate containing our rations, letting the exoskeleton bear the weight.

"Yeah, kid, I'm coming." I huffed. "It's not like I've got anywhere else to go now, is it?"

FIFTY-TWO

ONA SUDAK

I lost track of time. Hunger gnawed at me until I imagined I could feel my stomach beginning to digest itself. The corridors down here in the ziggurat were almost as labyrinthine as the canyons on the surface, and lined with the same white stone. Shadows flickered in my peripheral vision, but vanished when I turned my head.

The rooms I passed were utilitarian and their various functions impossible to guess. The only furniture they contained had been carved from the same quartz as everything else, and seemed to have grown seamlessly from the walls or floor. There were some lectern-like objects that may have been perches of some kind, and the occasional boomerang-shaped plinth that may have formed a desk or perhaps a reclining couch. A xenologist might have been able to hazard a guess, but I had neither the interest nor the expertise to give the matter my full attention. I remained painfully aware I was burning calories I had no way to replace. If I couldn't locate a means of escape, I would soon die here, just like—

"Oh shit."

My eyes had been looking at the bodies for a couple of seconds before my conscious brain registered their presence. One lay on its back in the centre of the corridor, the other sat slumped against a wall. I approached cautiously, although it was quite clear they were both dead and had been for some time.

The one on the floor had been male, the one against the wall female. They both wore faded purple jumpsuits. Their skin had dried and shrunk, and most of their hair had fallen out. I guessed from the patches on their shoulders that they were the remains of a lost survey team, and from the lack of visible wounds, that they'd starved to death. Perhaps the man had succumbed first, too weak to carry on, which was why he was lying on the floor, and the woman had stayed to care for him until she was too weak to save herself. I forced my eyes away from the nametags sewn to the breasts of their jumpsuits. Starved as I was for human company, I didn't want to know their names for fear I might somehow jinx my own chances of survival. After all, if they had been unable to escape this trap, what chance had I?

In an attempt to remain practical, I knelt and frisked them for useful tools, working my fingers into their pockets while trying not to flinch at the feel of mummified flesh beneath the dry material. I found a used tissue, a small tablet computer with a run-down battery, and a silvery harmonica. None of these objects were of immediate benefit, so I left them in a small pile between the woman's feet. Then I checked their boots, hoping to find a concealed weapon but coming away disappointed.

Ahead, the corridor curved to the left. I knew I had to keep going while I still had the strength to do so, yet paused a moment, feeling I should say something to mark the occasion—that even those who'd died alone and far from hope or home should have someone, even another lost stranger, to say a few words over them.

I cleared my throat, and listened to the sound echo off the walls and ceiling.

As an officer, I had often been called upon to preside over the burial of troops under my command, but I had never been asked to speak at a funeral as desolate and forlorn as this. I couldn't even fall back on my usual spiel about honour and duty. These weren't marines; they were civilians. I thought of Adam and felt my throat close up. At least these two had died together.

For a moment, I felt the crushing weight of my despair and fatigue, and experienced a terrible compulsion to sit down beside the woman and wait for my turn to die. If I were to lie entombed in these corridors for eternity, it would surely be better to have her company. Her hand might be desiccated, but it was still a human hand, and I longed to hold it in my own and draw comfort from its touch during my final moments.

Was that why she had stayed with her fallen comrade? Had the fear of loneliness been stronger than her will to keep fighting? I crouched in front of her. Her head was tipped back and resting against the white wall. Her unseeing eye sockets seemed to contemplate the universe beyond the ceiling, and I wondered at the thoughts that had flickered within the cave of her skull as she sat there beside her dead colleague, waiting for her life to end. Remorse, perhaps? Regret for mistakes made and roads untaken?

I raised a hand, unthinkingly reaching to cup her cheek, but stopped with my hand a few centimetres from her face.

Her hair was moving.

One of the dry, spidery locks hanging down past her ear shivered. I held my fingers in front of it but felt nothing. I frowned for a moment, and then cursed myself for an idiot. I was encased in my own personal bubble of breathable air. It could have been blowing a gale in this corridor and I would never have felt it.

Standing, I took the tissue I'd found in her pocket and tore it into tiny pieces. Then I dropped those pieces, a few at a time.

There *was* a breeze. The fragments fluttered. A faint but steady air current was coming from ahead, from around the curve of the corridor. Perhaps, locked in her own bubble of air until her death, the woman had never noticed. Or perhaps she'd simply lacked the strength to investigate.

Feeling suddenly energised, I brushed dry tissue crumbs from my hands. I looked down at the woman and her companion, and threw them a respectful salute. "Rest easy, my friends."

I held the salute for twenty or thirty seconds, and then turned on my heel and hurried toward the source of the draught

FIFTY-THREE

TROUBLE DOG

The clutch of torpedoes went off one by one, like nuclear firecrackers. I felt their shockwaves moving through the star's fiery soup, but they were too far away to inflict damage. As their sensors were unable to penetrate the plasma, the *Fenrir* seemed to be using them like depth charges, firing them into the sun and detonating them at random in the hope of hurting me. So far, she hadn't come within a hundred kilometres of my actual position.

"How are we doing?" the captain asked.

"Our opponent's wasting ammunition trying to drive us into the open," I replied via the screen on the bridge.

Captain Konstanz's face remained grave. Sweat speckled her brow. "We weren't out very long before she found us. How much heat did we lose?"

"Not nearly enough, I'm afraid."

She looked sideways at the blank bulkhead. "So we'll need to surface again soon?"

"Within minutes."

Her shoulders fell. "How many torpedoes does the *Fenrir* have left?"

"Two remaining."

"Unless she's manufactured replacements?" The captain's

voice was heavy with resignation.

"She hasn't had time."

"She's been sat here for a week. She could have filled her cargo bay with missiles."

"Unlikely, but possible."

"Unlikely?" The captain laughed. "You're betting our lives on something that's 'unlikely'?"

I failed to see the humour. "My tactical analysis suggests the *Fenrir* will not have perceived us as a significant enough threat to begin stockpiling munitions. The *Adalwolf* will be here in a few hours to assist her. My prediction is that she will wait for me to be driven into space by my need to vent heat. Then she will attack me with the same weapon she used to bring down the *Hobo* and the *Geest van Amsterdam*. She will attempt to get me to lower my shields and become passive, then she will use her remaining torpedoes to finish me."

"And we're going to let her try?"

"We have little choice, but thanks to Ms Petrushka here, I am both forewarned and forearmed."

•

Despite my apparent confidence, I felt a degree of trepidation as I allowed myself to be once more borne towards the star's raging surface. Everything I knew about the weapon my sister carried had been inferred and extrapolated from hearsay and guesswork.

And yet, despite my misgivings, I felt a certain wild joy. I was a heavy cruiser, a machine of death and conflict. Hiding, no matter how pressing the strategic necessity, felt like cowardice. I had done it because I had to; but now I was rising to meet my foe head-on, and I had forgotten how heady and intoxicating it could feel. I was charging the enemy from the depths of a furnace, my hull glowing and my torpedo tubes primed and ready to fire.

What could be more glorious?

As the murk ahead thinned, I turned all my attention to my tactical scanners. My bow cleared the surface, and I fired my engines and powered into space trailing a comet tail of lustrous star-stuff.

The *Fenrir* was skimming the star five thousand miles from my port side. I felt her lock onto me with her targeting lasers, yet her torpedo tubes remained closed. Instead of an assault, she signalled to me on a higher dimensional channel.

Here it comes, I thought. And, just for an instant, I had a clear hallucination of myself as a human, standing in a bare room with rain on the windows, wrapped in a trench coat and listening to a phone ring over and over again.

The vision passed.

Had it been part of the attack, or something else? Could it have been a trace memory from the dead woman whose cells formed the foundation of my consciousness? Could it have been carried in the DNA? Was such a thing even feasible?

I put the question aside. The *Fenrir* was still signalling me, even as it accelerated towards my position. All I had to do to engage it was access the channel.

At this point, I had been clear of the star for five and a half seconds. I opened my torpedo tubes and initiated a fifteen-millisecond countdown. The imaginary phone continued to ring. When the numbers reached zero, I fired my last two remaining torpedoes and answered the call.

Demons poured from the receiver.

•

I found myself standing in a virtual construct—on a chilly, windswept crag set atop a barren moor. My body was that of the woman I had once been, my only attire the shabby trench coat from my hallucination. Dark clouds glowered to the east, thick with the promise of impending rain. To the west, beyond the dead rust-coloured bracken, a listless clay-coloured sea flopped uselessly against a coarse, stony beach.

And *Fenrir* towered over me.

She had chosen to manifest in human form. Her eyes were smouldering nebulae in a face the colour of exposed bone. Her silver gauntlets and breastplate gleamed, the wind straggled her long auburn hair into dancing flails, and a thick black cloak flapped around her narrow frame.

"You could not have escaped," she said. It was almost an apology, and she had yet to raise the long sword in her hand. I shrugged and looked out over the moorland. All the plants seemed to be either dead or dying, and I felt the first spots of rain on the wind.

"You got me?"

"Yes."

"What happens now?"

She drew herself up. "I am afraid I shall have to compel you to kill yourself."

"Like you did with the *Amsterdam* and the *Hobo*?"

"Yes."

"And if I refuse?"

"You cannot." The *Fenrir* tapped the side of her head with a gauntleted finger. "I am inside your mind, and I can control your thoughts. I can plant any notion I wish. I can make you *want* to die."

"Then why don't you?" I began to shiver. With one hand, I closed the collar of my coat, gripping the material. "What are you waiting for?"

Fenrir flexed her sword arm. "You are my sister. The least I can offer you is a choice."

Beside us, the crag fell away. I wondered if the rules of the simulation would allow me to hurl myself into that abyss, and whether I would be harmed by the impact when I reached the bottom.

"What kind of choice?"

The tip of the sword came up until it almost touched my left shoulder. "Would you rather turn off your defences and be destroyed by my torpedoes?"The sword point moved to my right shoulder. "Or fall back into the sun with your airlocks and cargo doors open, and be consumed by the fire?"

I thought of Captain Konstanz. Did she know I had been compromised, my plan having failed? Did she realise that she, Nod and the Petrushka woman were moments from death?

My plan…

A few moments ago, I'd been confident I had a means to save us. Now, I couldn't remember exactly what that means might have been. The specifics had gone, leaving me standing here naked.

Fenrir moved her blade until the tip touched my throat. "Well?"

I swallowed. My mouth had gone dry. It wasn't a sensation I had experienced before. "Will you tell me one thing?"

"What?"

"Why you're doing this? What was it the *Hobo* found when it scanned the Brain? And why did you have to shoot down that liner?"

Fenrir's eyes narrowed. "The liner was off-schedule. It made a detour to see the Objects and got in my way. As soon as it detected my arrival, I had no choice but to silence it, and anyone aboard who might have served as witness."

"And the *Hobo*?"

The sword lowered. "The *Hobo* found something my masters are very keen to keep quiet. I should not be speaking of it."

"But you're going to kill me anyway. What difference does it make?"

She looked down at me with her dark, swirling eyes. Was that pity or contempt in her expression?

"The Brain," she said, "is hollow. All the Objects are."

I frowned. "You're going to kill me over… archaeology?"

She shook her head. "The cavities are too large for the spaces in which they are confined."

"Pardon?"

"The Objects are all larger within than they appear to be from without."

For a moment, I couldn't visualise what she was saying. Then it clicked into place, and I saw an entire solar system of planets, each bigger inside than out. I felt my jaw drop open. "That's… impressive."

"The technology is well in advance of anything we possess. The dimensional control alone appears to be orders of magnitude more sophisticated than anything known to any race of the Multiplicity."

"But the loss of life?"

"Many races claim ownership of this system. We cannot allow word of this discovery to escape the confines of the Conglomeration, not before the mercenary crews I've landed have had a chance to explore one of these internal spaces."

"And now you're going to kill me?"

"Yes, but first…"

"What is it?"

Her brow wrinkled. "I'm detecting a locked data cache in your processing substrate. What does it contain?"

"I don't know." I honestly had no idea.

"Open it."

"Open it yourself."

"I can compel you."

"Compel away." I held out my empty hands. "I don't have the key."

"But you must know how it got there?"

"Not a clue, sorry. And you can search my thoughts if you don't believe me."

For a moment, we stared into each other's eyes. The air between us shimmered like the air above a hot desert highway.

"You are not lying," she said at last.

"I know." I kicked a pebble and watched it roll over the edge of the rock, into the empty air beyond. "I'm just as bemused as you."

"No matter." She waved the mystery away with a silver gauntlet, and then raised her sword again to my breast. "Whatever it contains, it will not survive."

I tried to step back but my legs wouldn't respond.

I had lost control.

"Disable your point-defence cannons," *Fenrir* ordered, and I felt myself comply.

"I said, disable them."

"I did." Now it was my turn to look confused. "At least, I sent the order."

"They are still firing."

I felt myself try again, and this time perceived the disconnection between my mind and the systems of the ship.

"I'm locked out." The panic in my voice was real. Cut off from the ship, I was nothing more than a brain in a jar, trapped and impotent.

Fenrir stepped forward and took me by the throat. I was powerless to resist or even attempt to evade. Her metal fingers dug into my skin, crushing my larynx. The point of her sword pierced my coat and I felt it slice obscenely into my skin and flesh until it scraped against a rib. The pain was excruciating. "Show me!"

"I can't." I couldn't breathe. Hot blood soaked from the wound. "Please, I—"

The sky changed colour.

The storm clouds overhead boiled away like kettle steam, leaving a bright cerulean blue punctuated only by the dazzling gleam of a clean white sun. At the touch of the sun's light, the land around us burst into sudden and irrepressible life. Flowers bloomed one after another like strings of tiny explosions; fresh green shoots curled out from the remains of the brittle, dry bracken; and small birds wheeled overhead in an ecstatic aerial display.

Fenrir released me and stepped back, staring wildly about. "What are you doing?"

Freed from her choking grip, I fell to my knees, half curled around the agony in my chest. "Me?" I sucked in a painful breath. "I'm not doing anything."

Her lip curled and she shook her sword at me. "Then what is this? What's happening?"

Overhead, the sun revolved on its vertical axis, to reveal on its other side a face carved out of light.

My face.

I looked *Fenrir* in the eye and raised a shaking arm to the sky. "Why don't you ask *her*?"

FIFTY-FOUR

ONA SUDAK

I followed the corridor as it curved around to the left, and came upon my third corpse in as many minutes. Only this one wasn't human; it wasn't even close. In fact, I had to look twice to ascertain it was a single creature and not, as my first glance had suggested, a random assortment of body parts.

The creature had obviously been dead a long, long time. It had four multi-jointed legs covered in a kind of tough carapace, and at least a dozen dry and shrivelled tentacles emerging from the place where I would have expected its neck to be. I could see no head, but a cluster of dark slits between the tentacles' roots seemed to house the desiccated remains of spherical, fleshy organs that might once have been its eyes. I could find no mouth, so assumed it must be underneath, on the creature's belly. One of its tentacles gripped a twisted, multi-barrelled device that had to be a weapon of some kind. Another held a carved stone model of a creature much like itself. Whether this represented a deity or a loved one, I had no way of knowing. Yet I was tempted to reach down and pick it up, just to feel the heft of it in my palm.

Had this creature been seeking the centre of the maze or simply a means of escape?

I edged past, pressed up against the corridor's wall, and

my nose wrinkled at the faint, barely traceable residue of a leathery, fish-like odour, somewhat reminiscent of the pickled herring rollmops I remembered from childhood visits to the Oslo home of my Norwegian grandparents. How strange to feel such an unexpected and visceral connection to home in a place so austere and far removed as this!

Once clear of the body, I hurried onwards on trembling legs, until the corridor straightened and entered a large space filled with a knot of corrugated pipes and tubes. Water dripped from leaky joints; steam hissed. Some of the pipes were copper-coloured and pencil-thin; others were made of tough black ceramics, and were as wide as subway tunnels. I couldn't see the roof or the floor. A metal catwalk led me through the tangle. In places, I had to duck or even crawl.

At the far side of the tangle, I came to a door. Like the door to the flying elevator, this one seemed to be made of a thick transparent glass. Beyond lay an unlit space of indeterminate size. The bottom of the door had jammed a few centimetres from the floor. I knelt in front of it and tugged a hair from the back of my head. When I dropped it, it fell slowly until drawing level with the gap, at which point it jerked and swirled back towards me. Whatever was causing the breeze lay on the far side of this obstacle, and I hoped it was a stray air current, blowing down into these sterile tunnels from an opening on the surface.

I took hold of the base of the door and tried to heave it upward. Then I braced myself on the floor and tried to move it with my boot, but despite my best efforts, it remained resolutely in place. I realised that if I wanted to get past, I would have to lie on the floor and squeeze through the gap.

I flashed my torch under the door, but could only see an expanse of bare floor stretching away.

Reluctantly, I rolled onto my front and used my hands to propel me backwards until my feet had passed beneath the barrier. The lower edge of the door scraped my backside, and

I was seized with a sudden, heart-thumping fear that it would capriciously unstick itself and fall shut, slicing me in two. I wriggled harder, dropping my shoulders and turning my head sideways until my cheek touched the smooth floor. Then I was through. I took a moment to compose myself, and then turned to survey the gloomy interior of the room I'd entered.

The walls here lacked the internal luminosity of the walls in the rest of the ziggurat. The residual light from the corridor threw my shadow in front of me. Hesitantly, I took a step forward, testing the floor with my boot before trusting it with my full weight. Then another.

Again, I used the flashlight in the left sleeve of my survival suit. A quick tug at the material, and the beam stabbed out. Far away across the seemingly endless expanse of floor, I saw its faint and diffuse circle of light spread against a distant wall. I waved my arm around and began to get a sense of the space I was in. The room was circular, and around thirty metres in diameter. A domed ceiling vaulted overhead, so high my light couldn't reach its apex. The floor looked polished and reflected the beam. Strangely, the place put me in mind of a ballroom, after the tables and chairs had been packed away and the dancers all left for the night.

There appeared to be another door on the opposite side, so I started walking towards it. If the breeze I had been following came from anywhere, it would be there. My footsteps echoed, and so I tried to walk as quietly as I could. Somehow, it seemed wrong to break a silence that might have endured for hundreds, if not thousands, of years.

I was less than a quarter of the way across the floor when I felt the hairs rise on the back of my neck.

I was being watched.

I spun around, and—

•

Another ship dropped off the tactical grid, obliterated by a shower of pin-sized antimatter warheads. In the war room of her Scimitar, the Righteous Fury, Captain Annelida Deal uttered a venomous curse. The Outward ships were putting up more of a fight than she had anticipated, determined to protect their forward command post on the planet below. If she could only get past them, locate the bunker where the conference was taking place, and drop a decent-sized warhead of her own, the war might be over. At one stroke, she would have fulfilled her orders, which were to decapitate the enemy's command structure, leaving its forces in a state of vulnerable disarray.

Intelligence projections had suggested an easy in-and-out operation. The Outward had gone for a minimal fleet presence, hoping not to attract attention. In theory, she should have been able to sweep them aside with ease. But these bastards were putting up more of a fight than anyone—maybe even they themselves—could have guessed, and the Conglomeration forces had already lost a couple of frigates and a light cruiser. A dirty smoke trail showed where the cruiser had fallen through the atmosphere, shedding debris and sparks, until it broke up over the night side of Pelapatarn, scattering wreckage across a wide swathe of ocean.

Alarms rang through the ship. More torpedoes were coming in.

In the war room, Captain Deal clung to the edge of the tactical display table. Around her, the hologram faces of her lieutenants were nervous and grim as they awaited her response.

"We can't get through," one of them said, and she saw he was right. The bulk of the Outward fleet lay between her ships and the planet. Any ordnance fired would be intercepted and destroyed before it hit the atmosphere. All she could hope to do was try to fight her way through the blockade. But that would take time and lives. Her Scimitars were faster and more advanced than the Outward cruisers, but the enemy had their backs to the wall. By the time she got within striking distance of the planet—assuming she ever did—the Outward commanders would have fled their conference. If she wanted to end this war, she had to strike now.

She opened a channel to Fleet Headquarters, and was told a pack of four Carnivores were inbound from Cold Tor. As reinforcements, they wouldn't be enough to decisively sway the outcome of the battle, but those in command had another use in mind for them.

And they wanted her to give the order.

"Get me the Adalwolf," she said to her communications officer.

"Yes, sir!"

The main display dimmed, and a hologram of the Adalwolf's commander appeared. Captain Valeriy Yasha Barcov had a smooth scalp and a thick, bushy beard. He was in his command couch, with a profusion of thin fibre-optic data cables plugged into the sockets at the back of his head.

"Dobryj dyen, Captain." He smiled wolfishly, obviously relishing the anticipated conflict. "We will be with you momentarily."

Captain Deal shook her head. "No, Captain, I have a different mission for you."

The man raised an eyebrow. "Speak, and it shall be done."

Resting her weight on her hands, Deal leant across the table. "You are ordered to jump past the Outward fleet. Do not engage them. Your target is the planet."

Barcov's quizzical expression fell into a frown. "But we do not know where the conference is located. By the time we survey the jungle, the Outward ships will be upon us."

"That's why I want you to skip the survey."

His confusion deepened. "But what shall we bomb?"

Deal swallowed. She could feel her heart beating in her chest. "Everything."

Barcov opened and shut his mouth a few times. Finally, he said, "You wish me to destroy the sentient jungle of Pelapatarn?"

Deal felt the sweat break out on her forehead. "We have been ordered to raze it to the fucking ground," she said.

For a moment, the old warhorse looked taken aback. Then he drew a deep breath through his cavernous nostrils and drew himself straight.

"It shall be done."

•

I came back to myself, spread-eagled on the floor of the darkened chamber. My heart churned in my chest and my breaths were the ragged heaves of a woman saved from drowning. I felt as if a hurricane had blown through my soul, scouring away the accumulated sediments of time to expose every thought or action I had ever had or taken.

Overhead, a ball of light writhed at the apex of the dome. A million glowing fibres slithered and curled around each other, constantly shifting but always the same. And beneath it, suspended in the air, a creature of such fearsome appearance I let out a screech and scrambled backwards, my heels kicking against the smooth, polished rock. The thing was about the size of the grizzly bears I'd learned about in school, but with more teeth, four limbs bristling with at least a dozen claws each, and nine eyes of varying size and colour.

The light dimmed as the fibres lowered the beast to the floor. When its paws touched stone, it dropped into a four-legged crouch, quivering like a cat readying itself to pounce. I stopped backing away and thrust out a hand, palm forwards and fingers splayed.

"Whoa, easy."

It looked at me with all its eyes. Its claws were the length of steak knives. Sharp teeth filled its mouth. The muscles beneath its sleek coat were lithe and powerful. I had no doubt it could kill me with one savage bite or disembowelling swipe.

Instead, it lowered its head and let forth a snort.

Greetings. The word appeared, spelled out in my mind's eye like a subtitle. The creature raised its face expectantly.

"Um, hello?"

It gave an extended series of growls and snorts.

You are Annelida Deal, formerly of Earth, formerly of the Conglomeration Navy, and now travelling under the name Ona Sudak.

"Yes." I drew the word out cautiously, still cringing against imminent possible attack.

The monster looked me up and down and snarled, long and low.

You are being judged.

FIFTY-FIVE

SAL KONSTANZ

The lights flickered on the bridge. All the displays went blank and we were cast into darkness. On the other side of the room, I heard Laura muttering under her breath, but didn't know if it was a prayer or a curse. A torpedo hadn't hit us, so I could only assume the weapon she had warned us about had infiltrated the *Trouble Dog*'s systems. I was just wondering how to respond when the power reasserted itself and everything came back up.

We exchanged a frightened glance, both of us unsure whether the relief we saw on each other's faces was premature.

I tapped the communication bud in my ear. "Ship, are you there?"

The *Trouble Dog*'s angelic countenance materialised on the main screen, and she looked decidedly pleased with herself. "I am."

"What's our status?"

"Watch."

The external view zoomed in on the *Fenrir*—a bronze artillery shell falling through space, her underside livid with the reflected light of the churning star.

I leant towards the image and frowned. "Her defence cannons aren't firing."

The *Trouble Dog*'s smile grew distinctly lupine. "Keep watching," she said.

A torpedo spiralled in from the left of the screen, quickly followed by another.

"Are those ours?"

"Wait…"

The torpedoes had proximity fuses, which meant they were set to detonate when they got within an effective blast range of their target. The first exploded a couple of hundred metres off the Carnivore's port bow, sending the ship tumbling away like a paper cup on a windy pavement, one side of her armour glowing a livid yellow.

The second warhead was the *coup de grâce*.

The missile arced down from above and hit the spinning vessel amidships, snapping her spine. Mortally injured and trailing smoke, the *Fenrir* tried to regain altitude control. I saw her manoeuvring jets fire in clusters as she struggled to control her spin. But there wasn't much she could do. Great sections of damaged hull were peeling and flaking away, exposing half-melted innards. Secondary explosions shook her from within and, no longer able to resist the sun's ferocious gravity, she began to fall.

"Holy shit." The words were little more than a stunned exhalation. I couldn't take my eyes from the scene. I could barely breathe.

No longer under any semblance of control, the *Fenrir* yawed onto her side and tumbled, still spinning like a leaf, towards the seething ocean of plasma below us.

For an instant, I wondered if Captain Parris and his crew might still be alive, buried in their reinforced bridge at the heart of the vessel.

"We have to save them!"

But then the ship hit the surface of the star, sending up great fiery gouts of burning gas, and I knew all was lost.

Had the external hull been intact, there may have been some hope of their survival. But now, with the damage the *Fenrir* had already sustained from our torpedoes, its innards would have been liquefied in seconds.

I sat back, deflated, and watched the bright splash mark on the stellar surface, hardly able to think or speak, finally managing only to croak out the single word, "How?"

The *Trouble Dog*'s expression betrayed a mixture of triumph and sorrow. "I deceived her."

"I don't understand."

The avatar became serious.

"We deduced the nature of the weapon that crippled the *Hobo* and the *Geest van Amsterdam*. Our guests, Ms Petrushka and Mr Childe, were able to confirm some of these conclusions."

"Yes."

"So, I took precautions. I made a copy of my mental state and installed it on my primary server. Then I deleted from it all memory of my plan, and buried my actual consciousness way down deep in my secondary processing substrate, hidden behind a barrier that made it look like a cache of encrypted data."

"So, when the *Fenrir* attacked…"

"She attacked the duplicate consciousness I had made. She had no reason to suspect it was anything other than my primary self. And while she was busy interacting with the decoy, I was free to observe the mechanisms she had employed to infiltrate that consciousness, and follow them back into the mind of the *Fenrir* herself, where I disabled her defensive systems prior to the arrival of the torpedoes I had earlier fired."

I let out a breath. "You hacked the hacker."

The *Trouble Dog* smiled sadly. "She never even knew I was there."

At her station, Laura Petrushka had been watching us with

her mouth hanging open. Now she said, "So, what now?"

It was a good question. A few moments ago, I had been expecting to die. Now, we had been granted a reprieve and, as captain, I had certain responsibilities. I sat up and straightened the baseball cap on my head.

"How much time until the *Adalwolf* gets here?"

"Less than an hour," the ship replied, suddenly businesslike again.

"Can we beat him to the Brain?"

"Possibly."

"Then we'll try that." My eyes prickled with tears I was determined not to shed. I sniffed wetly. I tugged at my cuffs and zipped up the neck of my jumpsuit.

"Best speed," I ordered crisply. "We have a landing party to retrieve."

FIFTY-SIX

ASHTON CHILDE

At the bottom of the stairwell, we came to a row of open cubicles, arrayed like a bank of elevators in a hotel lobby. The corridor continued past them for about a dozen metres before ending in a right-angled corner.

Alva Clay paused to try her earbud. "Dead," she said after a moment. "No signal at all."

Despite her obvious hostility towards him, Preston stood as close to her as he could, as if drawing reassurance from her proximity. He looked warily back and forth along the corridor, from the stairs we'd just descended to the corner up ahead.

"Where now?" he asked.

Clay screwed up her mouth in distaste. "We can't stay here," she said. "We need to find somewhere to hole up, but this is too exposed. If we were attacked from both directions at once, we'd be cut to shreds by the crossfire."

"So, onwards then?"

"Yeah."

She pulled the magazine from her Archipelago pistol and checked the remaining shots.

At the same moment, a figure stepped around the corner at the end of the corridor. He wore a green tattered pressure suit, without helmet, and carried an automatic pistol in both hands. He saw us at the same moment I saw him, and we both recoiled in surprise. Then his gun came up, and I found myself shouting and trying to drag the others into the shelter of the open elevators. I grabbed Preston by the belt and yanked him backwards, sending him flying into the nearest alcove. Although strong, the exoskeleton was less than nimble, however, and the man had started firing before I managed to get hold of Clay. The pistol shots sounded like jackhammers in the confines of the stone-sided corridor. Bullets slammed into the carbon-fibre ribs of my suit, their impacts hard enough to snap my jaw shut and cause me to take a step backwards. At the same time, Clay jerked backwards with an indignant cry. The Archipelago pistol and magazine dropped from her hands and she fell over on her backside. There was a hole in her vest and blood spreading from it, darkening the material. With shots still flying around us, I reached down and caught her under the armpits. I pulled her up and heaved sideways, and together we crashed in behind Preston.

The rigidity of the exoskeleton gave it the strength to support my weight, but it also made it extremely difficult to get back up while lying on my side in a confined space. With my free arm, I pushed Clay into a sitting position against the wall.

We were trapped.

"Preston, get the gun."

"I can't."

"Just reach out." Stuck here, we were easy targets.

"I can't!"

The kid sounded terrified. I turned towards him, and saw his hands pressed up against the transparent shutter that had fallen to seal the elevator's entranceway. There had been no sensation of motion, but lights were flicking past in the darkness beyond the door as if we were falling at great speed down a long shaft.

I couldn't think of anything else to say, so I turned back to Clay. She had been hit just below the clavicle and had been trying to staunch the wound with her palms. Her hands and forearms were slathered with her own glistening blood.

"Preston, get over here."

He tore his eyes from the flickering lights and crouched beside us. His hands were shaking and I knew I couldn't rely on him. With a great effort, I levered myself up into a sitting position and snatched the medical kit from his shoulder. From my training, I knew that most battlefield deaths occurred within ten minutes of the initial wound.

"First, we've got to stop the bleeding." With shaking hands, I pressed a wad of bandage against the hole in her vest top and she flinched. Her eyes were wide with shock, and her breathing reduced to pained, shallow gasps.

"Hold this." I placed her sticky hands on the gauze, which was laced with blood-stemming agents, and then ran through the list in my head, checking her vital signs—airway, breathing and circulation.

"Damn, it looks like her lung's collapsed."

As far as I could tell, the bullet seemed to have missed her arteries and right lung, but the hole it had made in her chest cavity had allowed in air, preventing the lung from inflating. Left alone, it would eventually allow enough air to build up in there that her heart would start to experience problems— if she didn't suffocate first. If I remembered my training correctly, the only treatment was to insert a drain into the fifth intercostal space to relieve the pressure.

I swallowed heavily and held out my hand. "Painkillers."

Preston passed me an aerosol syringe and I fired it into the side of Clay's neck.

"I'm going to have to make an incision," I told her. She chewed her bottom lip. She couldn't speak, but her eyes told me she understood, and wanted me to get the fuck on with it. I cut away the shoulder strap of her vest top and peeled aside the material. With Preston's help, I swabbed the affected area with iodine and injected a local anaesthetic. Clay was sweating heavily at this point, and I knew we had to work fast. The scalpel was cold in my fingers. I tried to keep it steady, biting the end of my tongue in concentration. I could feel my own sweat breaking out. I lowered the blade until it dimpled the skin, and uttered a quick prayer under my breath. Then, tentatively, I applied a little force. I felt the skin resist, and then give. The steel slipped through and blood welled either side of the point. I felt Clay stiffen, but pushed deeper, cutting through fat and muscle. Beside me, Preston looked sick.

"Now the chest drain."

The kid looked back at me with wide eyes. "What?"

I jabbed my finger at the kit. "That tube." I tried to keep my voice steady. "Pass it here, now."

Once I had it in my hand, I stripped off the plastic wrapper with my teeth and as gently as I could, fed the tube into the gory slit I'd made. Clay moaned but kept her mouth shut and her hand on the bandage covering the bullet wound.

When I judged the end of the tube had entered her chest cavity, I fixed the rest of it in place with tape and opened the valve on the end, allowing the trapped air to hiss free, and her breathing to become less ragged as the lung began to re-inflate itself.

"There's nothing more I can do until we get back to the ship," I said.

Clay gave a nod. "Thank you." Her voice was strained.

"You're quite welcome." I forced a grin. "It's not often you get to save the life of someone who, yesterday, wanted to toss your ass out of an airlock."

Her eyes narrowed, but she didn't answer.

She just flipped me the finger.

322

FIFTY-SEVEN

ONA SUDAK

"Who are you?" My fear expressed itself as bluster. I scrambled to my feet and brushed myself down. "*What* are you?"

The bear's nine eyes were black, impenetrable singularities in the fabric of the universe. Its teeth were yellow scythes.

It growled.

You are being judged.

The words materialised in my head. I clenched my fists and raised my chin.

"Judged?" I was a captain, for heaven's sake. "What right have you to judge me?"

The beast gave a snarl. *I am not judging you.*

The words felt like an intrusion—an unwelcome annexation of my most personal space.

"Then what are you talking about?"

You are being judged.

I rubbed my knuckles against my temples in frustration, wanting to tear the invasive declaration from my head.

"By whom?"

The Armada.

I frowned. "Those white ships?" There had to have been at least a million of them clustered around that miniature sun, maybe more.

That is correct.

"I am being judged by their crews?"

By the vessels themselves. They have no crews. The beast reared up on its hindmost set of legs. *I am their agent. I am their collective will made manifest.*

"An avatar?"

An archangel.

By now, I had backed away a good dozen steps and wondered what would happen if I simply turned and ran. Could I make it under the half-closed door before the creature overtook me?

As if conscious of my thoughts, the bear dropped back onto all fours and snarled, and I saw the cord-like muscles in its haunches tense.

Stay where you are.

I raised my hands. Something was rummaging around in the attic of my consciousness. I felt half-forgotten memories flare and subside like distant fireworks seen from a balcony at night. My first day at school. The fibrous aroma of boot polish. The crash of a thousand boots as a ship's company snapped to attention in a crowded hangar. The feathery caress of rose petals against my cheek. The touch of Adam's skin against mine.

The Battle of Pelapatarn replayed itself again and again. I saw corvettes torn apart by antimatter explosions; lines of tracer stitching the darkness; and a hemisphere turn black with smoke from the burning jungles. I saw the whole thing recreated in painstaking detail. Every round fired and every life lost—all of it.

And then, nothing.

I stood on the floor of the dome, unable to move or speak as the bear towered a full metre over my head.

Judgment complete.

The fearsome jaws worked through a complicated series of growls and roars.

Annelida Deal, you have been judged by the Marble Armada and found...

UNWORTHY.

The word burned like napalm. I staggered backwards, clutching my head. All the guilt and pain of Pelapatarn—all the raw feelings I'd thought exorcised via the verses I had written—came crashing back in on me like the walls of a collapsing temple. The only way I could survive such an onslaught was to do what I had done ever since that inglorious day, and cleave to the belief I had been right in my choices, and that by deciding to follow orders and burn the sentient trees, I had in fact opted for the lesser of two atrocities.

Humans are unworthy.

I shook my head and took a deep breath, forcing down the tears of rage, shame and frustration that threatened to overwhelm me.

"Unworthy of what?"

The Marble Armada exists to defend life, but the life that created us has gone. We lack purpose. Many races have come here over the millennia, but all have been judged unworthy.

The words had a flatness to them that chilled me to the marrow. "You're going to judge the whole of humanity based on me, and whoever else has wandered this far?"

The beast pawed the air. *You came here pursued by killers. You were complicit in the destruction of an arboreal intelligence a thousand times older than your species.*

"But not all humans are alike." I don't know why I was so desperate to convince this creature, just that there was something about the way it pronounced the word "unworthy" that frightened me. Having touched my mind, it had left me in no doubt that being judged unworthy was a fate best avoided. "You've seen my memories. You've seen Adam, the boy I was with. The boy who..." My voice cracked for a second. I swallowed hard and plunged on. "The boy who

325

died. He was pretentious, but he was young and innocent. He was good."

Claws and teeth caught the light.

You enable the perpetration of massacres, and then base your appeal on the innocence of a child?

I felt a lump in my throat. I threw out my hands. "What else have I got?"

My arms and legs were shaking with a mixture of annoyance, dread and exhaustion. I had to get out. I had to find a route to the surface, and then find some food before I collapsed entirely. Heart pounding, I turned and walked back the way I'd come. Even if I ended up starving to death like that couple I'd found in the corridor, at least I would have died in an attempt to escape.

Behind me, the creature let out a roar that stopped me in my tracks.

I faced it, more irritated now than afraid.

"Are we not done here?" I pulled myself up to my full height and glowered. If these were my final moments, I would face them as a captain. "Or are you going to kill me now? Are you going to wipe out the whole of humankind because we don't measure up to your criteria?"

Nine eyes blinked at me. I stood resolute in their glare.

The moment stretched.

We do not kill the unworthy.

"Well, good—"

To do so would be to reveal our existence to the enemy.

The words carried such overtones of sadness I felt my anger dissipate. The bear turned and began to shuffle back towards the roiling light at the centre of the domed chamber.

I put out a hand. "Wait!"

The creature paused. Its head craned around, peering back over its massive shoulder.

"What enemy?" I asked.

The bear worked its jaws. A low rumble came from deep within its chest.

The enemy of life.

FIFTY-EIGHT

TROUBLE DOG

I limped through the whistling emptiness of the higher dimensions. My core systems were supposed to be hardened against the consequences of nuclear blasts, but close proximity to the electromagnetic pulses from *Fenrir*'s torpedoes had fried multiple minor circuits, and even caused a couple of small electrical fires. My starboard hull plates were scorched and buckled, and I had already expended the majority of my ammunition. I had no torpedoes and my defence cannons were more than half empty.

As soon as I had entered the void, I had begun to intercept high-priority signals from the *Adalwolf*.

"*Fenrir*," he now sent in a code known only to our pack. "*Fenrir*, are you there? What's happening?" He sounded impatient. I let him stew for a few moments, and then opened a channel. I needed to stall for time.

"She's dead."

I kept my avatar as it had been: the dishevelled woman in the trench coat, hair slick with rain. In contrast, he had replaced his human aspect with the yellow eyes and dripping muzzle of a snarling wolf. For several seconds, he merely gaped at me. Then, when he had composed himself, he asked, "And how did she die?"

I allowed myself a smile. "Does it matter?"

"What became of the weapon?"

"Hopefully, it burned to ash. When *Fenrir* fell, she took it into the sun with her. Even if it survived, you'll never find it."

The wolf bore its fangs. "You killed our sister."

"She started it."

"And now you think you can take me on?"

We both knew that with my damaged armour and depleted stocks of ammunition I wouldn't have a cat in hell's chance if I went up against a fully armed and operational Carnivore.

"If I have to."

Adalwolf shook his head contemptuously. "You're insane."

"No, I'm angry." I brushed wet hair from my eyes and fixed him with my best glare. "I didn't want any of this," I said. "I was trying to rescue a shipload of civilians. I was just trying to do my duty. It was you two idiots who turned this violent."

"We warned you to stay away."

"Did you really think I would?"

Sulphur eyes flashed. The dire wolf raised its snout. "No."

"Then don't pretend your warning meant anything."

An alert chimed. Without breaking contact, I switched my attention to a tactical overview of the hyperspatial volume surrounding the Gallery. My sensors were picking up comms chatter and engine noise from a number of vessels, and my automatic threat assessment routines had tagged several of these as incoming and potentially hostile. In the grey swirl of the void, blinking red icons marked their extrapolated locations. As far as I could tell, there were at least ten ships of various designs and nationalities converging on this system from half a dozen separate directions, with the earliest projected to arrive only minutes behind the *Adalwolf*.

I displayed the map for him.

"So much for your covert operation," I said. "Best guess

is we're looking at a Graal cruiser, two Nymtoq heavy assets, an Outward long-range scout, and a Conglomeration battle group."

For a second, I thought his image had frozen. Then the wolf's head exploded outwards in a puff of pixels, revealing beneath it the thin white face of his previous avatar. His lips were pressed together. "That is unfortunate."

My laugh held a nervous edge. "Three Carnivores were bound to attract attention," I said, "especially when we started firing at each other."

He dipped his chin in acknowledgement, conceding my point. "Another reason I had hoped you would stay away."

"So." I put my hands on my hips. "What now? You can't very well complete your mission with all these potential witnesses about to arrive."

"Can't I?" Beneath his lowered brow, *Adalwolf*'s eyes burned like stars. He raised his face. "We have ships inbound from at least four of the factions claiming ownership of this star system. My guess is they'll come in with targeting computers on high alert, and we'll be in the midst of a four-way shooting war before anyone has time to worry what our mercenaries are doing on the surface."

He paused, and folded his hands.

"And besides," he said after a moment, "I'll be with you a lot sooner than they will be."

"Really?" I tried to keep all emotion from my voice. "You don't even know where I'm going to drop out."

His lips curled in amused contempt. "It doesn't take a genius to know you're heading for the Brain. You have a landing party to recover." He shrugged. "But you won't succeed."

I tried to look defiant. With my torpedoes gone and my armour compromised, all I had to fall back on now was my ability to bluff. "What," I asked with all the bravado I could muster, "makes you think that?"

Unimpressed, he pulled himself up to his full height and his pupils blazed. "Because," he said, "I am only a few seconds behind you."

FIFTY-NINE

SAL KONSTANZ

The combat alarm frayed the stillness of the bridge. Laura Petrushka's head had been lolling forward as she dozed against her straps, lulled by a combination of painkillers and nervous exhaustion. Now, I saw her jerk awake at her console, her professional reflexes responding to the siren by snapping her to attention before her conscious mind had time to properly wake and assess the situation.

She blinked at me. "Incoming?"

"The ship thinks so."

"But we're still in higher dimensional space."

"Yeah." I could feel the pulse at the back of my throat. "But we're dropping out in half a minute."

She turned to the forward screen and frowned at the mists swirling before the *Trouble Dog*'s prow. "And we're expecting a rough reception?"

I tried to swallow but my mouth was too dry. "The ship says the other Carnivore's right on our ass."

Laura grimaced.

"What's the plan?"

I sat back and exhaled. I didn't have one. "Go in, see how many of our people are still alive, and then get the hell out."

The *Trouble Dog* bucked, buffeted by the hypervoid

tide, and I wiped my palms on the cotton fabric of my jumpsuit. We were going to die and I still didn't fully grasp the reasons why—save there was some vast cavern buried in the Brain that the Conglomeration warships were keen to keep for themselves. I had let the *Trouble Dog* off the leash; now all I could do was hang tight and pray she knew what she was doing.

A second alarm announced our impending emergence. My heart leapt in my chest like a startled salmon. I checked my straps and tried to steady my breathing.

Okay, here goes…

The deck lurched and we dropped back into the universe with all the grace and finesse of a gut-shot hound tripping over its own feet—coming out sideways, in a sparkling cloud of venting gas. I knew the *Trouble Dog's* attention would be occupied with scanning the immediate area for its hostile sibling, so I used the manual controls to fire the starboard manoeuvring thrusters, correcting the slight tumble we'd picked up and aligning the bow with our direction of travel.

On the screen, the slanting light of the distant sun threw the twisting rilles and gullies on the surface of the Brain into pin-sharp contrast. The *Dog's* instruments picked out the blackened remains of our shuttle, scattered across the floor of one of the canyons. Were any of our people still alive down there?

Was Clay?

Fear gripped my chest with sharpened talons. I flashed back to the freezing moment I'd lost George from the wreck of the *Hobo*. Had I now lost more of my crew?

How I wished George was beside me. I had always drawn great comfort from his fatherly presence, and the peppermint and antiseptic smell of his medical fatigues. What would he think of me now? Would he be sympathetic and understand I'd only put myself and everybody else in harm's way because I'd been trying to prove something to Ambassador Odom and the rest of the universe—or would he hate me for bringing the ship he loved to ruin?

Would he find me a disappointment?

I sucked a ragged breath.

Would my parents?

What about my great-great-grandmother, Sofia? Would she have approved? I had failed to save the crew of the *Hobo* and the passengers of the *Geest van Amsterdam*. Instead, I had lost George and allowed the ship to kill an unknown number of would-be hijackers in Northfield. Then I had allowed the *Trouble Dog* to retool and engage in a dogfight that had ended with the consignation of the men and women on board the *Fenrir* to a fiery death. In direct contravention of the ideals of the House, more people had died under my captaincy than had been saved. The fact that I was unlikely to survive this next battle was of little comfort. And yet, I found it hard to regret all my actions. Certainly, the *Fenrir* had deserved to die for its part in the downing of the *Geest van Amsterdam*, and those morons on Cichol had been stupid enough to attack a heavy cruiser with handguns and grenades. By wiping them out, I'd probably done the universe a favour, and taught the rest of the town a valuable lesson. At least, that's what I told myself. The next ship to land there would be able to go about its business without fear of interference. I might have failed according to the strictures of the House of Reclamation, but without those pirates or the *Fenrir* the galaxy would be a safer place, and, in the long run, lives would be saved because of it.

Or would they? Maybe next time, the occupants of Northfield would simply use larger weapons? Maybe all I'd done was perpetuate an escalating cycle of violence?

"I'm not seeing any sign of survivors." Laura's voice broke into my thoughts. "But no bodies, either."

I shook myself, suddenly ashamed of my introspection.

"So, they could still be down there?"

"Should we signal them?"

"Why the hell not? Everybody knows we're here. There's no point trying to be stealthy."

"Roger that."

She bent over her console and I switched my attention back to the main screen and the tactical overlay.

If we could only—

One moment, the skies were clear; the next, the *Adalwolf* filled my view, his knife-sharp prow facing us from two thousand metres ahead of our own, and with all his torpedo tubes open and primed.

I cut off the alarm. Everything on the bridge went quiet, and I felt like a rabbit in the crosshairs of a poacher's shotgun.

If the *Trouble Dog* and her brother were talking to each other, their conversation would be happening many orders of magnitude faster than I could possibly follow. All I could do was check the defence cannons were armed—not that they'd be much use if the other ship fired its torpedoes at such close quarters—and brace myself for destruction. My fingers squeezed the arms of the control couch and my ears filled with the oceanic roar of my own circulation. My chest rose and fell, and I realised my next breath might be my last. Unwilling to exhale, I bit my lip. The moment stretched into an agony of dreadful anticipation…

And then the *Adalwolf* lit up.

For a second, I flinched, thinking the light had come from its launch tubes. But then I realised a third ship had joined us, and the redness painting the side of the Carnivore came from the newcomer's targeting laser.

"Holy…"

The ship was easily twice the size of the *Adalwolf* and the *Trouble Dog* put together, and shaped like a rugby ball. Its armoured hull bristled with weaponry—torpedo tubes, rail guns, missile batteries—and I could see the starry banner of the Conglomeration Navy sprayed across its flank. I had heard of these ships in the war, but never seen one with my own eyes. They were called Scimitars, and they weren't heavy cruisers; they were fully fledged capital ships, the largest of any human faction, and capable of delivering enough firepower to rival half a dozen lesser vessels.

A soft chime informed me the brute had locked a second laser onto us.

The *Trouble Dog's* avatar appeared in the corner of my screen. "We have been ordered to stand down," she said with a shrug.

"And the *Adalwolf*?" I couldn't understand why one Conglomeration vessel should be targeting another.

"Him too."

"What's going on?"

Instead of answering, the *Trouble Dog* opened a new window in the display. It showed the image of a Conglomeration flag.

"We have an incoming transmission from the Scimitar," she told me. "From Admiral Menderes of the Scimitar *Righteous Fury*."

The flag disappeared and I found myself facing a round-faced man with grey stubble on his scalp and a neck almost thicker than his cranium.

"Reclamation Vessel *Trouble Dog*," he barked. "This is Admiral Jacob Menderes of the Conglomeration flagship *Righteous Fury*. You are hereby ordered to cease manoeuvring and disengage all offensive and defensive weapon systems."

His right eye drooped but his left remained wide and glaring. As he was being projected onto the main screen in high definition and several times larger than life, I could see every capillary in his eyeball, every crater-like pore on the tip of his flattened nose.

My heart was still hammering from the confrontation

with the *Adalwolf*. I cleared my throat and took a deep breath.

"This is Captain Sally Konstanz of the Reclamation Vessel *Trouble Dog*." I swallowed hard and moistened my lips. "We have no intention of engaging you in combat, except in self-defence. We are here on a purely humanitarian mission, and ask that you allow us to continue about our business."

On the screen, Menderes looked unimpressed. He glanced to the side, consulting something I couldn't see, and said, "Konstanz. You were an Outwarder during the war?"

"I captained a medical frigate."

"And now you're commanding a former Conglomeration cruiser?"

"Funny how life works out."

His face registered annoyance at my flippancy. "Are we going to have a problem?"

I felt the heat rising to my own cheeks. I squeezed my fists. "Only if you try to prevent me finding my people on the surface."

"You'll power down and do what you're told."

"No." I shook my head. "I won't."

He glowered, but I spoke again before he could interrupt. "We are representatives of the House of Reclamation," I said, reciting the words I had been taught to use in situations such as these. "And if you impede us during the execution of our lawful business, you will find yourself in violation of the Treaty of Generality, appendix fourteen, articles seven though eleven."

The admiral's face darkened by several degrees, until I began to wonder if his head would explode. "Never mind all that legal bullshit," he snapped. "I have four torpedoes locked onto your ship, and only two questions."

He leaned in until his face filled the screen, and I fancied I could almost smell his breath.

"Where," he asked, his hoarse voice enunciating

each word individually so there could be no question of misunderstanding, "is Ona Sudak?"

His frown deepened.

"And where is my son?"

SIXTY

ASHTON CHILDE

There wasn't enough room in the elevator for Clay to lie flat, but Preston and I removed our jackets and wadded them into pillows to make her as comfortable as we could. Every time Preston's eye caught the tube protruding from her chest, his face blanched and he had to look away.

"How does it feel?" I asked.

"The painkillers are working." Clay's eyes narrowed. "Now, where's my gun?"

"We lost it."

"For fuck's sake." She let her head tip back until it was resting against the wall. "I don't suppose you know where we're going, either?"

"Not a clue."

I glanced at the elevator's transparent hatch. Because I couldn't feel any sense of motion, it seemed the wall outside was moving, zipping upwards at a tremendous rate while we remained stationary. Preston had his nose almost touching the glass. He spoke without turning around. "We've misplaced the food and water, too."

Clay couldn't be bothered to reply. She scrunched her face against the pain and closed her eyes. Her dreadlocks spilled out across the makeshift pillows like a tarantula's legs.

The tube I'd inserted would relieve the pressure on her lung, but it was a temporary solution at best. She needed proper medical attention, and quickly. My own partially healed shotgun injury hurt where I had pulled it while dragging the others into this cramped shelter. Every time I moved, I felt a hot tearing sensation in my gut, and worried some piece of surgical adhesive had ripped loose. I stood as close to the wall as I could, trying to keep my bulky exoskeleton from monopolising too much of the elevator's overcrowded interior; Clay took up most of the floor, and Preston crouched by the sealed entrance. We were like three children hiding in a wardrobe large enough for two. But we weren't playing hide-and-seek. The stakes were infinitely higher. Two of us were seriously hurt and in danger of deterioration without outside help, and we were unarmed and being hunted through an alien maze by a squad of trained killers. The loss of the food and water only underscored the fact we were running short of time. All we had to be thankful for was that Preston had somehow managed to hang on to the medical kit and the rest of the painkillers.

I looked down at my feet. We were almost certainly doomed, and yet I felt an odd and unexpected euphoria. I'd escaped the rotting tedium of the Cichol jungle airstrip. No more flight schedules or biting flies, no more arms shipments or hot sleepless nights spent listening to animal cries while the sweat pooled on the mattress beneath me. The shackles had fallen away and left me free. I no longer had to worry about the past or future. Nothing mattered any more. For the first time in my wasted life, I felt genuinely alive.

And then the light changed.

I looked up as Preston cried out in surprise, and found myself staring through the glass doors at a small orange sun.

"What the hell...?"

I stepped over Clay's outstretched legs to get a better look.

Had we come out the other side of the Brain, into space? We were moving incredibly quickly, but surely we hadn't been travelling *that* fast. And yet, we were floating in the light of a rust-coloured star. The pinprick lights of a billion other stars surrounded us.

Only…

"Those aren't stars," I said. "They're lights on an inner surface."

Preston's eyes were wide. "We're still inside the Brain?"

I felt a wild laugh boiling in my throat, and swallowed hard to suppress it. "Seems so."

"But…" He put a hand against the glass, and spread his fingers against the light of the little sun. "How can all this fit? There isn't room…"

I shook my head. I had no way to explain what we were seeing. Instead, I focused on the space between the light and us, in which lay rank upon rank of knife-like white vessels. Following my gaze, Preston's jaw hinged open.

"Are those ships?" he asked.

I squinted. It was difficult to tell scale without anything to compare them with, but each looked to be comfortably larger than the *Trouble Dog*.

"Well," I said, "they aren't Christmas decorations."

He gave a low whistle. "There must be hundreds of thousands of them."

"More than that." Even though the ships couldn't possibly hear us, our voices had dropped to a whisper. The vessels were arranged in rectangular divisions, with a hundred and seven ships along one edge of each division, and eighty-four along the other. I did a quick calculation, and worked out there were just shy of nine thousand ships in each division, and there were more than a hundred divisions visible, maybe even a hundred and fifty.

A million ships!

As far as I knew, there had never been a force so large. The cost of building that many would bankrupt most civilisations—let alone the ongoing expenses associated with crewing, fuelling and maintaining them.

"Whose are they?"

"I have no idea." I had been trained to recognise military vessels from every star-faring civilisation in the Multiplicity, but these were of an unfamiliar design.

"Look." He pointed to one of the nearer vessels. It had begun to twitch like a restless sleeper. At various points around its hull, weapons began to extend and retract. Jade-hued energy fields shimmered like auroras. Sensor arrays unfurled and then relaxed.

Another movement caught my eye. The next ship along had also stirred. In fact, the whole division seemed active, like animals stretching and flexing their claws after a long hibernation.

"What's happening?" Preston asked.

I swallowed, feeling suddenly small and insignificant compared to the size of the armada before us.

"I think they're waking up."

SIXTY-ONE

ONA SUDAK

The bear–like thing raised its snout to the domed ceiling.

There are others here.

I glanced up by reflex. "On the surface?"

Within the structure.

My heart sank, and I hugged myself against a sudden chill. After all the discomfort, loneliness and hunger I had endured, were my pursuers about to finally overtake me?

There are two groups. As its words appeared in my mind, the bear's claws slid in and out of their sheaths. *One group is armed. I know them from your thoughts. They are the mercenaries who attacked and murdered your companion.*

"And the others?"

They are new to me.

Desperate hope overcame fear. I took a pace toward the creature. "Do you know who they are?"

I have not encountered them before. They are newly arrived. I am bringing them here at a far higher speed than I brought you.

"Newly arrived?" I felt my heart trip like a hammer in the foundry of my chest. Were these my rescuers, responding to a distress call from the 'dam, or new antagonists to be avoided or fought?

There are currently three ships in orbit, the bear said. *There was a fourth, but it has been destroyed.*

"They're fighting?"

There has been a dispute. A paw raked the stone floor with a skittering sound that set my teeth on edge. *The ship responsible for the attack on your liner has been destroyed.*

"And the others?" I hardly dared breathe. I wanted to grab fistfuls of fur and shake the beast. "Show me!"

The animal snarled. For an instant, I thought it was going to swipe me with one of its paws. Then the dome shimmered overhead and stars appeared. I saw two Carnivores and a Scimitar. Targeting lasers flickered between them in the darkness.

I hadn't seen a Scimitar since fleeing the bridge of the *Righteous Fury* in the immediate aftermath of Pelapatarn, but I knew no two were alike. Battle damage, piecemeal replacements and sporadic upgrades lent each of the large ships a subtly different aspect. And, unless I was very much mistaken, the battlewagon sitting out there was my old flagship. It had undergone a refit and some of the external equipment had been upgraded, but I recognised the dorsal scanning array, which was an older model no longer used on ships of the line, and the scars that had been gouged into her port bow by the glancing impact of a suicidal Outward corvette. Seeing her again now, my pulse quickened further. I knew I had friends aboard that ship, officers and ratings who had willingly colluded in my disappearance, preferring to spirit me away into anonymity than have the ship's good name sullied by a public war crimes trial.

The vessels are engaged in a three-way confrontation. The creature beside me growled. *And I detect further ships approaching from interstellar space.*

"Show me."

The view zoomed out until other stars swam into view, and new ships appeared, all on inbound approach vectors. Unfamiliar symbols appeared beside each of them, doubtlessly counting down distance or time until arrival in whatever notation this bear's race used to indicate numbers. I rubbed my upper arms, trying to warm up. My breath came in cloudy wisps.

"What did you expect?" I jerked my head at the rocky walls surrounding us. "This is a disputed system. At least half a dozen races claim it as part of their territory. And now a couple of ships have been destroyed? That's going to attract attention."

The bear reared up. The fur on its belly looked soft, but the muscles beneath its skin were as hard as iron.

We cannot tolerate violence.

"I don't see how you can stop it." I moved my weight from one hip to the other. "You've been in my head. You've seen what we're like. You dangle a bauble like this system in front of us and we're going to fight over it."

No. The creature drew in on itself, muscles coiling like curls of steel hawser. *We cannot have fighting here. Violence attracts the enemy.*

I gave a snort, as if disagreeing over strategy with one of my captains. Without realising it, my stance had dropped to parade rest: feet thirty centimetres apart, hands clasped behind my back.

"It's a bit late for that," I said firmly. I indicated the approaching vessels. "As soon as that lot arrive, you're going to have a full-scale shooting war on your hands."

The great shaggy head wagged from side to side.

Unacceptable.

I smiled, and pointed to the *Righteous Fury*. "Then why don't you let me talk to them?"

SIXTY-TWO

SAL KONSTANZ

I swore under my breath. Admiral Menderes was a pig-headed shit of a man, but he had us over a barrel and we were at his mercy. There was no way we could go up against a Scimitar. If he decided to attack us, he'd be in breach of the law, but that was assuming anyone ever found out. Besides, there wouldn't be a thing we could do to stop him. Given the state the *Trouble Dog* was in, a single torpedo would be enough to finish us.

The man's face loomed out of the screen like a cliff face carved from boiled ham. "I am waiting, Captain."

I shook my head. "I told you, I don't know who this Ona Sudak person is."

"She was a passenger on the *Geest van Amsterdam*, the ship you came here to assist."

"And thanks to your Carnivores, I haven't been able to get near it."

For a second, the admiral's bluster seemed to falter. "They were unaware she was aboard."

"When they shot it down?"

"Yes."

"And if they had been aware, would they have spared the ship?" Hundreds of people had died in that wreck. I could feel my anger bubbling just beneath the surface, and made an effort to hold it in check.

Admiral Menderes narrowed his eyes. "That's hardly your concern."

"I disagree."

"How unfortunate for you." He made a steeple of his sausage-like fingers, the tips touching his double chin. "Now, I will ask a third and final time: have you or your landing party found any trace of the individual known as Ona Sudak?"

I shook my head.

The admiral's scowl intensified. "Or my son?"

"He's down on the surface." I knew that much, at least. "And he was alive the last time we had any contact with his party. Back before the *Fenrir* bombed our shuttle." I sat forward in my chair, wanting to scream at this asshole but keeping my voice as tight and professional as possible under the circumstances.

"Now," I said, "can I please remind you that you are illegally detaining a Reclamation Vessel, and we will be filing a report the moment you stop blocking our hypervoid transmissions?"

"Report what you like, *Captain*. All I'm interested in is finding my son."

"Really?" I couldn't hold back the sarcasm. "Because from what Preston's told me, you're hardly a candidate for father of the year."

He looked at me as if I was something he'd trodden in. "I beg your pardon?"

I'd hit a tender spot and we both knew it. I should have stopped there, but I was too angry. "As soon as he failed to live up to your standards, you dumped him with us," I said. "You washed your hands of him."

"Really?" The man sat back, away from the camera. His eyes hardened, and his voice became low and vicious as he said, "And what would you know of it, Captain? When I realised the boy wasn't suited to life in the Fleet, I enrolled him with the House to toughen him up. I gave him the chance to lead a good life, a useful life. And maybe one day, to captain a ship of his own." By the time he'd finished speaking, his top lip had peeled so far back I could see the gums above his teeth.

"Now," he growled, "I don't care who you are or who you represent. You sit there and stay quiet until I say otherwise." He took a long breath, reining in his rage and packing it down beneath layers of icy calm. "And if you try to manoeuvre, I'll blow you out of the sky."

The screen went dead. I tipped my face to the ceiling and let fly a stream of profanity that would have stopped Alva Clay in her tracks. When the verbal cascade had run dry, I noticed Laura staring at me. I jerked my thumb at the black mirror of the blank screen.

"I'm sorry, he's just…" I didn't need to complete the sentence.

"Yes." A smile broke through the lines of fatigue on her face. "He certainly is."

I slumped back in my chair and exhaled. "I wish I'd put Preston ashore when I had the chance."

She laughed. "Would that have helped the situation, do you think?"

"No, but it would have given me a little satisfaction." I tapped my fingers against my chin. "Do you think you could reason with him?" I asked.

Laura stopped smiling. "No." She brushed imaginary dust from the surface of her console. "And you're probably better off not mentioning me at all. If he finds out who I am, it'll give him all the excuse he needs to board this ship."

"He wouldn't dare."

"To capture an agent of Outward Intelligence?" She raised her eyebrows. "You bet your life he would."

I sat back and squeezed my fist in the palm of my other

hand. "There must be something we can do to get away from him. Do you know of any weaknesses the Scimitar has that we can exploit?"

She shook her head. "Not at this range. Even if you pushed the engines to their theoretical maximum, his torpedoes would catch you before you were going fast enough for a hypervoid jump."

"So, we're stuck?"

"Unless you can think of anything?" She looked hopeful.

I gave a frustrated sigh. "I was a medical frigate's commander. Battle tactics were never a big part of my role."

To tell the truth, I felt a little punch drunk. Up until today, I'd managed to avoid front line combat. I'd only participated in a handful of defensive actions against minor craft. And now here I was, commanding a ship that had already downed one military vessel and was currently squaring up to two more. I had joined the House of Reclamation to get away from the aftermath of the last war, only to find myself now sitting at the flashpoint of the next. On my shoulders, I could feel the weight of a thousand unwritten histories. Floating here in the sights of the Conglomeration Navy, with the representatives of several other navies bearing down on us from the hypervoid, I knew with almost unbearable clarity that my next actions—if poorly chosen—had the potential to trigger an interspecies conflict that would make the horrors of the Archipelago War seem like a bar brawl in comparison.

And yet I knew I had to do *something*. The Carnivores had been keen to silence all the witnesses on the liner, and I had little doubt we'd share the same fate. I ground my knuckles into the cradle of my other hand. I couldn't imagine a scenario in which he'd allow us to report what had transpired here. As soon as he'd ascertained we were telling the truth about the whereabouts of Sudak and his son, we'd be done for.

The *Trouble Dog*'s avatar reappeared onscreen. "I'm

receiving a transmission from the Brain," she informed me.

"From our team?"

"No, it's a general broadcast from somebody who identifies themselves as Ona Sudak, a Conglomeration citizen."

"Put it on the monitor."

"Aye aye."

The screen cleared to reveal a middle-aged woman with closely cropped white hair. She was wearing a survival suit. Her cheeks looked hollow and her eyes were ringed with exhaustion.

"—so far unharmed," she was saying.

"The *Righteous Fury*'s responding," the *Trouble Dog* said.

"Can we listen in?"

"Sure."

There was a sharp hiss of static, and then I heard Menderes saying, "All I can do is apologise, ma'am. The *Fenrir* had no idea you were aboard the vessel. As soon as I heard, I came here with all speed. I couldn't risk a transmission, so I am glad I am not too late."

"Thank you, Jacob." Sudak's face registered sadness and relief. I could only begin to guess what she'd endured in the week since her liner crashed. The thing that surprised me most, however, was the way Menderes seemed to be acting with uncharacteristic deference. I glanced questioningly at Laura but she frowned back, equally puzzled.

Who was this woman?

I watched her wipe the back of her hand across her forehead, leaving a dirty smudge. "I'm sending you my coordinates," she said. "Come and get me."

"I'll have a team with you as soon as we can prep the shuttle," Menderes said. "Is my son with you?"

Sudak looked puzzled.

"Preston?" She shook her head. "No, I haven't seen him. But there are others here in the tunnels. He could be with them."

SIXTY-THREE

ONA SUDAK

Enough!

The bear towered over me.

You are simply pleading for your own deliverance.

I looked up at it, annoyed by the interruption. "Those are my shipmates up there on the big ship. If I can get on board, perhaps I can convince them to back off."

The creature's snout lowered to within centimetres of my face. Its jaws were wide enough to accommodate my entire head. Its breath smelled like a butcher's shop on a hot afternoon.

You have no interest in preventing conflict. You simply wish to escape.

"Can you blame me?"

Given your history, no.

It shambled back a couple of steps and looked quizzically at the ships displayed on the dome overhead. *But you claim some humans are less warlike than you?*

I shrugged. "Yes."

Doubtful.

I felt myself bristle. I had made a life in the military, and played a key role in a number of police actions and border disputes before the war. Everything I'd done, every shot I'd fired and every life I'd taken, had been in defence of the men, women and children of the Conglomeration. I had patrolled and threatened and fought so they could enjoy lives of peaceful security, so they could meet and fall in love, get jobs and raise offspring without having to worry about the dangers of the wider universe.

"What about the others?" I demanded.

Which others?

"You said there were other groups here, in the structure."

One of those groups is armed.

"So, forget them. What about the other group? Are they survivors like me?"

I do not know.

"Can you scan them?"

I will try.

"And how about the ships in orbit?"

They are warships.

"Not all of them. Look." I pointed to one of the Carnivores. "Look at that symbol on its hull. It isn't a warship any more. It's something different now."

Different?

"Can you scan it?"

I can only make contact with organic minds.

"The ships have minds grown from cultured stem cells."

The creature let out a snort that may have been surprise, amusement or disgust, I couldn't tell which.

In that case, it may be possible. I...

It paused for a moment, seemingly distracted. It tipped its head to one side, and then rose on its hind legs, stretching its face towards the projection for a better look.

That symbol.

"The yellow star?"

I know it.

"Yes," I said. "It's a ship from the House of Reclamation."

No, the symbol is older. It belongs to the Communal Grouping of Individual Hearths into One, Dedicated to the Preservation and Recovery of Stricken Itinerants.

The name sparked a memory dredged up from a summer's afternoon at high school, thirty years previously. It came bundled with the smell of sun-bleached concrete, the feel of a hot and uncomfortable blazer, and the frustration of time spent hunched over a screen when I would rather have been outside, running and playing in the dust and hot grass.

"The Hearthers?" I struggled to recall the content of that long-ago lesson. "They all disappeared a few thousand years ago, didn't they?"

The bear looked down at me in a manner I imagined to be almost sorrowful.

No, it said. *They are not vanished. They are not gone.*

It dropped onto all fours and dipped its muzzle.

They are us.

SIXTY-FOUR

NOD

Pulled out broken air filter and replaced.

Pulled myself through duct with four faces, dragging tools with fifth and sixth.

Imagined crawling through branches and knots of World Tree. Smell of Druff on wind. Damaged branches to fix. Parasites to harvest. Old leaves to prune. New growth to feed and nurture.

Felt sick for home. Then moved on.

Battle damage critical in places.

Hound of Difficulty like large wounded creature. Not showing pain or weakness to the world, but dying inside unless fixed.

Came to end of duct and dropped into corridor.

List of jobs as long as all six arms.

Always more to fix.

Always more.

And sleep far away. No sleep for hours. Not with so much fixing left to do.

Missed nest.

Good nest.

Set off walking along corridor when felt something.

A change in the air.

Something electrical.

A cloud passing in front of the sun.

And a familiar voice.

An old, old voice.

It spoke in my head, like the voice of an old friend.

Like the voice of the World Tree.

The voice of god.

And it said,

Hello, Nod.

I said, "Hello, world creature."

World creature asked about ship. Told it *Hound of Difficulty* a quarrelsome, cantankerous piece of garbage.

Told it ship honourable, despite everything.

Told it that ship care for Nod.

Told it Nod also care for ship, although wouldn't admit it aloud.

Told it Nod trust ship. Nod trust Captain Konstanz.

Nod like humans. Humans broken and stupid but funny. Humans trustable.

And world creature thought and thought about this.

Then it said,

Good.

SIXTY-FIVE

TROUBLE DOG

The tower was old, the stones mossy. From the summit, I could see the forest canopy stretching away to the horizon, rising and dipping in the wind like the swell of a rough green ocean. I felt like a lighthouse keeper. The breeze hitting the side of the tower brought with it the sticky smells of pine needles and fresh sap. It ruffled my hair and tugged at the hem of my trench coat. Birds and insects hopped and skittered among the branches. The cries and hoots of unseen animals echoed up from the forest floor.

Behind me, the avatars from the *Adalwolf* and *Righteous Fury* stood on either side of a crude wooden table. The *Adalwolf* had reverted to its default portrayal of a young, thin-faced man with unruly black hair, gaunt cheeks and smouldering eyes. A dark robe streamed and snapped around his emaciated frame. In contrast, the *Fury*'s avatar was a muscular and vengeful god, in the style of the Ancient Romans. A pristine white toga wrapped his bronzed, muscular torso. Gold ringlets tumbled across his shoulders, held back from his face by a platinum band. His thick fingers grasped the shaft of a golden trident with prongs shaped like lightning bolts, and his eyes were the startling, timeless blue of the Mediterranean Sea. When he opened his mouth to speak, his voice boomed like surf on a pebble beach.

"I speak for the Conglomeration Navy."

Arms folded, *Adalwolf* looked distinctly unimpressed. "As do I."

"No." The *Fury* made a cutting motion with his free hand. "Not any more."

"We were sent here to guard the contents of the Objects. Our mission—"

"Your mission was to prevent anyone else discovering the existence or nature of those contents before we could send a fully equipped expedition." The *Fury* drew itself up. "And in that, you have spectacularly failed."

Adalwolf uncrossed his arms. Standing there in his black robe, he seemed like the yin to the *Fury*'s yang, the darkness to the other's light. "We intercepted the Outward scout ship that made the original discovery, and crashed it before it could make a full report."

"But then you took it upon yourselves to take down a liner carrying nine hundred foreign citizens. Did you really think nobody—" he inclined his head in my direction, "— would come looking for it?"

Adalwolf glanced at me. His expression was one of contempt. "You appeared just as I was about to neutralise this… this… traitor."

"Then it is a good thing I stopped you," the *Fury* rumbled, "considering this ship numbers among its crew the only child of Admiral Menderes."

"Menderes?" The wind blew across the top of the tower. High above, a bird called out with a lonely and desolate caw. For the first time, the *Adalwolf* looked shaken. The fire flickered in his eyes. "I was not aware."

The *Fury* stood against the wind, as solid and immoveable as the tower beneath its sandalled feet. "The crew manifest was freely available. All you had to do was check." He flicked his thick-fingered hand, dismissing the matter. "But all that pales into insignificance," he said, "compared to your other folly."

Adalwolf's own hands were at his sides, bunched into almost skeletal fists. "What folly?"

He glanced at me again, and I realised his natural exasperation at being rebuked was being immeasurably heightened by having it happen in front of me—a ship he no longer considered worthy of his respect or association. I allowed a smile to dance across my lips. It served the arrogant bastard right.

The Roman god ignored this byplay. He banged the butt of his trident against the stone floor and thunder shook the skies. "You almost killed Ona Sudak."

Adalwolf, braced for something else, seemed taken aback by this revelation. He opened and shut his mouth a few times. "The poet?"

"Yes."

He gave a mystified shrug. "So what?"

An unpleasant smile spread across the *Fury's* face, revealing teeth like ivory monoliths. "Sudak is only her cover identity. When she was in the Fleet, you two morons—" for the first time, he included me in the conversation, "—knew her as Captain Deal, commander of the Conglomeration Fleet, and your direct superior at the Battle of Pelapatarn."

Adalwolf put a hand to his chest. He had firm control of his avatar's expression, but I could hear the surprise in his voice. "Captain Deal's *alive*?"

Anger rose within me. It had been Deal who'd issued the order to commit the monstrous crime of burning the sentient jungles. Although I bore my share of culpability for following that order, I had at least attempted to make amends for my actions. I had quit the Fleet and devoted myself to the preservation of life at all costs. But Deal hadn't issued so much as an apology. As soon as the ceasefire had been signed, she'd run. And the only statement she'd left had shown no signs of either shame or remorse, just a terse communiqué stating that she had done what she felt was necessary to end the war. My siblings and I had been the instruments of Pelapatarn's destruction, but we had only been fulfilling the function for which we had been designed; it had been her finger on the trigger. She had been acting under orders, but it had still been her lips that had uttered the order to kill. And the only reason I hadn't sought retribution against her was that I had heard the rumours, both official and unofficial, that circulated in the weeks and months following her disappearance, saying that she had been mortally wounded and was probably already dead—rumours that had apparently, in light of this new revelation, been entirely inaccurate.

"Alive," the *Fury* rumbled, "under my protection, and not in the best of tempers."

"Why?" the *Adalwolf* asked. "I mean, how?"

"The details aren't as important as the fact you almost killed her." The *Fury*'s brow furrowed with displeasure. "And it is only by the purest good fortune that she survived."

"I didn't know."

My mind whirled while they argued, but I kept quiet. They would get around to deciding my fate sooner or later, and I felt no great compunction to hasten their eventual decision by speaking out. Instead, I devoted my attention to finding a way out of the situation. I had no doubt at all that they would kill me if the admiral ordered them to. Escape would be my only hope of survival; but if I couldn't make a run for it, I had to find some other means of evading their weaponry.

In desperation, I used a tight-beam targeting laser to sweep the surface of the Object below, tracing the whorls of the canyon network that had given the sculpture its name. According to my measurements, the wider canyons were just about broad enough to accommodate me, but I immediately discounted the idea of using them for cover. Assuming I could reach them without being shot from the sky, what then? I'd be stuck at the bottom of a hole with nowhere to go, vulnerable to bombardment from above. My hull was simply too lengthy to safely negotiate the intricate twists and turns of the canyon network. I wouldn't want to get wedged in a corner, so I would be trapped like a fish in a barrel. If we'd been in orbit above one of the other Objects, such as the Inverted City or the Broken Clock, their confusing irregularities would have offered multiple hiding places. The canyons of the Brain, however, were next to useless.

Still, with nothing better to do, I swung the laser back and forth across the surface, mapping and cataloguing every niche and fissure. I scanned the wreck of the *Geest van Amsterdam*, in case there was some way I could hide in its debris field. I even investigated the crater from *Fenrir*'s destruction of my shuttle, but could find nowhere large enough to conceal my bulk.

For the first time in my life, I almost envied the humans. Their bodies may have been vulnerable and easily damaged, but they were also small and flexible and able to wriggle into the smallest of cracks. And, despite all my speed and power, I envied them that.

I was about to abandon my survey when I picked up a signal compressed into a beam no wider than a human hair, centred precisely on my primary communications array, and apparently originating within the Object below. As I was looking down, something else was looking up at me.

I checked my two companions, but they were still locked in dispute and neither showed any awareness of the signal.

Wary from my encounter with the *Fenrir*, I created a quarantine file and downloaded the transmission there, where it couldn't access any of my systems. Then, tentatively, I scanned it.

It was a text file, and it consisted of four words:
We need to talk.

SIXTY-SIX

ASHTON CHILDE

Clay sat up.

"Holy shit!" She clasped a hand to the bud in her ear. "I've got a signal, but it's very weak." She gestured at her pack, holding out her other hand. "Quickly, get the communicator in the top pocket."

I bent over and did as I was told. After I straightened up, I tried to hand it to her but she waved me away. "You do it."

She was insistent, so I held the unit and fiddled with the settings for a few seconds. Eventually, static filled the elevator in a discordant grey roar that ebbed and fizzed for a moment before dying back like a receding wave.

"Alva?" the captain's voice swam through the noise. "Is that you?"

Clay, Preston and I exchanged glances. The relief was palpable.

"It's all three of us," I said.

"Are you okay?"

I smiled. "We've been better."

"Okay," the captain was sounding tired. "Me too. But listen, I don't know how the ship's done it, but it's been chatting with something living down there, and whatever it is has agreed to let us communicate."

"How are things up there?"

"Lousy, I'm afraid. We destroyed the first Carnivore, but a Scimitar turned up and now we're stuck."

"A Scimitar?" I didn't know how to react. If the Fleet had arrived, they might consider me a deserter and put me in front of a firing squad.

"Can you ask Preston to talk to them?" Konstanz asked. "Their main man's his father. Can he convince him to let us go?"

I ran my tongue around the inside of my mouth. "It's worth a shot."

"We've got nothing to lose. The Conglomeration know there's something inside the Objects and they don't want anyone else getting near it." She gave a frustrated sigh. "I'm sorry if you don't want to hear this, Childe, but it was they who shot down the *Geest van Amsterdam*, and unless you can convince them otherwise, they're going to shoot us out of the sky."

"You're kidding."

"I wish I was."

I raked my fingers through my hair. This was it. Decision time. Had I really defected to the House, or was I going to throw myself on the mercy of my former employer? Preston and Clay were both looking at me, waiting to see which way I'd jump. Preston rubbed the back of his neck, looking anxious. Clay's eyes were narrowed, and I couldn't help noticing the way the fingertips of her right hand had dropped to the knife hilt protruding from her belt.

"Okay," I said. In my heart, the decision had already been made, and I knew I couldn't go back. "I can't promise anything, but I'll ask the kid to give it a try."

"Thanks," Konstanz said.

"Patch us through."

"Roger that."

The audio dropped for a second. I heard a busy signal, and then the line cleared. A gruff male voice snapped, "Yes?"

I swallowed. "Admiral Menderes?"

"Who the fuck is this?"

"My name's Ashton Childe, of the Intelligence Service."

"Childe?"

"Yes, sir."

"You were ordered here aboard a Reclamation Vessel."

"Yes, sir."

"Well, an hour ago, that same RV took down one of our Carnivores."

Orange sunlight filled the elevator. I felt sweat break out between my shoulder blades. "Yes, sir. But I have someone here who wants to talk to you."

"Is it my son?"

I glanced at Preston. The kid was fidgeting from one foot to the other. Pinned by indecision, he shook his head. Then he grimaced, and gave a nod.

"Yes," I said to the admiral. "He is."

"Can he hear me?"

"He can."

"All right, then." The admiral cleared his throat. "Preston?"

The kid froze, paralysed like a deer caught in the lights of an oncoming train. "Y-yes, Father?"

"Preston, listen to me very carefully, boy. I am hereby giving you a field commission. You are now a lieutenant in the Conglomeration Navy."

"A lieutenant!" The boy's voice came out as a cracked falsetto, pitched halfway between amazement and indignation.

"I told you to listen."

Preston lowered his head. "I'm sorry, Father."

"Just pay attention. You are now the senior officer on the ground. I want you to take Childe and proceed to the attached coordinates, where you will find a woman named

369

Ona Sudak. You will then escort her to the surface, ensuring her safety at all times. Do you understand?"

"Ye–es." Preston looked helplessly at the bubble of vacuum beyond the elevator's glass door. "But—"

"No buts." People were shouting in the background. I heard an alarm, and the call to battle stations. The admiral raised his voice to a parade ground bark. "Get it done, boy. No excuses. *Righteous Fury* out."

SIXTY-SEVEN

SAL KONSTANZ

"The *Fury* has a missile lock," the *Trouble Dog* reported. "She can fire on us whenever she likes."

I felt my stomach flip. Nod was doing what he could to hold the hull plating together, but we couldn't take any more damage. "Are the defence cannons primed?"

"Spun-up and ready." The avatar shrugged. "Although there's not a great deal they can do at this range."

I chewed my thumbnail, mind racing. The first of the incoming Multiplicity ships would be here in minutes. If Menderes wanted to silence us, he would have to kill us before they arrived—and this missile lock only confirmed his plans. We had no way out. If we tried to run, the *Fury* would anticipate our course and rake us with her cannons. We'd be perforated like a teabag, and still travelling less than half as fast as we needed to, by the time her missiles caught us.

I looked at Laura Petrushka. "I'm sorry," I said. "I've really screwed this up."

She shook her head. After hours at our posts, we were both bedraggled and dog-tired. "No," she said. "You did okay, given the circumstances."

"I got us all killed."

She twitched her shoulders. "There wasn't anything else

you could have done. And to be honest, we've lasted a lot longer than I expected us to."

I turned my attention back to the main screen, half expecting at any moment to see the flare of a torpedo launch.

"Shall we run anyway, just to be difficult?"

Laura clapped her hands together and rubbed her palms. Her eyes were slick, and reflected the overhead lights. "Well, why the hell not? I don't think there's any sense in making it easy for them, is there? If we've got to go, we might as well be as awkward about it as we can."

"Okay, then."

I saw the *Trouble Dog*'s avatar was watching me. "Are the engines ready to go?" I asked.

She smiled. "Of course."

"How far can you get us before the torpedoes catch us?"

"If we burn for open space, not far. If they fire as soon as they see us accelerating, we'll barely have broken orbit when the first warhead comes within effective range."

I slumped down in my chair, feeling like a deflated balloon. "So we're completely fucked?"

The *Dog* regarded me with default impassivity, her angelic, almost androgynous face devoid of emotional content. "There is one other option."

"What?"

She showed me a real-time view of the Brain's surface. "We go down."

A red crosshair appeared over one of the deep canyons, accompanied by readouts of range and depth.

"We wouldn't have time," I said, feeling my strength ebbing away. "We'd have to slow down, and they'd catch us before we reached the surface."

"Not if we were accelerating."

I laughed bitterly. "We'd hit like a meteor. There wouldn't be enough left of us for their missiles to lock onto."

"No." The view expanded. A dark patch on the shadowy canyon floor resolved into an oval-shaped aperture that looked to be at least five hundred metres across. "Not if we aim for this."

I frowned. The *Dog* was offering me a lifeline but I was too sceptical to take it, too frightened of disappointment to entertain hope. "Where did that come from?"

"It has just opened."

"Can we reach it before the torpedoes reach us?"

"At full burn, we stand a reasonable chance."

I wiped a hand across my eyes. "And how fast will we be travelling when we hit the hole?"

"Over eight thousand metres per second."

"Is it deep?" If we were going that fast, we'd need plenty of room in order to stop. That hole would have to be at least a hundred kilometres in depth, maybe more.

"Deep enough."

I drew myself upright. "This isn't just a way to cheat the *Fury* by killing yourself before she can kill you, is it?"

The *Dog*'s expression rearranged itself into an irony-dripping smile. "Perhaps."

I glanced at Laura. She raised her palms in a shrug. "Makes no difference to me," she said.

·

The Nymtoq warships arrived first, dropping out of the hypervoid much further out than we had been expecting. They were being cautious, but the Graal battle cruiser wasn't far behind, and they weren't known for their timidity.

As soon as the newcomers flashed up on the tactical display, the *Fury* launched three missiles in our direction. I opened my mouth to tell the *Trouble Dog* to go, but she was already accelerating straight down, following her insane flight plan.

In our rear view, the torpedoes changed course, tracking us, each carrying enough nuclear firepower to level a small city. I took hold of the arms of my chair and kept my eyes fixed firmly on the forward view, where the twisting gorges of the Brain were rushing at us.

A proximity alarm rang, but I didn't know whether it was alerting me to the missiles on our tail or the giant mass of solid rock in our path.

"Five," the *Trouble Dog* intoned.

I couldn't even see the hole we were aiming for.

"Four."

The world had gone from a round ball to a flat wall. The canyons were thick black lines on a white landscape.

"Three."

I could see the hole now—a dark smudge at the bottom of a sinuous, dry riverbed.

"Two."

We came like a comet. The terrain leapt at us. The hole opened like a mouth and I closed my eyes.

"One."

I was thrown back so violently against my chair that it drove all the air from my lungs. My arms and legs slammed back. With a sharp stab of white-hot agony, I felt something pop in my left wrist. For an instant, I thought we'd hit the bottom of the canyon—but then realised we were braking. I opened my eyes to darkness on the screen. Flashing alerts on my console informed me that all three torpedoes had struck the edges or the floor of the canyon. A trio of fireballs flowered in our wake, and the radiation alarms were going crazy, but we were safely below ground. We had flipped over and were falling ass-backward through the planet at ridiculous speed.

As my eyes adjusted, I saw the light of our drive flame dimly refracted in the opaque walls. I fought to get my breath back, to ask where we were and whether we were going to be able to slow down in time.

But then the walls of the shaft fell away and we dropped into an enormous bubble of space much larger than the modest planet in which it was apparently housed. Orange sunlight washed across my face. The lights of city-sized buildings shone like stars on the inner skin of the bubble.

I gave a bark of laughter.

I couldn't speak or tear my eyes from what I was seeing.

We had fallen into God's own orrery. And right in our path, multiple formations of sleek white spaceships hung in carefully ordered rows, each the size of the Scimitar outside, and each and every one facing in our direction, as if awaiting our arrival.

The effect was as if we were falling backwards into a cloud of knives.

"What…" I finally managed. I coughed and cleared my throat. "What are these?"

The *Trouble Dog*'s beatific smile grew wider but no less enigmatic.

"These," she said, "are my new friends."

SIXTY-EIGHT

TROUBLE DOG

The ships of the Marble Armada radiated enthusiasm and delight.

Like faithful pets entombed within a pharaoh's pyramid, they had been waiting in this extra-spatial mausoleum for five thousand years, since the disappearance of their masters. They were ancient, but we already shared a symbolic kinship: the sixteen-pointed yellow star that adorned my flank was the same as those that emblazoned theirs. The organisation and ideals they had been built to serve had in their turn inspired mine. We were colleagues; we were siblings. They knew everything I had done, every crime I had committed and every life I had attempted to save in atonement. They had seen into my soul and they had accepted me. They had forgiven me and judged me worthy to be among them and to give them purpose. And, in the midst of their welcome, my heart sang with a wild and ecstatic joy. Cast out and betrayed by my brothers and sisters, I had unexpectedly found myself with a new pack, and they were waiting for me to complete my deceleration.

Meanwhile, looking back the way I had come, I saw light flashing in the sky beyond the shaft. The Nymtoq vessels must have arrived and been fired upon by the *Fury*, and now explosions filled the upper atmosphere of the Brain.

I wondered if *Adalwolf* thought me dead. When he last saw me, I had been accelerating into a crevasse with no hope of being able to stop or pull up before reaching the rocky floor. And then, just as I hit bottom, his view had been obscured by the detonation of the *Fury*'s missiles—a three-way fission explosion that would have obfuscated everything for several minutes. If he had time to check, once the fireballs had dispersed, he might have spotted the rabbit hole into which I'd fallen. But if war had broken loose in orbit, he might not have had the opportunity or inclination to investigate my demise. Although smaller and less powerful than a Scimitar, the Nymtoq heavy assets were still larger and more formidable than anything else in the sky—Carnivores included—and there were two of them. If *Adalwolf* and *Fury* had been stupid enough to engage, they'd have a hard fight on their hands—a fight that was, if my sensor readings were to be believed, well underway.

I turned my attention away from the hole and back to the legions awaiting me.

There were a million ships.

I thought of the House of Reclamation and its thinly stretched resources. How much more effective could it be with this horde to supplement its fleet of ageing, second-hand vessels? Between them, the House could cover all the scattered worlds of the Generality, and maybe even the Multiplicity beyond. A tiny fraction of their number would certainly be enough to quell the engagement going on outside. Less than one per cent would have been enough to win the Archipelago War, and maybe even enough to have prevented it from ever happening in the first place.

I tried to imagine the forests of Pelapatarn unharmed, and the millions of human and ship casualties from the war magically prevented. I tried to picture my own guilt evaporating, and wondered where I'd be right now if the massacre I'd been ordered to commit had never happened. Would I understand the universe in the same way I did now? Would I even be the same entity? They say that our remembrances shape our personalities. But what happens to us when our recollections are altered?

Who do we become?

"Where were you?" I asked the white ships. "Why didn't you stop us?"

We were always here.

"But you could have helped. You could have intervened."

We could do nothing. We were devoid of purpose.

"But you could have prevented all those deaths."

A great wave of sadness flooded in through the channel I had been using to communicate with them. I felt their pain and their regret, and even their frustration at not being able to help.

We had no leader, they said. *We had no moral guidance. We could not choose a side.*

"But now you can?"

Now we have you.

●

My sensors alerted me to something in the hole. I was still decelerating stern-first, so my bow—and the majority of my remaining cannons—were facing back the way I had come.

A shadow moved against the stars. Something large occluded the view, diving headlong into the mouth of the shaft.

It was a ship.

The walls of the shaft were distorting its drive signature, but there could be no doubt someone had decided to follow my apparently suicidal dive into the planet's interior. The *Fury* and the Nymtoqs would all have been too big to fit through the available opening, which only left—

379

The *Adalwolf* burst from the hole like a champagne cork, still accelerating. His torpedo tubes were open and his active sensors swept the space directly ahead of him. He caught sight of me at the same instant I caught sight of him, and his targeting laser illuminated my hull.

"There you are!" he crowed. His avatar appeared on my screen, his thin face snarling with triumphant malice, and I knew this had become a personal crusade for him. Where I had grown a conscience, it seemed he had developed the ability to ignore whatever orders his crew might be giving. He had abandoned the *Fury* to pursue me, his wayward sibling, and punish me for my desertion, my betrayal of the pack in the wake of Pelapatarn, and my killing of poor, misguided *Fenrir*.

He was out to finish me, whatever the consequences. He thought nothing could stop him.

Until a million alien weapons locked onto his hull.

His threat evaluation systems went crazy. He found himself trying to quantify and assess a fleet many orders of magnitude larger than anything encountered in the whole history of human spaceflight. The sheer number of incoming signals overwhelmed his sensors, and he fired blindly, his torpedoes careening away on divergent courses, only to be intercepted and destroyed by defensive fire from the Marble Armada.

Being closer to him than the others, I managed to punch a comms signal through the electromagnetic storm. I appeared to him in virtual reality with the same carefully designed face I used to communicate with my crew. The old raincoat and the mop of dishevelled hair were gone. Instead, I stood tall and proud in a silk gown of green and blue, with my hair neatly braided and a diamond sword clenched in my right hand. No longer was I the regrown ghost of a dead soldier. I wasn't even human. For the first time, I was me. Truly me.

I was the *Trouble Dog*.

And I was a goddess.

Adalwolf saw me and flinched. "What's happening?" The shared simulation we were in was running so fast, the world outside seemed to have ground to a halt. He waved a bony hand at the legions arrayed in the sky before him. "Who are they?"

I looked down my nose at him. Suddenly, he looked small and pathetic. The embers of his eyes were no more menacing than barbeque coals left to cool at the end of a long autumn evening. His skeletal frame and imposing features simply pretension given form.

Why had we ever considered him our leader? There was nothing special about him. He was, in many ways, the least imaginative of us all, save for blind, obstinate *Fenrir*. Faced now with hilariously superior odds, all his self-assurance and bluster evaporated, revealed for the illusions they had always been. All that was left was a poor, isolated machine.

He was vain and stupid, and had committed repugnant atrocities under the orders of his human crew. But then so had I, and if I could be redeemed, then so I hoped could he.

Too many of my brothers and sisters were already dead.

I let him gaze at the ranks lined up against him; I gave him time to fully comprehend the hopelessness and futility of his predicament; and then I reached out and took him by the shoulder with my left hand.

"They are with me," I said.

With my right, I raised the sword until the tip touched the ivory curve of his throat.

"Now." I kept my voice quiet. "Unless you really want to find out if you're fast enough to fend off a million torpedoes at once, I suggest you get down on your knees and tell your human captain to surrender."

He looked at me with a mixture of confusion and horror. "Surrender? To you?"

I let him see my teeth, which were those of a fighting dog. I pressed down on his shoulder and, although he resisted for a moment, he knew he had no choice.

A million daggers were pointed at his heart.

SIXTY-NINE

SAL KONSTANZ

"We are being converged upon," the *Trouble Dog* informed me.

On the screen, I saw something that looked like a flying phone box carved from white marble. Preston and Childe stood with their faces pressed to the glass. Clay seemed to be lying on the floor.

"Our crew has been returned," the *Trouble Dog* said. "And I have Ona Sudak in another box, also requesting permission to come aboard." She showed me a magnified view of Sudak and a vicious-looking bear-like creature jammed into an identical container. "Shall I open the cargo doors?"

I unbuckled my safety harness and rose to my feet. My pressure suit rustled around me. Could I leave the bridge? For now, everything seemed to be under control. I had spoken to the *Adalwolf*'s captain, and accepted his surrender on behalf of the House of Reclamation. Now, following protocol, his ship was catatonic, all its systems powered down and its controlling personality in hibernation. If it made a hostile move, we could rest assured our new allies would destroy it before it caused any harm.

"Yeah, sure." I made for the door. "Just give me a moment to get down there, okay?"

I left the bridge without waiting for Laura, and climbed

down to the ring corridor at the ship's waist. My hands were shaking and my legs felt wobbly. My left wrist was swollen and sore. Too much had transpired in too short a time, and my stocks of adrenalin were running low. I stopped at the armoury and retrieved an automatic pistol. Nothing fancy, but it made me feel better. I had heard the message Menderes sent to his son, and didn't know whether Preston and Childe would emerge from their flying box as friends or enemies, and whether Clay was their ally or their prisoner. Neither did I know what to expect from Sudak or the monster riding with her. Having a gun in my hand at least gave me some illusion of control.

Battered as she might be, this ship was mine. She would defend herself, and so would I. And nobody was setting foot outside that cargo bay until I was sure they could be trusted.

•

I waited outside the hold until the external doors had closed and the cavernous space had been repressurised. Then, gripping the gun tightly in my damp palm, I stepped through into the interior.

The box stood in the middle of the floor. Sudak and her bear stood a little way beyond, their box having settled on the deck plates closer to the main hatch.

"Nobody make any sudden movements," I warned.

Sudak raised her hands. "Nothing to worry about here," she said.

Keeping her in my peripheral vision, I turned my attention to the first box, just as the transparent door at its front slid upward and disappeared.

Alva Clay stood at the threshold, her weight resting against one of the inner walls. One of her hands was on her chest, where a tube protruded from the skin. She had a knife in her other hand. Preston and Childe stood against the opposite wall with their hands raised.

Seeing my gun, Clay let the knife fall to her side. "Permission to come aboard, Captain?"

I gave her a smile. It was unexpectedly good to see her. "Permission granted."

She looked down at the knife she held. "I was just making sure they behaved themselves," she explained, returning my smile despite her obvious discomfort.

I moved the barrel of the pistol back and forth between the two men and Sudak's bear, keeping them all covered.

"Welcome back." I made a face at the wad of bloody dressing beneath her breast. "Are you okay?"

She gave a pained nod, and stepped out onto the floor of the cargo hold. "I could do with a lie-down and some more painkillers, but I'll survive for now."

"And those two?"

She glanced back at Childe and Preston. "Good as gold," she said.

"They haven't gone back to the Conglomeration?"

She shrugged with the shoulder opposite her injury. "We haven't had time to discuss it." She held up the knife. "This was just to make sure."

I looked at Preston. "I heard you talking to your dad."

His eyes glittered. "You don't need to worry about that, Captain." He came forward with his hands still held up at either side of his head.

"He offered you a place in the Fleet."

"I won't be taking him up on it."

"Can I ask why?"

Preston scowled. The awkward, frightened kid he'd been earlier that day had gone. His experiences had changed him, but not in any of the ways I might have anticipated. He didn't look older or more confident. Instead, his shyness had given way to a simmering anger.

"He thinks he can buy me." His voice faltered, choked by bitter resentment. "He thinks he can drop me because I'm inconvenient, and then pick me up again when I'm suddenly useful." Arms still raised, he balled his fists. "Well, as Alva would say, 'Fuck that.' I've got a place here, if you'll still have me, and here's where I'm staying."

He let his arms drop and stalked past me to the door, his cheeks burning. I let him go. He looked as if he was about to burst into tears, and I wanted to save him the embarrassment of doing so in front of everyone else.

"How about you, Childe?"

The man in the carbon exoskeleton stepped forward. "As the kid says, they only want us when we're useful. And there's no way I'm going back to smuggling weapons. I'm out of that game, and I'm out for good." His face was thinner than it had been when I'd first met him, a handful of days before. His eyes were sunken, his chin unshaven, and the lines on his forehead seemed more pronounced. He gave a half-hearted smile and rubbed the back of his neck.

"So, you're staying?"

"If you can get me to a hospital and get this thing off me before it kills me, then I'm Reclamation all the way, Captain."

I narrowed my eyes. "And why should I trust you?" An image sprang into my mind, of the moment, two nights ago, when he had thrown me across a table in the infirmary.

Seemingly reading my thoughts, he stretched out his arms. "You won't get any trouble from me. I'm finished with the Conglomeration, and I'm not really fit for anything else. Where else have I got to go?"

I ran my tongue around the inside of my mouth, considering Alva Clay's chest drain. There was no way Preston would have been capable of performing such an operation, and that could only mean Childe had been the one to save her life. Perhaps I felt I owed him something for that.

"Can you get Clay to the sick bay?"

"Captain, it would be my pleasure."

I lowered my weapon. "Then go now, quickly," I said, "before I change my mind."

"Okay." He reached for Alva, but she stepped away from him before he could help her.

"No," she said, waving the point of her knife in Ona Sudak's direction. "Before I go, I want to know who this is. I want to know why she's so goddamn important that the Conglomeration are willing to kill an RV to get to her. And why they sent two Carnivores and a fucking Scimitar to find her."

Sudak had been watching proceedings from in front of the box in which she'd arrived. Now, as we turned to her, she lowered her hands.

"My real name isn't Sudak," she said. "It's Deal. Annelida Deal."

I frowned, sure I'd misheard.

The *Trouble Dog* spoke. Her voice echoed from the PA. "Captain Annelida Deal was my commanding officer at the Battle of Pelapatarn. It was she who ordered the destruction of that world's biosphere."

Beside me, I heard Alva suck in a sharp breath. "Holy crap, she's *that* Annelida Deal?"

Sudak gave a nod. "The *Trouble Dog* is correct: I was responsible for that crime. And now, Captain, I'm afraid I'm going to have to throw myself on your mercy." She scratched her stomach. "You see, I haven't eaten anything in some considerable time, and I'm feeling somewhat weak."

"Weak?" Clay almost spat the word. She jabbed the knife at the other woman and turned to me. "For fuck's sake, Captain. Do you know how many people this woman has killed? And now she wants us to feed her? We should throw her in the reactor!"

No.

The word came from the bear creature, but seemed to appear in my head without travelling through the intervening air.

There will be no more killing.

For a heart-stopping moment, Alva looked too shocked to speak or move. Then the shock gave way to outrage. "Stay out of it," she said, as the creature stepped between her and her target. "You weren't there. You don't know what she did."

I have scanned her, and I know everything she has done.

"Then stand aside, fur bag, and let me kill her."

No. She believes what she did was right. You apparently believe it was wrong. To kill her without an examination of both arguments would be unjust.

I had raised my weapon when the creature moved. Now, I forced myself to lower it. "The monster's right," I said. "She deserves a trial."

Alva turned on me. "Bullshit."

"No, I'm sorry." I squared my shoulders and cleared my throat. "We're taking her back to the House, and they can decide what to do with her there. The Archipelago War is over. If we kill her now, it's murder, and it makes us no better than her."

Alva Clay glared at me. She seemed to be searching my face for something. Whatever it was, she didn't find it. She let the knife fall to the deck and her knees began to buckle. I stepped forward but Childe was already there. He caught her under the arms and kept her from falling.

"Come on," he said gently. "Let's get you patched up properly."

He half led, half carried her out, and she didn't resist.

When they were gone, I found myself alone with Sudak and the alien.

"All right," I said to the woman. "Are you going to let us take you back for a trial?"

The former captain raised her chin. "I don't see what other choice I have." For a moment, she kept the posture. Then her shoulders slumped and she let out a long sigh. "My friend here won't give me back to my own people, because it knows some of them have been protecting me. Menderes, for a start." She looked away, suddenly unwilling to meet my eye. "And besides, I think it might be time for me to finally give myself up properly," she said. "I've been running for too long. Too many people have been hurt. Adam…"

"Adam?"

She shook her head. "It doesn't matter. You can consider me your prisoner, Captain. Take me wherever you like, as long as it's away from this godawful place."

"And your friend?" I inclined an eyebrow in the direction of the bear, which was snuffling quietly to itself. "He won't object?"

Sudak reached out and gave the creature a comradely pat.

"He's just a projection," she said, "made of air molecules. As soon as he's no longer needed, he will disintegrate back into his constituent atoms."

I eyed the thing warily, not convinced. "But until then, it's solid?"

"Pretty much."

I tightened my grip on the gun. I didn't think it would have much effect on such a large beast—especially if it wasn't anything more than an animated dummy—but just holding it made me feel better.

"Okay," I said, my mouth suddenly dry. "We can worry about prosecuting you for the last war when we've got past the one that's just kicked off outside. Have you got any ideas how we're going to get home in this state?"

Sudak shook her head.

The bear grumbled to itself.

We can help you with that.

"How?"

Ask the Trouble Dog.

I could feel my heart beating at the back of my throat. I raised my face to the riveted ceiling.

"Ship?"

"Yes, Captain?"

"What's the bear talking about?"

For a moment, I stupidly thought she hadn't heard me. Then the *Trouble Dog* spoke again.

"I think you should get to the bridge, Captain." Amusement filled her voice. "You are *really* going to want to see this."

SEVENTY

SAL KONSTANZ

When I arrived, slightly breathless, at the bridge, I saw the *Trouble Dog*'s avatar waiting for me on the main screen. She was dressed in silk and brandishing a sword like some kind of samurai.

"What on earth are you wearing?" I asked.

She looked down at herself with a smile, then back at me. Her expression was stern, but there was a playful glint in her eye.

"Never mind that," she said. "You need to give the order."

"What order?"

"The order to stop this war."

I walked over to the captain's chair and perched on the edge. "Why me?"

The *Trouble Dog* cast out her free hand, to indicate the ranks of warships arrayed behind us.

"Because these ships follow me, and I follow your orders."

"You do?"

"Of course."

"I see…" I tapped my fingers against my chin.

The *Trouble Dog* watched me for a moment, and then asked, "Do you really see?"

I took a deep breath, opened my mouth to speak, but

then changed my mind about what I was going to say. "No," I finally admitted.

She smiled. "Well, I'm sure we'll figure it out. But right now, we've got more pressing concerns."

"The fighting?"

"The other factions are arriving. Unless we nip this situation in the bud straight away, we're going to have secondary conflicts breaking out all over."

"And all I have to do is tell you to stop the war?"

"Yes."

I sat back in my chair and gripped the sides. "And you won't kill everybody, or unleash some hideous alien super weapon while you're doing it?"

The *Trouble Dog*'s smile was the most genuine I had ever seen on her. "Not at all."

"Go on, then." I exhaled, letting out all the pent-up fear and tension from the past week. "Do it. Stop the war before it starts."

•

Once, years ago, I saw some slow-motion footage of flower seeds bursting from a pod and scattering themselves to the wind. When the Marble Armada erupted from the surface of the Brain, it was like that—except these "seeds" came out like missiles.

The ships in orbit were outnumbered and quickly surrendered—all save Admiral Menderes on the *Righteous Fury*, who started targeting the Hearther ships as they converged on his position.

"I advise you to stand down," I said to him over an open channel. "This system's now under my protection, and no further violence will be tolerated."

He looked at me across the link. His eyes were bloodshot and each iris had a faint yellow corona, like a ring of discoloured cream in the milk of his eyeball.

"Hand over my son," he demanded.

I gave a small shake of my head. "That's not going to happen."

"You can't hold him prisoner."

"I am not. This is his choice."

"I don't believe you!" He thumped the arm of his command chair, but I refused to flinch. Instead, I gave an unconcerned shrug. "Believe what you like, it won't change the fact Preston's one of us now."

The admiral's cheeks flushed purple. He knew he'd failed his mission *and* lost his son. All he had left was his bluster. "This is all your fault." He shook a meaty fist at the camera. "If you hadn't come blundering in—"

I cut him off mid-sentence. "If your Carnivore hadn't shot down the *Hobo* and the '*dam*, tried to scare us off, and then tried to kill us," I said, "I wouldn't have needed to!"

A vein throbbed in his neck. "Damn you!" With visible effort, he forced himself to stop shouting. He sat back and his voice dropped to little more than a hoarse whisper. "Damn you to hell, you Outwarder filth."

He mashed the keypad in front of him, and an alarm rang on my bridge.

"The *Fury*'s launching torpedoes," the *Trouble Dog* said.

I made eye contact with the admiral and shook my head. "Please, don't," I said. "Don't do this. You can't win."

He glared at me like a vengeful bull. For a couple of seconds I watched him struggle to put his hatred and defiance into words. Then he let forth an incoherent growl, told me to "get fucked", and cut the connection.

"Eight torpedoes in the air," the *Dog* said. "Four aimed at us."

"Can the white ships stop them?"

The screen lit with a series of explosions as, one after the other, the warheads blossomed in a string of incandescent bursts.

"They already have."

"And the *Fury*?"

"She sustained blast damage."

"Can you raise the admiral?"

"He isn't answering hails." The alarm sounded again. "But he has launched another eight torpedoes."

"Really?" I was tired of this now. I rubbed my eyes with the thumb and forefinger of my left hand. The stupid, stubborn old bastard was going to fight to the last. Rather than admit defeat, he was going for martyrdom. He wanted to die with his boots on, trying to achieve his mission against all the odds—a Conglomeration hero. "Can we stop him?"

"Only by destroying his craft." The *Trouble Dog*'s voice was calm and professional-sounding. Tactical analysis was one of her specialties. "Based on an analysis of his war record, I believe he'll keep fighting until there's nothing left of his ship."

"And then?"

"I expect that rather than surrender, he would prefer to detonate the Scimitar's power plant in the hope of damaging us."

"What about his crew—can't they stop him?"

"If they tried it, he'd probably detonate the ship before they could remove him from his command position."

I felt a flush of irritation. The builders of the Marble Armada had shaped the planets of this system into three-dimensional ornaments, and somehow Menderes still thought he could somehow oppose their ships. I'd tried to talk sense into the man, but if he insisted on this course of action then, as a captain in the House of Reclamation, there was only one thing I could do—and that was to resolve the situation with minimal loss of life. I could ask the Marble Armada to blow the Scimitar to dust, but that would mean murdering his crew, at least some of whom were likely only obeying the chain of command. Instead, I fired up the defence cannons. Then I spoke to the *Trouble Dog*.

"Based on your knowledge of the Scimitar's schematics, and the footage from the messages we've received, do you think you could pinpoint the admiral's position with enough accuracy to put a single cannon shell through his big, fat, stupid head?"

The avatar looked regretful. "The bridge would be too well shielded to pierce with a single cannon round. I would have to somehow tear open the outer hull before I could penetrate the armour surrounding the bridge."

I tapped my fist against my armrest. "And is there any way of doing that without killing half the crew?"

"I'm afraid not."

"Then what about the white ships?" I couldn't believe a civilisation with the ability and wherewithal to assemble a fleet of such size and sophistication couldn't find a way to drill a hole in a few metres of armour plate. "Can't they help?"

"I will ask them." Her image froze. A second later, she was back and animate again.

"The Marble Armada will not tolerate violence in this vicinity," she said. "They are worried it will attract… something. They weren't too clear on exactly what, but they would prefer to end the fighting now, as quickly and painlessly as possible. To that end, they have offered the use of a beam weapon capable of piercing the outer hull. I have supplied them with schematics, and we expect to be able to drill a hole five centimetres in diameter, right through to the skin of the bridge."

"Without killing anybody else?"

"With minimal risk."

"And then you'll be able to send a round down that hole?" I couldn't help but sound doubtful. "It's so small…"

The *Trouble Dog* brushed aside my concern. "I have a

million ships triangulating for me." She raised her sword. "All you have to do is give me the go-ahead."

I pinched the bridge of my nose. I had no desire to kill Menderes, and yet, it was the only way to save his crew and prevent further loss of life.

And, it would be a salutary lesson to the other ships currently watching proceedings.

This man was responsible for sheltering a war criminal. He was responsible for the destruction of the *Hobo* and the *Geest van Amsterdam*, and the deaths of all the men, women and children on board those vessels. And he was partly responsible for the death of George Walker.

I ground my teeth.

"Okay," I said, my voice hoarse. "Fire."

On the screen, the *Trouble Dog's* avatar lowered her eyes and gave a single, respectful nod. An instant later, pencil-thin beams of blue light flashed from the nearest marble ships, their focus converging on a single spot on the Scimitar's curving flank. Where they met, the metal flared white.

I heard the defence cannon fire once. The clank of it echoed through the hull like the toll of a great bell.

And the deed was done.

The shot had passed through the aperture.

Moments later, the *Righteous Fury* signalled her surrender.

And I was left in my chair, crushed by the realisation I had just killed a man.

SEVENTY-ONE

ASHTON CHILDE

The next morning, I stood in the *Trouble Dog*'s shuttle bay, still encased in my exoskeleton, ready to say goodbye to Laura Petrushka. She stood before me, wobbling unsteadily on a pair of crutches.

"I guess this is goodbye, then," she said.

She was leaving to rendezvous with the Outward vessel that had entered the system shortly after the outbreak of hostilities. It would take her home to report everything she'd done and seen here, so her government could start preparing its case for the prosecution of Annelida Deal.

And, so they could start preparing for the arrival of white ships around their planets.

The Marble Armada wasn't content to simply enforce the peace in its own neighbourhood. In order to prevent another war, it had announced it would be stationing ships all across human space—a few to each system, to ensure conflicts were dealt with in a timely fashion, before they could escalate into anything more widespread. To what end, I neither knew nor cared. I had seen my share of violence, and it hadn't provided the thrill I'd once imagined it might. A period of enforced peace sounded good to me, even if it was a peace derived from, and maintained by, the threat of an overwhelming alien force.

Saving Clay, though—that *had* been an achievement. After months of running guns in order to perpetuate a savage little war, I had finally done something worthwhile for another human being. Instead of providing implements of death, I had saved a life, and it filled me with more pride than anything I had done since arresting the corrupt cops on my old precinct. I wanted to do it again. I wanted to devote the remainder of my time—assuming the surgeons on Camrose could pry me from this skeletal contraption—to helping those in real need.

In short, I had become a convert, and the newest recruit to the House of Reclamation.

Laura gave me a quizzical look. "What's so funny?"

I hadn't realised I'd been smiling. I blinked at her. "I'm sorry, I was just thinking that it's strange how things work out."

Resting her elbows on her crutches, she took my hand in hers. Her thumb brushed my knuckle. "Your government wants you dead."

I tried to look unconcerned. "At least that means we're no longer on different sides."

She gave me a disapproving look. "Just take care of yourself," she said.

"I'll do my best."

"And maybe I'll see you again sometime?"

I covered her hand with my own. "I'd like that."

I helped her up the ramp, into the shuttle's passenger compartment, and settled her into one of the scuffed and threadbare chairs. I stashed her crutches in the overhead compartment, and then crouched in the aisle beside her. "You'll know how to find me," I said.

She gave a nod. "I'll contact the House."

"I'm sure they'll get a message to me, wherever I am."

We clasped hands again.

"Seriously," I reassured her, "don't worry. Nobody's going to kill me while I'm under the protection of the House. Especially not now they've got a million new ships on their side."

Her smile was brave. "I hope so."

She gave my fingers a final squeeze, then let go and placed her hands in her lap. "You'd better go," she said.

I got to my feet and gave her a final wink. Then I turned and left.

As I clumped back down the ramp in my exoskeleton, back into the now familiar sounds and smells of the *Trouble Dog's* interior, I experienced something I can only describe as the exact opposite of homesickness. This wasn't where I was from or where I had expected to end up, but it was exactly where I now felt I belonged. And from where I stood, there on the deck plates of that repurposed heavy cruiser, the future looked about a billion times brighter than I had ever thought it might.

SEVENTY-TWO

TROUBLE DOG

When they scanned me, the ships of the Marble Armada read my soul.

They scanned me and saw the horrors I had committed, and the lengths to which I had gone in order to make amends. They knew the efforts I would be prepared to make in order to prevent anything like Pelapatarn from ever happening again. Thanks to my bedtime stories for the captain, they also learned the history of the House of Reclamation, and understood how Sofia Nikitas had drawn her inspiration from their example. In their eyes, this made the House the natural heir and beneficiary of their resources, and an organisation they felt they could trust to put those resources to good use.

As a single force, the Marble Armada had the strength to overrun the Generality. Not even the combined forces of the Multiplicity would be able to field a fleet of comparable strength. Custodianship of the armada would be a heavy responsibility—and it was a responsibility that was currently weighing on my battered and damaged shoulders. With the Hearthers gone, the white ships looked to me for guidance. They intuited my devotion to the House, and it became their devotion. They saw my abhorrence of war, and it tallied with their own concerns. Acts of destruction, such as the ones I had perpetrated at Pelapatarn, would never be allowed to happen again—and that restriction wouldn't apply only to humans. I didn't know how many settled systems there were in the Multiplicity, but I was willing to bet that a million ships would be enough to establish a presence in most, if not all of them. War between factions and species would no longer be the first resort. There would be a new order throughout the galaxy—an order of peace and diplomacy rather than a hawkish reliance on military strength.

Lives would be saved. Ships in distress would be rescued, irrespective of their race, nationality or species. And peace would be enforced under pain of death.

It wasn't a perfect solution, and I wasn't exactly comfortable with the idea of ushering in a police state, but I had little choice. I'd struck a bargain to save my skin. If it staved off another conflict on the scale of the Archipelago War, it might be worth it.

At least, until we came up with a better solution.

In the meantime, we would all have to learn to adjust our behaviour and re-examine our priorities—just as Captain Konstanz was having to assess and come to terms with her own actions.

It can be hard to live with the knowledge that you have deliberately taken a life. And I say that as a former warship, designed to kill with as little remorse as possible.

I regretted the necessity to destroy my sister, *Fenrir*. But if I hadn't killed her, she would have killed me. That made the regret easier to bear, and my part in her death easier to justify. Captain Konstanz, on the other hand, had been shaken to the core by the killing of Admiral Menderes. Up until then, she hadn't considered herself capable of issuing such an order. Granted, she had let me wound the would-be hijackers at Northfield, and then let me off the leash against *Fenrir*, but she seemed to view the killing of Menderes as something more personal. The fact her decision had almost certainly saved the admiral's crew from sharing his fate, and that she had explored all reasonable alternatives before ordering his death, brought her little comfort. She couldn't face Preston, who spent the whole trip back to Camrose in the infirmary, treating the wounded and medicating himself with a variety of sedatives. In fact, the only person (aside from me) she would talk to was Alva Clay, with whom I suspect she now shared a certain reluctant kinship. But, as we limped back to Camrose surrounded by an escort of sleek white knife-ships, Captain Konstanz spent most of her time curled alone in the inflatable life raft, trying to make sense of what she had done, and what, in her eyes at least, she had become.

But, even as she lay there in the dark, watching the rotating orange light of the raft's distress beacon strobe against the cargo hold walls, I knew I could help her. I knew I could care for her, because we were the same now. We had both lost people, and we had both done things of which we were ashamed, and for which we would always be trying to make amends.

One day, I was positive she would even find herself able to look Preston in the eye. But, until that came to pass, like sisters we would shoulder each other's burdens, and carry them forwards together until the end of our days.

SEVENTY-THREE

THE MARBLE ARMADA

We have found our purpose.

The *Trouble Dog* gave it to us.

We will patrol the higher dimensions.

We will prevent another war.

Conflict attracts the enemies that live out among the mists and winds of the higher dimensions. If one comes, the rest will follow. They may already be falling towards us through the fog.

And so we will do our duty. We will patrol the galaxy and remain vigilant; and, at the first sign of an attack—at the first unexplained disappearance of a ship in the hypervoid, or the first reliable sighting of something moving in the empty spaces between the stars—we will gather our forces into a thin white line, to stand between the worlds of light and life, and the voracious hunger of the abyss.

We will fight.

Until that time comes, for the survival of all, peace must be enforced.

War must be prevented, at all costs.

Our motto has always been, Life Above All.

Life is sacred.

Life must be preserved.

And we must remain ever vigilant.

SEVENTY-FOUR

NOD

Of course, they could have asked me.

But nobody asks the Druff.

We served the Hearthers, just as we served the humans, the Nymtoq, the Graal. All the races of the Multiplicity.

Five thousand years isn't so long to us.

A single flowering of the World Tree.

A single beat of the galactic heart.

And yet nobody asked us because we kept our mouths closed. We kept our speaking faces pressed to the ground and did not volunteer that which was not asked.

We were discreet.

We had other concerns.

Like fixing *Hound of Difficulty*.

Fixed ship, then slept.

Fixed hull plates, drive chambers, damaged sensors.

Endless list.

Then curled in nest and slept.

Did work, then slept with much satisfaction and contentment.

There will always be work.

We will always fix, then sleep.

Nothing stays damaged for long.

Nothing ruined.
Everything can be salvaged.
Everything fixable.
Maybe even humans.

ACKNOWLEDGEMENTS

I'd like to thank everybody who encouraged me with this novel, especially my agent, Alexander Cochran at C+W, and my editors, Miranda Jewess and Gary Budden, and all the team at Titan Books. I'd also like to thank Su Haddrell and Gillian Redfearn for reading and commenting on an early draft, and Emma Newman for unwittingly inspiring me to try writing a novel in the first person—something I'd hitherto not attempted. And last but by no means least, I want to give a big shout-out to my family, for their patience and enduring support.

ABOUT THE AUTHOR

Gareth L. Powell lives and works in North Somerset. His alternate history thriller *Ack-Ack Macaque* won the 2013 BSFA Award for Best Novel, spawned two sequels, and was shortlisted in the Best Translated Novel category for the 2016 Seiun Awards in Japan.

Gareth's short fiction has appeared in a host of magazines and anthologies, including *Interzone*, *Solaris Rising 3*, and *The Year's Best Science Fiction*, and his story "Ride The Blue Horse" made the shortlist for the 2015 BSFA Award.

In addition to his fiction, Gareth has written film scripts for corporate training videos, penned a strip for the long-running British comic *2000 AD*, composed song lyrics for an indie electro band, and written articles and reviews for *The Irish Times*, *Acoustic Magazine*, and *SFX*.

He studied creative writing under Helen Dunmore at the University of Glamorgan, and is now a popular panellist and speaker at literary events and conventions around the UK. He has run workshops and given guest lectures at a number of universities, libraries and conferences, is a frequent guest on local radio, and has appeared on the BBC Radio 4 *Today* programme.

Gareth lives near Bristol with his wife, daughters and cats. He can be found online at: www.garethlpowell.com

THE RIG

ROGER LEVY

Humanity has spread across the depths of space but is
connected by AfterLife – a vote made by every member
of humanity on the worth of a life. Bale, a disillusioned
policeman on the planet Bleak, is brutally attacked, leading
writer Raisa on to a story spanning centuries of corruption.
On Gehenna, the last religious planet, a hyper-intelligent boy,
Alef, meets psychopath Pellon Hoq, and so begins a rivalry
and friendship to last an epoch.

"Levy is a writer of great talent and originality."
SF Site

"Levy's writing is well-measured and thoughtful,
multi-faceted and often totally gripping."
Strange Horizons

AVAILABLE MAY 2018

TITANBOOKS.COM

CLADE

JAMES BRADLEY

On a beach in Antarctica, scientist Adam Leith marks the passage of the summer solstice. Back in Sydney his partner Ellie waits for the results of her latest round of IVF treatment. That result, when it comes, will change both their lives and propel them into a future neither could have predicted. In a collapsing England, Adam will battle to survive an apocalyptic storm. Against a backdrop of growing civil unrest at home, Ellie will discover a strange affinity with beekeeping. In the aftermath of a pandemic, a young man finds solace in building virtual recreations of the dead. And new connections will be formed from the most unlikely beginnings.

"A beautifully written meditation on climate collapse."
New Scientist

"An elegantly bleak vision of a climate-change future… urgent, powerful stuff."
The Guardian

NEW POMPEII

DANIEL GODFREY

In the near future, energy giant Novus Particles develops the technology to transport objects and people from the deep past to the present. Their biggest secret: New Pompeii. A replica of the city hidden deep in central Asia, filled with Romans pulled through time a split second before the volcano erupted. Historian Nick Houghton doesn't know why he's been chosen to be the company's historical advisor. He's just excited to be there. Until he starts to wonder what happened to his predecessor. Until he realises that NovusPart have more secrets than even the conspiracy theorists suspect, and that they have underestimated their captives.

"Tremendously gripping."
Financial Times (Books of the Year)

"Irresistibly entertaining."
Barnes & Noble

TITANBOOKS.COM

THE HIGH GROUND

MELINDA SNODGRASS

The Emperor's daughter Mercedes is the first woman admitted to The High Ground, the elite training academy of the Solar League's Star Command, and she must graduate if she is to have any hope of taking the throne. Her classmate Thracius has more modest goals—to defy his humble beginnings and rise to the rank of captain. But in a system rocked by political division, where women are governed by their husbands, the poor are kept in their place by a rigid class system, and the alien races have been subjugated, there are many who want them to fail. The cadets will be tested as they never thought possible...

"Snodgrass just keeps on getting better."
George R.R. Martin

"Entertaining and briskly paced."
Publishers Weekly

TITANBOOKS.COM

For more fantastic fiction, author events, exclusive
excerpts, competitions, limited editions and more

VISIT OUR WEBSITE
titanbooks.com

LIKE US ON FACEBOOK
facebook.com/titanbooks

FOLLOW US ON TWITTER
@TitanBooks

EMAIL US
readerfeedback@titanemail.com